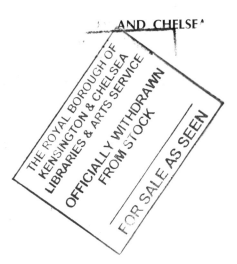

YOU STOLE MY HEART AWAY

Molly Bennett and Nellie McDonough are very happy with their lot in life. Their rock-solid friendship has lasted over twenty years, through good times and bad, and never once have Molly and Nellie fallen out. They love a bit of excitement, so when they learn there is a wedding in the offing which will bring the Bennett, McDonough and Corkhill families even closer, it gives the intrepid pair a good reason to save up for a visit into Liverpool, to the shop selling wedding hats. As Nellie says, 'It had better be a posh wedding to match me posh new hat.'

YOU STOLE MY HEART AWAY

YOU STOLE MY HEART AWAY

by

Joan Jonker

Magna Large Print Books
Long Preston, North Yorkshire,
BD23 4ND, England.

British Library Cataloguing in Publication Data.

Jonker, Joan
    You stole my heart away.

    A catalogue record of this book is
    available from the British Library

    ISBN   0-7505-2605-X
    ISBN   978-0-7505-2605-0

First published in Great Britain in 2006 by Headline Book Publishing

Published in Large Print 2006 by arrangement with
Headline Book Publishing Ltd.

Magna Large Print is an imprint of Library Magna Books Ltd.

Printed and bound in Great Britain by
T.J. (International) Ltd., Cornwall, PL28 8RW

I dedicate this book to all my readers, for without them where would I be?

I would like to say a huge thank you to my niece, Jean, for allowing me to use her wedding photograph on the front cover of this book. She was such a pretty bride and is still as beautiful to this day.

Hello again to my friends

Here is another Molly and Nellie story and the fearless mates are in good form, so sit back and enjoy the fun.

Take care now.

Love

Joan

PS – A little bit of gossip: some of you might remember Brian, my gardener, who pestered me to mention him in one of my books. Well, his wife had a baby recently and I swear his head and chest have grown about six inches. Honestly, you'd think he'd performed a miracle! His wife is called Sam, and she's very pretty, and the baby is Thomas.

Chapter One

Molly Bennett carried the breakfast dishes out to the kitchen and put them on the draining board. There weren't many these days, since three of her children had flown the nest. All in the space of two years. She didn't half miss them, especially at mealtimes when the room would be alive with voices shouting to be heard above the din, and laughter. Lots of laughter.

Leaning back against the sink, Molly let her mind go back over those days. And she told herself she shouldn't be feeling sorry for herself, she should be glad the three children were happily married and settled down so close to her. She saw them every day, and two of them had made her a grandmother. 'I should be counting me blessings,' she told the gas cooker, 'instead of standing here feeling sorry for meself. So pull yerself together, Molly Bennett, and get some work done.'

She walked back into the living room, and bending over the table she gathered together the four corners of the white tablecloth. Then she took it out into the yard and gave it a good shake before folding it neatly and putting it in the cupboard of the sideboard. While she was doing this with one hand, the other hand was reaching for the maroon chenille cloth which would cover the table until dinnertime. When that task was complete, she tried to put some spark into herself,

13

but she couldn't raise her spirits.

Sighing softly, Molly told the empty room, 'It's Monday morning blues, that's what's wrong with me. Just the thought of that tub full of washing is enough to give me the willies. Still, the clothes have been in steep all night, so I'll only have to rinse them in clean water before putting them through the mangle. And from the look of the clear blue sky, it's going to be a good day for drying. So, all being well, I should have the clothes pegged out on the line in an hour, and they'll be dry enough for ironing before Jack and Ruthie get home from work.'

'Who are yer talking to, girl?'

Startled, Molly spun round, to find herself looking down into the face of her mate, Nellie McDonough, who looked as though she didn't have a care in the world. This didn't go down well with Molly, whose heartbeat was racing with shock. 'Nellie McDonough, yer gave me the fright of me life! What d'yer think ye're playing at? And how the hell did yer get in anyway?'

'Yer door was ajar, girl, and I thought yer'd left it open on purpose. You know, like yer were inviting me in for a cup of tea.'

'Yer must think I want me bumps feeling! It's Monday, Nellie McDonough, washday! Yer know damn well I won't let yer in for a cuppa on a Monday morning until me washing is on the line, me beds are made, and the place is cleaned and tidied.' Molly shook her head. 'Nellie, it's no good looking sorry for yerself and pulling faces, 'cos it won't work. Yer can just turn round and go out the way yer came in. And make sure yer close the door properly on the way out, 'cos I don't want any more unexpected visitors.'

Nellie pouted her lips and dropped her head as she turned towards the door. But it wasn't her little girl lost look that caused Molly to follow her, it was curiosity. 'Why were yer passing my door at eight o'clock in the morning, anyway?'

Nellie kept her head down so her mate couldn't see the crafty look in her eyes. 'I was on my way to the corner shop for an aspirin, girl, 'cos I've got a splitting headache, and I don't feel so good.'

As Nellie had anticipated, Molly found herself in a dilemma. She was used to her mate playing the fool to get some sympathy, but as Nellie was a good actress, you could never tell whether she was telling the truth or not. So Molly was torn, and decided to take the middle road. 'I'm sorry about that, sunshine, and I can't help yer 'cos I don't have any aspirin. I've got a Beecham's powder, though, and they're very good for headaches.' She put an arm round Nellie's shoulder. 'Sit at the table and I'll mix yer a powder, then I'll make yer a cup of tea. Yer'll be as right as rain then, and yer can go home and leave me to get me work done.'

When Molly bustled out to the kitchen, still wondering if her mate was telling the truth or not, Nellie carried the carver chair from the wall by the sideboard to the middle of the room. After using a foot to kick one of the dining chairs out of the way, she placed her trophy at the head of the table. She told herself that she deserved to be comfortable after being clever enough to make up that cock and bull story so quick. Mind you, she didn't fancy having to take a Beecham's

15

powder, 'cos she hated them.

'Here yer are, sunshine, get that down yer while I see to the kettle.' Molly put the cup down in front of her mate. 'Yer'll feel better in no time.' Then she bustled out to the kitchen again.

Nellie pulled a face when the cup neared her lips, and she shivered with distaste. It was no good, she couldn't drink it. But what the heck could she do with it? She couldn't tell her mate now that she didn't have a headache, because she'd be sent home without a cup of tea. 'I can't drink this, though,' she muttered under her breath, 'I'd make meself sick. I'd throw it away if there was anywhere to throw it.' Just as she was saying that, her eyes lighted on Molly's pride and joy, the aspidistra plant that stood on a little table in front of the window. Now even Nellie knew that plants never got headaches, but they did like a drink now and again. In fact they died if they didn't get watered, so she'd be doing it a favour.

Her eyes narrowed to slits, Nellie cocked an ear to the kitchen. She could hear her mate getting the cups down, so she'd have time to make it to the aspidistra while Molly was busy, and no one would be any the wiser. Except the plant, of course, but that wouldn't be able to snitch on her. So slowly scraping her chair back, Nellie put the cup down while she used her two hands to push herself to her feet. Then, after a furtive glance towards the kitchen, she picked up the cup and began the slow, silent walk towards her goal.

In the kitchen, the kettle began to boil and Molly switched it off. But she didn't pour the water into the teapot, for there was a little niggle

16

in her mind that was telling her to keep an eye on her mate, for the tale she told didn't ring true. In the twenty-odd years of their friendship, she'd never once known Nellie to have a headache. So she walked into the living room just in time to see her mate's arm moving upwards, with the cup in her hand tilted ready to pour the contents on to Molly's pride and joy. 'Don't you dare, Nellie McDonough, or so help me I'll never speak to yer again as long as I live.' Molly took the cup from Nellie's hand and glared down at her. 'My ma gave me that plant twenty years ago, and I've treasured it ever since. And you, you sneak, were going to kill it off! What the hell were yer thinking of?'

'I wasn't going to kill it off, I was only going to give it a drink, like what I've seen you do plenty of times.' Nellie put on her innocent face. 'I was doing you a favour, girl, that's all!'

'I'm lost for words, Nellie. I thought I was past being surprised by anything you do. But this little lark takes my breath away. Even you should have known the powder I put in that cup was to clear your headache, not to kill off me plant.'

'Oh, don't be getting yer knickers in a twist, girl, not this early in the morning. If yer look in the saucer, yer'll see I poured half the ruddy water in there! So the drop what's left in the cup wouldn't have done the bleeding plant no harm. In fact it might have done it the world of good. Yer might have come down tomorrow morning and found flowers growing, what yer've never had in the twenty years yer've had it.'

With her nostrils flared and teeth ground

17

together, Molly said, 'Nellie, aspidistra plants don't have flowers.'

Nellie turned her head slightly, telling herself Molly was weakening: she could see it in her eyes. 'What good is a plant what doesn't ever flower, girl? Waste of space if yer ask me.'

'Nobody is asking you, Nellie McDonough, certainly not about a plant what yer nearly murdered.' Molly leaned forward and looked closely at Nellie. 'Yer haven't got a headache, have yer? In fact yer never did have one and when yer said yer weren't feeling too good, that was a lie as well, wasn't it?'

'Are yer asking me or telling me, girl?' Nellie shook her head slowly, for she didn't want to wake her chins up. 'If yer don't calm down, it'll be you what's got a headache and not feeling too good. But yer wouldn't have to worry, girl, 'cos help is at hand. There's enough Beecham's powder in me saucer to clear the headache, and the kettle's been boiled once, so it won't take me long to make yer a nice cup of tea.' Nellie's chubby face beamed. 'So yer see, girl, there's no need to get yerself all worked up, which I keep telling yer is bad for yer heart. That's your trouble, girl, yer worry about things what are not worth worrying about. Like that ruddy plant! I know yer ma gave it to yer and yer think the world of it, but just ask yerself, what is more important? Your life, or me poisoning that bleeding plant?'

'Oh, I was never worried about the aspidistra, Nellie.' Molly kept her face straight. 'Yer see, the only thing in the cup was a drop of water out of the tap, with a spoonful of cold tea added to

18

make it look like I'd put a powder in. Yer see, sunshine, I never really believed the tale yer came up with, about having a headache and not feeling too good. Yer never have a headache, and if yer did get one, yer wouldn't be going to the corner shop for an aspirin, 'cos Maisie doesn't sell them. So now we've sorted the truth out, I'd like you to get back home and leave me to get me washing out. But I still want to know how you got in here. I'm sure I closed the door after seeing Jack and Ruthie off to work.'

'Well, ye're not as clever as yer think yer are, girl, 'cos I hear your door getting banged every morning. Regular as clockwork, you are. And I heard yer closing it this morning. But I've got sharp ears, girl, and I didn't hear the lock click into place like it usually does. So I knew yer hadn't banged it hard enough. Easy mistake to make, girl; I've done it meself before today.'

'Now I know you watch me every movement, sunshine, I'll be extra careful. But don't keep looking at yer chair, 'cos it's not going to have the pleasure of your company for at least two hours. I'll see yer at half ten.'

Nellie was very reluctant to lift her feet off the ground, and Molly had to take her arm and escort her to the door. All the time Nellie was muttering, 'She's a miserable bugger, even if she is me mate. There's a ruddy good chair going to waste in there. And even though she wouldn't agree, I bet it's missing me, 'cos me backside keeps it nice and warm.'

Thinking of all the work she had to get through in two hours, Molly started to close the door.

19

'See yer at half ten, Nellie, and I'll have a couple of custard creams for yer to have with yer tea.'

She shut the door and leaned back against it, then chuckled when she heard her mate saying, 'Two fiddling custard creams! She's killing me with bleeding kindness, that's what she's doing, the miserable beggar. Thinks she's doing me a big favour with two biscuits what I'll swallow so quick me throat won't even know they've passed through.'

While Molly went back to her kitchen and the dolly tub, Nellie walked slowly to her own house three doors away. She really felt down in the dumps. It wasn't often she failed to get round her mate, but she had today and it was her own fault. She'd really put her foot in it over that ruddy plant. She wouldn't give it house room herself. 'I mean, what good is it? It doesn't speak or laugh, to brighten up the place. It just stands there, day after day, doing sweet bugger all. And it expects to be given a drink twice a week, and dusted once a week. Molly doesn't half fuss over it, even washes its leaves with a damp cloth every Saturday without fail. And she even goes as far as moving the ruddy thing away from the window when the sun is shining on it! I mean, that's going a bit too far. She needs her head seeing to,' Nellie muttered finally as she used the doorframe to pull herself up the two steps. Then, puffing and red in the face from exertion, she waddled half-way down the tiny hall before coming to a halt just long enough to kick her leg backwards to shut the front door. And when Nellie shut the door, well, the door knew only too well that it had been shut, for it shuddered for a few seconds with the impact.

The first thing that met her eyes when she entered the living room was the fireplace. It hadn't been cleaned out, and the ashes were spread across the grate and hearth. And the sight added to Nellie's woes. Pointing to it with a chubby finger, she said, 'And as for you, ye're as useless as that bleeding plant of me mate's. Ye're just bone idle.' After a few huffs, she added, 'And yer can stay like that for all I care. I'm going to give me washing a quick rinse out, while the kettle's warming up. And I've no intention of pulling me guts out by putting the clothes through the mangle, either, 'cos it's too much like hard work. I'll wring as much water out of them as I can with me bare hands, then put them on the washing line to drip dry. The kettle will have boiled by then, and I can make meself a cuppa.' Once again she pointed to the grate. 'If I've got any time to spare after that, I'll give yer a quick going over with the hand brush and shovel. But only if I've got time, mind, 'cos I've got to be at me mate's by half ten. I know it's only two custard creams, but even that is better than a kick up the backside. And credit where credit is due, she makes a better cup of tea than I do. Don't ask me how, but I think it's got something to do with the way she holds her mouth.' She held up an open hand. 'Anyway, don't argue with me 'cos the way I'm carrying on, it'll be bedtime before I get me ruddy washing on the line.'

Nellie waddled into the kitchen, a hand on each hip. And she put a question to the dark, empty room. 'Shall I make a cup of tea first, or see to me washing?' Then she tutted. 'What's the point of asking you? I'm more likely to get an extra biscuit off me mate than I am to get an answer from you.' She began to laugh, and her eighteen-stone body shook. If the floor had been a wooden one, it would have joined in the laughter because floorboards had a sense of humour. But concrete was too thick to see the funny side of anything. 'I've often heard people say it's like talking to a wall, and here's me doing it meself. I must be going barmy.'

Rolling her sleeves up, Nellie put the plug in the sink and turned on the tap. While she was waiting for the sink to fill, she had a word with the window. 'I've changed me mind about making meself a cup of tea. I'm going to wait until I get to me mate's. I don't enjoy sitting at the table on me own with a cup in me hand and no one to talk to, or have a laugh with.' She saw the sink was now half full, and turned the tap off before bending over the dolly tub and pulling out a pair of her husband's working trousers. She wrung as much water out as she could over the tub, then quickly transferred them to the sink, where she dunked them up and down in the clean water.

Now Nellie didn't believe in wasting time on any job, so the trousers were only given the one rinse before being carried, dripping wet, out to the yard, where they were thrown haphazard over the line, while Nellie went back for some pegs. The next item to receive the same treatment was a double sheet, followed by two shirts belonging to her son Paul. And last but not least came a pair of her own bloomers. And it was when she was hanging these out that she heard her mate's voice from three yards away and called, 'Is that you, girl?'

'It is, sunshine. I was just passing the time of day with me next door neighbour, seeing as we are both putting our washing out. I was saying it was a good job out of the way. Have yer got yours out yet?'

'Of course I have, girl. I don't mess around, yer know that.' Nellie's eyes went towards the heavens, and she said, very quietly, so her mate wouldn't hear, 'That's only a white lie, St Peter, not worth yer making a note of. I'll be putting the rest of me washing out later, after I've had a little break. You wouldn't understand, being a man, but a woman's work is never done.'

Molly's voice floated over the walls. 'Did yer say something, sunshine?'

'Yes I did, girl, but it wasn't something I want the whole world to know, so I'll tell yer later. I'll be in yours in fifteen minutes.' With that, Nellie moved as speedily as she could up the step into the kitchen and banged the door shut. She didn't want to hear her mate's reply.

Molly had called out once and got no reply, so she shouted louder. 'Half an hour, Nellie, and not a minute sooner. I haven't made me beds yet.'

'She mustn't have heard yer, Molly,' the neighbour, Irene, said. 'Is Nellie hard of hearing?'

Molly didn't know whether to laugh or cry. But she did know she'd better get in and make the beds in ten minutes flat. 'Irene, I'm going in, sunshine, and I hope the weather stays dry for us.

See yer later, perhaps. Ta-ra.'

Ten minutes later, Molly was puffing when she stood on the landing. She'd never made the beds so fast in all her life. What with a line full of washing out, pushing the heavy mangle back into the space in the corner of the kitchen, cleaning the grate and dusting the living room, she felt worn out and it was only quarter past ten in the flipping morning! Just wait until Nellie Mc-Donough came. 'I'll give her a piece of me mind. It's all her fault that the day's routine has been turned on its head.' And she'd tell her so, as well.

Holding on to the banister, Molly took her time going down each stair to allow her heartbeat to slow down. And as she reached the last stair, she was telling herself this would never happen again. In future, no one would get over the doorstep until she'd done all her housework and was ready, and willing, to receive visitors. Even the Queen wouldn't be allowed in. But standing in the hallway she decided she'd weaken in her resolve on one condition, and only one. And that was if the person knocking on her front door was Robert Taylor. Now that was something that would make her very happy. And she'd make sure Nellie didn't get a foot over the doorstep that day, for she'd hog the limelight and no one else would get a look in.

Molly's wishful thinking was brought to an abrupt end when there came a loud knocking on her door. She didn't have to open the door to see who it was, 'cos her mate was the only person she knew who was so heavy-handed. 'Yer can wait until I'm ready, Nellie McDonough,' Molly said as she sat on the second stair. 'Yer've upset me whole day with yer shenanigans, and I've a good mind not to open the door to yer! If I set eyes on yer, I'm sure I won't be able to stop meself from throttling yer.'

Nellie knew she was in her mate's bad books, so she thought she'd better do a bit of crawling. Bending down, she opened the letterbox and peered through. She could see Molly sitting on the stairs and said, coaxingly, 'Come on, girl, open the door. Yer know yer'll get a headache if I keep on knocking. And besides, it's not like you to go back on yer word.'

Molly sat with her chin cradled in her two hands. 'What word was that, Nellie? Quite a lot of words were spoken this morning, and most of them childish and unnecessary. So I think the best bet for us is not to see each other at all for the rest of the day. Let's cool off, and we'll feel better tomorrow. Yer see, right now I feel like marmalizing yer for ruining the whole day for me. It's only half past ten and I'm worn out.'

Nellie called through the letterbox. 'Is that all it is, girl, half past ten? Well, fancy that! I'm just in time for our usual cup of tea and two custard creams. So yer can't tell me off for coming too early.'

It was on the tip of Molly's tongue to shout back that Nellie's eight o'clock call had ruined the usual daily routine, and now everything had gone to pot. But she knew if she did it would just be a waste of breath. She knew her mate well enough by now to know that if Nellie was determined to get in, then there was nothing more certain than that she would get in. Even if she

25

had to climb over the back yard wall. It wouldn't be the first time. Mind you, it was many years ago now, and both she and Nellie were a lot younger then. Molly had told her mate not to come in one day, because she wasn't feeling so good. It was not long after Tommy was born, and she wanted to feed him before putting him down to sleep for a few hours. She wanted a break, so she could put her feet up while he slept.

These thoughts took Molly back in time, and although it had happened over twenty years ago she could see it in her mind as though it was only yesterday. She'd fed Tommy, nursed him until he dropped off to sleep, then laid him in his pram in the hall. Then, looking forward to putting her feet up for a few hours, she'd walked back into the living room and flopped on the couch. She was just about to swing her legs round, to stretch out full length, when she saw, through the back window, a sight she thought must be an illusion. She'd rubbed her eyes with the heel of her hands, thinking she must be seeing things, for that couldn't be Nellie sitting astride her back yard wall, surely? She thought she was imagining it at first, until her mate waved to her. It turned out that Nellie had asked her neighbour for the loan of her stepladder. The neighbour was very dubious, but Nellie could talk anyone into thinking the sun was shining when in fact there was two foot of snow on the ground. Anyway, Nellie had ended up on the wall, but couldn't get down into Molly's yard. And to add to her dismay, the neighbour had taken her steps back in, saying she wasn't going to be involved with Nellie's falling and breaking her neck. So, armed with a chair, Molly had had to forgo her rest to rescue her mate. Remembering it now brought a smile to Molly's face as she pushed herself off the stair. Nellie had been a ruddy nuisance at times, and caused Molly much embarrassment, but those times had been few compared to the number of occasions she'd had Molly doubled up with laughter at her antics. And not only Molly, but all their friends and families.

The letterbox rattled, and Nellie shouted, 'Come on, girl, those ruddy biscuits will be stale by the time I get them. And me throat is parched with shouting.'

'Well stop ruddy well shouting, yer silly nit.' Molly was feeling a lot more relaxed as she walked towards the door. She should take a lesson from her mate and not worry so much. If she lived at a slower pace, she'd live longer.

Her jaw dropped when she opened the door to see Nellie kneeling on the second step. 'In the name of God, sunshine, what are yer doing down there?'

'I had to get down here to look through the letterbox, girl, and it's taken yer so long to move yerself me knees must be locked, because I can't get up now.' Nellie was holding on to the edge of the wall to keep her balance. 'It's your fault I'm down here, so the least yer can do is give us a hand up.'

Molly saw the funny side and chuckled. 'Seeing as it's you, and ye're me best mate, then I'll give yer me two hands.' She pulled Nellie upright, then stepped back to let her enter the hall. 'But don't think that means I'm taking any responsibility for yer being on yer knees, 'cos I'm not. Move along now so I can close the door, unless yer want to stand tummy to tummy while we chat.'

'How many times do I have to tell yer that sarcasm doesn't suit yer, girl?' Nellie asked as she waddled into the living room. 'Yer've got the wrong face for it.'

Molly had just closed the door, and was about to follow Nellie, when there was a rap on the knocker. With a sigh of resignation, she wondered aloud, 'Who can this be now?'

But when she saw who was standing outside, her face lit up. 'Hello, sunshine, this is a nice surprise. Do yer want me to get something from the shops for yer, when me and Nellie go shopping?'

Doreen was Molly's second daughter, and lived in the house opposite with her husband Phil, baby Bobby and ninety-year-old Victoria Clegg, who had lived in the house alone for about fifty years. She had offered a home to Doreen and Phil when they got married, and it was a happy arrangement. 'No, I'm going out to do me own shopping, Mam, to give Bobby some fresh air. I've come over because I thought there must be something wrong, with Auntie Nellie shouting through the letterbox. I could hear her shouting but couldn't make out what she was saying. Are you all right?'

'Of course I am, sunshine. It was just me and Nellie playing silly beggars. I'll tell yer about it some other time; it's nothing exciting.' Molly called through to the living room, 'Are yer listening, sunshine? I'm just telling Doreen we've been

28

playing silly beggars.'

'I can't answer yer, girl,' Nellie croaked, ''cos me mouth is as dry as a bone.'

Molly winked at her daughter, and very quietly whispered, 'Tell her a Beecham's powder is good for a sore throat.'

Doreen whispered back, 'But a Beecham's is no good for a throat. They're more for colds, or headaches.'

'I know that, sunshine, but do it anyway, and see what me mate has to say about it.'

Doreen shrugged her shoulders, then called out, 'Try a Beecham's, Auntie Nellie, that'll ease yer throat.'

Nellie's voice came back as a growl. 'Ha, ha, very funny. Yer look like yer mam, and now ye're beginning to take after her for being sarky.'

Doreen passed her mother and went into the living room. 'I wasn't being sarcastic, Auntie Nellie, I was trying to be helpful. It sounds to me as though ye're getting a cold, 'cos yer voice is really gruff. And the best medicine for a cold, I've always found, is a Beecham's powder.'

'I'll clock the next one who mentions that bleeding stuff again. I've heard nothing else since eight o'clock this morning.'

Doreen's eyes widened. 'Eight o'clock this morning? You weren't up and about at that time in the morning, surely? If yer were, Auntie Nellie, then ye're definitely sickening for something.'

'Oh, I'm sickening for something all right, and that's a ruddy cup of tea and two custard creams. I was promised them by your mam at eight o'clock, when she threw me out of the house without any pity. She's a hard woman is your mam, and if she doesn't stop messing around, and get me tea and biscuits, then she'll be a hard woman with two black eyes.'

Molly chuckled. 'You better go home and see to Bobby, sunshine, and me and Nellie will see yer later. As soon as she gets an injection of tea and biscuits, she'll brighten up and be back to her lovable, happy self.'

Doreen bent to kiss Nellie's cheek before walking to the front door. 'Aunt Vicky will wonder what's keeping me. She'll be on pins, thinking there's something wrong, like I did.'

'Oh, I'll tell yer the whole tale later, sunshine.' Molly looked down at her daughter from the top step. 'All in all it's been quite an eventful morning so far. It seems like a week to me; I can't believe it's still only half past ten. Still, by the time we get across to yours, me and Nellie will be back to normal.'

Doreen grinned. 'When ever has Auntie Nellie been normal, Mam? I'd think there was something wrong with her if she was.' She turned to cross the cobbles. 'Give us a knock before yer go shopping. Add a bit to the story to make it more exciting. It'll give me and Aunt Vicky something to talk about. Our life is very dull compared to yours.' She waved when she got to her front door. 'I can hear Bobby complaining because he's due for a feed. See yer later.'

Molly closed the door and walked through to the living room. 'Did yer hear that, sunshine? Doreen wants an exaggerated account of our shenanigans. So while I'm making the tea, you put yer thinking cap on.' She hesitated at the kitchen door. 'But keep it clean, sunshine, 'cos Victoria enjoys a laugh as long as there's no swearing or tales of what happens in your bedroom.'

Nellie jerked her head back, confusing her chins. They were used to swaying from left to right, even enjoyed the up and down sensation when she nodded, but the quick backward jerk of her head had them flying all over the place. 'If I'm not allowed to swear, or mention my George's lust for me voluptuous body, then I'll have nothing to say. So I'll leave the talking to you while I sit yawning. 'Cos yer have to admit, girl, that you can't tell a tale like what I can.'

'Don't yer mean I'm not as good a liar as you, sunshine? Because surely yer don't think for one minute I believe half the things you come out with? Your George, who I have the greatest sympathy for, would have to be Tarzan and Hercules rolled into one to keep up with you. Have yer ever heard the word "stamina", Nellie?'

Nellie gazed at her with eyes as wide as she could get them. 'I've never heard of half those words, girl, and I'm sure yer make them up as yer go along. When I get the tea and biscuits yer promised me hours ago, then we'll go across the road and yer can repeat it word for word to your Doreen and Victoria. And they'll tell me whether yer were making little of my George's staying power in the bedroom.'

'I'll make the tea, sunshine, and then we'll sit quietly and enjoy our biscuits while I explain about Hercules and Tarzan. And then perhaps we'll see a smile on yer face.'

31

Nellie opened her mouth in surprise. 'Oh, I know who Tarzan was, girl. He was a man and a half, he was. And did yer say my George reminded yer of him?'

Molly knew when it was time to give in, or they'd be late getting out. Not that they weren't late now, but she'd be best keeping quiet about that. 'Yes, I did mention your George in the same breath as Tarzan, sunshine. I think it was the eyes, and the shape of their faces. In fact I'd go as far as to say they could easily be taken for brothers.'

Nellie gave this some careful thought. 'The eyes and the shape of their faces, yer say? So the only resemblance, as you see it, is from the neck upwards?'

Molly's mind told her to choose her words carefully or she'd be digging a hole for herself. 'Well, no, Nellie, I don't think that's the only resemblance. But yer have to remember I have nothing to compare Tarzan with. While I've seen his chest and his arms, I haven't seen him from the waist down. And as for George, well, I have only seen him from the neck up. So yer must understand why I can't compare them from head to toe. George is too much of a gentleman to walk round without a vest and shirt on, so chances are I'll never know properly how alike the two of them are.' She smiled, chuckled, then doubled over with laughter. 'If yer were wanting them to look alike, yer could buy George a monkey and call it Cheeta.'

'Very funny, girl, very funny. But if yer take a good look yer'll see I'm not laughing. And d'yer know why I'm not laughing? It's because I haven't got the energy. Not a drop of water has touched my lips since half past seven this morning. And not a crumb has touched my mouth. I'm so weak, I couldn't get off this chair even if yer held out a cream slice to me.'

'Oh, dear, you must be in a bad way, sunshine, if yer haven't the energy to lift yer hand for a cream slice. I'd better put a move on in case yer conk out on me.' Molly reached the kitchen door, then pulled up sharp. 'Aye, buggerlugs, ye're not the only one hungry and thirsty, so I don't know why I'm feeling sorry for yer. I haven't had a drink or bite to eat since eight this morning, thanks to you. In fact, let's face it, Nellie, your shenanigans have ruined the whole day for us. Our routine has gone to pot. So when we eventually get our tea and biscuits, we'll have to make up for lost time. We'll do everything at the double, so no stopping to gab to everyone we pass. D'yer hear me?'

Nellie let her head drop on to the table. In a muffled voice, she said, 'I can't hear yer, girl, I'm too weak.'

Molly took the hint, and in seven minutes flat the two mates had a cup of tea in front of them, and a custard cream between their fingers. Nellie had noted there were six biscuits on the plate and her spirits had lifted. She was feeling very generous. 'Yer know, girl, if I asked George to take his shirt off one day, when he was going down the yard to the lavvy, he would do. And I could give you the wire and yer could come up and see him for yerself. Yer see, if I told yer he knocked Tarzan into a cocked hat for brawn, yer wouldn't believe me, would yer? But if yer saw it with yer own eyes, then yer'd have to believe me.' As she moved her head to look into Molly's face, she moved her hand at the same time, towards the plate with the last biscuit on. 'He's very obliging is my George.'

'I'm sure he is, sunshine, but in this case I'll take your word for it. And I won't forget to tell Jack tonight. But so I get it right, let me make sure. George knocks Tarzan into a cocked hat for brawn. Have I got it spot on, sunshine?'

'Dead on the nose, girl, dead on the nose.'

'Right, then, let's make tracks.' Molly pushed her chair back as she asked herself who was the daftest, her or Nellie? And the answer came right away. She was dafter than her mate, for she was the one who'd be coming back to these dirty dishes. 'We'll go up to Jill's first, see if she wants us to do any shopping. Then we'll call over the road later. Doreen said she was getting her own shopping, anyway, to give the baby some fresh air.'

Leaving the cups on the table, the two mates left the house, made sure the door was firmly closed, then linked arms and walked up the street with their shopping baskets over their arms.

Jill's face lit up when she opened the door. 'Me and Auntie Lizzie were just talking about you, Mam. We were hoping you would call to see the new tooth your granddaughter's got.'

'Oh, has she?' Molly looked delighted until she felt herself being pushed aside by her mate. 'Ay, what was that for?'

Nellie put on her fierce expression. 'Have you

34

and Jill forgotten that I'm also young Molly's grandma? If it hadn't been for my son Steve, there wouldn't have been no baby. So just think on in future.'

Jill stepped down on to the pavement and hugged her mother-in-law. 'I hadn't forgotten you, Auntie Nellie, how could I? If it hadn't been for you I wouldn't have the most handsome, wonderful husband in the world. So come in and see yer granddaughter. You and me mam are in for a surprise.'

Under her breath, Molly muttered, 'Today's been full of surprises.'

'Did yer say something, girl?' Nellie asked as she pulled herself on to the top step. 'If yer said what I think yer did, then I agree with yer. Today's prices are terrible.'

'No, sunshine, yer heard me wrong. I was talking to meself really, just saying how I fancied one of Hanley's pies.'

Nellie turned, her chubby face one big smile. 'It's funny how you and me think alike, girl. That's exactly what I had in mind. We'll get one each for our lunch, eh?'

'Whatever yer like, sunshine, but will yer move in now, so I can see the baby, and Lizzie.'

The word surprise came up again, but this time it brought cries of delight and pride. For crawling across the floor towards her two grandmas was baby Molly, gurgling with eagerness to get to the two women, who she knew would pick her up and tickle her tummy.

Molly turned her head to hide the tears that sprang to her eyes. They weren't tears of sadness,

35

but of happiness and emotion. For young Molly, eight months old now, brought back memories of when her eldest born, Jill, was the same age as the baby who was now squealing to be picked up. Same vivid blue eyes and blonde hair. Please God the baby would grow up to be as beautiful and kind as her mother.

'D'yer know, girl, this takes me back over twenty years,' Nellie said. 'She's the spitting image of your Jill, and Doreen. And they all take after you.'

Molly swallowed the lump in her throat and tried to keep her tone light. 'Are yer trying to tell me in a nice way, sunshine, that me and my daughters are as ugly as sin?'

'I'm not that daft, girl,' Nellie said as she bent to pick the baby up. 'I'd have to say me grand-daughter was ugly, wouldn't I?' There weren't many things that Nellie became emotional over, but her two grand-children brought out the very best in her. She wasn't a real grandma to Bobby, for they weren't related, but telling that to Nellie was like asking for a thick ear. Anything that her mate had, she had to have as well. So when Bobby was born they'd settled on making her his adopted grandma.

'Can I have a nurse now, Nellie?' Molly asked. 'Let's have a look at her new tooth.' The baby pulled at Molly's hair and her nose, gurgling with laughter. 'She doesn't seem to be bothered by it, so she can't be in pain.'

Lizzie Corkhill had offered a home to Jill and her then boyfriend, Steve, when she heard they wanted to get married the same day as Doreen to make it a double wedding, but had nowhere to live. And she told herself every day that it was the best thing she ever did.

'She's the most pleasant, placid baby I've ever known,' Lizzie said. 'My Corker cried the whole time he was teething, and look at the size of him now. He'd go mad if he heard me telling yer that, but it's the truth.'

'We won't snitch on yer, Lizzie,' Nellie said. 'Not if Jill is going to make us a cup of tea, like I'm sure she is.'

Molly tutted in the baby's face. 'Can you hear yer grandma McDonough? She's a cheeky article, always on the cadge. But nobody minds, really, 'cos she's very funny and makes us laugh. I'd tell yer I love the bones of her, but she'd hear me and get big-headed.'

Nellie held her arms out. 'Let me have another cuddle, girl, just for a few minutes. I want to give this little princess a few tips on life. She may as well start early, and who better to teach her than a woman of the world like meself?' The baby was punching and kicking as she tried to grab hold of Nellie's nose. 'Never mind that now, sweetheart, you just listen to what I've got to tell yer. When yer grow up, yer haven't got to be afraid of asking for something if yer want it. If yer don't ask, then yer don't get. Like now, I've asked for a cup of tea because I feel like one. And with me cup of tea I'd like a few biscuits. Custard creams if possible, but yer have to take what people give yer, 'cos some folk are miserable and take offence if yer ask. But I'll give yer more advice as yer grow older, put yer on the right track, like. And now lesson one is over, I'll pass yer back to Grandma Lizzie, 'cos I can see yer mam coming through with a tray. If yer were a year older, I'd scrounge a custard cream for yer, but ye're a bit too young yet. But don't you worry, princess, I'll see yer never go short. And if yer take after yer grandma McDonough, then yer'll soon learn the tricks of the trade.'

Molly rolled her eyes to the ceiling. 'Heaven help her if she takes in everything you tell her, Nellie. Pass her over to me now, and you sit and have yer tea. I'll try and undo any damage you've caused. I know she didn't understand a word yer said, but I'm not taking any chances.' Molly held the baby in front of her, so they were looking into each other's faces. 'Hello, sunshine, this is yer grandma Molly. And for every lesson yer get off Grandma McDonough, yer'll be getting one off me.'

Little Moll, as the family called her so there was no confusion with big Molly, was gurgling and chuckling happily. She was a beautiful child, and Molly's heart was filled with love for her. And with her dad, Steve, being as kind and gentle as her mother Jill, she wouldn't go far wrong in life. And she would know what it was to be loved, for she was idolized by all the Bennett and McDonough families. Plus, she had a great-grandma and granda, who seemed to have taken on a new lease of life since the birth of Bobby and little Moll.

'Here, you go to Grandma Lizzie now, sunshine, before my mate empties the plate of biscuits.' Molly passed the baby over to an eager Lizzie, then took a seat at the table. 'I see yer've left me an arrowroot and a custard cream, Nellie. That

38

was big of yer.'

'Never look a gift horse in the mouth, girl. And if yer knew the agony I've gone through, resisting the temptation, then yer'd appreciate what a good mate I am to yer.'

'Ah, I do feel for yer, sunshine. It must have been painful having to sit with yer eyes glued to those two biscuits. And I'll enjoy them all the more, knowing how much you wanted me to have them.'

'Have yer been to Doreen's this morning, Mam?' Jill asked. 'Or are yer going there from here?'

Molly glanced at her mate, and wondered whether to tell her daughter and Lizzie about the events of the day so far. But she decided it would take too long, and they'd never get to the shops in time. So she settled for saying, 'I saw Doreen in the street for a few minutes, sunshine. I asked if she wanted any shopping, but she said she would get her own as she was taking Bobby out for some fresh air.'

'Oh, I'll go with her, Mam, 'cos Moll could do with some fresh air too. Will yer give Doreen a knock on yer way past, and tell her to wait for me? I won't be long getting the baby ready, and can have her in the pram in ten minutes. I feel like a walk, and me and our Doreen can have a good natter. Will yer do that, Mam?'

'Yes, of course I will, sunshine. Me and Nellie have to pass her house to go to the shops. I'll tell her to wait for yer.'

'What are yer having for dinner, girl? Have yer decided yet?' Nellie's eyes narrowed as she looked at her mate. 'Yer've had all morning to think about it.'

'I'm having sausage and mash, sunshine, with lots of fried onions. What about you?'

Nellie feigned surprise, shaking her head as she looked over at Lizzie Corkhill. 'This is unbelievable, Lizzie, and a stranger would think I was telling fibs if they didn't know I never tell lies. But me and me mate know exactly what the other one is thinking. Every day, I can guess what Molly is having for her dinner. Like today, I'd made up me mind that my George, and Paul, would love sausage and mash for their dinner, with lots of fried onions. That was at seven o'clock this morning, and I never mentioned it to Molly. And lo and behold, yer've just heard what me mate said. Isn't that just amazing?'

Catching Molly's wink, Lizzie looked suitably impressed. But she was also blessed with a sense of humour. 'It certainly is, Nellie. It's more than amazing.'

Jill was leaning back against the sideboard with a smile on her face. She was used to the tales told by the woman who had once been her much-loved Auntie Nellie, and was now her mother-in-law. And she was also getting used to the woman who had given her and Steve a home. For she too was good at telling tales. Not quite up to Nellie's standard, but enough to keep the house alive. So when Lizzie held her eyes for a few seconds, Jill knew she was being asked to play along.

Lizzie was nodding her head slowly at Nellie. 'I'll tell yer why I think it's more than amazing, Nellie. Now you just listen to this.' She raised her brow and asked, 'Jill, tell yer mother-in-law what

40

we've decided to have for dinner tonight?'

Jill bit on the inside of her mouth to keep the laughter at bay while she answered. 'You know what we're having, Auntie Lizzie. We're having sausage and mash, with lots of fried onions.'

The loudest laugh came from Nellie. 'I don't know who's the best bleeding liar. Must be me, I suppose.'

Molly wiped a tear away with the back of her hand. 'It's about time someone played you at your own game, sunshine. Good on yer, Lizzie.'

Nellie pretended to be put out. 'Wait until tomorrow I'll have the last laugh. And I hope yer all burn the sausages tonight for spite.'

Little Moll didn't understand a word, but she understood laughter. And her loud chuckles, and clapping hands, told the four women she enjoyed the joke.

Chapter Two

'It smells good, Mam,' Paul McDonough said, his dimples deepening when he smiled. 'I didn't know how hungry I was until yer opened the front door.'

Nellie came through from the kitchen carrying a dinner plate in each hand. 'Yeah, I knew you and George would enjoy them. I told Molly that when we were in the butcher's and she said it was a good idea, and she bought the same for her dinner.'

Her husband, George, left his fireside chair and moved to sit at the table. He was a well-made man, with black hair and a black moustache, both of which were now speckled with grey. He was a jovial soul, with a smile never far from his face. Which was just as well, seeing he was married to Nellie. He loved her dearly, for she'd given him three children, and had made their home one that was warm and happy. Two of the children were married: Steve their eldest, and Lily the middle one. But both lived in the street with their families, and they were able to see them every day. Paul, their youngest, was twenty-two, and had been courting Phoebe Corkhill for nearly two years now.

Nellie put the plate in front of her husband. 'I've been talking to you, and me fingers were burning holding on to that ruddy plate while you were in dreamland.'

George grinned up at her. 'D'yer want me to kiss yer fingers better, love? I'll do that if it makes yer happy. As long as yer wash yer hands first, 'cos how do I know where they've been?'

'Ay, buggerlugs, don't you be getting sarky with me. It's bad enough when Molly is, but I don't mind it so much with her being me best mate. It's coming to something, though, when the man what married me, and promised to love, honour and obey me, forsaking all others till death do us part, starts being sarcastic. I've a good mind to pick that plate up and hit yer on the head with it.'

'If ye're going to do that, Mam,' Paul said, brown eyes twinkling, 'give us time to take the sausages off first. It's no good wasting them.'

George pulled a face. 'Thanks for that, son, it's nice to know we men stick together. I'll remember that when I come to make me will out.' This caused laughter, for it was well known that George liked his pint, and Nellie liked her cream cakes, so there wasn't likely to be any money over for putting away for a rainy day. None of them were good at saving money; it burned a hole in their pockets. George was generous but not stupid, and would probably have a bit put by if it wasn't for his wife. He knew if she bought anything for herself, she doubled the price when she asked him for the money. He was soft with her and couldn't refuse because he always saw her in his mind as the lovely, slim girl, full of life, who had first caught his eye. He'd fallen for her then, and loved her just as much now.

'Are yer not having any dinner yerself, love?'

'Of course I am, soft lad. Yer don't think I'd stand over a hot stove for hours just to feed you and Paul, do yer?'

Paul had his mother's sense of humour. In fact all her three children took after her for being quick-witted, which is why their house was always filled with laughter. Now he asked, in a matter-of-fact way, 'Haven't you had yer dinner, Mam? I thought yer had.'

'What made yer think that? My plate's in the kitchen. I'm just going to get it.'

As Nellie turned towards the door, her son pulled on her arm. 'I hate to be the bearer of bad news, Mam, but ye're growing a moustache.'

Nellie nearly pushed the table over in her haste to get to the mirror over the fireplace. But she couldn't see anything below her hair. She stood on tiptoe and jumped up and down, but to no avail. 'This bleeding mirror isn't a ha'p'orth of good, George McDonough, I can't see anything but the top of me head. I'm fed up asking yer to move it. I haven't seen me face since the day we moved into this house twenty-five years ago. I don't know what I look like, and wouldn't know meself if I passed meself in the street.'

George chuckled. 'There's not many people could say that, love, and even less would understand even if they could.'

Paul had been holding the laughter in, but now he let it rip. 'Oh, Mam, ye're a case. And all yer have to do to get rid of the moustache is stick yer tongue out.'

Nellie glared at him. 'Ay, smarty pants, any more lip out of you and your sausage will find its way to your head. Yer might be bigger than me, but yer'd never win if it came to blows.' She took up her fighting stance, with feet apart and hands made into fists. 'Come on, big boy, let's see what ye're made of.'

Always game for a lark, Paul pushed his chair back. He got to his feet, and at six foot he towered above his mother. Nellie was lashing out with her fists, and moving around as though shadow boxing, and saying, 'Come on, clever clogs, let's see how brave yer are when ye're up against a professional.'

Keeping a space of two feet between him and his mother, Paul stretched out his arm and put an open palm on Nellie's forehead, leaving her throwing blows into the air and dancing on the spot. She looked so comical, George was convulsed with laughter. He took a hankie from his trouser pocket and wiped away the tears running down his cheeks.

'Oh, dear, oh, dear! I think ye're fighting a losing battle, love, so if I were in your shoes I'd give in before I ran out of steam.'

Paul thought it was hilarious. 'Hey, Dad, there's a key on the mantelpiece belonging to the clock. If yer pass it over, I'll wind me mam up.'

George had an idea of how to put a stop to it. 'Nellie, didn't yer hear the bell go for the end of the first round? Yer've been disqualified now for breaking the rules.'

Nellie's punches slowed down, as did her breathing. She looked up at her son with the fiercest expression on her face she could muster. 'Think yerself lucky, son, 'cos if the bell hadn't gone, I'd have made mincemeat of yer.'

Paul opened his arms and Nellie walked into them. 'Mam, ye're a smasher and I love yer to bits. I pity anyone who hasn't got you for a mother, 'cos a house without laughter is a miserable house.'

'Ay, watch what yer say, son.' Nellie wagged a chubby finger. 'If the Bennetts and the Corkhills heard yer saying that, they'd have yer guts for garters.'

'Oh, I don't mean them, Mam, 'cos I always think of the McDonoughs the Bennetts and the Corkhills as one big family. They have been all my life, and always will be.'

George banged on the table with the handle of his knife. 'Can you two break it up, please, and eat yer dinners, which must be stiff by now. It's

45

yer own fault if they are, and I'm going to put me foot down and say yer'll eat them even if they choke yer. I can't stand to see food wasted, so get them down yer.'

'Ooh, er.' Nellie pulled a comical face as she walked towards the kitchen. 'The master has spoken, and he must be obeyed.'

She came back with a plate between her hands. 'It's still warm and eatable.' She put the plate down and pulled out a chair. 'I've got two things to say before I start on me dinner, though, 'cos if I leave it till after, I'll have forgotten.' Her finger came into play again when she pointed it at Paul. 'I hope yer don't think yer won that fight, son, 'cos if the bell hadn't rung, I'd have knocked spots off yer.' She gave a sharp nod of her head, and her chins followed her example to show they were in agreement with her. Then she looked across the table at her husband. 'I like it when yer go all domineering on me. It reminds me of what Mae West said in that picture me and Molly went to see.' She pushed her chair back. 'I'll have to stand up, 'cos it won't come over the same if I'm sitting down.'

Once again the dinners were forgotten, and this time George didn't worry about a few sausages going in the bin, for Nellie impersonating Mae West was well worth starving for a few hours. Nellie was about a foot shorter than the famous film star, so although they probably weighed the same, the distribution of flesh was somewhat different. Anyway, Nellie took a few seconds to get her left hip out as far as she could, then put a hand on it. The other hand went to the right side of her head, as though she was patting her hair.

46

And then, swaying her hips in what she thought was a seductive movement, she curled her lips and said, 'It's not the men in my life, darlin', it's the life in my men.'

As the words left her lips, there came a rat-tat on the front door knocker. She looked down at herself, then at the plates on the table. 'Who the hell can this be? Just look at the state of the place.' She jerked her thumb at Paul. 'You go to the door, son, and tell whoever it is that there's no one at home.'

'Don't be ridiculous, Nellie!' George said. 'How can he say there's no one in, when he's opened the door, and the light's on! It would be best if you went; ye're better at making up lies than me or Paul. If yer don't want anyone in, then you be the one to tell them.'

The letterbox rattled then, and a female voice called, 'I know ye're in, Mam, so open the flipping door.'

'Oh, it's only our Lily,' Nellie said, relief in her voice. 'Open the door, Paul, you're the nearest.'

As she went to sit down George said, 'Aren't yer going to clear the table? It doesn't look good for visitors to walk in and the first things they see are dirty plates.'

'It's only our Lily, she won't mind. She's seen the place looking ten times worse than this before today.'

'That's no excuse, Nellie. Yer could at least take the plates out.' George moved away from the table and sat in his fireside chair. 'I bet Molly would be ashamed if she was in your shoes now.'

Nellie stuck her tongue out. 'Well she's not

47

here, is she, misery guts? I don't see you getting off yer backside to take the plates out. Talk about moan-a-bit isn't in it.'

'Who's moan-a-bit?' Lily asked as she entered the room, followed by her husband Archie. 'Our Paul just told us yer've been having a good laugh, but you look as miserable as sin.' She noticed the dinner plates on the table and said, 'Oh, I'm sorry, Mam, have we come when ye're in the middle of yer dinner?' Then she bent closer. 'Mind you, it doesn't look very appetizing.'

That remark got Nellie's dander up. 'It was more than appetizing when it was put on the table, girl. Even I couldn't make a mess of sausage and mash.'

'I'll second that, Mrs Mac,' said Archie, who thought the world of his mother-in-law. 'Yer knock spots off the cook we had in the army. He used to say that if sausage weren't black, then they weren't cooked proper.'

George took his wife's side, too. 'There was nothing wrong with the dinner; the sausages were fried just as I like them. I was enjoying it until Paul and my dear wife decided to have a boxing match. Fortunately she only lasted the one round and was disqualified.'

Paul was leaning back against the sideboard, his brown eyes shining with laughter, and his dimples deep in his handsome face. 'Yeah, I was saved by the bell. Me mam said I was lucky she didn't hear it, because if it went to the second round she would have made mincemeat of me.'

'But that doesn't explain why yer haven't eaten yer dinner,' Lily said. 'I don't know much about boxing, but I always thought a round only lasted three minutes.' She took after her mother for being quick-witted and having a good sense of fun. 'Anyway, Mam, how come yer didn't knock our Paul out in the first minute?'

The quivers in Nellie's tummy and mountainous bosom were the first signs of the laughter to come. 'I won't tell yer, girl, 'cos yer wouldn't see the funny side. But if you and Archie sit on the couch out of the way, me and Paul will show yer. Are yer game for a bout, son?'

Paul moved away from the sideboard, saying, 'Mam, I'll have a bout with you any time.' And a minute later, the room was filled with laughter. Nellie put her heart and soul into the role. With her feet apart, head bent, fierce expression on her chubby face and fists clenched, she played the part well. Meanwhile, all Paul had to do was keep his hand on her head, and make sure he kept a safe distance.

Nellie, for all her eighteen stone, didn't run out of steam, and in the end it was George who brought it to a close. 'Yer missed the bell again, Nellie, and that means yer've been barred from the stadium.'

'They can't do that,' Nellie said, her face doing the most amazing contortions. 'They can't, can they, Archie?'

Archie wiped the smile off his face before answering. 'I'm afraid they can, Mrs Mac. One bell a warning, two bells out.'

'Damn and blast!' Nellie stamped a foot and woke the floorboards up. 'And I've been saving to buy meself a new pair of boxing gloves. Just in case I ever come across Elsie Flanaghan in the street, like.'

'Nellie, are yer going to take those plates out?' George asked. 'I'm sure Lily and Archie don't want to be staring at cold sausages and mashed potato.'

'I'll give yer a hand, Mam.' Lily took her coat off and gave it to Archie to hold. 'We're not pushed for time, we're only going to last house at the Astoria.' She picked up a plate and was reaching for another when she noticed the meal on it hadn't been disturbed. 'Mam, haven't yer had anything to eat? This plate hasn't even been touched.'

'Ah, well, I can tell yer why that plate wasn't touched,' Paul said with a chuckle. 'Me mam wasn't herself, yer see. She was Mae West. It's the way she thinks, yer see. She decided to change her profession. If she couldn't be a boxer, she'd be a film star.'

'Look, I enjoy a laugh as much as the next person,' Lily said, 'and goodness knows there's always been laughter in this house. But it isn't more important than starving me dad and Paul, when they've put in a day's work.'

'Don't be getting yer knickers in a twist, girl,' Nellie said. 'I'll warm those dinners up, and they'll be as good as new. We won't starve.'

'Mam, these dinners won't be very appetizing warmed up, they'll only be fit for the bin.'

Archie came to the rescue. 'I've got a solution that will please yer. Bin those dinners, and I'll nip down to the chippy. It won't take me long, and it'll solve the problem of hunger. How about fish, scallops and peas? Does that sound good?'

Nellie rolled her eyes as she rubbed a finger in the dimple on her elbow. 'Sounds bloody marvellous to me, lad. Just what the doctor ordered.'

Lily looked at her husband as though he'd gone mad. 'Have yer forgotten we're going to the pictures? Yer'll never make it back from the chippy in time.'

'I'm a good runner, pet; I'll be back before yer've had a chance to miss me. Besides, it wouldn't be the end of the world if we gave the flicks a miss. We could always go another night.'

Nellie's head and chins were on Archie's side. They could almost smell that wonderful aroma that comes from a chip shop. But Nellie's hopes were to be dashed. And her chins, of course.

Lily was standing with the plate still in her hand. 'You're not soft, are yer? Yer didn't want to go, 'cos yer don't like romantic films. You'd rather have a cowboy film, or a murder mystery, with people getting shot and blood everywhere. Going to the chippy is a good excuse to get out of it.'

The sight and smell of the chippy was getting fainter, and Nellie's spirits were sinking. 'There's no need to take off on Archie, girl, he's only trying to do us a favour.' She decided to pile the agony on, and make it a real sob story. 'I think it's very good of him, wanting to stop us from starving.'

From his fireside chair, George listened to the exchanges, his head moving from one to the other. Paul leaned back against the sideboard, his head in time with his dad's. And in both their minds, they were thinking alike. They reckoned it

51

was ten to one on Nellie winning.

'Put the plate down, girl, and you and Archie go on yer way.' Nellie thought she was on safe ground, because she knew her daughter wouldn't enjoy the film if she did go. 'I'll fry up the sausage and mash, it won't take me long, and it won't kill us. So you and Archie poppy off and enjoy yerselves.'

That did it, of course. George and Paul knew Nellie's words had clinched it, as did her chins, which were wanting her to nod her head so they could celebrate with a quickstep.

Archie had a mind and humour that matched his mother-in-law's, and he was laughing inside. She was a smasher was Mrs Mac, the funniest woman on two legs. He'd hopped in lucky when he married the girl he adored, and found out her mother was full of fun, always ready with a joke. There was never a dull moment when you were in her company.

Lily wasn't behind the door when it came to giving out humour, and she knew her mother inside out. And she loved every inch of her. 'Okay, Mam, yer can drop the sob story. But I still think it's criminal to throw good food in the bin. In future, eat yer dinner first, then have yer boxing match, and leave Mae West until suppertime.'

Archie got to his feet, a tall, dark, handsome man, who would stand out in any room. He ran two fingers down the crease in his trousers, then said, 'If we're not going to the flicks, we may as well have a game of cards. How about it, Mr Mac? Are yer in the mood for a few hands?'

George nodded. 'Suits me, Archie.'

'I'm seeing Phoebe,' Paul told them, 'and she can't play cards. Well, she can play, but she's not very keen. So you can count me out.'

'Yer need some food in yer,' Lily told him, 'so yer can stay in long enough to eat it.'

'I'll get going then,' Archie said. 'And I'll get meself a bag of chips while I'm there.' He grinned at his wife. 'I know I've not long had a good dinner, love, but I can't resist chips from a chippy.'

'Ye're like a big soft kid, Archie Higgins, with eyes bigger than yer belly.' Lily grinned. 'But seeing as ye're going to a chippy, yer can get me a few scallops. If the batter looks a nice golden colour, I'll have four.'

As Archie headed for the door, George followed him. 'Here's a ten bob note, lad. Yer can't be expected to pay for the lot.'

Archie waved it aside with a smile. 'Mr Mac, yer got me out of going to see a picture I didn't want to see, and there's nothing I like better than chips from a chip shop. They're not the same when they're made at home. So keep yer money in yer pocket and try not to let me win it off yer when we're playing cards.'

'Makes no difference where the money goes, lad, as long as I've got enough for me ciggies and the odd pint. If you won't take it for the chips, I'll either lose it at cards or Nellie will talk me out of it. She's good at talking, is my wife, and it's much easier to give in to her at the beginning than end up with a splitting headache.'

Archie stepped down on to the pavement and turned round to ask, 'Would you part with her for all the money in the world, or swap her for

53

another woman?'

'Not on your life, lad. I know what side my bread is buttered. Nellie is everything I would want in a woman.'

'And her daughter is everything I ever dreamed of for my wife. So you and me have got it made, Mr Mac. Two very happy, and lucky, men.' Archie waved a hand and began to walk down the street, then came to an abrupt halt to add, 'I'm not frightened of her, but if I'm not back from the chippy pretty sharpish, she'll batter me.'

George chuckled as he closed the door. His daughter had picked a good one when she married Archie. And his eldest son, Steve, had a wonderful wife in Jill. There was only Paul left now, and heaven only knew when he was going to get married. He'd been courting Phoebe Corkhill for a few years now, and it was about time he made an honest woman of her.

When Molly answered the knocker the next morning, she smiled down at Nellie and opened the door wide. 'Good morning, sunshine. I hope you are feeling good this fine morning?'

Nellie brushed past and made straight for the living room and her carver chair. She was sitting with her two chubby arms folded and resting on the table when Molly came in.

'Nellie,' Molly said, 'it's manners to answer when someone passes the time of day with yer. And it is also manners to wait until ye're invited, then walk in in a ladylike manner. Yer don't push past without a by your leave.'

As though Nellie hadn't heard a word Molly

said, she pointed to one of the wooden dining chairs. 'Sit down, girl, while I tell yer what a marvellous time we had last night. Yer missed a treat. It was great, and I bet yer could kick yerself for not being there.'

Molly pulled a chair out and sat down. 'Yer've lost me, sunshine. I don't know what ye're talking about. Why would I want to kick meself over something I know absolutely sweet Fanny Adams about?'

'It's a wonder yer didn't hear us, girl.' Nellie was getting het up because her mate's attitude was taking some of the shine off what she had to say. 'It wasn't a proper party, like, 'cos it only happened because I was acting daft with our Paul, and we let the dinners go so cold they weren't fit to eat. Our Lily went off the deep end at first, but Archie, God bless him, calmed her down, and the fish and chips were better than sausage any day.'

Molly's face was a picture no artist could paint. She couldn't make head or tail of what her mate was taking about. 'Nellie, will yer calm down, sunshine? I haven't understood one word yer've said. So start at the beginning and tell me what happened when yer put the dinner plates on the table. That seems a good place to start.'

'Yer don't want me to go through the whole lot again, do yer? Not before yer make me a cup of tea, anyway, 'cos me mouth is dry as it is. I can't talk no more until I've had a drink to quench me thirst. And it's yer own fault, girl, for not listening proper to what I was saying.'

'Nellie, I am not moving from this chair until I know how your Lily and Archie come into it.

55

Then I'll make us our usual cup of tea and two biscuits, and your thirst will be quenched so yer can tell me the rest of the story.'

The look of disgust on Nellie's face had Molly laughing inside. One thing her mate wasn't blessed with was patience. 'Go on, sunshine. The sooner yer start, the sooner yer get the usual tea and biscuits.'

Her eyes narrowed to slits, to show she wasn't at all pleased with the arrangement, Nellie began her tale. And halfway through her showing Molly how she was shadow-boxing with Paul, the two mates were laughing their heads off. Words weren't needed when Nellie was in action, her body language spoke for itself. She was wiping the sweat and tears from her eyes when she told her mate, 'So that's how the dinners came to be ruined, girl. And now can I have a cup of tea, 'cos I think I deserve it. And yer'll get a laugh when I tell yer how our Lily and Archie got involved.'

Molly slid her chair back and with hands on the table she pushed herself up. 'And will I still kick meself for not being there, even though I wasn't invited?'

'Oh, I didn't have no time to invite yer, girl, 'cos everything happened so quick. One minute we were going to have sausage and mash for our dinner, then me and our Paul wasted a bit of time by larking around. The next thing I know, we're all sitting down to fish, chips and scallops! It all happened so fast I almost missed it. If it hadn't been for a bit of fish sticking in me tooth, I'd have thought it was all a dream. Mind you, I'd soon have known it wasn't a dream when my George

56

raised the roof when he won the kitty. He said it was the first time he'd won anything in his life, except the odd argument now and again with his mates in work. Half a crown he won, but he didn't keep it; he shoved it across to Archie to put to the money he'd forked out in the chippy.'

Molly couldn't take it all in. 'Nellie, I'm completely lost now, sunshine, so I'll go and put the kettle on. And while I'm waiting for it to boil, I'll try and get me head together.'

While Molly was in the kitchen, Nellie sat swinging her legs under the chair and running her fingers over the chenille cloth. She couldn't make out why her mate didn't understand what she was telling her. After all, she was talking in English, not some foreign language. Perhaps Molly was getting a bit deaf, and couldn't hear proper. But she shouldn't be going deaf, not at her age.

'Here yer are, sunshine, tea and biscuits.' Molly put the wooden tray on the table. 'Yer couldn't get better service if yer went to one of the posh hotels in Liverpool centre. And just think what it would cost yer there, to getting it off me for nothing.'

It was on the tip of Nellie's tongue to say if she was in a posh hotel, she'd be getting a nice cake stand with cakes and a selection of expensive biscuits, but perhaps it was best if she held her tongue on that subject. 'Ooh, I'll drink that tea right off in one go, girl, 'cos me mouth is parched. I hope yer've filled the kettle, so I can have an extra cup?'

'What are yer talking about, Nellie? Yer always have two cups of tea!' Molly glanced at the clock. 'We haven't got time for a long drawn out

57

account of what you and yer family got up to last night, sunshine, so tell me the part from when your Lily and Archie called. Tell it nice and slowly so it sinks in. Then we'll do our shopping, and when we get back yer can tell me the rest. And I'll treat us to a cream slice each, for afternoon tea. How about that, sunshine?'

Nellie perked up right away. 'Sounds good to me, girl, sounds good to me.' Her chubby faced creased into a smile. 'We can have two cream slices each, girl, 'cos I cadged a shilling off George. He gave it to me out of the money Archie made him take back.'

Molly gave her head a few quick shakes. 'I don't know what's wrong with me this morning. I don't seem to be able to think straight. I can hear yer talking, sunshine, but none of it makes sense. Did yer tell me George won half a crown playing cards?' When Nellie nodded, Molly went on, 'And didn't yer say he'd given the winnings over to Archie to help pay for the fish and chips?'

Nellie had a knowing look on her face when she answered. 'Ye're doing well so far, girl. Yer can go to the top of the class now.'

'No, hang on a minute. If George gave his winnings to Archie, how come you're offering to buy cream slices with it? Something doesn't add up, Nellie.'

Nellie's huge bosom and tummy rose to accompany the deep sigh she let out. 'I'm getting bleeding fed up now, girl, and me head is beginning to throb. I'm sorry now I didn't eat our dinner when I put it on the table last night instead of acting the goat with our Paul.' Another deep sigh

58

had her tummy lifting the table off the floor. 'I made a rod for me own back by thinking that you, being me best mate, like, yer'd get a laugh out of it and we'd both be doubled up with tears running down our cheeks. I should have kept it to meself. Kept me big mouth shut.'

Molly patted her mate's hand. 'Don't take this the wrong way, sunshine, but there's a way out of it, if that's what yer want. Drink yer tea, forget all about last night, and we'll get cracking on our shopping. As soon as we walk in Hanley's, and yer see the cream slices, the sun will come out and yer'll feel on top of the world. So drink up and we'll be on our way. I'll wash the cups when we come back.'

In the butcher's shop, Tony was putting a tray of mincemeat in the window when he spotted the two friends on the pavement opposite, waiting for a break in the traffic to cross over. 'Yer mates are on their way, Ellen,' he called through to the stockroom. 'Just seeing them cheers me up, 'cos I know we're in for a laugh.'

Ellen came through wiping her hands on a piece of muslin, and she stood beside her boss and watched as her neighbours, and close friends, darted across the wide, busy road. 'Ay, just look at Nellie. She's as light on her feet as a fairy, for all the weight she's carrying.'

Tony chuckled. 'Two Ton Tessie O'Shea's got nothing on Nellie. Oh, I know Tessie's got a smashing voice, but I bet she hasn't got the same humour as Nellie.'

The two mates were linking arms when they

59

tried to get through the shop doorway, and when they got stuck it was Molly who had to give way. 'Why don't yer get this bleeding door made wider?' Nellie asked. 'Honest, yer must think all yer customers are as thin as beanpoles.' She tutted in make-believe disgust. 'Have a bit chopped off by the time we come tomorrow, or we'll take our custom elsewhere.'

Molly glared down at her. 'If yer didn't insist on linking me, we'd have no trouble getting through. It's not the door that's the wrong size, Nellie, it's you.'

Nellie's gasp of horror was so overdone it was hilarious. 'Well, I like that! I've never been so insulted in all me life. And by my supposed to be best friend.' She appealed to the two people behind the counter who were having trouble keeping their faces straight. 'You heard that, Ellen, and you, Tony. Don't yer think she had a ruddy cheek?'

'Oh, yer can leave me and Ellen out of it, Nellie,' Tony said. 'We can't take sides between customers, 'cos if we did we'd soon have no customers left. And don't forget, Nellie, I've got a wife and four children to fend for.'

'Flipping heck, Tony, that was quick!' Nellie leaned her elbows on the counter and squinted up at the butcher. 'Yer wife's had another baby since Saturday, has she? Blimey, yer didn't even tell us she was expecting. Ye're a dark horse, Tony, keeping a thing like that to yerself and not telling me and Molly, what are yer two best-paying customers.' She was really enjoying this and her eyes were bright with mischief. 'Come on, lad, spill the beans. Is it a boy or a girl?'

'I think yer must be getting me confused with someone else, Nellie.' Tony was stumped. 'My wife hasn't had a baby. Or if she has, she's kept it very quiet 'cos she hasn't told me!'

'Well there's something fishy going on, Tony, and if I were you I'd be demanding she comes clean. Yer've had a wife and three children for over ten years now, and suddenly yer've got a wife and four children. She must be very crafty, that's all I can say. And you must be bleeding short-sighted if yer didn't notice she'd slipped another child in.'

Tony was nodding his head and looking thoughtful. 'Fancy you noticing that, Nellie. And now you've brought it to my attention, I can kick meself for being a fool. I thought there was a bit of a crush at the table when we're having our meals, but it never entered me head to count the number of chairs.'

Molly was moving from one foot to the other. 'Well, now Nellie has sorted that out, Tony, can we talk about what we're going to have for our dinner?'

'I'll serve yer, Molly,' Ellen, her next-door neighbour, said. 'Tony can see to Nellie. What is it yer want?'

Molly sighed. 'I can't make up me mind. Honest, yer get fed up trying to give the family something different every night.'

Nellie was all ears, waiting for her mate to say what she wanted, then Nellie would have the same. But now, unknowingly, Tony put his foot in it. 'I've just made some beef sausage, Nellie, but I've remembered yer had sausage last night.'

The little woman's face lit up. 'Ooh, ay, Tony, wait until I tell yer what happened to those sausages, and what a smashing night we had because of them.'

Molly groaned, and put a hand over Nellie's mouth while she told a startled butcher, 'That's two mistakes yer've made since we came in the shop, Tony. One was adding an extra child to yer family, and the other was mentioning sausages. As I don't want to be here all day, Ellen can serve me with a breast of lamb. A lean one, out of the tray in the window. You can see to me mate.'

Nellie pushed Molly's hand away, and narrowed her eyes to slits. 'Copycat, Molly Bennett. Yer saw me looking at that tray in the window, and it was me what gave yer the idea. So bring that tray here, so I know there's no favouritism. I want to see the two breasts of lamb on the counter, to make sure one isn't leaner than the other.'

Tony's shoulders were shaking with laughter. 'Ellen, will you get the tray from the window, please, while I fetch a tape measure. Nellie is bound to want them measured, as well as weighed.'

Nellie and Molly both saw the funny side of that remark, and Nellie called after him, 'Too bleeding true I will! If yer can't be trusted to keep track of how many children yer've got, I'm not going to trust yer with my breast.'

Two customers walked into the shop as Nellie was shouting, and hearing the last six words immediately turned their eyes to her mountainous bosom. Then their noses wrinkled in disgust. Molly heard one say, in a whisper, 'Common as

62

muck. Just look at the state of her.'

Fortunately for the two customers, Nellie didn't hear what was said, or they would have had cause to regret their words.

'Where are we going to now, girl?' Nellie asked after they'd left the butcher's. 'Is the next stop Hanley's?'

Molly shook her head. 'The greengrocer's first, sunshine. I want some carrots, a swede and an onion. I'm not roasting the breast of lamb, I'm going to cut it into strips and cook it with all the sliced veg, on the top of the stove. And I've got some pearl barley at home; I'll put some of that in to thicken it.' She squeezed her mate's arm. 'Me mouth is watering just thinking about it.'

'I'll get the same as you in the greengrocer's, girl, but will yer lend me some of yer barley, 'cos I haven't got none of that at home?'

As they ambled along, arms linked, Molly asked, 'Are you sure you had an English teacher when yer were at school? I mean a teacher who taught you English?'

'Of course I did, girl, her name was Miss Henderson. I didn't like her, she was a tight cow. The least excuse and she'd send me to the head-mistress to get the cane.' Nellie squinted up at her mate. 'What made yer ask that? It's thirty years since I left school.'

'Nothing in particular, sunshine, except your Miss Henderson didn't do a very good job on yer. Not that it matters now, 'cos it's too late to find her and ask for yer money back.'

'What money, girl? I didn't give her no money

because me mam was always skint. And even if we did have money, I wouldn't have given her none, 'cos she was horrible.'

'Well, I'll give yer a reason for me asking about whether yer were taught English or not. And don't get a cob on over it, because it's the lack of good English that makes what yer say so funny. Just for an example, let's start with you asking me to lend yer some barley. Now, I can't lend you barley, can I?'

'Why can't yer, girl? Yer said yer had some in the house, so why can't I borrow some?'

'What will you do with it, sunshine?' Molly could hardly control her face or voice, for she was longing to laugh.

'Yer know what I'll do with it, girl, I'll put it in the bleeding water with the lamb and the veg. That's what!'

'Then how are yer going to give it back to me? Remember yer only asked to borrow it. So tell me how I'll get it back off yer?'

Molly had seen Nellie's face going through some weird shapes over the years, but her mate's expression now defied description. Her mouth was screwed up and nearly touching her nose, and her frown of concentration brought her forehead down to cover her eyes. They'd come to a halt while Nellie tried to figure out how she could give Molly the barley back, if she'd boiled it. In the end she shook her head, put her face back to normal, and said, 'Yer got me there, girl, I give in, so what is the answer?'

Nellie's face looked so woeful, Molly felt awful. She'd only started on the subject for a laugh, but now she was ashamed of herself for using her best friend as a figure of fun. 'There's no answer, sunshine, it's just me being sarky, as you call it. But the joke's on me, Nellie, for thinking I could be more funny than you. Yer knock spots off me, sunshine, but don't start getting big-headed because I say so. And as for that Miss Henderson, well, if I ever meet her, she'll get the length of my tongue for being the cause of you getting the cane.'

Nellie's bust grew two inches and stood to attention. This was praise indeed from her best mate. And because Molly had been so good, if they ever did bump into Miss Henderson, then Nellie would stand shoulder to shoulder with her mate, and give her ex-teacher the length of her tongue as well.

'Here's the greengrocer's, Nellie, but if you wait outside, I'll get enough veg for both of us. I'll be quicker going in on me own, and it'll save time. Then we've only got Hanley's to go to for our bread and cakes.'

Nellie licked her lips in anticipation of the luxury to come. 'Hurry up, girl, and don't stand jangling if there's any of our neighbours in there. Tell them ye're in a hurry.'

Molly's mouth opened in surprise. Her mate was the last person to tell someone not to jangle, when she herself would stand and gossip every chance she got. Even if the unlucky recipient of her tongue didn't know Nellie she'd have to stand and listen if she valued her front teeth. 'I'll be in and out in no time,' she said, 'so just stay where you are and don't talk to anyone.'

With a tray of cream slices going through her

mind on a conveyor belt, Nellie was only too happy to agree. And when Molly came out of the shop with the now heavy basket over her arm, it was to find her mate glued to the same spot she'd left her in. 'We'll take turns with this basket, sunshine, 'cos it is heavy. I'll carry it to Hanley's, and then you can take over and carry it home.'

'We're getting two cream slices each, aren't we, girl? I'm buying two, anyway, because George gave me the money. And I know he won't be asking me for change out of the shilling, so I can afford to treat you as well.' Nellie tilted her head, her face one huge beaming smile. 'We'll go mad and have a party, eh, girl? Just the two of us, on our own, living it up. Like my ma used to say, we'll break eggs with a big stick.'

Molly smiled down at her. 'Don't get carried away, sunshine. If you had your way, yer'd be suggesting we have a bottle of milk stout with our cream slice! I know you, Nellie McDonough, give you an inch and yer'd take a yard. Yer'd lead me into bad habits.'

They were outside Hanley's shop when Nellie chuckled. 'A cream slice and a bottle of milk stout wouldn't be a bad habit, it would be heaven on earth.' She rolled her eyes up to the sky. 'If ye're listening, St Peter, I was only kidding. Don't give me a black mark for a little joke.'

'You are always telling me St Peter is a very good friend of yours, sunshine, and if that is the case then he'll enjoy a joke. Any friend of yours, meself included, would have to have a really good sense of humour or yer'd drive them round the bend. And I should know because I've been yer mate for twenty-five years. And there's many a time yer've driven me to distraction.'

Nellie's eyes slid from side to side. Where the hell her mate got these big words from she'd never know. I bet she makes them up, the little woman thought, just to confuse me. 'Go and get the cakes and bread before they sell out, girl, or yer'll drive me to disfaction.'

Molly opened her mouth to correct her friend, but decided it wasn't worth the bother. 'Oh, I'd hate to drive yer to disfaction, sunshine, so I'll go and get the cakes. Four cream slices and two loaves.' She was on the step of the shop when Nellie called, 'Don't forget to pick the cakes with the most cream in. Don't let Edna palm yer off with the thin ones, 'cos she's crafty if yer don't keep yer eye on her.'

Molly was smiling when she walked over to the counter. 'Good morning, Edna.'

'What are yer grinning at?' Edna asked, reaching for two loaves on the rack behind her. 'Has Nellie been up to something?'

Molly's grin widened. 'Yer could say that, Edna. I've never known my mate not to be up to something. She's picked on you today; you are her chosen subject. You, meaning you yourself, and subject being your cream slices. She reckons that if I take me eyes off yer for one second, yer'll give me the thin slices and save the fat ones for yer favourite customers.'

'But you two are my favourite customers!'

'I know that, Edna, but it won't be so easy convincing Helen Theresa McDonough.' Molly leaned across the counter. 'Are yer busy, sun-

67

shine, or have yer got time for a laugh?'

'I've always got time for a laugh, Molly, 'cos we don't get so many we can afford to lose one. What caper are yer up to now?'

'I'm going to have a little game with Nellie. And you of course.' Molly looked out of the shop window to make sure her mate was still standing where she'd left her. 'How many cream slices have yer got, Edna?'

The shopkeeper looked at the cakes in the glass case. 'There's six, Molly. How many do you want?'

'Are they all the same, with plenty of cream in?'

'There's four the same, but two got squashed and the cream came out. Well, not all of it like, but they're not fit to sell to you.'

'I'd like to put the squashed ones in a bag, and when we get home tell her they're hers. It would be worth it to see the faces she'd pull. But the four nice creamy ones will have to go in a box, and she'll twig I'm playing tricks on her. With my luck, she'd end up with the box, and I'd be stuck with the squashed ones. I never win with Nellie, yer know. She has some sort of sixth sense, and I end up with egg on me face. So just put the four in a box for us, Edna, and I'll take our two loaves. How much is that altogether, 'cos I know it's an extra penny for the box.'

'I've been watching Nellie through the window, Molly, and I'll swear her mouth is watering.' Edna started to make up the box. 'I won't charge yer for the box, Molly, and seeing as Nellie buys cream cakes every day, I'll put the two squashed ones in a bag and yer can have them on the house. So altogether, with the four cakes and the bread, it comes to two shillings and tuppence.'

'Yer'll never be rich if yer start giving things away, Edna. You have to work hard for yer money.'

There were customers standing near, so Edna winked and held out her hand. 'That's two and tuppence, Molly. Give my love to Nellie.'

Nellie raised her eyes to the sky and huffed when Molly joined her. 'Blimey, you've taken yer time. I could have baked the bleeding loaf meself by now.'

'Don't you be getting a cob on with me, Nellie McDonough, or I'll think twice about passing on the good news.'

Nellie was torn between moaning about her arm being numb with carrying the heavy basket for so long, or hearing what her mate had to say. Then she told herself to be crafty. Hear the good news first, and perhaps she wouldn't need to moan. 'What good news is that, girl?'

'Edna has been kind enough to give us a treat.' Molly decided to drag it out, then enjoy the look of bliss she knew would shine on her mate's face.

'What d'yer mean, girl, give us a treat? Has she picked out the cream slices with the most cream in? Nice fat ones, what will ooze cream right up to me nose?' Nellie's tongue popped out to lick her lips. 'Ooh, I hope that's what ye're going to tell me, girl.'

Molly chuckled. 'Better than that, sunshine, much better. She really surprised me.'

Nellie moved from one foot to the other. 'Listen, girl, I'll be giving you a surprise if yer don't put a move on and tell me what Edna's treat is. I've had me legs crossed for the last ten minutes 'cos I'm dying to go to the lavvy. So either hurry up or be made a show of.'

'I won't be made a show of, sunshine, because I'll just walk away and pretend I've never seen yer in me life before. But before I did, seeing as ye're me best mate, I'd give yer this bag. Inside are two cream slices what got a bit squashed. Edna gave us them for nothing, and she didn't charge for the box either.'

Nellie's face was transformed, her need for a lavatory forgotten. 'Yer know, girl, I've always liked Edna. Kind and generous, that's what she is. The salt of the earth. They don't come any better than Edna Hanley.' Nellie's chins couldn't keep up with her head nodding one minute, then shaking the next, so they settled for a gentle swaying.

Molly burst out laughing. 'Nellie's McDonough, ye're a two-faced article. Yer were calling Edna fit to burn not so long ago.'

As Nellie was waving to Edna through the window and mouthing, 'Thank you', she said under her breath, 'I know that, girl, and you know that. But there's no need to bleeding well tell Edna that, or she'll come and take the cakes back off us. So wave to her, and look cheerful. Yer can pull her to pieces when we get home and are licking the cream out of the slices she gave us.'

'Ye're all heart, Nellie,' Molly said. 'All heart.'

Chapter Three

'The weather is picking up a bit,' Jack said as he tucked into his plate of very tasty stew. 'It's been like a spring day. At least as far as I could tell in the short time we get for our dinner break. I sat on the wall with a few of the men, and we ate our sandwiches there. Better than being stuck in the factory with the smell of the machines.'

Molly nodded. 'It has been a nice day. I washed a few things through and put them on the line before me and Nellie went to the shops. They were dry in a couple of hours, so I'll put the iron over them in the morning.'

'Did yer wash my blue dress, Mam?' Ruthie asked from the opposite side of the table. 'I want to wear it tomorrow night to go to the dance.'

'Yes, sunshine, I washed yer dress. When I was hanging it on the line, I noticed a few stitches missing on the hem. If yer don't sew it before yer wear it again, then more stitches will come loose and the hem will drop down. There's pale blue cotton in the drawer, so yer could do it tonight.'

Molly's sixteen-year-old daughter leaned forward and asked in a coaxing voice, 'Do me a favour will yer, Mam, and sew it for me?'

'Not on your life I won't! Ye're quite capable of doing it yerself, sunshine; you're old enough now,' Molly tutted. 'Don't be putting that woebegone face on, because you'll not get round me.

71

Jill and Doreen were seeing to their own clothes when they were your age.'

There was laughter in Ruthie's eyes when she pointed her fork and said, 'My two sisters have got a lot to answer for. They've ruined my life, being so goody-goody. Didn't they ever do anything wrong, or get into trouble?'

It was her father who answered. 'They never did anything to bring trouble to out door, pet. Doreen was inclined to answer back, and like you she wanted to grow up too quickly. But Jill has always been the quiet one.' He chuckled. 'She was the referee between Doreen and yer mam. Always calm and gentle, she would stop an argument before it got out of hand.'

Ruthie was nodding her head. 'Everyone loves our Jill, yer can't help loving her. And I can remember our Doreen getting a cob on when she wanted to stay out late, and yer wouldn't let her. But she's not like that now, she's more like our Jill.' Her infectious giggle filled the room. 'I've just been reckoning up, and our Tommy is seven years older than me. Then there's two years between him and Doreen, and one year between her and Jill. So I'm the baby of the family.'

'And the cheekiest,' Molly told her. 'You get away with more than the others ever did. Tommy was the apple of my eye, being the only boy. He was never a ha'p'orth of trouble and look what a fantastic man he's turned out to be.'

'Yeah,' Ruthie agreed. 'He's not half handsome, our Tommy.'

'We're a handsome family,' Jack said, laughing. 'Your mam's beauty passed down to her three daughters, and how could Tommy be anything but handsome when he came from such fine stock as the Bennett family?'

'Can we stop patting each other on the back and finish our dinners?' Molly said. 'Looks aren't anything to go by, it's what the person is like inside that counts.' She laid her knife and fork down on her empty plate. 'I enjoyed that, it was very tasty. Unfortunately there's none left, the pan is empty.'

'I'll clear the table, Mam,' Ruthie said, 'and I'll help yer with the dishes. You wash and I'll dry.'

'Are yer going out tonight, sunshine?'

'Only to Bella's. We're staying in tonight and having a game of cards. Tomorrow we're going to the dance at the church hall.'

'Are yer going with Gordon?'

'Yeah, and Peter's coming with Bella.'

Molly collected the dishes and scraped her chair back. 'Keep yer promise, Ruthie, sunshine, and clear the table. And don't forget to shake the cloth in the yard before putting it away. Then come and dry the dishes for me. Yer dad can put the chenille cloth on, he's not helpless.'

Jack poked his head into the kitchen. 'What's the sudden rush, love? Are yer going out?'

'I'm slipping round to me ma's for an hour. I've seen Doreen today, and Jill, so now I want to see Tommy and Rosie, and me ma and da. I'll sleep easier once I know all the family are well.'

'I'll walk round with yer, love,' Jack said. 'I haven't seen them for a few days. Except Tommy, of course, I see him every day in work. But it's not the same as seeing him at home.'

'As soon as I've finished out here, yer can swill yer face. Get here before Ruthie, 'cos she takes ages getting herself ready, and we'd be going out when it was time to come home.'

'Ah, ay, Mam, I'm not that bad!' Ruthie said. 'It takes me about ten minutes, that's all.'

Molly huffed. 'And the rest, sunshine. Anyone would think yer were going to the Adelphi, the time yer take titivating yerself up. I bet Jean Harlow didn't take as long as you.'

Jack came to stand at the kitchen door. 'I think that is a very unfair comparison, love. Jean Harlow didn't have to do anything but sit there and let others do her make-up and hair. She probably didn't even dress herself.'

'What's got into you?' Molly asked, putting the plates Ruthie had dried on a shelf. 'I didn't know you were so knowledgeable about the life of a film star. Ye're a dark horse on the quiet, Jack Bennett.'

'Ah, well, it's good to have an air of mystery, love, it adds to my attraction. That's why you have always been so madly in love with me.' Jack leaned against the kitchen wall and chortled. 'Sounds good, doesn't it, love? A man of mystery.'

'Is that why I fell for yer?' Molly said, pulling him over to the sink. 'I've left yer a drop of water in the kettle, so yer can put that in the bowl to warm it up. I'd hate a man with so much going for him to have to get washed in cold water.'

Ruthie was sitting by the living room table waiting for her turn to get to the sink. 'I wish we had a bathroom, Mam, then we wouldn't have to take turns. Most of the girls in work live in houses

74

with bathrooms. And there's a toilet in them, as well. D'yer think we'll ever get a bathroom?'

'We've managed in this house for twenty-five years, sunshine, and brought four children up in it. I love my little house, it holds a lot of wonderful memories, and I can't see meself moving to another house just because it's got a bathroom. Not that I wouldn't like the luxury of one, and an inside toilet, but if I was offered a choice, I'd opt to stay in this two-up two-down house where me and yer dad raised four children who have turned out to be a credit to us.'

Ruthie was sorry she'd mentioned a bathroom now, for it must have sounded as though she didn't like the house she lived in and would like something better. She hadn't meant it to sound like that, for she wouldn't want to move to another house, even if it did have a bathroom. Just imagine not living near Auntie Nellie, and her friend Bella; it didn't bear thinking about. 'Ye're right, Mam, this is a lovely little house. And like yer said, it holds all the memories of us as babies. No, I bet the girls in work don't have a big family like ours who all love one another. And they definitely don't have a neighbour like Auntie Nellie.'

'That is a certainty nobody could deny, sunshine, 'cos there isn't another Auntie Nellie in the entire city of Liverpool. She's a one-off, is Nellie.'

Jack came into the room drying his face. 'I've always said that Nellie wouldn't be as funny without you, love, you know that. Ye're a double act, and yer bounce off each other.'

'It's me mate's actions that make her funnier than me, sunshine. Half the time she doesn't have to say a word, her face does the talking for her.' Molly smiled as she saw a picture in her mind's eye of Nellie and her aspidistra. And the woeful look on her face when Molly refused to let her stay. 'She would have made a fantastic actress. You've got to be with her every day to know exactly what she can get up to. When we've got some time to spare, so I can do justice to her acting, I'll tell you about Monday morning, when she was giving me plant a Beecham's powder, to give yer an idea of what she gets up to.'

Jack looked startled. 'Nellie wanted to give the plant a Beecham's powder? Are yer having me on?'

'I'm not having you on, sunshine, and that's only the half of it. But there's no time to tell it now, or we'll never make it to me ma's before she goes to bed. I'll tell yer tomorrow night.' Molly raised her brows to Ruthie. 'You mustn't repeat anything I tell yer, sunshine, not even to Bella. Not one word, do yer hear?' She waited for her daughter's nod before saying, 'It wouldn't be fair to laugh behind Auntie Nellie's back. She probably wouldn't turn a hair. But she's my best mate, and while I don't mind my family having a laugh at her expense because I know they all love the bones of her, I would be very annoyed if I heard anyone outside of our group making fun of her.'

'Bella wouldn't make fun of her, Mam. She really loves her.'

After combing his hair, Jack told his daughter, 'Do as yer mam tells yer, pet, and don't repeat anything you hear in this house. Least said, soonest mended.'

Molly was standing with her coat on, her front

door key in her pocket and her purse in her hand. 'Come on, Jack, put a move on. Honestly, men take longer to get ready than women. I wouldn't care if they looked any better for it, but they don't!'

'Ah, now, love, that's hitting below the belt. Men would look well with their hair curled, and powder and lipstick on their faces. I admit that women are better-looking – prettier, like – but most of them need help to look that way.'

Ruthie's eyes were going from one to the other. Her mam would have to retaliate, 'cos she never used any make-up, didn't need to for she had a lovely complexion. And she never needed to curl her blonde hair, either.

'Let's not get into that, eh,' Molly said, 'otherwise you'll raise the roof if I told yer how much money I spend on powder, rouge, perfume and having me hair done every week.' She held back the smile of mischief which wanted to put in an appearance. 'I just couldn't bear you to tell me off for being so extravagant. So come on, let's get round to me ma's before me lipstick wears off.'

Jack put his arms round her and held her tight. 'You've never needed powder, rouge or lipstick since the day I set eyes on yer, love. If yer'd looked like a painted doll, I wouldn't have given yer a second glance. In my eyes you are the most beautiful woman in the world, and always will be.'

Ruthie sighed with emotion. When she got married, she hoped it would be to someone as loving as her dad. And she would want him to show his affection openly, so she could show hers in return, without feeling embarrassed. Another big sigh came. It would be wonderful to love, and be loved, like her mam and dad.

'We're going, Ruthie, so don't forget to take a key with yer. And make sure yer bang the door shut behind yer. We'll be back before ten, and that's late enough for you to be out.'

Molly stepped down on to the pavement and waited for Jack to close the door and join her before linking her arm through his. 'I feel as though we're courting again, sunshine. It's not very often we walk out together arm in arm.'

Jack laughed. 'It feels like it did when we were courting. It's hard to believe that it's about twenty-eight years ago. The time seems to have flown over.'

'Don't be putting years on me.' Molly let out a gasp of surprise and pulled Jack to a halt, for leaning against the wall of a house three doors from her own was her mate Nellie. 'What are yer doing out here, sunshine? Are yer getting some fresh air?'

Nellie stepped away from the wall. 'When have I ever been interested in fresh air, girl? I know it's good for yer, and it's free, but it doesn't do a thing for me.' Her chins quivered at the very thought. 'No, I'm not here for the good of my health, girl, I'm here because I'm curious. That's the only reason.'

Molly would have had a bet on what was going to happen next, for she knew her mate inside out. She gave Jack's arm a slight jerk, to warn him to listen carefully. 'What are yer curious about, sunshine?'

'Well, if yer must know, I'm curious to find out

78

whether my best mate is playing a dirty trick on me.'

'As I'm supposed to be your best mate, Nellie, I'm cut to the quick that yer could even think I'd play a dirty trick on yer.' Events were turning out as Molly's mind had predicted, and she gave another little jerk to let Jack know he would be interested in what was to happen. 'What have I done to upset yer?'

'Sneaking out without telling me, that's what. I've been with yer all day, yet yer never cracked on yer were going out tonight. Not a dicky bird out of yer. And if I didn't have good ears, what can hear a pin drop at the Pier Head, then yer'd have got away with sneaking past me window.' The shoulders went back, the bosom pushed forward, and the head gave a quick shake. 'And yer deserve to be cut to the quick.'

Molly could feel Jack's body shaking with silent laughter, and she hoped he could keep it in a little longer. 'We're only going round to me ma's, Nellie, to see how the family are. There's nothing wrong with that, surely?'

'Yes, there is, misery guts. I'd like to know how yer ma and da are, 'cos I'm almost like one of the family. And when I tell them how yer nearly got away with sneaking past me house, they'll be very upset.'

'What d'yer mean by saying we nearly sneaked past? We don't have to sneak, sunshine, we're not thieves.'

'Don't be twisting me words, Molly Bennett.' Nellie's chins agreed she was right to point that out. 'Yer nearly did get past, but yer didn't, 'cos

79

ye're still here. And yer wouldn't be still here if yer had! Now do yer see what I'm getting at?'

'What ye're saying is as clear as mud, Nellie. But what I can understand is that me and Jack are going to have company on our walk to me ma's house. I'm right, aren't I?'

Nellie's whole body became alert. 'Of course ye're right, girl, yer always are. And I won't keep yer waiting, 'cos I've got me coat ready on the floor behind the front door. I knew yer wouldn't want to be held back.' Quick as a flash, Nellie bent over the steps to put her hand inside the door to get her coat. In the process, she showed a glimpse of blue bloomers, elastic garter and bare leg.

'Don't you dare laugh, Jack,' Molly warned, 'or I'll clock yer one.'

By this time Jack's sides were sore because he wanted, not just to laugh, but to bend over and roar. However, his wife's tone of voice told him it would be unwise.

Molly took the coat off Nellie and held it open. 'Here yer are, sunshine, slip yer arm in. But yer do know ye're a flipping nuisance, don't yer? And a ruddy cheeky one at that.'

'Yes, I do know that, girl. But I'd rather get a telling off from you than have to sit with me mouth shut all night while George reads the *Echo*.' Somehow, she managed to get between Molly and Jack, and she linked arms with them. 'I know every man likes to read the paper, and I don't begrudge it to them. But where most men read from the front page to the back, then fold it and put it away under a cushion, my George

80

doesn't. Once he's read it from front to back, he reads it again from back to front.'

As the trio walked towards the next street, Nellie's hips were swaying from side to side. Jack was pushed towards the gutter with one sway, then jerked back when Nellie's other hip had Molly wiping the passing window ledges with her coat sleeve. The little woman was four foot ten inches, against Jack's six foot, and she had to drop her head right back to look up at him. 'It's no good me talking to you, lad, 'cos yer wouldn't hear me. So don't think I'm being rude, and leaving yer out of our conversation. But that's yer own bleeding fault for growing into a giant. It's like out Paul, he's a six-footer. I have to stand on a chair to give him a clout now.'

Jack bent down to say, 'Nellie, seeing as ye're Molly's best mate, and one of my favourite people, I'll stand yer on a chair if yer ever want to clout me, or give me a thick lip.'

Nellie beamed. 'Ay, did yer hear that, girl? I've always known your husband had a soft spot for me. Like I keep telling yer, but yer won't believe me, there's no man what can resist my voluptuous body.'

They were nearing the Jacksons' house when Molly pulled them to a halt. 'Let's get this straight, sunshine. There are three words you must not mention tonight. They are voluptuous body, sausages and Beecham's powder. Have yer got that?'

'Yes, girl, I've got it. I've got a terrible memory though, yer know that. So I might have to ask yer to repeat them a bit later on. And just as a matter of interest, like, is Beecham's powder counted as one word or two?'

Molly tutted as she knocked on the door of the house where her parents lived, together with her son Tommy and his beautiful wife Rosie. 'Just behave yerself, Nellie, that's all I ask.'

'Will it be all right with you if I enjoy meself, girl?'

When Tommy opened the door it was to see three people he loved shaking with laughter. 'Don't tell me Auntie Nellie's garter has snapped? Not outside our front door? Ooh, me grandma won't like that, having all the neighbours talking about her keeping a rowdy house.'

Molly stepped into the hall and kissed her son on the cheek. 'She'd make a saint blush, would yer Auntie Nellie, sunshine, but this time her joke was very mild. Not that she's slipping, like, she's just taking a short break.'

When Molly saw her ma and da sitting side by side on the couch, her heart filled with love and emotion. She could never find enough words to describe her devotion to them. Her childhood had been wonderful, thanks to her Irish-born mother and her loving father. Although Bridie had lived in Liverpool since she met and married Bob, her first love, she still had that lovely Irish lilt in her voice. 'Oh, it's yerself, me darlin'.' Bridie lifted her face for Molly's kiss. 'Sure it's lovely to see yer. And Jack and Nellie, too! Sure ye're as welcome as the flowers in May, and that's the truth of it.'

Bob Jackson kept hold of his wife's hand when he stretched his neck for Molly's kiss. In his seventies now, he'd had to pack in work long before he was due to retire because of a heart attack. He'd never really recovered from it and Bridie had looked after him ever since. They were as much in love as the day they were wed, and weren't afraid to show it. Molly and Jack had given them four grandchildren, whom they adored, and now they were proud great-grandparents to Bobby and little Moll. And it wasn't only Molly's family who filled their lives. For a fourteen-year-old Irish girl, a friend of one of Bridie's old friends back in the old country, had asked if she could live with them until she found a job. There was no work in Ireland, and times were hard. That's when Rosie O'Grady came to be part of the family. A real Irish beauty, she had taken a shine to Tommy. But he was young and girl shy, and avoided her like the plague. However, Rosie persisted, even though he would run a mile rather than talk to her. And her patience paid off when one of Tommy's mates fell for her and asked for a date. That caused Tommy to look at her more closely, and she was quick to steal his heart. They were married now, and as much in love as Bridie and Bob, who had opened their home to the newly-weds.

Rosie came running down the stairs when she heard the familiar voices. She hugged and kissed Molly and Jack, then turned to Nellie. 'Oh, I didn't hear your voice, Mrs Mac. Is it yerself that's not feeling too good?'

Nellie hung her head. 'I've been told to be quiet and behave meself, girl.' She turned her head slightly and winked at Rosie. 'I've had strict instructions that I am not to use three words what my mate doesn't like. And I've forgotten them now.' She narrowed her eyes, a sure sign of mischief. 'What were the words, Molly?' Without giving her mate time to spoil her fun, she went on quickly to say, 'Oh, I've just remembered! I must not, under any circumstances, say sausages, voluptuous body, or Beecham's powder.' Her face lit up. 'I got them right, didn't I, girl? Or have I left one out?'

Molly's lips were twitching as she passed her coat over to Rosie to hang up. 'How about aspidistra, sunshine? That's one word yer've probably forgotten.'

'Ah, now, Molly Bennett, I'm not deaf, and I know yer didn't say that word. And yer wouldn't, would yer, 'cos yer'd need to put it into a sentence. Yer couldn't just say "aspidistra", and stand there like a lemon, or people would think there was something wrong with yer. What yer'd need to say is that I tried to poison your aspidistra with a Beecham's powder.'

This sounded like one of Nellie's pranks, and Bridie sat forward with anticipation. 'Nellie, pull a chair out and make yerself comfortable. It sounds as though you and Molly have either been having a joke, me darlin', or a little disagreement, perhaps?'

When Nellie pulled a chair out from the table, Molly and Jack followed suit, and the only chair left was taken by Rosie sitting on Tommy's knee. 'I'm sure it wasn't a disagreement, so I am,' Rosie said. 'Auntie Molly and Mrs Mac are like sisters, they never fall out.'

'We do have the odd disagreement, sunshine,' Molly told her, 'not many, just now and again. But

84

I'll let my mate tell yer this tale, for she's a better actress than me. She's better at exaggerating too.'

Bridie was eager, and gripped Bob's hand as though she feared he'd be spirited away from her. 'We're all ears, Nellie, me darlin', so go ahead and start at the beginning.'

The little woman was as pleased as Punch. She was never happier than when she had an audience. 'I may need a drink halfway through this story, 'cos it's a long one.'

'The kettle is on now, Mrs Mac,' Tommy said. 'When you're ready we can have the tea ready before yer can say Jack Robinson.'

'Ay, I wish I'd known that Jack Robinson. He must have been very popular, 'cos everyone talks about him.'

'Nellie, he died before yer were born. So if yer had known him, yer wouldn't be sitting here tonight keeping everyone waiting for yer to start talking.'

'Oh, you knew him, did yer, girl? And yer never let on? Ye're a dark horse, Molly Bennett.'

'I didn't tell yer, 'cos it would have sounded as though I was bragging.' Molly was thinking that if yer can't beat them, then join them. 'He used to live next door to a girl I went to school with.' She raised her brow at her mother, who nodded to say she understood. 'You remember Elsie, don't yer, Ma? We used to play ball or skipping in the street. Bright red hair and freckles, she had.'

'Of course I remember Elsie, me darlin'. She was a nice girl.'

'That's funny,' Bob said, laughing inside. 'I can't bring her to mind. And if she had red hair and freckles, well, yer'd think I'd remember someone like that.'

Molly could see Nellie's frown deepen and her eyes narrow. She hated not being the centre of attention, but Molly wanted to get one more dig in. 'You were at work, Da. By the time you got home Elsie had gone in for her tea.'

That did it for Nellie. She banged an open palm on the table and glared at each one in turn. 'I thought yer were all interested in a little tale I had to tell yer. And yer would have been if my mate hadn't stuck her big nose in. Her with her friend what had red hair and bleeding freckles. And of course she'd know Jack Robinson, 'cos she's man mad is Molly Bennett, and she wouldn't care if he was as old as the hills as long as he could stand on his two feet.' She shook her head slowly when she looked at Jack, allowing her chins the option of a waltz or a slow foxtrot. 'I'm sorry, lad, but you must be the only one who doesn't know your wife is a maneater.'

'Oh, I've known that for a long time, Nellie.' Jack did a good job of keeping his face straight. 'I'm covered in bite marks, all over. That's why I could never wear a swimming costume. But when I found out the truth about Molly, it was too late, we were already married.'

'Well I hope yer had the sense to ask for the seven and six back, what yer paid for the marriage licence. If ever there was a waste of money, that was it. I know I keep harping on it, lad, but it's only because me heart bleeds for yer. Why didn't yer choose someone with a voluptuous body like mine? Oh, I know there's not many around, they're few and far between. But if yer'd waited, someone like me would have come along. And yer wouldn't have had to ask for yer seven and six back, lad, yer'd have been leaving them a tip!'

'Stop putting ideas into Jack's head, Nellie, or I'll never be able to keep him on the straight and narrow.'

'Listen, girl, yer told me to be quiet and behave meself, but you're doing more talking than me. Six times I've opened me mouth to start telling me tale, what all these people are waiting for, and each time you've butted in. So d'yer think yer could pipe down, and give me a chance?'

When Molly nodded, Nellie's eyes went round the table. 'I hope ye're all wide awake, 'cos me story starts off at ten minutes to eight on Monday morning. And because I think it would be more interesting to act the scene, I'm going to ask Molly to act her part. Are yer game, girl? Words and actions?'

'Well, it's very short notice, sunshine, but I'll try. I'll have to start off by doing what I was working on when you came into it. And for that, I'll have to stand up and go through the motions, words and all.'

Tommy squeezed Rosie's waist. 'This should be a hoot, sweetheart.'

'Better than going to the pictures, me dearly beloved husband,' Rosie whispered back. 'And it's more comfortable, so it is, and doesn't cost a penny, even though we're in the best seats.'

Nellie feigned annoyance. 'When you two love-birds stop being lovey-dovey, we can get the show

87

on the road.'

'Sorry, Auntie Nellie,' Tommy said. 'I have heard that all actors are nervous before the curtain goes up, and I should have remembered.'

Nellie's eyes turned from the loving couple, and they all heard her mutter under her breath, 'He might take after his dad in looks, but he takes after his mother for being a gasbag.'

'I'll pretend I didn't hear that, sunshine,' Molly said. 'Now into the hall with you until you hear your cue.'

With her back to the sideboard, Molly explained. 'This is ten to eight on Monday morning, and I'm talking to meself about whether to make meself a cup of tea, or start the washing. You'll have to use yer imagination.' She fixed her eyes on the mantelpiece and repeated as much as she could remember of the conversation she had held with her living room on Monday. Her audience were enthralled, for Molly was a good actress. When she jumped with fright when a voice behind her asked, 'Who are yer talking to, girl?' then the audience were startled too. And as the enactment continued, with Nellie not feeling well, and Molly falling for it, the two amateur actresses were so convincing, you could have heard a pin drop.

Fortunately for Nellie, Bridie had a huge aspidistra on a small table in front of the window. It was her pride and joy, and although Nellie's actions with the supposed Beecham's powder brought roars of laughter from the other family members, Bridie didn't know whether to laugh or cry. But her humour was soon restored when it came to the part where Nellie was banished from the house by Molly, and told not to come back until half past ten.

The part where Nellie was kneeling on the step looking through the letterbox, and Molly answering her from her seat on the second stair, brought the loudest laughter. Bob and Bridie were wiping their eyes on neatly folded hankies as white as snow, while Tommy and Rosie clung to each other, tears falling on their shoulders.

And Jack was so proud of his wife he left his chair to embrace her. He wasn't usually a demonstrative man, but his kiss now let all the family know how much he adored her. 'That was good, love. Better than a pint of bitter any day.'

'Ay, lover boy,' Nellie said, hands on hips and chins waiting to see which way her head turned. 'What about me? If I'd known it was going to be an orgy, I'd have brought my feller with me.'

'Ah, yer poor thing,' Molly said, putting on a sad face. 'Give her a hug, Jack, before she starts crying.'

When Jack walked towards her with arms outstretched, Nellie's chubby face was a sight to behold. She ducked under his arm to tell Molly, 'Yer've cooked yer goose now, girl. Once he gets hold of my voluptuous body, he'll never be satisfied with someone what is flat-chested and pigeon-toed.'

With a hand covering her mouth, Molly doubled up. She might be able to take Nellie's words with a pinch of salt, even tell her off about them, but the faces her mate could pull, well, unless you were devoid of humour, you couldn't help but laugh at them. And she could hear the others laughing, even Jack.

'I don't know why you're laughing, lad,' Nellie told him. 'If I was in your shoes I'd be crying at the unfairness of it. Yer've been swingled.'

'Oh, dear, oh, dear,' Molly used the back of her hand to wipe her eyes.

'Ye're coming up with some big words, sunshine. Yer haven't gone and bought a dictionary, have yer? Not at your age?'

'I'm the same age as you, girl, give or take a few months. So don't be putting years on me. And another thing, ye're not the only one what can come out with big words. I'm far from being hignorant.'

'I know ye're far from being hignorant, sunshine, 'cos ye're beginning to use words even I don't know.'

Nellie grew two inches in stature, and her bosom blossomed before their eyes. 'What word didn't yer know, girl? Or was it more than one?'

'Well, for one thing, Nellie, I never knew there was an h in ignorant. But that's an easy mistake anyone could make. What I'm dying to know is what the word "swingled" means. It sounds a jolly word, like, you know, a happy jingle.'

Nellie beamed. 'Yeah, it does, girl, now as I come to think of it. Isn't it wonderful that yer have all these words in yer head that yer don't know are there?'

'What does swingled mean, sunshine, so I can keep a note of it? It might just come in handy some time.'

Nellie's chins shook when she moved her head.

90

'It means diddled, girl. You know, like yer've been had.'

'Oh, I've got it now, sunshine, you mean swindled!'

Nellie tutted, then blew her breath out through her teeth. 'That's what I said, soft girl. Are yer going deaf?'

'Not that I know of, sunshine. I've heard everything you've said, so there can't be anything wrong with me hearing. Have yer got any more big words in yer head that can baffle me with science?'

'How soft you are, girl!' Nellie pooh-poohed the question. 'I give you some of the big words what I've got in me head, and tomorrow yer'd be in the butcher's shop, swanking to Tony and Ellen using my words! Yer must think I was born yesterday! Find yer own words, Molly Bennett, seeing as ye're so clever. I mean, why did yer have to bring fortune-telling up? What's that got to do with words and the price of fish?'

The group round the table looked at each other, baffled by Nellie's words. 'Yer've lost me completely now, Nellie,' Molly said. 'Who mentioned fortune-telling? I most certainly didn't!'

'Oh, come off it, girl! Everyone heard yer, didn't they, Jack? Go on, lad, tell her! Don't be frightened, I won't let her hit yer.'

Jack was still waiting to give Nellie a hug. Not that he wanted to give Nellie a hug, mind, but he didn't want to upset her by sitting down. 'I couldn't tell yer, Nellie, because I haven't been taking a lot of notice. But I do know Molly doesn't like fortune-telling, she thinks it's unlucky.'

Nellie's eyes went to Tommy and Rosie, who shrugged their shoulders, and she got the same reaction from Bridie and Bob.

'This is a stitch-up,' the little woman said. 'Ye're all ganging up against me.' With her feet apart, she took on her fighting stance, much to the amusement of those looking on. 'If my mate tells me she never mentioned one of those things where silly buggers sit in the dark, hold hands and ask to talk to people what are dead, I'll clock her one.'

Molly jumped to her feet. 'Oh, yer mean a séance, sunshine! Why didn't yer say that, and I'd have known what yer were going on about?'

'It was you what said it, girl, so yer didn't need me to tell yer.' Her head down, looking at her feet, Nellie muttered, 'She might be me best mate, but she can be as thick as two short planks sometimes.'

While Nellie was muttering, Molly was going over in her head what she'd said to bring the conversation from her being deaf. Then it came to her in a flash. 'Nellie, I said science, not séance, yer silly nit!'

'What's the difference, girl? Sounds like the same ruddy word to me.'

'Ay, Nellie, I'll give yer a good word to try out in the butcher's,' Molly said. 'I came across it in the dictionary ages ago, and I bet there's not many people know there is such a word, 'cos I'd never heard of it. D'yer want to know what it is, so yer can show off in front of Tony and Ellen?'

'I'll have it if I can get me tongue round it, girl.

92

But if not I'll let you be the clever bugger.'

'What is the word, Mam?' Tommy asked. 'I bet I could tell yer what it means.'

'Oh, he could that, Auntie Molly,' Rosie said. 'Sure he's very clever is my ever-loving husband.' Her beautiful face was aglow. 'He proved how clever he is by marrying me.'

'Go on, Mam,' Rosie's ever-loving husband said. 'I'll have a go and I bet I'm right.'

Nellie was glaring at him. 'Don't be so ruddy cocky, Tommy Bennett. And before yer answer yer mam's question, yer can answer one for me.'

'Auntie Nellie, I'll do anything for you.' Tommy, the spitting image of his dad, grinned. 'Yer just have to say the word and it'll be done.'

'Well, just tell me, seeing as how ye're so bleeding clever, how come we've been here half an hour, and yer haven't even boiled the kettle yet? Yer don't get all this entertainment free, yer know, there's a price to be paid.'

Rosie loosened her arm from Tommy's, and jumped to her feet. 'It's right yer are, Mrs Mac. Come on, beloved, help me make the tea.'

'There's plenty of biscuits in the pantry,' Bridie called. 'And isn't Nellie partial to a custard cream or two?'

'Ay, not so fast.' Tommy held Rosie back. 'Let's sort this word out first. It'll haunt me in bed, and I'll not be able to sleep if I don't find out what it is. Have a bet with me, Auntie Nellie?'

'Sod off, lad! If I had money to spare, I'd spend it on cream slices, not on flaming words I don't understand.'

'What is the word, Mam, before Auntie Nellie

clouts me one?'

Molly had to bite on the side of her mouth to stop herself from falling apart with laughter as she looked at the faces waiting for her to speak. One last sharp bite, and out it came. 'Serendipity.'

There was complete silence, then Tommy, who had been so sure of himself asked in a croaky voice, 'Say it again, Mam, but slowly this time.'

'I'll spell it out.' Molly was hoping her son knew what the word meant, for he'd feel stupid after bragging. 'S-e-r-e-n-d-i-p-i-t-y.'

'This is a joke, isn't it, Mam! There's no such word,' Tommy said.

'I'm sorry, son, but I'd be telling lies if I said there wasn't. Try it on yer workmates, and get a laugh out of it.'

'Sure I've never heard a word like it in all me life,' Bridie said. 'It's a foreign word, so it is.'

'What does it mean, Mam?' Tommy asked, looking sheepish. 'I was always top of the class in English, but I'm blowed if I've ever heard that. Are yer pulling our legs?'

'I'm not pulling yer legs, sunshine. I can't remember what it said in the dictionary, but I promise there is such a word. And I've got a vague idea it means something nice, like magic.'

Nellie tilted her head, and asked Tommy, 'D'yer think you and yer ever-loving wife could do something magic with the kettle and teapot, lad?'

Rosie took control and pulled Tommy out to the kitchen. 'You see to the kettle and I'll get the cups and saucers ready. Sure it'll be time for our visitors to leave before they've had a drink, so it will.'

In the living room, with Bridie and Bob still

sitting at the table holding hands, and Jack leaning against the sideboard, Nellie was looking up at Molly. 'I like the sound of that word, girl, and I could have some fun with my George and Paul. That's if I can get me tongue round it.' Her face creased into a smile. 'Ay, I can just see meself in the butcher's, coming out with a word like that when the shop was full of customers. They wouldn't half think I was clever. And it would be one in the eye for smarty-pants Tony. Say it again, girl, nice and slow so I can get used to it.'

'Well listen carefully, sunshine, 'cos I can't keep repeating it.' So very slowly, with her mouth exaggerating every letter, Molly said, in a singsong voice, 'Ser-en-dip-ity.'

Nellie beamed. 'Ay, yer could dance to that.' She grabbed a startled Jack by the arms and began pulling him around. 'Sendipity, sendipity,' she sang, moving the letters about as she saw fit. 'Densipity, densipity.' There was no respite for poor Jack, who was thrown against the chairs and table. All he could do was appeal to his wife with his eyes. If it carried on, there wouldn't be a spot on his body that wasn't black and blue.

'That's enough now, Nellie,' Molly said, seeing her husband being bashed about. He was the only one not enjoying it, though, for she thought it was hilarious, as did Bridie and Bob, and Tommy and Rosie were in stitches. And it really was because there was no sign of the original word now. Serendipity had been torn apart and thrown out, and Nellie was singing any words that came into her head. She was like a bouncing ball, with a hot and bothered Jack wishing she'd run out of breath and energy.

It was Molly who brought Nellie to a stop. 'Enough is enough, sunshine, so pack it in. My husband has to go to work tomorrow, don't forget. Just look at him; he's worn out. He won't have enough energy to get out of bed.'

A slow, wicked smile crossed Nellie's face. 'Yer should be thanking me, then, girl, 'cos you could have a lie-in with him, and he'd soon recover his energy.'

Molly's hand was quick to cover her mate's mouth. Heaven only knew what was coming next, and with Tommy and Rosie only married a short time, she didn't want them to be embarrassed. And she herself would be embarrassed in front of her ma and da. 'Sit down, Nellie, and behave yerself. The tea's poured out, and yes, there's a plate of biscuits. So plonk yer backside down. Yer've had enough fun for one night.'

'I don't know where yer get the energy from, Nellie,' Bridie said. 'It's tired I am just watching you.'

Bob agreed. 'I was breathing for yer, Nellie, and yer you seem as happy as Larry and not in the least puffed.'

Nellie was feeling full of devilment, and was about to tell him she only ever ran out of puff in the bedroom. She actually had her mouth open, but was thwarted when Molly pushed a custard cream into it. 'Ay, girl,' she croaked, 'what did yer do that for?' With crumbs flying everywhere, she spluttered, 'Yer neatly choked me, yer daft article. Yer'd have something to say if I did it to you. The foot would be on the other boot then, wouldn't it, ay?'

The little woman didn't know why there was a burst of laughter. 'What's so bleeding funny about me being choked to death?'

Molly struggled to keep her face straight. 'There wouldn't be anything funny, sunshine, not when the foot would be on the other boot. Painful, perhaps, but definitely not funny. On the other hand, though, if the boot was on the other foot, then it wouldn't be painful at all.'

They could practically see Nellie's brain working by the shapes her face was making. They'd lost her now; she didn't know what they were talking about, turning things round about and upside down. They were daft, the lot of them. She was the only sensible person at that table. She scratched her head. The best way to treat someone what was doolally was to be nice to them and keep them calm.

'These are nice custard creams, girl.' Nellie smiled sweetly at Bridie. 'Not that me mate's are not nice, 'cos they are.' She sent the same smile across the table to Molly. 'Listen, girl, d'yer know tomorrow morning, when we're having our morning cup of tea and biscuits...' Another sweet smile, then, 'Well, will yer write that word down for me, so I don't forget?'

'What word is that, sunshine?'

'I don't know, girl. I've forgot!'

Chapter Four

As Molly stepped down on to the pavement she almost collided with the young couple coming out of next door. 'Oh, I'm sorry, sunshine, I nearly knocked you over.' She smiled at Nellie's son, Paul, and his girlfriend Phoebe Corkhill. 'I should look where I'm going.'

'Or look before yer leap, Auntie Molly,' Paul said. 'Yer came down those steps like a bat out of hell.'

'Take no notice of him, Mrs B.' Phoebe's shy smile came with a wink. 'He never looks where he's going, even when he's on the dance floor. I bet there's many a girl gone home with sore toes.'

'Is that where ye're off to now?' Molly asked. 'Going to Blair Hall, or the Grafton?'

Paul, who had long black eyelashes any girl would die for, and deep dimples, lifted both arms out. 'See, Auntie Molly, no dance shoes tucked away. My girlfriend is keeping me in order, and I'm only allowed to go dancing once a week. With her, of course, not on my own. She's getting really bossy, and I'm wondering if she'll give me a dog's life after we get married.' His dimples appeared when he chuckled. 'What d'yer think, Auntie Molly? Shall I cancel the wedding?'

Phoebe punched his arm. 'The way you're carrying on, Paul McDonough, there'll never be a wedding!' She pretended to be exasperated.

'Money goes through yer hands like water; you can't spend it quick enough. It's about time yer grew up and showed a bit of responsibility.'

'Oh, dear,' Molly said. 'I hope ye're not going to have a row in the middle of the street? If you are, then can yer just hang on for a minute while I knock for me mate? Yer mam would go mad if she missed a bit of excitement, Paul.'

'It won't come to that, Mrs B.,' Phoebe said. 'Me and Paul are on our way to the pictures. And before he gets a chance to tell yer why we're going to the pictures, I'll tell yer. It's cheaper than going dancing. And although yer'd never notice, we're supposed to be saving up to get married.'

Paul grinned, and looked a bit sheepish. 'I do try, Auntie Molly, but yer know what they say about a fool and his money being soon parted? Well, it's true. I'm hopeless at saving up, but I'm going to try and turn over a new leaf.'

Phoebe pointed a stiffened finger. 'You better had, Paul McDonough, because if we don't get married this year, then there won't ever be a wedding.' Again the finger was pointed. 'And don't think I'm not serious, because I am.'

Molly knew this was an idle threat, for Phoebe had loved Paul before she was old enough to know what true love was. She was a shy, gentle, pretty girl, and there'd never been any other boy in her life. 'Are you listening to what Phoebe's saying, Paul? Well, now you can listen to me. If you do your mam out of having an excuse to buy a wedding hat, she'll stand on a chair and knock spots off yer. And d'yer know what, sunshine? When yer mam's finished with yer, I'll have a go at yer. Yer see, Paul, I'm partial to wedding hats meself.'

Phoebe chuckled. 'There you are, see! If you don't marry me before the summer's over, I'll set the whole street on to yer.'

Paul gaped. 'The summer?' He pretended to stagger backwards. 'You said before the year's out! Now ye're saying before the summer's over! That's not going to give me enough time to save up ten bob!'

'Ten bob will only pay for the flowers, dear.' Phoebe smiled. 'My bouquet and the bridesmaids' posies. Oh, and buttonholes for the men.'

Molly had been intending to cross the road to visit her daughter when she'd bumped into the couple, so now she said. 'Seeing as yer've got as far as the buttonholes, I'll leave yer to it. I promised to go over to Doreen's, and she's probably looking through the window, wondering what I'm standing here gassing about. So I'll love yer and leave yer. But I hope yer enjoy the picture.'

'Oh, we won't be going to the pictures now, Auntie Molly,' Paul said. 'We can't afford it. A seat in the picture house costs as much as a buttonhole.'

Phoebe thumped him. 'Don't be acting daft. We are going to the pictures because Cary Grant is on, and he's my favourite film star.' Then with a broad wink at Molly, she added, 'But we're not getting the bus there, we'll walk.'

'I'm getting frightened now, Auntie Molly,' Paul called out as Molly knocked on her daughter's front door. 'I don't think I'll enjoy being married.'

Doreen heard Paul's remark when she was

opening the door. 'What's Paul on about, Mam? Yer've been talking to him for ages.'

'Wedding nerves, I think, sunshine. He doesn't know whether he likes the idea of marriage now, or if he's gone off it.'

Doreen had grown up with Paul, and there was only six months' difference in their ages. 'Don't knock it until yer've tried it, Paul Mac,' she called. 'Yer don't know what ye're missing.'

Phoebe answered. 'And he will be missing it if he doesn't buck his ideas up. He's playing hard to get.' She lowered her voice so the neighbours wouldn't hear and think they were being serious. 'But I'm up to his tricks, and when we're married he'll find I've a few tricks up my sleeve. I'll soon knock him into shape.'

Molly and Doreen laughed when they heard Paul say, 'I'll soon sort you out, Phoebe Corkhill. I'll set me mam on to you.'

'You are going to miss the start of the big picture,' Molly told them. 'And then yer won't know what it's about.'

Paul waved as he cupped Phoebe's elbow. 'Come on, Phoebe. And we're getting a bus there, so don't argue. I'll let you buy the tickets if yer behave yerself.'

Molly and Doreen watched them walking down the street, then went into the house. 'Paul is just like Nellie, never serious.' Molly said. 'I think we'll be going to their wedding in the not too distant future.'

'Are they still saving up for it?' Doreen asked. 'Last time Phoebe mentioned it, she said Paul couldn't put money away, it went through his hands like water.'

Molly walked into the living room to see Victoria rocking gently in her chair, a welcoming smile on her face. 'On your own, Molly? Where's Nellie?'

'Keep yer voice down, Victoria,' Molly said. 'I didn't tell her I was coming. But it wouldn't surprise me if she comes knocking, because she listens for me closing the front door.'

Phil, Doreen's husband, popped his head out of the kitchen, his chin covered in shaving cream. 'Yer'll have to excuse me, Mrs B. I'm shaving now so it isn't such a rush in the morning.' He waved the shaving brush, saying, 'You women are lucky you don't have to shave. It's a nuisance.'

'You don't have to do it every day, being so fair-skinned,' Molly told him. 'Jack goes through it every day, sometimes twice if we're going out.' She winked at Victoria before adding, 'Women don't have to shave, sunshine, but we have to make sure our hair is neat and tidy, and that takes as long as a man shaving.' Molly looked at Victoria's hair, which was almost pure white, and very sparse. But Doreen combed it for her, and she always looked the perfect lady, which she was. She was turned ninety now, but was always well dressed, and she still possessed all her faculties. 'Men think women have an easy life, but they'd soon find out different if we swapped places with them for a week. They wouldn't know what had hit them.' Molly slipped her coat off and laid it on the couch. 'I'd give them a week, and I bet they'd either take to their bed pleading tiredness, or spend the week's housekeeping money in the first day buying easy to cook food.'

'And that's putting it mildly, Mam,' Doreen said. 'What about if they had to look after an eight-month-old baby, on top of all the housework?'

Phil's head appeared again, free now of shaving cream. 'I'll surrender, Mrs B., come out with my hands up. I wouldn't last a day if I had to do what Doreen does. Bobby is a handful on his own, before she starts on her housework, shopping and cooking. I wouldn't...' Phil's words tapered off when there was a loud knocking on the front door.

'I bet this is Nellie,' Molly said, shaking her head in frustration. 'Yer'd better open the door, sunshine, before she knocks it down and wakes the baby.'

Nellie bustled in, arms folded, head quivering and eyes narrowed. 'What sort of mate are you, Molly Bennett, what sneaks out without telling anyone? If I hadn't heard yer talking to our Paul and Phoebe, I'd have missed yer, and yer'd have got away with it.'

Victoria put a hand on each of her chair arms and pushed herself back into a comfortable position so she could enjoy what was bound to come. It reminded her of when she was younger, able to go to the pictures, and waiting for the big feature to start. The two women standing in the middle of the room now, facing each other, were as comical as Laurel and Hardy.

'Nellie, what d'yer mean, I'd have got away with it?' Molly asked. 'I haven't done anything to get away with! All I'm doing is visiting me daughter, and I can't see anything wrong with that. I would have liked to have been here early enough to see the baby, but I had to darn a hole in one of Jack's socks, 'cos he needed it to wear tomorrow for work. So that made me too late to see Bobby.' Molly lowered her head so her eyes were on a level with Nellie's. 'Now, can I ask what you're doing here, or is it a secret?'

Shaking her head, and her chins, Nellie looked at Doreen. 'Your mam can be very sarcastic when she wants. I've told her it doesn't suit her, 'cos her top lip curls over, but she doesn't take no notice of me.'

'Nellie, yer haven't answered me question,' Molly said, 'and I'm not letting yer talk yer way out of it. Just tell me what ye're doing here.'

The little woman jerked her head at Doreen. 'See what I mean, girl? See how the top lip turns up?' She turned her attention to Victoria, and then Phil. 'Yer both must have seen the face on her, as though she was smelling milk what had gone sour.'

'I'm afraid I didn't notice anything, Mrs Mac,' Phil said, trying to keep his face straight. 'But I'm sure my mother-in-law wasn't intentionally sarcastic.'

'Oh, you would say that, wouldn't yer, lad? Got to keep on the right side of her, haven't yer? Well, I can understand that, 'cos she can be a bad-tempered beggar when she feels like it.'

'Oh, dear, Nellie, why don't yer just tell us why ye're here?' Molly asked. 'Yer must have had some reason for leaving yer own house and coming over here. Unless ye're walking in yer sleep, sunshine, but yer look wide awake to me. Or perhaps it's just because ye're a nosy article, and are frightened of missing anything.'

Nellie took a deep breath and let it out slowly. 'This could go on for a long time, and me feet are getting tired. Particularly me little toe, what has a corn on. So if there's no charge for sitting down, would yer mind if I take the weight off me feet?'

Phil jumped to his feet, like the gentleman he was, and pulled a chair out. 'Here you are, Mrs Mac. Sit down and rest your legs.'

Nellie wrinkled her nose at Molly before turning to Phil with a beaming smile on her face. 'Thanks, lad, ye're very kind. Not like some people I know what are not a million miles away from here. They wouldn't tell me to sit down and rest me weary feet while they make me a cup of tea.' Phil received the benefit of another smile. 'I like me tea strong, lad, and two sugars. And if yer happen to see a stray biscuit when ye're in the pantry, stick it on me saucer, there's a good lad.'

'You cheeky article!' Molly said, pulling a chair out and facing her mate across the table. 'Yer walk in as though yer own the place, and cadge tea and biscuits. I don't know how yer've got the nerve.'

Nellie lifted a finger. 'I asked for a biscuit, girl, not biscuits. And yer should be thanking me for asking Phil to make me a drink, 'cos it means you'll get one as well. Mind you, I'll be thinking, not out loud, like, but in me head, that I hope it chokes yer for being so miserable.'

'I'm not miserable, sunshine, I'm feeling quite cheerful as it happens. But if it makes you happy to think I'm miserable, then I think we should agree to disagree.'

This left Nellie feeling very confused. How could they agree to disagree? Honestly, where did that leave them? And to look happy when ye're miserable, well, that was a tongue twister that was. But it would be in her own interest not to rub her mate up the wrong way, or she'd not be able to get round her to find out what she wanted to know. So Molly would relax over a nice cup of tea and they'd be back to being best mates. 'So yer missed seeing the baby, did yer, girl? It's a pity, that, but yer'll see him tomorrow.'

Victoria set her rocking chair in motion, while thinking the two mates were quiet tonight. That was a disappointment, for she always enjoyed the pretend spats they had. Still, she shouldn't expect them to be able to turn the laughter on like a tap, just to please her.

'Tea up, Mam.' Doreen put the tray on the table. 'I've poured the tea out and put milk in, so all you have to do is put yer own sugar in.'

'You've forgotten something, girl,' Nellie told her. 'There's no biscuits on the tray.' She could feel Molly's eyes glaring at her, but she'd risk a telling off for a couple of custard creams.

'Biscuits coming up, Mrs Mac.' Phil put the plate down with a flourish, then bowed from the waist. 'At your service, madam.'

'Is he being sarky, girl?' Nellie asked. 'If he is I'll clock him one. After I've eaten the biscuits, of course.'

'Oh, that goes without saying, sunshine. Yer pretend to be dumb, deaf and daft, but not where goodies are concerned.'

As Nellie bit on a custard cream, she eyed her

106

friend through lowered lids, looking for a sign that there might be a thawing out, but Molly's face was blank, giving nothing away. And that was unusual for Molly, who never stayed annoyed for long. So the little woman, who couldn't bear to fall out with her best mate, decided to go for it and take a chance. Silence was something she couldn't live with. 'I saw yer talking to our Paul and Phoebe, girl. Yer were having a long conversation with them, which surprised me, 'cos they were supposed to be on their way to the pictures. What were yer talking about what took yer so long?'

Molly gazed into her mate's face, and after a few moments' reflection she decided it was time to get her own back. And it would serve Nellie right to be on the receiving end of a joke. 'Oh, we were talking about this and that, you know how it is. Actually, it was mostly about their wedding. Phoebe was talking about the flowers for her bouquet and the bridesmaids' posies. Oh, and red carnations for guests' buttonholes.' She paused to control the urge to laugh. 'It should be quite a wedding, the way they were talking. And it's not long off now, sunshine, so you and me had better start looking for wedding hats and dresses.'

Doreen's eyes were wide, and moving from side to side. From what she'd heard in the street a short time ago, there was no prospect of a wedding in the near future. Victoria and Phil, who were believing Molly's words, were looking happy at the idea. But Nellie was speechless. As she gazed at Molly's face, her own expression was set. She was utterly taken aback by what her mate

107

had hinted. After a few gulps, she said, 'There's no need to be buying hats and dresses now, girl, 'cos it'll be ages before they get married. They haven't got enough saved up yet.'

Sounding cool and casual, Molly answered, 'I may have heard wrong, sunshine, but I thought Phoebe said before the summer. And that isn't long off, only a matter of weeks.'

By this time, Doreen had realized her mother was pulling Auntie Nellie's leg, and wondered how long it would be before her auntie twigged. She was very crafty, and looking at her now you could practically hear her mind ticking over. It should be very interesting to see who came off best. She certainly wouldn't like to bet on it.

'Anyway,' Nellie said, 'we don't have to look for dresses 'cos Doreen always makes them, don't yer, girl? It would be daft to buy them when we can have them made for nothing.'

Molly tutted. 'It would be very nice if you were to ask Doreen, instead of taking it for granted. I think she's got enough on her plate with the baby to look after, and cooking, cleaning, shopping, and doing the washing. She doesn't have any spare time on her hands.'

'I wouldn't worry about that, girl,' Nellie said, the devilment shining in her eyes. 'Yer see, by the time my son gets married, the baby will be starting school. Take no notice of this married before the summer lark, they're pulling yer leg. Same as you've been pulling my leg for the last half-hour. But I don't mind, 'cos yer've got to get yer own back sometimes. Yer can't let me win all the time. So shall we call it quits, girl, and while

Phil puts the kettle on for a fresh pot of tea, I'll tell yer the truth about this wedding. Take no notice of what our Paul ever tells yer, 'cos his head is in the clouds most of the time.'

Ten minutes later, with a fresh cup of tea in front of them, Molly said, 'Bring Victoria's chair nearer the table, Phil, so she can hear what we're saying without having to lean forward. And she can see the contortions that Nellie makes with her face when she gets stuck for a word.'

Nellie was in her element with an audience hanging on to her every word. 'It's a pity we haven't got any cream slices, girl, 'cos then we could have a little party.'

'Nellie, I told Jack I'd only be out for half an hour, and it's well past that now. So will yer get on with it, please?'

'Sod Jack, girl! That's what I say! Sod Jack and George, if they'd rather sit on their backsides than come and join us.'

Molly sighed. 'Nellie, if yer've got anything interesting to tell us, then get on with it. But if ye're making things up in yer head as yer go along, just so we'll be here longer, then forget it. Tell the truth and shame the devil.'

'Oh, yer can't shame the devil, girl, 'cos yer don't get the chance to see him face to face. And I'm buggered if I'm going to cut me throat just so I can go to hell and tell him he's not very popular with us.'

'I know this is changing the subject after I've just told yer to get on with the story, sunshine, but I've just had a thought. Yer know I say a little prayer every night, to ask God to look after all me

109

family and friends? Well, so far, God has been good in answering me prayers. Like, for instance, he brought Tommy, Steve and Paul home safe from the war. And he made me da better when he had that heart attack.'

'Yeah, we know all that, girl, yer don't need to tell us again. Yer can't half talk a lot and yet say nothing.'

'If yer won't listen, how d'yer know I'm saying nothing? All I was going to say, if you'd only give me the chance, is why don't you set up a line with the devil, like yer have with St Peter? That way, ye're covering yerself for every eventuality. A friend in heaven, and a friend in hell!'

Nellie huffed. 'How soft you are, girl! Yer must think I want me bumps feeling, if yer think I'll fall for that.' Her eyes landed on Doreen first, then Victoria. 'Did yer hear that? What sort of mate would sit on the front row in heaven, with a harp and a halo, knowing her best mate was sweating cobs, shovelling great big lumps of coal on to a bleeding fire what never goes out?'

'Why are you so sure that Molly will be on the front row in heaven, sweetheart?' Victoria asked, while hoping that God wouldn't be displeased by their conversation. 'None of us know where we will eventually end up.'

Much to the delight of Doreen and Phil, the little woman's face was so contorted it seemed to be made of rubber. Then she tapped the side of her head, and said knowingly, 'Oh, my mate will be going to heaven, no doubt about that. She never does nothing wrong. Doesn't tell lies, never swears, she's bound to get in. If she didn't I

110

would demand to know why, because there must have been dirty work at the crossroads somewhere along the line. I'd have to have serious words with my friend St Peter, that's what. I'm relying on Molly getting in, so she can put in a good word for me.'

Phil cleared his throat before asking, 'Why don't yer hedge yer bets, Mrs Mac?'

She narrowed her eyes. 'What d'yer mean, lad?'

'Keep a foot in both camps. Yer say ye're already mates with St Peter, so try and get in the devil's good books as well.'

Nellie nodded her head slowly, much to the delight of her chins. 'Good thinking, lad, good thinking. So if I don't make it up there, I can ask the devil for an extra shovel for me mate.'

'Don't be so flipping generous, sunshine,' Molly said. 'I don't want any favours from the devil. I'll bring me own shovel!'

And soon the two mates were back to normal, and Victoria was able to go to bed with a smile on her face.

The following morning when Molly opened the door to Nellie, she waited until they were in the living room before speaking. 'Sit yerself down, sunshine, and I'll put the kettle on.' She watched her mate carry the carver chair from the wall to the table, then added, 'But I might as well tell yer now that I haven't got a biscuit in the house. So yer can moan as much as yer like, it won't do you any good. What I haven't got, I can't give yer.' With those words, Molly walked towards the kitchen, where she put a light to the gas ring

111

under the kettle. She was humming softly as she set the cups and saucers on the tray, and was unprepared for the tap on her shoulder.

'Nellie, I wish yer wouldn't creep up on me like that! One of these days yer'll give me a heart attack.'

Nellie wasn't concerned about a heart attack; she had other things on her mind. 'Haven't yer even got one biscuit in the tin, girl? Did yer have a good look, 'cos yer could easily have missed one.'

Molly shook her head. 'There's not even a crumb in the tin, sunshine. Ye're out of luck.'

With her shoulders drooping, and a downcast look on her face, Nellie shuffled back to the living room. But she didn't sit down, she stood by the table while her mind ticked over to find a solution. And after a few seconds a smile creased her chubby face, and back she went to the kitchen. 'I'll tell yer what I'll do, girl, to help yer out. If you give me threepence, I'll nip down to the corner shop and ask Maisie to give us threepence worth of mixed biscuits. That's a good idea, isn't it, girl? I mean a cup of tea doesn't taste the same without a biscuit.'

'Of course yer can go to the corner shop, sunshine, for threepennyworth of biscuits. Just as long as the threepence comes out of your purse. I've no money to waste on luxuries, besides which it won't upset me very much if I have to do without a biscuit for once. But don't let me stop you having what yer want, sunshine. You run down to the corner shop and the tea will be waiting for yer when yer get back.'

With a face as innocent as a newborn baby, Nellie said, 'I haven't got me purse with me, girl. You lend me the money and I'll pay yer back later.'

Molly gazed down into her mate's face. 'D'yer know when we were talking about St Peter and the devil in our Doreen's last night?' She waited for Nellie's nod. 'Well, right now the devil must be rubbing his hands in glee, while St Peter will be feeling really let down.' And because she was into her stride now, Molly piled the agony on. 'You've let him down badly, sunshine, and yer've always said he was a good friend of yours. Some friend you've turned out to be.'

'I think ye're going off yer rocker, girl, if yer ask me. What are yer bringing all that up for? Anyone would think I'd committed a murder, or robbed a ruddy bank, to hear you talk. All this for the sake of a biscuit! It's not a sin to want a biscuit, is it?'

'It is if yer tell a lie to get it, sunshine.'

Nellie looked shocked and hurt. 'I haven't told no lie, girl, so don't be making me out to be a liar.'

'You did tell a fib, sunshine, I'm not deaf.' In her mind, Molly was giving her mate ten out of ten for acting. 'As bold as brass, you stood there and told a barefaced lie.'

'What did I say, girl? Go on, tell me what it was and I'll say it's you what's telling lies. Go on, I dare yer!'

'Why did you want to borrow money off me, sunshine, to buy the biscuits?'

'Well, Maisie wouldn't give me them for nothing, would she? And if I just walked in the

113

shop, grabbed a handful of broken biscuits and scarpered, she'd have set the police on me and I'd have ended up in a cell.'

Molly thought they'd wasted enough time. If she left it to her mate, the morning would be over without them getting anywhere. So she took the bull by the horns. 'Nellie, I can see your lie, so why keep it up?'

'How the hell can yer see a lie, girl? Yer might be able to hear one, but yer can't never see one.'

'I can see yours, sunshine, so why don't yer give in? Lift yer hands in surrender, and I'll get on with our cups of tea.'

'What can yer see, girl? Yer've lost me now.'

'I'm too old for guessing games, Nellie, and there's work to be done. We've lost half an hour for no reason at all. But we'll waste more time if I don't ask yer now, what is that sticking out of yer pocket?'

Nellie's hand went to the left pocket in her coat. 'There's nothing there. It's empty.'

Molly sighed. 'Don't be playing the innocent, sunshine, because I'm beginning to lose the will to live. Try the other pocket why don't yer?'

Lips pursed, head down, and muttering under her breath, Nellie slowly moved her hand across the mound that was her tummy to the right pocket. Then, feigning surprise, she looked up at Molly with her eyes and mouth wide open. 'Well, did you ever! Just fancy that, girl! Who would have thought I'd forgotten I'd brought me purse out with me? Aren't I a silly billy? I must have picked it up off the table without noticing. Honest, I'm getting really forgetful in me old age.' Her chubby

114

face beamed. 'Ah, well, all's well what ends well. So come on, girl, let's be having yer. Get that tea poured out, I'm parched.'

Molly grabbed her mate's arm. 'Aren't yer going to the corner shop for some biscuits, now yer've got the money?'

'No, I won't bother now, girl. Yer know what it's like when Maisie starts talking, yer can't get away from her. And I'd hate to let the tea go cold.'

'It wouldn't be Maisie that kept yer gabbing, she's too busy with customers,' Molly told her. 'It's you that's the gasbag. Any poor woman who was unlucky enough to be in the shop the same time as you would have the head talked off her. She wouldn't be able to get a word in edgeways, and yer'd keep her prisoner until another unfortunate customer came in. You talk to them whether they want yer to or not. Even if yer've never seen them in yer life before. And yer don't talk to them, sunshine, yer talk at them.'

'All right, girl, don't harp on it. I'm only being friendly with people, that's all. And you're a fine one to talk, Molly Bennett, 'cos once you start, yer forget to finish. Like now, I've hardly opened me mouth. It's nearly half an hour since I came in, and you've never stopped! I mean, we've had St Peter, what is a friend of mine, no matter what yer say, and I've been put with the devil, what is no blinking friend of mine! So can yer put a plug in it now, girl, and let me drink me tea in peace? Me head is buzzing, and I'm not surprised. What with a mate in heaven, the devil himself, and the customers what come in Maisie's shop, I'm dead tired. I feel as if I've put in a day's work down at the docks, and it's only half past ten in the morning! Perhaps I should have stayed in bed today, eh?'

Molly was facing her mate across the table, and she couldn't help but chuckle at the changing expressions on Nellie's face. 'I'll say something to cheer yer up, shall I, sunshine?'

'Don't tell me yer've remembered that there are some biscuits in the tin after all, 'cos I couldn't stand it.'

'No, sunshine, I was just going to say six words that would bring a smile to yer face.'

'They'll have to be good, girl, 'cos I haven't got a smile in me right now.'

'Well, close yer eyes, sunshine, and let yer imagination take over. Cream slices, cream slices, cream slices. Can yer see them in yer mind, Nellie?'

Her head nodding, the little woman's face took on a look of bliss. 'I can see them, girl. And when we go to Hanley's for our bread, I'll buy those three cream slices what I saw in me mind and what are making me mouth water. And d'yer know what I'm going to do, Molly Bennett? I'm going to eat them in front of yer, so yer can see me licking the cream out of the sides of them. And I won't even ask yer if yer want a lick. I'll make you suffer like what you've made me suffer this morning.'

'You wouldn't do that to me, would yer, sunshine? Don't forget it was me who cheered you up with the mention of the treat when we go to Hanley's. Because I've been hard on yer for being a liar, which yer can't deny because yer were

116

found out, then I'll mug you to a cream slice. Now I can't say fairer than that, sunshine, can I?'

Nellie's chins were in full agreement with her nodding head. 'I'm quite happy with that arrangement, girl, 'cos that shows how sorry yer are for being so bleeding miserable. For a while there, I expected yer to put me through the mangle, that's how bad I felt.'

Molly reached for the teapot for their second cup of tea. As she poured, she said, 'I'll admit to being hard on yer, if you'll admit yer knew darn well yer had yer purse with yer all the time.'

'That's no problem, girl, 'cos I had to know I had me purse with me, didn't I? It was sticking out of me pocket for all the world to see.'

'So now we're all done and dusted, let's drink our tea and then be on our way to the shops. I haven't got a clue what to get for the dinner, sunshine. Don't yer get fed up with trying to think of something different for a change? If I give Jack and Ruthie stew again, I think they'd throw it at me. They have it so often it's coming out of their ears.'

Nellie perked up and leaned across the table. 'Ay, I know what we could have for a change. Last night I slipped over to our Lily's, 'cos she promised she'd make me a tray of fairy cakes, and when she opened the front door the smell of her dinner had me sniffing up like the Bisto Kids. They were having shepherd's pie, and it didn't half make me feel hungry. We could have that today, girl, for a change.'

'That's a very good idea, sunshine, 'cos it's a while since we've had shepherd's pie. See, yer do

117

come in handy sometimes. If you hadn't gone to your Lily's we'd have been scratching our heads wondering what to get. That is a load off our minds.'

Nellie drained her cup. 'Hurry up, girl, that cream slice yer promised me is calling, telling me that if I don't come quick, then someone else will snaffle it up, 'cos it's thick with fresh cream oozing out of both sides.'

'It doesn't take much to make you happy, does it, sunshine? One cream slice and you're as happy as a kid with a bucket and spade, on yer way to the shore in New Brighton.'

'When I was a kid, girl, my mam didn't have the money for a bucket and spade, and I've never been on a shore in me life. I've heard of New Brighton, 'cos our Paul went dancing in the Tower there. That's before he started courting Phoebe. But I've never been. Never did me no harm though, being poor. All the kids in the neighbourhood were the same, but we had fun.' Nellie's bosom and tummy shook when she laughed. 'I had a mate called Doreen, and we used to share a gobstopper. She'd have three sucks, then she'd pass it to me to have my three sucks. We enjoyed life, even though we had nowt. Not like the young ones today, who want everything handed to them on a plate.'

'Oh, it's not that bad, sunshine. Our kids don't expect everything they'd like. Unless they work for it, which ours do.'

Nellie pushed herself up off the chair. 'I still think life was better before the war, girl, when people were nicer and helped each other.'

118

'Time marches on, sunshine; nothing stands
still. We'll never get the old days back, but we
can't complain, Nellie, we've got good families,
and are better off than some poor beggars.' Molly
walked into the hall for her coat, and as she
slipped her arms into it, she said, 'I'll rinse the
cups when I come back.' She picked up her key
from the glass bowl and put it in her pocket, then
took her basket from the pantry. 'Ay, sunshine,
where's your basket?'

'I didn't bring it, girl, 'cos we don't need two. I
can share yours.'

Molly's eyes rolled to the ceiling. 'Nellie Mac,
yer've got the hide of a flipping elephant, you
have.'

Nellie's face beamed. 'No I haven't, girl, 'cos
my George said I've got lovely soft skin. And he
should know because…'

Her words were cut off when Molly pushed her
towards the door. 'I don't want to know any
more, sunshine, so out yer go. And I'm not carrying all the shopping; we'll take turns with the
basket, d'yer hear?'

'I heard yer, girl, and so did half the street. And
I bet there's a feller down on the docks, pushing
a trolley with heavy boxes on, who can hear yer
as well.'

Molly was shaking her head as she pulled the
door to behind her. Was there ever a time when
her mate was lost for words? She couldn't
remember one in all the twenty-five years they'd
known each other. That should go down in the
Guinness Book of Records.

'Here they come, Ellen,' Tony called to his assistant. 'They're just waiting to cross the road.'

Ellen came through from the storeroom wiping her hands on a piece of muslin. 'I've never known anyone like them,' she said. 'They've stuck together through thick and thin. Good times and bad times. And it's funny, really, because they're as different as chalk and cheese.'

'Look at Nellie hurrying across the road,' Tony chuckled. 'She bounces like a ball. I hope she brings a bit of life to the shop, 'cos it's been really quiet in here this morning.'

'They'll all come in at once, you'll see,' Ellen said, 'and in the meanwhile Nellie and Molly will brighten the place up.'

When the two mates came in, Ellen told them, 'We've just been talking about you two. It's been as quiet as a graveyard in here this morning. We've only had half a dozen customers in since we opened, and we're hoping you can cheer us up, give us a laugh, and put some money in the till.'

'Well, we can put some money in the till,' Molly said, 'but we can't promise to cheer yer up. Unless Nellie can come up with something. And while she's trying, you can serve us, Ellen. We both want half a pound of mincemeat.'

Nellie's face was going through the motions as she tried to think of a trick she could play on the butcher. 'Are yer any good at words, Tony? Long ones, I mean, what are hard to get yer tongue round?'

'Yeah, not bad, Nellie. As long as they're English, of course, 'cos I can't speak Chinese.'

'Oh, very funny, I must say. Well, I've got a

120

word what I bet yer haven't heard before. It's a humdinger, this one, what Molly told me.'

Tony pushed his straw hat back, and folded his arms. 'Okay, Nellie, let's be having it.'

Nellie opened her mouth, closed it again, then said, 'I can't say the bleeding word meself now.' She put a hand to her chin. 'Give me a minute, and it'll come to me.'

While her mate was deep in thought, her mouth moving silently, Molly said, 'This should be good. Nellie has a problem with words consisting of more than three letters.'

Nellie came to life then. 'That one will do, girl, save me racking me brains.'

'What one was that, Nellie?' Molly frowned. 'I can't read yer mind, sunshine, so yer'll have to tell me.'

Nellie got agitated. 'If I could say the bleeding word, girl, I wouldn't need you to do it for me! Yer've just told soft lad here that I can't say words what have more than three letters in. But yer used a big word to tell him.'

Molly saw the light. 'Oh, you mean consisting, sunshine, don't yer?'

Nellie jerked her head back in disgust, frightening her chins who weren't expecting to be disturbed. 'That's the one, girl, so now ask soft lad here what it means. And I bet he won't have a clue.'

'I'm sorry to disappoint yer, Nellie,' Tony said, 'but I do know what consisting means.' His smile was like a smirk of confidence. 'It means, Nellie...' He tapped his chin, and thought how he could best explain it to her. 'Let's see how I can

121

put it. I know – the word consisting means made up of.' Tony looked pleased with himself. 'So yer see, I do know what it means.'

'Oh, yer must think I'm as thick as two short planks! No one can trick me like that, soft lad. When yer say "made up of", what d'yer mean. What is made up of what?'

Molly thought they'd be there all day if she didn't step in, for Tony was beginning to look confused. 'Nellie, we're having shepherd's pie tonight, aren't we?' She waited for a nod, then went on. 'Well, to make the pie, we need potatoes, mincemeat, onions and an Oxo cube. There's a lot more ingredients yer can use, but I'm just talking about us. Our pies will consist of the mince and the other things I've mentioned. So have yer got it now? D'yer know what consist means?'

'Yeah, I know what it means. I knew all along, girl,' Nellie lied. 'I was only pulling Tony's leg 'cos he thinks he's so ruddy clever.' She turned her head to wink at her mate. 'But I've got a word what will stump him. Are yer ready for it, Mr Clever-clogs?'

Tony chuckled. 'Ready when you are, Mrs Mac.'

'Right, me lad, just get an earful of this.' Rising to her full height, Nellie said, 'Sentity.'

Tony frowned. 'Never heard of it, Nellie. Spell it for us?'

'Sod off, lad! If I could spell that, I'd not be standing in a ruddy butcher's shop right now, I'd be standing in a classroom full of kids, with a cane in me hand to wallop kids what got their spelling wrong.'

And the little woman couldn't understand why Molly doubled up, Tony and Ellen burst out laughing, and the two customers who had been standing at the back of the shop for a few minutes had smiles on their faces. 'What's so bleeding funny?'

'Nellie, because I'd like to finish me shopping, and because there's two customers standing behind you waiting to be served, I'll hurry things along.' Molly put her arm across her mate's shoulder. 'The word you were trying to stump Tony with wasn't sentitity. You should have said serendipity.'

'That's what I said, girl! Yer want to try washing yer ears out! And you, Mr Butcher-man, I bet yer don't know the meaning of it. Or you, Ellen Corkhill, standing there trying to look intelligent when ye're as thick as I am.'

One of the waiting customers very foolishly thought she'd try to help. 'I could explain what it means, Mrs McDonough.'

Nellie spun round and glared at the poor woman. 'Who are you when ye're out? Nosy, aren't yer?'

'I think it's time we were on our way, Ellen, so will yer pass our meat over, before war breaks out! Here's five bob. Yer can take for Nellie's as well, and she can pay me later.'

Ellen passed the two parcels of meat over, and the change from the five shillings. 'Take Nellie with yer when yer go, Molly, because the way she's going on we're going to lose two good customers.'

'Not to worry, we'll be on our way,' Molly told

her. 'All I need to say to get her running is "cream slice", and yer won't see her heels for the dust.'

'Oh, before yer go, Molly.' Tony nodded to a customer he'd just served, then walked down the counter. 'What does that ruddy word mean? I've never heard it before.'

'Ooh, I got it out of the dictionary, Tony.' Molly crossed her fingers before telling him, 'I couldn't remember what it said if yer paid me.'

'Ay, take a gander over there.' Ellen was nodding to the back of the shop. 'Hurry before yer miss it, 'cos yer might never see the like again.'

Molly was expecting to find her mate in an argument with the lady who had offered to help, but to her amazement, what she saw was Nellie looking up at the woman and actually smiling. So Molly moved closer, and was in time to hear her mate saying, in a voice as sweet as honey, 'Oh, thank you, dear, that was very kind of yer.'

'Think nothing of it, Mrs McDonough. I'm glad to have been of some assistance to you.'

Molly took her mate's arm, and said, 'Come on, Nellie, we're running late.' She smiled at the two women. 'We'll leave you to get served. Ta-ra.'

'Ay, there was no need to drag me away like that,' Nellie said, as she was pulled sideways through the shop door. 'She was very nice, that woman, what's named Mrs Maudsley. Told me all about the word and what it meant. She was a bit posh, like, but nice just the same.'

'Nellie, sunshine, yer were ready to knock spots off the woman five minutes ago,' Molly said, basket over her arm. 'Now yer think she's a very nice lady! Which she is, of course, and she's also

124

very well known in the area, and popular. And another thing, sunshine. Because a person is well spoken it doesn't mean that they are toffee-nosed snobs.'

'Yer don't need to tell me that, girl, because haven't I been your mate for twenty-five years?'

'What on earth has that got to do with anything?' Molly queried. 'Yer go from one subject to another, and yer lose me sometimes. I can't keep up with yer.'

Nellie did a hop, skip and a jump to keep in step with her mate. 'Well, it's like this, girl. You're a bit posh, aren't yer? And I know you're a nice person, 'cos yer've always been me mate. And yer use big words and don't swear.'

'And that make me posh, does it, sunshine? I don't know whether to feel flattered or battered! But we'll discuss that another time, for we're nearly at Hanley's. And as I promised to buy yer a cream slice, I think I'll join yer and make it two cream slices. And we'll be daredevils and eat them in the shop, eh?'

Nellie stopped dead in her tracks. 'Ay, girl, I've changed me mind about you. Yer were right, ye're not posh. I mean yer'd never see a posh woman like Mrs Maudsley standing in a shop eating a cream slice, with cream on her chin and nose. No, girl, ye're not posh. Ye're just the same as me, as common as muck.'

Chapter Five

Molly raised her brow when she opened the door one morning and found her daughter standing outside. 'I wasn't expecting you, sunshine, I thought yer were Nellie. She's usually here by now, so I don't know what's keeping her.'

'Shall I give her a knock, Mam, to make sure she's all right? Perhaps she's not well.'

'No, she'll be along any minute, you'll see. If she was out of sorts, George would have knocked when he was passing on his way to work.' Molly stepped back into the hall. 'Aren't yer coming in, sunshine?'

Doreen shook her head. 'No, I won't come in, Mam. I only wanted to tell yer that I called to see little Moll last night, and Jill said if it was a nice morning, we could take the babies out in the prams for a walk. A bit of fresh air would do them good. So I thought I'd let you know, save yer knocking. Aunt Vicky will probably have a nap while we're out. And we'll get our shopping in.'

'It's good to take the babies out, sunshine, when the weather is decent. Best to make the most of it. Besides, it's nice for you and Jill to get out of the house so yer can have a good natter. It means the babies can get used to each other as well.' Molly popped her head out and looked towards her mate's house, three doors away. 'I can't understand Nellie not being here, 'cos she's

126

usually here before half ten. It's not like her at all. She knows I put the kettle on at twenty past, so the water's boiled when she knocks on the door.'

'Mam, why don't yer give her a knock? It's no use walking up and down, wondering and worrying. I'll knock if yer like, just to make sure.'

Molly sighed. 'I won't rest until I know she's all right, so I may as well go and see. I've got a key to her front door, so if she doesn't answer, I can let meself in. I've had her key for years, in case of emergency, but I don't like going into her house.' She grinned at her daughter. 'Yer wouldn't think I'd be afraid at my age, would yer, but I'm a bit of a coward.'

'Get the key, Mam, and I'll come in with yer.' Doreen nodded her head. 'Go on, Mam, let's get it over with. Our Jill will be coming down soon, and I want to be ready so we can go straight out. And I'd rather know Auntie Nellie was all right before we left, otherwise she'd be on me mind all the time.'

'Right, I'll get the key, sunshine. I'd rather have someone with me than go in on me own.'

Armed with the key, Molly led the way to Nellie's. 'I'd better knock first, in case we barge in and find her standing there in her nuddy.'

Doreen chuckled. 'It doesn't bear thinking about, Mam. Go on, knock hard.'

The first knock was quite soft, but when there was no reply Molly knocked harder. 'I'm getting worried now, sunshine,' she told her daughter when there was still no sound from inside. 'She would have heard the knock if she was in, and I know for a fact she wouldn't go to the shops without me.'

'I'll try and peep through the window,' Doreen said, 'see if I can see anything.' But she couldn't see clearly through the net curtains. 'I can't see anything, Mam; it's dark in there. I don't think Auntie Nellie is in, 'cos I'd have been able to see if someone was moving around. Yer'd better use the key and go in, it's the only way.'

It was with trepidation that Molly turned the key in the lock, for she felt like a trespasser. She was taking the key out of the door when she nearly jumped out of her skin with fright as a voice called, 'And about bleeding time, Molly Bennett.' The voice sounded strangled, and Molly and daughter looked at each other before making for the McDonoughs' living room. They were both expecting to see Nellie lying on the couch with a headache or perhaps an upset tummy, but nothing prepared them for the sight that met their eyes. And they didn't know whether to laugh or cry

Nellie had broken the seat of the fireside chair, and her bottom had fallen through. It was inches from the floor, and Nellie's body was folded together, her knees on her chest. Her arms were flat on the arms of the chair, and they were the only thing stopping the chair from collapsing completely.

'How the hell did yer do that, sunshine?' Molly asked, as she weighed up the situation, and wondered how to get her mate out of the chair without hurting her. 'How did yer come to break this chair, 'cos yer never sit on it with it being George's.'

'If ye're after me life story, do yer have to have

it now?' Nellie snorted and narrowed her eyes. 'I'm in bleeding agony, and you're asking me stupid bloody questions! Just get me up instead of standing there as though I'm a monkey in a zoo. And a fat lot of good it was bringing yer daughter with yer, she's bloody hopeless, standing there with her mouth open.'

'Nellie,' Molly said, a hand cupping her chin. 'If you were standing where I am, and I was in the predicament that you're in, then you'd not only have yer mouth wide open, but yer'd be killing yerself laughing. And being your usual crafty self, you'd be selling tickets to the neighbours.

'Doreen, you get a grip on the back of the chair and hold it down, then I'll try and pull Nellie up.'

Molly put her hands under Nellie's armpits and heaved, but she couldn't move her mate. She tried again, but it was no use, for Nellie's bottom was stuck tight. 'I think it would be better if yer came round to the front, Doreen, and we can take an arm each. I'll never be able to manage on me own.'

'Stop flapping about, will yer?' Nellie's back was hurting where she'd scraped it when she fell through the seat, and every time she moved it was agony. 'Just give one big pull, and I'll try and help yer by pushing on the arms. Don't worry about whether ye're hurting me, just get me up. And move yerselves, don't stand gawping. I don't want to still be like this when George comes home from work.'

'Well, you asked for it, sunshine, so yer can't blame me or Doreen if we hurt yer.' Molly looked at her daughter and nodded. 'When I give the sign, sunshine, let's make a big effort and pull like mad.'

With much grunting and groaning from Nellie, and heavy breathing from her two would-be rescuers, Nellie was pulled to her feet, but she was still bent over because the chair was stuck to her bottom. And no matter how hard Nellie pushed, and Molly and her daughter pulled, the chair wouldn't budge an inch. 'It's certainly taken a fancy to you, sunshine,' Molly said, thinking it was the funniest sight she'd ever seen. Oh, she'd seen something similar in slapstick comedies on the pictures, but never in real life. And she could see Doreen was thinking the same as herself, but neither wanted to hurt Nellie's feelings. 'Well, yer've got yerself in a right mess now, sunshine, and no mistake. I don't know what to do for the best. If the men were here, they'd probably separate you from the ruddy chair in no time.'

'We'll have to think of something quick, Mam,' Doreen said, ''cos I saw our Jill going past the window ages ago. She'll wonder where I am. And I left Bobby crawling round the floor. Now, I can think of something that might get Auntie Nellie off the chair, but it won't be very ladylike, and might hurt.'

'And what's that, sunshine? 'Cos I'm blowed if I can see any way out.'

'Don't worry about me getting hurt, girl.' Nellie's voice sounded hoarse. 'The way I am at the moment isn't exactly comfortable. And I don't give a bugger whether it's ladylike or not. Just get me out, that's all, and to hell with what I look like, or if it hurts or not. And be bloody quick

130

about it 'cos me back is killing me.'

Doreen flexed her arms. 'Right, here goes, Mam. You stand in front of Auntie Nellie, and I'll stand at the back. I'm going to put me foot on her bottom and push like hell. So be ready, Mam, 'cos she might come out quick.' Doreen bent down and patted Nellie's back. 'Before I do it, I want a firm promise from yer, Auntie Nellie, that yer won't clout me, or fall out with me, if I hurt yer during this operation.'

'You get me out of here, girl, and yer'll be me friend for life.' Even though she must have been suffering, Nellie could still manage a joke. 'I mean, yer can understand why I'm keen to be parted from this chair, can't yer, girl? I've got two hungry men coming in from work at six o'clock, and if they walk in and see me, they'll think I'm the humpback of Notre Dame, whatever his name is, and they'll run like hell.'

'We'll have yer back to normal before then, sunshine,' Molly said. 'Even if I have to find a workman with a saw. Then I'll give yer back a good massage and yer'll be as good as new when George sees yer. I can't say the same for his chair, but we'll see how it goes.'

Doreen lifted her foot, nodded to her mother, then took hold of the feet of the chair to give herself some leverage before putting all the strength she possessed into one huge push. She was red in the face with the exertion, but it did the trick and set Nellie falling forward into Molly's waiting hands.

'Oh, thank God for that,' Nellie puffed. 'I had visions of going to me grave in that ruddy chair.'

131

She was putting a hand on each knee to hoist herself up when Molly stopped her.

'Don't try and stand up straight, sunshine, or yer'll be in agony. Just stay as yer are, while I tell Doreen she'd better go now, or Victoria and Jill will be worried sick.'

'Yeah, I'll buzz now, as long as Auntie Nellie is all right. Me and Jill don't have to go out though, yer know. We can go later.'

Nellie turned her head as best she could under the circumstances, and said, 'Thanks, girl, ye're an angel. And with a kick like you've got, yer should be playing for Liverpool or Everton.'

Doreen chuckled as she bent to kiss Nellie's cheek. 'You take care of yerself in future. Always test the chair before yer sit on it.'

'I won't be getting up to any mischief today, girl, I won't have the energy. My lower regions must be black and blue, and me back feels as though it's broken.'

'Listen, sunshine,' Molly said to her daughter, 'just in case Nellie isn't fit to walk to the shops, would you get our shopping for us? Yer'll have the pram, so yer won't have to carry it.'

'Of course we will! Have yer decided what yer want for dinner?'

'I'll see what me mate says. It'll have to be something easy, in case I have to do Nellie's as well as my own.' Molly bent and pushed her mate's hair back behind her ears. 'How about bacon, egg, tomatoes and fried bread? Would George and Paul be happy with that?'

'I'm not worrying about whether they'll be happy, girl, they'll get it and like it. If it's good

132

enough for Jack and Ruthie, then it's good enough for my two. And yer know I like nothing better than a bacon butty with fried bread.'

'That's sorted, anyway. So it's a pound of streaky bacon, six eggs, a pound of soft tomatoes and a large tin loaf. That will do both houses. But have yer got enough money, 'cos I haven't brought me purse.'

Still bent over, and obviously in pain, Nellie said, 'My purse is in the sideboard drawer, girl, take the money that yer need. Oh, and when ye're in Hanley's getting the bread, bring us a cream slice back with yer. I might as well get some pleasure out of me agony.'

Molly saw the surprise on her daughter's face, and chuckled. 'Don't try and figure out what the connection is between pleasure and agony, 'cos only Nellie knows what she means. But get two cakes, sunshine, because I'm not sitting here licking me lips while Nellie is moaning with delight.'

Doreen handed the purse over to her mother. 'I don't like going in the purse, Mam, so you take some money out. As much as yer think yer shopping will come to.'

Nellie could hear Molly laughing as she opened the purse, and she asked, 'What's so bleeding funny, Molly Bennett?'

'For twenty-five years I've wanted to see the inside of this purse, to see if there were any hidden compartments. And what better time than now, when ye're out of action.'

'I won't always be out of action, soft girl, so just watch what ye're saying. As soon as I can stand up straight, I'll sort you out.'

'Well in the meantime, I'm taking a ten bob note, which is all the money in the purse, sunshine.' Molly waved the note where her mate could see it. 'I'll settle up with yer later, when Doreen brings the shopping back.' She gave the note to her daughter. 'Here you are, love, and don't tell Jill or Victoria what's happened. Just say Nellie's got a bad headache, and I'm staying with her for a while to keep her company.'

'We'll only be out for an hour,' Doreen said, 'and I'll bring your shopping over before I take me own in. So it won't be long before yer get a cake, Auntie Nellie, and I'll be careful not to squash them.'

'Carry them careful, girl – I don't want more cream stuck to the paper bag than there is in the cake. I know I could lick the cream off the bag, but yer mam thinks it's not ladylike, and the look on her face is enough to put me off.'

Molly went to the door with her daughter. 'As I said, sunshine, don't tell anyone what happened here, 'cos although it might give them a laugh, there's nothing funny about it. Nellie must be in pain and although she'd make a joke of it herself, I don't want anyone laughing at her behind her back. She'll tell everyone herself, to give them a laugh, but I don't think it's up to us to do it.'

'I'd clock anyone that laughed at her, Mam, unless she was there herself.' Doreen nodded to a house on the opposite side. 'There's our Jill's pram; she'll be wondering what's happened, so I'd better get over there. I'll see yer later. Ta-ra.'

'Ta-ra, sunshine, and thanks for yer help. I'd

134

have been lost without yer. I'll see yer later.'

When Molly went back into the living room, it was to find Nellie still bent and holding on to a chair back with both hands. 'Any chance of a drink, girl? Me mouth is parched.'

'Just let me massage yer back, Nellie, to see if there's any real damage been done. I'll do it very lightly, and I'll stop as soon as yer tell me to. If anything is broken, we'll have to call the doctor out.'

'Not on your bleeding life, girl! There's no doctor coming in this house and telling me to take me clothes off so he can examine me. Sod that for a lark, girl. You rub me back, like yer said, and I'm sure I'll be as right as rain in no time.'

Molly flexed her fingers and rolled up the sleeves of her cardi. 'Right, sunshine, I'll start very slowly and see how we get on. With a bit of luck there'll be nothing drastically wrong, and you'll be fine in no time.' With her hands flat on Nellie's back, she moved them gently down from her waist to the bottom of her spine. 'How's that, sunshine? Am I making the pain worse, and does it hurt more in any particular spot? It can't be that bad seeing as ye're not screaming in agony when I touch yer, so I'll carry on for ten minutes and we'll see if the massage is helping. Then I'll put the kettle on and yer can have a drink.'

'That feels good, girl. Yer must have healing hands.' Nellie closed her eyes and her body became relaxed. Although she would never admit it, even to Molly, she'd had a fright. She'd been trapped in that chair for two hours before her mate came, and she'd had visions of being there all day. Thank God Molly had a front door key, and the sound of the door being opened, then her mate's voice, well it was the sweetest sound she'd ever heard.

'Ye're quiet, sunshine. Are yer still in pain?' Molly asked because she'd never known her mate be so quiet for so long. 'Can yer feel any improvement, or is it still painful?'

'It's sore, girl, I've got to admit, but I'm not in agony. A cup of tea would go down a treat.'

'I'll make one now. But for heaven's sake don't try to stand up straight all in one go. I'll help yer do it a bit at a time. For now, just stay as you are until I've made the tea. Like yerself, sunshine, my mouth is dry. I'll only half fill the kettle so it won't take so long.'

'It would be a lot quicker if yer'd only stop talking, girl! Don't ever tell me I talk too much, 'cos I'd have to go some to beat you.'

There was water in the kettle, so Molly put a light under it and turned the gas full on. And by the time she'd got the cups ready, and filled the milk jug, the kettle was whistling away. 'Any minute now, sunshine. I'm just trying to find where yer keep the sugar.' She was too occupied to hear her mate muttering that she was too slow to catch a cold. Not that she'd have been put out if she had heard it, for Nellie was Nellie, and there was little you could do but not take to heart what she said.

'Here yer are, sunshine, but don't try to stand up. I'll hold the cup for yer and see how yer get on.'

'Oh, sod that for a lark, girl! How can I drink

136

when I'm stuck like this? Move the cup before I knock it out of yer hand, and I'll try and sit down on a chair, eh?'

'I can't stop yer doing what yer want, Nellie, but take my word and do it very slowly, or yer'll be sorry.' Molly pulled a chair out. 'Here, yer stubborn so and so, let me help yer to ease yerself down.'

Inch by inch, Molly lowered her mate down. And with each inch she expected a cry of pain. But although Nellie was in pain, she gritted her teeth and didn't utter a sound. For if Molly had her way, then she'd fuss over her, and Nellie didn't like being fussed over. That's what she thought until she leaned forward to pick the cup of tea up, and sharp pains shot up her back, and the tops of her legs. Still she kept quiet by biting on the inside of her mouth. 'Pass me the cup over, girl, and I think yer better hold it for me in case I spill it. Me hands are a bit shaky, yer see, with the shock I suppose. But I'm sure a drink will make me feel better.'

'It's a pity we don't have any whisky,' Molly said, holding the cup near to Nellie's lips. 'A drop in a cup of tea would do yer a power of good.'

'We haven't got the money for whisky, girl, 'cos a bottle would cost a fortune. I might get George to nip up to the pub when he gets in from work. He spends enough money in there; I'm sure the barman would let him bring a tot out in a glass. He wouldn't refuse, not when he knows he'd lose a lot of custom if he did. Corker must spend a couple of pound a week in that pub, and he'd have something to say.'

'Ay, I've got a good idea, sunshine.' Molly pulled her chair closer. 'The pub opens at twelve o'clock, and closes again at two. I could nip up there and ask him to put a measure in a glass for us. It's turned eleven now, and I could go up before they have any customers in. What d'yer think?'

'D'yer want the truth, girl?' Nellie turned her head, and because her chins were sorry for her, they didn't even quiver with the movement. 'I think it's the best bleeding idea yer've had since yer came in.'

Molly grinned. 'Yer don't need to thank me every few minutes, sunshine. I know ye're grateful, and are too shy to say so.'

Nellie actually chuckled, which made Molly feel better. 'If I thanked yer, girl, yer'd get such a shock yer'd faint. And a fat lot of good yer'd be then. You sprawled on the floor with yer mouth wide open, and me not able to enjoy the joke.'

'Yer sound a bit more cheerful now, sunshine, after a drink. So if yer can lean forward with yer arms on the table, I'll give yer back another gentle massage. It will help, I promise yer. The sooner yer loosen up, the sooner yer'll be back to normal, and then we'll have to see whether the chair can be fixed before George gets home from work. Personally, I think it's past redemption. For you to fall through the seat, yer must have broken the wooden supports.'

'Yer can be a miserable bugger at times, girl. Why don't yer look on the bright side first, instead of the other way round?' Nellie laid both her arms on the table and lowered her head when Molly began

138

to rub her hands gently up and down her back. 'That's nice, girl, that is. Bittersweet, if yer know what I mean. Like when we were kids and had a gumboil. Yer couldn't help touching it with yer tongue even though it was sore.'

'My God, Nellie, you're going back some years, aren't yer? I haven't heard of anyone having a gumboil for years.' Molly chuckled. 'I did have one once, when I was about eleven, and like yer said, I couldn't keep me tongue away from it. If I remember right, a lot of kids used to get them in those days.'

'We used to get a lot of things in them days, girl, what were not very pleasant. We used to have mice in our house, and in the end me man got a cat because I was frightened of going to bed in case a mouse got in bed with me.' Nellie remembered something from her childhood, and she was so eager to tell Molly she turned her body round too quickly and winced with the pain that ran up her spine. But she brushed it aside before she forgot what she was going to say. 'Ay, girl, d'yer remember when the nit nurse came to the school? Ooh, I hated her 'cos she used to be horrible to the kids what had nits. And they couldn't help it, 'cos if one child got them, they spread to every girl in the class. I kicked the nurse once, 'cos she said I had a dirty head.'

Molly gasped. 'Yer didn't, did yer?'

'Of course I did! I wasn't going to let her get away with calling me dirty. I got the cane for it, and was sent home with a note. But me mam gave me a hug and told me I'd done the right thing, 'cos having fleas didn't mean yer were dirty.'

'And she was quite right, Nellie, because I remember me ma saying that fleas "wouldn't be seen dead in a dirty head, and isn't that the truth of it?"'

Nellie laughed at Molly's attempted Irish lilt. 'Ye're good, girl but not as good as yer ma. She's still got the Irish accent she had the day she left the land of her birth.'

'We've covered some ground, sunshine.' Molly patted Nellie's back to tell her the massage was over for the time being, for her hands were getting sore. 'We've gone from having gumboils, then mice in the house, and finally on to the very pleasant subject of fleas! And the really important thing we should be discussing is George's chair!'

'Look, girl, don't fret over his chair. What I'll do is swap chairs. I'll put mine in his place, and the one what's broke can go in my speck. Then there'll be no problem, 'cos he won't know the difference.'

Molly's eyes nearly popped out of their sockets. 'Nellie, they're not matching chairs! Yours is floral, and George's is plain dark beige. They are not remotely alike.'

'He won't notice the difference when I've finished with them.' Nellie was beginning to look a lot better, and apart from the odd twinge, when she'd screw her eyes up, didn't appear to be affected by her mishap. 'I'll take the seat off my chair and swap it with the broken one.' The crafty gleam was back in her eyes. 'Yer see, girl, yer can do anything if yer put yer mind to it.'

'I hate to disillusion yer, sunshine, but yer can't

just swap the seat of your chair, because it's a fixture. It's fixed to the wooden slats at the sides and back. If yer take those off, which yer'd need a saw for, then the whole chair would collapse. I'm sorry to have to warn you that there's no way yer can get round it unless yer get someone who knows what they're doing to mend George's chair. It can be done, but it's finding the right person to do it. And yer don't stand a snowball's chance in hell of getting it done today.'

'Let's have a look at the bleeding chair,' Nellie said, trying to push herself up with her hands flat on the table. She only managed to stand up with Molly's help, and then she was still bent over. 'It must have been on its last legs to break just because I sat on it.'

Molly was tempted, but held back from saying that her mate's eighteen stone had something to do with the breakage. Also, Nellie never sat down gently like most people, she just dropped down. The groaning and creaking of chair legs didn't bother her. 'D'yer still want me to go to the pub for a tot of whisky for yer?' Molly asked. 'Or not?'

It wasn't often that Nellie was made such a fuss of, and she was lapping it up. It might never happen again, and she told herself she may as well make the most of it. So she decided to play the wounded soldier. 'Oh, I think so, girl, 'cos I did get quite a shock, yer know. And a shock to the system like what I got, well, it can bring on all sorts of things, like a stroke or a heart attack. So best be on the safe side and have a tot of whisky.'

'I'll go now then,' Molly said, reaching for her coat. 'Where d'yer keep yer glasses?'

'Oh, we don't have no glasses, girl. We used to, but somehow they all got broke. It won't take yer a minute to slip down to your house for one.'

'Yer don't half love getting waited on, Nellie. And fancy not having a glass in the house. I'm surprised at yer.'

'Well, we don't need no glasses, do we, girl? I mean, George goes to the pub for his pints, and if we have a party it's always at your house. So we have no need for glasses.'

Molly shook her head slowly. 'Don't yer ever listen to yerself when ye're talking, Nellie? If yer did, yer might realize that yer get away with murder. First, it's bad enough when yer tell me yer haven't got a glass in the house, so I'd better get one from my house to get the whisky in. Then yer have the nerve to tell me yer don't need glasses because when *we* have a party it's always in my house! The flaming cheek of yer!'

Nellie looked surprised. 'Well, we do have parties in your house, girl, so what are yer getting so het up about?'

Keep calm, Molly told herself, 'cos yer know darn well yer'll never get through to Nellie, and yer'll never win. But that little voice in her head egged her on to say what was in her mind. It wouldn't make a blind bit of difference to Nellie, who was never going to change, but it would make Molly feel better to get it off her chest. 'There yer go again, Nellie! Well, when Christmas comes round this year, we'll have *my* party in *your* house! How about that?'

With the innocent look of a newborn baby on her face, Nellie said, 'But we can't have the party

142

in my house, because I've just told yer, soft girl, we haven't got no glasses!'

Molly, torn between tearing her hair out or laughing, chose the latter, and her loud laughter brought a huge grin to Nellie's chubby face. 'That's better, girl, yer had me frightened for a while. I thought yer'd lost yer chuckle button. Why don't yer treat yerself and have a tot of whisky with me? It would warm the cockles of yer heart and cheer yer up. Go on, girl, go mad and tear paper.'

'It's too strong for me, sunshine. I don't like it.'

'Well, get yerself a sherry, then, if that's what yer like. I'll mug yer to one, how about that?'

'That's very kind of yer, Nellie, I appreciate it. I'll nip home and get two glasses, then go to the pub. Tell me where yer keep the purse with yer silver in, and I'll pass it to yer to get the money out.'

'Oh, I don't know what I've done with that purse, girl! It must be with the shock, I can't remember where I put it. You pay, and I'll settle up with yer later.'

'Not on your life, Nellie McDonough.' Molly slipped her coat off and laid it on the arm of the couch. 'How soft you are! And how convenient that yer can't remember where yer put the purse. I'm not forking out for drinks that I don't want anyway, knowing I'll probably never get the money back. And I hope yer don't try and pull any stunts on our Doreen when she fetches our shopping. She can't afford to be throwing her money away. So put yer thinking cap on, and remember where yer put that purse of yours.

Otherwise there'll be no dinner for George or Paul. And there'll be no cream slice for you, Nellie McDonough.'

'But I've already given Doreen ten shillings,' Nellie said. 'That's plenty for what shopping she's getting.'

'I know, sunshine, and I'll have to pay half of that for my shopping. The ten bob note will cover it all, at least I think it will. But I'm not paying my half until I know how much it all comes to. Regarding the whisky, I think we should forget it, 'cos yer seem to have perked up, and you don't need it.'

'You're wicked, Molly Bennett, d'yer know that? Fancy begrudging a mate what has just had a bad accident a dose of something what might do her good. But just wait, I'll get me own back on yer.'

A knock came on the front door, and Doreen's voice called through the letterbox. 'Open the door, Mam.'

Molly was taken aback when she opened the door to find Doreen was not alone. Standing next to her was Harry Watson, Bella's father, and he was carrying a workman's toolbox. 'I met Mr Watson on the main road, Mam,' Doreen said, looking pleased with herself. 'He was on his way to a job, and I happened to mention that Auntie Nellie's chair had caved in, and he very kindly said he'd have a look to see if he could fix it.'

'Oh, that's kind of yer, Harry. Come on in.' Molly held the door wide. 'Nellie will be delighted if yer can fix it.'

When Harry had passed her on his way to the

living room, Molly took the basket Doreen had taken off the pram. 'The shopping came to nine shillings and sixpence, Mam, so I got two extra cream slices with the other sixpence. I thought Auntie Nellie would appreciate an extra cake.'

'I'm glad about that, sunshine, because yer know what she's like with money. As it is, I'll give her five bob and we're quits. I'll nip home for it when Harry leaves.'

'How is Auntie Nellie, Mam? She certainly came a cropper.'

'She's improving by the minutes, sunshine. Can't yer hear her talking fifteen to the dozen down Harry's ear?' Molly stepped down on to the pavement to kiss Bobby, who chuckled and kicked with excitement when he saw her. 'Who's a lovely boy for his grandma, eh?' She cocked an ear and stood up. 'Is that banging I can hear?'

Doreen was grinning from ear to ear. 'Wasn't it lucky I met up with him, Mam? I'll be delighted if he can fix Auntie Nellie's chair for her, and I bet she'll be over the moon.'

'I won't go in yet, because I always blush when my mate tells lies, and she doesn't turn a hair. It'll be interesting to know what tale she's telling Harry about how the chair came to be broken. It wouldn't surprise me if she told him George had done it.'

Bella's father came out looking pleased. 'I've fixed it for Nellie, but I've told her to tell George not to stand on it again. Those chairs weren't made to stand on.'

'Yer've been a blessing, Harry. I bet Nellie's tickled pink?'

'I think you could say that. But it was an easy job, no trouble at all, and I was glad to be able to help. I'll be on me way, Molly, I've got a couple of jobs to go to. Ta-ra.'

'Ta-ra, Harry, and thanks again.' Molly waited until he was out of earshot, then dashed into the house, calling over her shoulder to Doreen that she'd be down to see her and Jill as soon as Nellie was sorted out with the shopping.

Nellie had a really smug smile on her face. 'How about that for service, girl? The chair's as good as new.'

'Nellie Mac,' Molly said, 'if you fell down the lavatory, yer'd come up with a gold watch. It's the luck of the devil you've got. He loves yer because ye're very good at telling whopping lies. Fancy telling Harry it was George who broke the chair by standing on it.'

'What George doesn't know won't hurt him.' Nellie's cheeky, chubby face looked so alive, Molly couldn't be angry with her. So when her mate asked, 'Has Doreen brought the shopping? A nice fresh cream slice will make my day perfect,' Molly brought in the basket from the hall.

'Ye're dead lucky, Nellie, 'cos Doreen bought us two cream slices each.'

Just the thought of two cream slices brought a look of bliss to the chubby face. 'All in all, girl, it's turning out to be a wonderful day.'

Chapter Six

Paul took Phoebe's hand and led her on to the dance floor. He was humming to the music as he took her in his arms and held her close, his cheek touching hers. The tune the four-piece band were playing was 'I Wonder Who's Kissing Her Now' and Paul whispered, 'This is my all time favourite song.'

Phoebe moved back a little, to look into those deep brown eyes that made her go weak at the knees. She was crazy about him, but wished he was more serious about their relationship, which was two years old now. 'One of these days you might have reason to hate the song, Paul Mc-Donough, for it may have memories that come back to haunt yer.'

'Why would it do that, babe? There's no reason why I'd ever go off the song. None that I can think of anyway.' His dimples deep and his brown eyes smiling into her face, he pulled her close. 'Yer've put me off me stride now, so don't blame me if I stand on yer toes.' When Phoebe held back he raised his brow and queried, 'I thought yer liked this dance? What's got into yer?'

'Trying to get through to you is like trying to get through a brick wall, Paul. And sometimes I get so mad I wonder why I bother. And when I said the day might come when this song brings back memories that will haunt yer, I wasn't joking. If things carry on much longer as they are now, with you being come day, go day, then yer might be left wondering who the boy is that's kissing *me!*'

'Don't be like that, babe, not in the middle of me favourite dance.' His dimples and brown eyes didn't work their wonder this time, and Paul's face became serious. 'Okay, you win, babe! Finish this dance as we always do, locked in each other's arms to show how much we love each other, and then we'll sit the next dance out, so we can have a good talk. You can get it all off yer chest, and I promise I won't act daft. But don't talk about any other boy kissing you, 'cos it ain't ever going to happen.'

The dance came to an end then, and Paul squeezed Phoebe tight as he steered her to the door leading to the entrance hall. There were quite a few people there, as smoking wasn't allowed in the dance hall, and he said, 'Let's get our coats and go for a little walk. We can't talk here, we'd need a loudhailer to make ourselves heard. You get yer coat and I'll meet yer back here in a minute.'

As Phoebe reached for her coat from the hanger in the cloakroom, she was curious. She'd often given Paul hints that she was not happy with his lack of real commitment, and he'd always joked his way out of it. Never before had he suggested leaving the dance floor, and as for going for a walk and maybe missing a dance, well, that wasn't a bit like him. Especially over the last few months since she'd told him she didn't like going dancing every night, there was far more to life. He'd reluctantly agreed to going just twice a week, but he was up for every dance.

He wanted everything his way, like when she said he could go dancing on his own, and she would go to the pictures with one of her friends from work. He wasn't happy about that, and because she could seldom refuse him once he set those eyes on her, it ended up with them going to the pictures together, and the dances. She knew she was too soft with him, and would probably end up regretting it one day. But when love rules the heart it's very difficult to refuse.

Paul walked towards her when she came out of the cloakroom. 'What the heck have yer been doing? I was worried yer'd climbed through the window and left me in the lurch. All on my lonesome, with no one to love me.'

'Ah, poor you! And for your information, Paul McDonough, there is no window in the cloakroom.'

'That's a very useful piece of information, that is. Yer never know, it might come in handy sometime. If I ever want to make a quick getaway I'll remember it's no good going to the ladies' cloakroom, 'cos there's no way out.'

As he pulled Phoebe's arm through his, he patted her hand. 'We won't stay out long if it's too cold for yer.'

'It's not cold at all, we're into spring weather now.' Her pretty face smiled up at him. 'Don't yer think ye're a bit on the big side anyway, to climb through a window? Yer'd be lucky if yer got yer head through, never mind yer shoulders.'

Paul came to an abrupt stop. 'As me mam would say, har you hinsinuating that hi have a big head?'

'Not at all! But yer must admit it would look big sticking out of a window. It would appear to be detached from the rest of yer body.'

'Can we skip all the frivolities now, babe, and go to where you want to tell me about finding yerself another man? I'm going to listen very seriously, I promise. Then I'll tell yer what my thoughts are.'

'I've told yer dozens of times, Paul, that I don't think you take our relationship as seriously as you should. We've been courting for two years now, and I'm getting tired of people asking me when we're getting married. I'm sure the girls in work think you're leading me on, with no intention of settling down. And there are times when I agree with them. Soft girl, me, I'm putting all the money I can spare each week, without fail, into the post office. It's mounted up now to eighty pounds, but you're saving hardly anything. So I'm just wasting me time. I could be buying meself new clothes with the money, 'cos heaven knows I could do with dolling meself up now and again.'

'Phoebe, you always look beautiful to me. Yer don't need to doll yerself up for me, 'cos I'd love yer just as much in a sack as I would if yer wore posh clothes! But I want you to be the most beautiful bride our street has ever seen, the day we get married.'

Phoebe chuckled. 'That's asking a lot, Paul, if yer think anyone can outshine the Bennett girls. I wouldn't even try.'

'I wish yer wouldn't run yerself down all the time, babe. The Bennett girls are lovely, and they're nice as well. They don't go around saying, "Look at me, aren't I beautiful?" Don't forget us fellers have different ideas on girls, we don't all think alike. Beauty is in the eye of the beholder, so they say. And in my eyes you are beautiful.'

'You're not missing a couple of dances just to have this conversation, are yer, Paul? Because if you are, we are both wasting our time.'

'No, not at all. And I think yer've done very well to have saved up eighty pounds.' He put a hand on each of her shoulders and turned her to face him, for he wanted to see the expression on her face when he told her, 'It's almost as much as my hundred pound.'

Phoebe's eyes were wide, as in her heart she was hoping what he was saying was true, and he wasn't pulling one of his practical jokes. 'Paul, yer wouldn't pull my leg over something like this, would yer? I'd never forgive yer if yer did.'

'As God is my judge, babe, I am telling yer the truth. I've been going to tell yer many times during the last few months when yer've been going on at me. But I stuck it out until I had a hundred pounds. That's enough to pay for whatever things the bridegroom has to pay for. Like presents for the bridesmaids, and all the flowers. I'm not sure about what my duties will be, seeing as I've never been married before, but I can ask our Steve. He'll put me wise.'

Phoebe's heart was singing with joy. 'All this time I've been nagging at yer, Paul. I'm sorry I've been such a moaner. But I can't wait to be married to yer, 'cos I love yer to bits.'

'I'll keep putting money away every week, babe,

so I'll have a nice little stack by the time we get married.'

'You won't need much more than a hundred pounds, Paul, in fact yer won't need anywhere near it. Me dad is paying for the wedding, but I'm insisting on buying me own wedding dress. I know exactly what I want, but I'm not telling anyone.' Phoebe clutched his arm. 'Oh, I'm so excited, Paul, me tummy is doing somersaults. This is the nicest walk I've ever been on. I've got so much to look forward to, and so have you. We'll have to get our parents together to include them in the arrangements. I know my mam and dad will be over the moon, and would like to be involved. And they'll want to set a date.'

'There is something I don't want them involved in,' Paul said, 'at least not yet. It's going to be my wedding present to you, but I'd like to keep it a secret from the families for now. It's got nothing to do with the wedding arrangements anyway, so I'm not leaving them out of anything.'

'Are you keeping it a secret from me as well?' Phoebe asked. 'Surely you can tell the future bride?'

'I'd like it to be a surprise, babe, so I'm not telling you. Have you any particular date in mind that you'd like to be married on? I know yer can't say a definite day because we haven't got a calendar, but have you any idea what month?'

'Paul, I can give you the month, the day, and the hour, that I'd like to get married on. But we can't always have what we want when there are other people to be considered, so we'll see what the families say. They'll be paying for most of it,

152

at least me dad will, so we'll all get together at a time that suits everyone, and make plans or offer suggestions.'

'No. Hang on a bit, Phoebe, it's not up to the family to say when we can get married. If you have a date in mind, then say so and we'll stick to that. After all, it's your wedding day.'

Phoebe chuckled. 'I had rather hoped you'd be there as well, Paul. It wouldn't be a wedding without the groom. I'd look a bit stupid standing in front of the altar on me own, with everyone feeling sorry for me.'

'No messing around, babe. I know yer think I've dragged me heels over setting a date for the wedding, but I wanted to save enough money to be able to do the job properly. But I've got that now, so I can concentrate properly. And for me the only thing I'm interested in, apart from making you my wife, of course, is to see you have the happiest day of your life. And if you have a day in mind, then for heaven's sake say so, and that is the day we'll choose, come what may. Are yer going to tell me, or not?'

'I'd love to get married on me birthday.' Phoebe shrugged her shoulders. 'But it sounds selfish, expecting everyone to fall in with what I want, so let's leave it until we can have a pow-wow with our parents.'

However, Paul stuck to his guns. 'If you want to get married on yer birthday, and I say that suits me fine, then no one is going to stop us.'

'But my birthday is on the eighteenth of September, Paul, and that's on a Friday. The men work on a Friday.'

'I bet you any money none of them will mind. They've taken days off for other weddings, so they'll think nothing of it. In fact, I'm sure someone else got married on a Friday, but I can't bring to mind who it was. Anyway, babe, forget everyone else. We'll get the parents together tomorrow night, tell them we've decided it would be nice to get married on yer birthday, and they'll be so flabbergasted they'll take half an hour for it to sink in.'

'We're not going back to the dance, are we? It's hardly worth it for one or two dances.'

'It's up to you, babe. I thought you might find it romantic to tell yer mates in work that I proposed to yer during the last waltz.'

'It would be nice to tell the girls in work, yes, it sounds dead romantic. But for me it's more than romantic. For every year, on me birthday, I'll be able to look back and relive my wedding day all over again.'

'Come, on, then, we'll have to have the last waltz, or yer'll spend the rest of your life telling fibs.'

Nellie and George had been invited to the Corkhills' house the next night, and when Nellie walked in and saw there was only Corker, Ellen and Phoebe there, she said, 'It's quiet, isn't it, Corker? I thought the room would be full.'

'We've sent all the kids out, Nellie, so we could talk in peace. Phoebe said her and Paul have got something to tell us.' The big man rubbed his hands together. 'She won't say what it is, but I've got high hopes.'

154

Nellie saw her son pass the window. 'Here's Paul now, so we'll soon find out what the mystery is all about.' She frowned. 'Hasn't my mate been invited?'

Corker slapped one of his huge hands on his forehead. 'Oh, lord, I forgot about Molly! It's been such a rush, me and Ellen haven't had time to think straight. But that's no excuse for leaving Molly out.'

Paul heard this, as he came in from the street. 'I'll knock for Mrs B., shall I? Ye're right, Uncle Corker, she should be here.' He chuckled. 'I almost gave the game away then, but I bit me tongue in time.'

'Ay, what about Jack?' Ellen said. 'Ask him as well, Paul. We can't leave him out, it would be mean.'

Nellie pulled a chair out from under the table, and despite the creaks and groans from the chair, who knew from old what it was about to suffer, she plonked herself down and spread her arms on the table. 'Ay, we could have a party when Molly and Jack come, 'cos all our gang will be here.'

'Apart from all the family, Nellie, and Maisie and Alec,' Ellen reminded her. 'And had yer forgotten Jill and Steve, Doreen and Phil, and your Lily and Archie? Our gang is getting bigger and bigger. We'll be needing a mansion for our parties soon. We had too many kids, that's the trouble.'

'I'll remind yer of that remark in about five years' time, love,' Corker told her. 'Our four will be married and flown the nest. There'll only be

155

me and thee, and yer won't know what to do with yerself. This house will be so quiet, yer'll be wishing the kids would come back again to liven things up.'

'Phoebe will only be living two doors away, when her and our Paul get married,' Nellie said. 'So yer'll still see her every day.'

Phoebe had been silent up until then, but she took to heart what her dad had said about the house being quiet when the four children were married. 'Mam, it won't seem as though I've left home when I'm only two doors away. Our Dorothy said she's not getting married for several years, and heaven knows it could be ten years before Gordon and Peter leave home. Then if ye're still feeling lonely and the house is too quiet for yer, me and Paul can come here and live with yer, so Mrs Mac can have her house back for a while.'

'Ay, don't mind me,' Nellie said, 'I'm only here to make the numbers up! Don't you be offering to come back and help yer mam out when ye're married to my son, 'cos I'm relying on you to help me around the house.' She screwed her eyes up and squinted at Phoebe. 'Before any deals are made here, I want to know whether I'm on the winning side or the losers'? So a few questions are in order. First, how are yer fixed for making fairy cakes? And are yer good at scrubbing the step and ironing men's shirts and trousers? And think before yer answer, girl, 'cos if yer tell me yer can do all these things, and then it turns out yer've never made a fairy cake in yer life, yer don't know how to scrub the step, and yer burn

156

everything yer put an iron to, well that would mean ye're a useless article like meself, and there's no room in our house for two of us.'

George was sitting on the couch next to Corker, and his eyes had been moving from Nellie to Phoebe. Now he said, 'Oh, I wouldn't say yer were a useless article, love. I remember yer mam telling me, before we got married, that yer were good at a lot of things. I can't remember them all 'cos there were so many. But I do remember one was that yer were good at breaking crockery, and another was that yer were a dab hand at burning toast. Those I remember because ye're still good at them.'

When the laughter had died down, Nellie was pointing a finger at her husband as Paul and Molly walked in. 'Yer all seem very happy,' Molly said. 'What have we missed?'

'Yer haven't missed it, girl,' Nellie told her. 'Ye're just in time to see me clock my feller for saying I'm good at breaking crockery and burning toast. The cheek of him, talking about his wife like that. Your Jack wouldn't talk about you like that, would he?'

Molly kept a straight face. 'No, he wouldn't, sunshine, and I'd be really annoyed with him if he did. But thinking about it, he would never have any reason to. Yer see, I'm very careful with crockery because I can't afford not to be. I can't remember the last time I broke a cup, because it's so long ago.' She looked thoughtful, as though puzzled. 'What was the other one now? Oh, yeah, it was burning toast. Well I don't do that either, sunshine, because me ma taught me never to waste food, for it was a sin when there are so many starving people in the world.'

Nellie's eyes were getting narrower by the second. When her mate had finished speaking, she folded her arms, tucked them under her mountainous bosom, and gazed up into Molly's face. 'Ye're too bleeding good to live, yer know that, Molly Bennett. Yer should be up there in heaven with the angels, them what were also too good to live.' Her head went from side to side as she thought up other ways of getting back at Molly. 'But I'm going to tell my friend St Peter that ye're a big sneak, and he'll pass it on to every angel up there. So yer won't get a good reception when yer arrive, and it'll serve yer right for telling lies about me.' With a sharp nod of her head, which frightened the life out of her chins, she ended by saying, 'Yer'll get paid back for telling everyone I burn the toast.'

'I didn't tell everyone yer burn the toast, sunshine, I've never mentioned it until you brought it up. But then again, I didn't need to tell everyone even if I'd wanted to, 'cos the whole street can smell the burning every morning. In fact, I was seeing Jack out to work one morning when the Millers' front door opened and Bill came out on his way to work. And I heard him shouting back to his wife, "Nellie's burnt the toast again, Vera."'

With her mouth wide, Nellie glanced at the captive audience. 'Who the hell are the Millers when they're out? I've never heard of no family of that name living in this street.'

'They're a make-believe family, Nellie. I made them up, like you've been making things up.

You've made a career out of it, and it's rubbed off on me now.'

George pulled on his wife's arm. 'Sit down, Nellie. We're invited guests here, and you've done nothing but yap. So behave yerself and sit down.'

Corker asked Molly, 'Where's Jack? Is he coming? I don't want to start until everyone's here.' He guffawed, then looked at his daughter. 'I'm sorry, sweetheart, this meeting of friends is for you and Paul. Don't let me spoil it by taking over.'

'I left Jack finishing the dishes, Corker. I didn't know it was a gathering of the clan, because Paul didn't say. But I'll go and get him, 'cos he won't want to miss anything.' She turned at the door and laughed. 'I love a little excitement and mystery, and it doesn't happen very often. I'll be back in two minutes flat, with my feller in tow.'

Five minutes later the parents and friends of Paul and Phoebe were all seated and looking at the couple with expectancy written on their faces. All were hoping that the reason for the gathering was an announcement that had been long in coming. The couple themselves were sitting holding hands. Phoebe was looking shy and nervous, while Paul looked the picture of happiness, and not in the least shy. 'Me and Phoebe have got something to tell yer. And to make it a bit more interesting, I'm going to tell yer how it came about.' He looked down at Phoebe and squeezed her hand. 'Everyone thinks my girlfriend is quiet and shy, which she is to a point, and it's why I love her. But behind that shyness is a strong personality which comes out now and again. And last night my girl really showed she has a mind of her own.'

In a quiet voice, Phoebe said, 'Get on with it, Paul. I'm sure no one is interested in the details.'

Nellie huffed. 'That's where ye're wrong, girl, 'cos we want to know every little detail. So stop blushing and let me son tell us why, and how, it all came about. Unless yer've got us here for a laugh, and in that case I'll box his ears for him.'

Paul sighed. 'Women, what would yer do with them? They can't keep quiet for five minutes.'

'Go on, son,' Corker said, 'and we'll all be as quiet as mice.'

'Thank you, Uncle Corker. Well, to get back to last night, me and Phoebe were dancing to my favourite song, "I Wonder Who's Kissing Her Now", and doesn't she go and spoil it by telling me that unless I buck me ideas up, I'll be singing that song for real, 'cos she will be kissing some other bloke.'

'Good for you, girl,' Nellie said, while Molly and Ellen nodded in agreement. 'It's about time yer put yer foot down with him.'

'Well, I wasn't going to take a chance of that happening,' Paul said, his brown eyes shining both with laughter, and with love for the girl sitting next to him. 'So I got down on one knee in the dance hall, and I proposed to her.'

Phoebe gasped. 'Paul!'

'Okay, so I'm adding a bit to make it more romantic. It doesn't matter how I proposed – you've agreed to marry me, and I'm holding yer to that.'

There was a loud burst of clapping and laughter, with kisses and congratulation in abundance. The only one who noticed that Nellie had tears in her eyes was Molly, and she quickly put an arm across her mate's shoulder. 'Save those tears for bed tonight, sunshine, and give yer son and future daughter-in-law a big kiss.'

'He's the last of me children, girl, me baby.'

'Hardly a baby, sunshine, and yer should be happy he's marrying a wonderful girl. Plus, Paul won't be leaving home, seeing as they're going to be living with you! Go on, give them a kiss.'

Nellie wasn't an emotional person, and always said she hated kissing because it was sloppy. The only exemptions she'd ever made were when Steve, her firstborn, married Jill, and again when Lily, her only daughter, had married Archie. And she was about to make another exception now, for her youngest. However, Paul didn't wait for his mother to come to him, he went to her with arms outstretched. Like his brother and sister, he loved his mother dearly for the warmth, love and laughter she'd given them all through their lives. And now, with his arms round her ample waist, he lifted her off her feet. 'Put me down, yer daft ha'p'orth, ye're showing everything I've got!'

His dimples deep, he said, 'Mam, whether yer've got yer pink or yer blue fleecy-lined on, it won't be the first time we've all seen them, so stop struggling. Give us a kiss, say ye're happy for me and Phoebe, and then I'll let yer down.'

Shaking her head and tutting, but secretly delighted, Nellie gave her son a kiss, then one to Phoebe who'd been waiting patiently. And in a whisper guaranteed to be heard by all, she said, 'Don't forget what I said about the fairy cakes, girl. Yer've got from now until yer get married to learn how to make them as good as our Lily does. Light as a feather, they are.'

Ellen thought she'd stick up for her daughter, because Phoebe wasn't one for bragging. 'She doesn't need any lessons, Nellie, because our Phoebe makes fairy cakes so light, they float off the plate towards the ceiling.'

'Ooh, er,' Nellie said, 'our Lily's don't float off the plate. I'll have to have words with her about that.'

'I think we should all settle down now,' Corker said. He didn't have much to say, but he was, without doubt, the happiest person in the room after Paul and Phoebe. 'Now Paul has proposed, and Phoebe has accepted, perhaps the couple have plans they'd like to tell us about?'

'Well, Uncle Corker, we haven't had time to discuss plans and arrangements. But one thing we have agreed on, and I'll let Phoebe tell you herself. Go on, babe.'

Phoebe's face went the colour of beetroot, and she would have backed out if Paul hadn't put his arm round her shoulder and whispered softly, 'Go on, love, it's what you want so go ahead.'

'I can feel me cheeks burning, and I'll probably stammer and stutter, but as Paul said, it's something I've thought about, and wished for, for a few years. I would love to get married on me birthday if it's possible.'

'Then you shall get married on your birthday, sweetheart,' Corker said. 'If you want it, then I'll make sure it happens.' He turned to Ellen. 'The first one to get married, eh, love? Like Molly's two girls, and Lily, we want to do Phoebe proud.'

'When is yer birthday, sunshine?' Molly asked. 'Not next month I hope, 'cos we all need time to buy new clothes.' Her hand went to her mouth. 'Oh, Nellie, yer'll be able to buy a new wedding hat! Oh, Phoebe, sunshine, yer've given us all something to look forward to.'

'I'm afraid my birthday is on the eighteenth of September, Auntie Molly, and it's on a Friday. But I can always have it on the Saturday if Friday is too inconvenient.'

It was George who first came to her aid. 'I can take the Friday off, love, no trouble. My boss can't refuse to give me the day off for my son's wedding.'

Corker was next to say, 'No bother for me to be off that day. Father of the bride, my boss wouldn't dare even pull a face.'

Jack grinned. 'Well, if me and Molly are invited guests, I'm damn sure I'm not letting her go on her own. So count me in, and thank you.'

'I know it's a good few months off, sunshine,' Molly said, 'but if yer want the reception at Hanley's yer'd be well advised to book early.'

'I lay in bed last night going over some of the details,' Phoebe said. 'I was so excited I couldn't get to sleep. I know in me mind what I'd like, and who I'd like, but as me dad is paying for the reception, and the bridesmaids' dresses and suits for Gordon and Peter, I'll be guided by him.'

'Ay, girl, we can't hang around, yer know.' This was Nellie on her high horse. 'As mother of the groom, I'm hentitled to know what's going on.'

'Yer mean entitled, sunshine, not hentitled. I can't see any chickens being invited guests. And

I'm sure Phoebe will keep you in touch with any developments.'

'I'll need you with me, girl, to tell me what all the big words mean. For I could end up in the back pew in the church, all on me own in me new wedding hat.'

'I doubt that very much, Nellie, 'cos ye're hardly the wallflower type. And being mother of the groom, plus a new wedding hat, well, I can see you throwing your weight around.'

'When we've got the house to ourselves later,' Phoebe told them, 'just me, Paul, and me mam and dad, then we'll make a proper list for yer to see. I know who I'd like as bridesmaids, and maid of honour, but I'll sort it out with me parents first.'

Paul chuckled. 'It's easy for a bridegroom, I only need a best man, and I'm hoping our Steve will fill that role.'

Molly jumped to her feet. 'We'll leave yer to let the happy news sink in. And yer can sort the arrangements out, plus who's doing what, without us chipping in. So on yer feet, Jack, and you, Nellie, with George. Let's leave these people in peace.'

Nellie didn't agree with that. 'I'll stay with our Paul, in case he needs any help or advice. You go home, Molly, and take Jack and George with yer. I don't mean take my feller home with yer, I mean when yer get outside, point him in the direction of his own home.'

'No, Mam,' Paul said. 'Me and Phoebe want to go over everything, and we can't do it with people around. We're better on our own.'

Nellie heaved a big sigh. 'It's coming to something when me own son tells me to sod off.'

'As soon as we've got our heads round all the people who will be involved, the main ones, like, then we'll let yer know. And as it's a few months off, yer'll have plenty of time for yer wedding outfit. In fact, Mam,' Paul said, 'yer'll be sick of the sound of this wedding before long, because yer'll be hearing about it every night when we're having our dinner.'

Phoebe touched his arm. 'Does yer mam know yer've been putting money away on the quiet? And how much yer've saved?'

Paul shook his head. 'I haven't told anyone. But seeing as you've brought it up, I'll never get any peace until she knows.' He raised his brow at his mother. 'Your son has saved the grand total of one hundred pounds.' He heard surprise in the raised voices, and went on to say, 'I know you thought I was spending all me money on enjoying meself, but yer were all wrong, yer see.'

Nellie was lost for words. 'A hundred pound! Why, that's a fortune! Ye're a dark horse, Paul McDonough, but I'm proud of yer.'

'And so you should be, Nellie, for that's wonderful news.' Molly told her. 'He's not my son, but that doesn't stop me being proud of him.'

Corker didn't say anything, but in his heart he was a very happy man, and a very relieved man. For he'd often wondered if Paul would ever settle down, and put a wife before his carefree lifestyle. What he'd seen and heard in the last half-hour had chased away any doubts he had. Phoebe would be safe in Paul's hands. And because he took after his mother for humour, then his daughter could look forward to a marriage filled with warmth, love and laughter. And no father could ask for more.

Ellen saw Molly and Nellie out with their husbands. As she returned to the living room, she found herself comparing life now to what it had been years ago. What a difference there was. Her firstborn was going to marry a boy she'd loved from afar since she was a schoolgirl. She'd been Phoebe Clarke then, and because her father, Nobby Clarke, was a drunkard and a wife-beater, they were looked down on by neighbours in the street. Ellen was never free of bruises and black eyes, and was ashamed for herself and her four children, walking round empty-bellied and in rags. Nobby Clarke spent all his wages on booze and horses while his family starved. It was his love of beer that finally killed Nobby. It was the day the war ended, and everyone was celebrating. Leaving his wife and children without a penny, he'd gone out to celebrate, and he got so drunk he'd walked in front of a tram and been run over.

All these memories came back to Ellen. She smiled at her daughter, while part of her mind was still thinking of those dark days. She would never have survived without the help of Molly and Nellie, to whom she owed everything. They had made her go out with her head held high, had dressed her and her children in second-hand clothes from the market, and even got her a job at the local butcher's. And Corker had come into her life then, helping to restore the pride and dignity that Nobby Clarke had robbed her of.

Corker was the best thing that had ever happened to her and the children, who had led a dreadful life with their drunken father who lashed out with his hands and feet if they dared to speak in front of him. When the giant of a man married their mother it was the happiest day they had ever known, and they were immensely proud when he asked them to call him Dad. He taught them to be open and honest, and he brought love and laughter into a house that had once been their prison.

All this flashed through Ellen's mind as she took her seat at the table. 'Well, now it's quietened down, we can hear ourselves think. I am so happy for you, Phoebe, and I couldn't have chosen a better man to be your husband.'

'I've just been telling them the same thing, love,' Corker said, stroking his beard. 'I have to admit there were a few times when I wondered whether Paul was serious, but now I know he's been saving up like mad, I have to admit I was wrong, and I'm happy to do so. Any man who can put that look on my beautiful daughter's face, well, he must have all the qualities she wants in a future husband, And what me and Ellen are most pleased about is that you'll be living next door but one. The Bennetts, McDonoughs and Corkhills are becoming an even bigger family, and nothing could please me more.'

Paul's guffaw told them a laugh was coming. 'I've been thinking about this for a while now, Uncle Corker, and I've worked out that the Corkhills and McDonoughs will be blood relations, but not the Bennetts! They'll be blood related to the McDonoughs through our Steve, but not to the Corkhills.' Again the dimples showed themselves at the same time as a guffaw. 'So I've worked it all out. I did it in bed last night actually, and 'cos there's so many now, I kept getting confused. But in the end I came up with the answer. If Ruthie Bennett marries your Gordon or Peter, then all three families will be blood related!'

Corker's loud guffaw could be heard as far away as Molly's house, where she and Nellie were standing discussing the happy and surprising news. George and Jack had left them to it, and gone to the pub for a pint. After all, what better excuse could they have than the announcement of a wedding? Even if it was months off!

'Listen to Corker,' Molly laughed. 'He is over the moon, yer could see it in his eyes. And I'll tell yer what, Nellie, he'll make sure Phoebe has the best wedding money can buy. He absolutely adores those children, all four of them, and he's a fantastic father. I never think about Nobby Clarke, haven't done for years, but I couldn't help but compare him with Corker tonight. Can you imagine Nobby ever giving those children the life that Corker has? I know I shouldn't speak ill of the dead, but that man was an out and out rotter.'

'Yer can say that again, girl, 'cos he was a real bad 'un. But when ye're talking about the wedding, yer should mention our Paul, yer know, 'cos he's playing as big a part as Phoebe. Without him there wouldn't be no wedding, so I want him to be included. Don't forget, girl, he's the last of me children.'

'You won't get left out, sunshine, don't you worry. But I know how yer feel about Paul, because I felt the same when our Tommy got married. I cried for weeks because me only son was leaving home. It still pulls on me heartstrings every time I go to me ma's and see him. I know it's daft, but I can't help it. None of us can help the way God made us. I love the bones of Jack, and me four children, and I don't care if anyone thinks I'm soppy.'

'Ay, girl, look on the bright side. Think of the time we'll have buying new hats and dresses. We've got something to look forward to.' Nellie's head gave a little shake, her back straightened and her bosom rose majestically. 'Mind you, girl, being mother of the groom, I'm going to have to look better than you. No offence, like, girl, but it's true, isn't it? Stands to sense that the people in the church will be looking out for me, to see what creation I'm wearing to me son's wedding.'

Molly's shoulders shook with silent laughter. She'd just been insulted by her best mate, but she didn't mind. Nellie thought she was going to be the star of the show at this wedding, and Molly wasn't going to burst her bubble. Then again, there were two ways of looking at this situation. One was that Nellie would be happy, and that was the good part. But on the other hand, Molly would hear nothing but the wedding for the next few months, and she'd end up with a headache every day. And it would be useless to tell Nellie she had a headache with having the wedding rammed down her ears every day. In her mind she could hear her mate's reply. 'Well, it's to be hoped yer don't have a headache on the day of the wedding, girl, 'cos yer'll look as miserable as sin, and yer would spoil my son's wedding. The happiest day of his life, and you pick the same day to have a bleeding headache!'

'What did yer say, girl?'

'I never said anything, sunshine.'

'I could have sworn yer said yer had a headache, girl.'

'No, yer must be hearing things, Nellie, 'cos I haven't got a headache. I'm expecting one soon, though.'

'Well, as long as it doesn't come on the day of the wedding, that's all right. Or the day I go for me mother of the groom hat, either! I want you to watch me trying hats on, and I'm counting on yer telling me which I look best in. You know what I mean, one what will catch everyone's eye, so they'll still be talking about it weeks after the wedding. What I don't want is to be looking in a mirror in Lewis's, expecting to see meself looking like a film star in a big, wide creation, and instead I see you behind me with a face as long as a fiddle.'

'That's a bit awkward, Nellie, because I haven't a clue how long a fiddle is! If yer tell me, then I promise I'll try and keep me face shorter than a fiddle. I can't do better than that, can I, sunshine?'

Nellie looked up at the sky for guidance before answering. 'I'm trying to work out whether ye're being sarcastic, girl, 'cos yer don't seem to be very excited about this wedding. It wouldn't be that ye're jealous, would it?'

'Of course I'm jealous, Nellie.' Molly had to think quickly. What could she say she was jealous of to put a smile of satisfaction on her mate's face? 'I'll be as mad as hell on the day of the wedding, because your hat will be twice the size of mine, and all eyes will be on you. I'll be like the poor relation.'

'Ay, girl, yer can borrow the hat I had for our Lily's wedding. It's a nice hat, as good as new, and it'll look nice on yer.'

'No, thank you, sunshine. The whole of the neighbourhood will be at the church, and they'll all recognize it as the hat you wore for Lily's wedding. No, I'll come up with something, even if it's only a beret!'

Nellie's nostrils flared. 'Ye're not coming to my son's wedding in a beret, Molly Bennett, or I'll pretend I don't know yer.'

'I'll have yer know that berets are all the rage in France. The height of fashion they are.' Molly would have loved to laugh at the expression on Nellie's face, but she wanted to keep the farce going a bit longer. Jack was in the pub, Ruthie was out with Bella, and she'd rather rile her mate up for a laugh than sit in the house on her own. 'The French are noted as the fashion capital of the world, sunshine, it's where all the models go, and their clothes are chic. So I might just give some thought to a beret. A nice bright red one, I think. Anyway, I can choose a colour when we go shopping for your mother of the groom hat. I could buy a nice red chiffon scarf to go with the beret, they'd go well together.' Molly clapped her hands and giggled like a schoolgirl. 'Ooh, I'm not half looking forward to it. I'm dead excited.'

'I don't know about excited, girl, but dead yer would be if yer turned up at the church wearing a bright red beret. I'd throw yer out of the church meself, and choke yer with me bare hands.'

Molly did her best to look horrified. 'I'm surprised at yer, Nellie McDonough, talking about murder in a churchyard! Whatever would Father Kelly say?'

'He'd probably send for the gravediggers, if he's got any sense. I mean, there'd be no point in taking yer dead body to a hospital, would there? He'd think I'd been very considerate, but being a priest, he'd have to hear my confession, and he'd probably give me six Hail Marys as a punishment.'

'Am I only worth six Hail Marys, sunshine? Surely I'm worth a lot more than that.'

'Yer might be now, while ye're still alive, but not when ye're dead, girl. And I'll make sure that ruddy red beret and scarf go in the coffin with yer. High fashion or low bleeding fashion, they're not allowed at my son's wedding.'

'Ay, Nellie, I've just thought of a good answer to that.'

'What is it, girl?'

'I wouldn't be seen dead in red, sunshine!'

'Oh, yeah, that was very quick-witted, that was. Not like you, 'cos yer usually take ages to catch on.'

Molly heard her husband's voice in the distance. 'Good grief, sunshine, here's the men back from the pub, and we're still standing in the same spot they left us in. They'll think we're real gasbags.'

'I don't give a bugger what they think, girl. I bet

172

we've had a better time than they've had, 'cos my feller is no good at making up jokes. He'll laugh at other people's jokes, but he doesn't know any of his own.' Nellie's whole body shook as she burst out laughing. 'He wouldn't see the funny side of me choking yer to death in a graveyard, all because I didn't like yer red beret. I know exactly what he'd say if I told him. And he'd be dead serious when he said, "Nellie, that's not a bit funny. There's many a true word spoken in jest." And he'd think I'd lost the run of me senses if I told him that berets were all the rage in France. Especially bright red ones.'

'Don't tell me you two have been here since me and George went to the pub.' Jack was amazed. 'Why didn't yer go in and talk in comfort?'

George came up behind him. 'My wife prefers to stand up when she's talking, don't yer, love? It gives her a feeling of power.'

'Ay, smart Alec, at least I don't need to get beer down me to be able to talk. It doesn't cost me nothing, either. Me and Molly have enjoyed our little chat, breathing in the cool, fresh night air.'

'I don't know how yer find enough to talk about,' Jack said, 'seeing as yer've been together most of the day. Me and George have got our work to discuss, and our workmates and bosses.'

Nellie didn't give Molly a chance to hit back, not when she had a quick retort on her lips. Putting the back of her hand to her mouth, she let out a loud and long yawn. 'Oh, dear, how bleeding dull can yer get? Ye're at work all day, and then it's the only thing you can talk about at night! Not like me and Molly. We've been talking about

173

clothes from the big French fashion houses. Most fashionable people in the world, the French are. They have models what walk on these catwalks what look like the planks of wood sailors used to have to walk on because they'd started a mutiny. Walking the plank they used to call it.'

George raised his brows at Jack, and shrugged his shoulders. 'Ye're as wise as me, Jack. I never knew Nellie had been to France – she never told me. And I certainly didn't know she'd crossed the ocean on a galleon that had a plank for sailors to walk to their death on.'

'I knew we'd have been better staying with the wives,' Jack said. 'At least the conversation wouldn't have been as flat as that beer was. There wasn't even a head on it!'

'Ooh, er, don't start talking about a head, Jack Bennett, unless yer want to be here all night. My mate here, your wife, has talked me hind leg off over what she's putting on her head for the wedding. She's going to make a holy show of herself if somebody doesn't talk some sense into her.'

'Nellie, it's the hind leg off a donkey,' Molly told her. 'Yer got yerself a bit mixed up.'

Nellie scratched her head. 'What flaming donkey are yer talking about, girl? I never mentioned no donkey, and I don't know no donkeys.'

'I know yer don't, sunshine, that's why I said yer got mixed up when yer said I'd talked the hind leg off yer. I couldn't do that 'cos ye're not a donkey.'

'And yer thought it worthwhile to tell me that? Don't yer think that I'd have noticed meself that I'm not a donkey?'

George was happy to add his two-pennyworth. 'I don't know so much, love. Yer might have been one at some time, but didn't notice because yer talked the hind leg off yerself.'

'No, I don't agree with yer there, George,' Jack said, his face deadpan. 'Even if Nellie had talked the hind leg off herself, she'd still have the "hee-haw". Every donkey I've seen nods their heads and snorts "hee-haw".'

'Yer wouldn't believe it, would yer, girl?' Nellie asked. 'You and me have spent our time having an intelligent conversation, about fashion and models in France, and outfits for my son's wedding. And these two roll up and act like children. They haven't got a brain between them. I bet if yer blew in one of their ears, yer breath would come out of the other end, 'cos there's nothing inside to stop it. Pig igorant they are.'

'It's pig ignorant, Nellie,' her husband said. 'Yer missed a letter out.'

Nellie rose to her full height. 'If you don't behave yerself, George McDonough, it won't be a letter missing, it'll be two of yer front teeth. And if you don't stop laughing, Jack Bennett, two of your front teeth will be lying on the pavement next to the silly sod I'm married to.'

'I think it's time we called it a day, Jack,' George said, 'while we've still got teeth in our heads.'

Jack nodded. 'Yeah, we'd better call it a day, 'cos our Ruthie will be home any minute.'

George put a hand on his wife's arm. 'Are yer coming, love? It'll be time for bed before we've had our usual cup of tea.'

Nellie shook his hand away. 'You go in and put

the kettle on. Me and Molly have got lots to talk about yet. Give me a shout when the tea is poured out.'

Jack pulled a face at George. 'I suppose that goes for me, too! Although it's beyond me that they've still got anything to talk about.'

'That's for us to know, Jack Bennett,' Molly said. 'And I expect me tea to be on the table when I come in. Just as I like it, with milk and one sugar.' She gave a sly wink at her mate. 'Now, where were we up to, sunshine, before we were so rudely interrupted?'

Chapter Seven

'When we've had our second cup of tea, girl, are we going over the road to tell Doreen and Victoria about our Paul getting married, before we go to the shops?'

'I've been wondering whether we should or not,' Molly answered. 'But if we don't tell them, somebody else will and they'll think we're dark horses. So we'll mention it when we go over. And come to think about it, there's no way yer could keep news like that to yerself.'

'Well, it's my son getting married, girl, so I've got every right to let folk know, 'cos it's a big occasion in my life.'

'It's a big step in Paul's life as well, sunshine. And I hope that every time you tell anyone that your son is getting married, yer'll mention it's

Phoebe he's getting married to! Yer can't leave her out, sunshine, 'cos the bride is more important at a wedding than the groom is.'

Nellie didn't agree with that, and she was quick to say so. 'She is not! There wouldn't be no wedding without a groom. Phoebe wouldn't like it if she was standing on her own in front of the altar.'

'She wouldn't be the only one, sunshine, because Father Kelly would think it was a queer goings-on. But don't be getting yer knickers in a twist, Nellie, because I mentioned the bride being more important than the groom. It's the wedding dress and veil and the bouquet that make the bride stand out. And her bridesmaids. Yer know yerself that most of the neighbours only go to see the outfits. Nobody takes much notice of the groom, because all men wear suits.'

'What ye're trying to tell me, Molly Bennett, is that a groom is only there to make the numbers up.'

'Paul isn't a wallflower, Nellie, he's very outgoing and also very handsome. He'll be noticed, don't worry, 'cos he'll be giving the after dinner speech, don't forget.'

'Oh, yeah, he'll be good at that 'cos he's always cracking jokes. And as I'll be sitting next to him at the table, nobody will be able to miss seeing me hat.'

Molly turned her head away for a few seconds so she could have a quick, quiet chuckle. When she turned back to her friend, she said, 'Nellie, there is one thing I'll be sure of over the next few months, and that is I can say without any fear of contradiction that your hat will not be missed by a single soul. Even next door's cat will see it.'

'Not if I've got anything to do with it, it won't. It's a mangy thing, that cat. I wouldn't touch it with a bargepole.'

'I should hope not, Nellie, because the old lady loves that cat. He's her only companion, and he keeps her company.'

'Well, she should have got married like what we did, girl, then she wouldn't have needed a companion.' Nellie's face took on a thoughtful expression. 'Come to think of it, girl, my George isn't much of a companion. He'd rather read the ruddy paper than talk to me.'

'Nellie, I wish you wouldn't pull George to pieces in front of me. And not in front of anyone else either! He's a smashing husband; yer don't know ye're born. I would sympathize with yer if I thought for one moment that he wasn't treating yer right. And yer might not like what I'm going to say, sunshine, but I'm going to say it anyway. Never, in all the years yer've been married, has George raised a hand to yer. And we both know there have been times when yer've deserved, not a hiding, but a ruddy good telling off. Yer want everything to go your way, and that's your biggest fault.' Molly stopped, to take a breath and to see what effect her words were having. 'Am I right so far?'

'I'll have to think about it.' Nellie's eyes rolled. 'Ye're always bleeding right, that's the trouble with you. Have yer finished telling me what a bad wife I am?'

'I have never said yer were a bad wife, sunshine, so don't be putting words in me mouth. You're a good wife and a wonderful mother. Your main fault is that yer want to be on the go all the time. Yer can't do with sitting down after dinner and reading or sewing. And when George comes home after a day's hard work, all he wants is to relax and read the paper. Like every other man in the street, he wants to sit quietly and have an hour or so to unwind. But you're just the opposite, Nellie, yer can't sit still, and yer expect George to be the same. He gives in to yer every time. If yer ask for money he never refuses, but yer don't appreciate it. You want company and excitement, while he just wants a bit of peace.'

Nellie looked at her across the table. 'My God, girl, yer can't half talk. I don't know whether to cut me throat, or ask yer if there's another cup of tea in the pot. And I don't care if it's not hot, I'll drink it anyway.'

'I think I'll add some boiling water to it, sunshine, I don't like tea when it's lukewarm.' Molly pushed her chair back and picked up the teapot. 'We can't spend all day drinking it, Nellie, 'cos we're late getting out as it is.'

Nellie called after her mate's retreating back, 'And whose fault is it that we're late, girl? You've taken up the time telling me off. It felt like being back at school and the teacher making me stand in the corridor because I was talking to the girl what sat next to me. I used to say it wasn't me talking, and the teacher couldn't be sure because she had her back to the class, writing on the blackboard. But the girl sitting next to me was a clat-tale-tit, and she always piped up like little goody two shoes and said it was me what was talking.'

Waiting for the kettle to boil, Molly leaned back against the sink and smiled as she listened to her mate.

'I always got me own back, though, girl. I never let the sneak get away with it. Every time she snitched on me, I used to kick her on the ankle before I went out to the corridor. And through the glass window, I used to see her bending down rubbing the place. So she got more punishment than me, 'cos it didn't hurt me to stand in the corridor.'

The kettle began to whistle, and as Molly was pouring the water into the teapot she called back, 'Yer haven't changed much, have yer, sunshine? Except we don't have a corridor, we've only got a tiny hall that yer can hardly turn round in.' She put the cosy over the teapot and carried it through to the living room. 'I'll tell yer what, though, sunshine, I wouldn't have liked to have been that girl who sat next to yer.'

When they sat facing each other, a cup of fresh tea in front of them, Nellie showed her serious side. 'That's why I'm as thick as a brick wall, girl, because I never listened in class. I didn't like school, didn't like the teachers and didn't like the lessons. It's me own fault I can't read or write proper, and I bet that girl what sat next to me is as clever as you are. I was the big-head then, who thought I was clever for skiving off lessons, but the other, Sylvia Clarkson her name was, she's the clever one now.'

'I'm not going to give yer a long lecture, sunshine, or say yer were wrong not to take in what you were taught. That's up to you; it's your life.

180

But, while it doesn't seem to have done yer any harm, 'cos yer've got a good life now, wouldn't it be better if yer had taken in some of the things yer were taught? Or shall we say what the teacher tried to drum into you?'

Nellie's chins felt sorry for her, so when she shook her head, they swayed very gently. 'I know that now, girl, when it's too late. If it hadn't been for you making friends with me when we both moved into the street at the same time, I'd have been lost.' She nodded as though agreeing with what was in her mind. 'You're the one what calmed me down, girl, otherwise I'd have had a row with every neighbour in the street. In fact I'd have probably given most of them a black eye, 'cos I was a bugger for fighting. Anyone who looked sideways at me, I'd have belted.'

'Don't I know it, Nellie! Yer picked a few fights with me over the children. That was when Jill was only a baby, and your Steve was just a toddler.' Molly smiled as her mind took her down memory lane. 'It seems daft now, but we were pushing and shoving each other one day, our fists clenched to do battle, when we looked at each other and burst out laughing. And that's the day we became best mates. We ended up in here, having a cup of tea. Not that it's all been plain sailing, sunshine, because it took me years to stop yer lashing out at anyone who said something yer didn't approve of. Half the time I think yer did it for fun, 'cos yer seemed to get a kick out of people being afraid of yer.'

'I remember that, girl, and I was lashing out at yer because I thought yer were a snob. Yer spoke

181

nice, and yer didn't swear. I'd be turning the air blue, but not once did yer swear. I never thought we'd be best mates because I was a fighting, swearing, common as muck, rough and ready, rowdy neighbour.'

Molly was chuckling inside. 'Ay, Nellie, yer could make a song out of all that. I can even put a tune to it in me head.'

'How d'yer mean, girl, I could make a song out of it? A song Out of what?'

'I'll try and put it to a tune, Nellie, but yer'll have to remember that my singing is hopeless. It'll sound better coming from you, when ye're impersonating Tessie O'Shea, or Mae West.'

'Well, get on with it, girl, or yer'll be moaning that it's me what made us late going to the shops.'

'I'll have to stand for it, sunshine, and don't laugh at me 'cos I'll stop and yer'll never know what yer've missed.' Molly scraped her chair back, and stood for a while ticking her fingers off while silently mouthing some words. Then she put her hands on her hips and, to the tune of 'Ragtime Cowboy Joe', swayed to a song she'd made up in her head from Nellie's words. 'I'm a fighting, swearing, common as muck dame. With rough and ready, rowdy ways.' Molly's voice rose at the end, as 'Ragtime Cowboy Joe' did. And she felt really chuffed with herself 'How about that, sunshine? If we could make up those few lines in a minute, we could easy add to it, and yer could have a new act for when yer do a turn. At yer son's wedding, perhaps?'

'Ooh, aren't you clever, girl!' Nellie was quickly on her feet. 'I'll have a go, now, girl, see if I can remember the words.'

'D'yer want me to go over the words for yer, sunshine? It took me all me time to get me mouth round them.'

'No, I remember them, girl.' With her hand on her hips, Nellie swayed to the tune that was running through her mind. Then when she'd got the hang of it she moved into the space between the table and the sideboard. 'I'll just get me hips going, girl, then I'll be ready.' And as she got going, a look of concentration on her face, her first sway sent her left hip banging into the sideboard, followed by her right hip nearly knocking the table over. If Molly hadn't been quick, cups, saucers and teapot would have ended up on the floor.

'Nellie, for God's sake watch it! Yer nearly knocked everything off the table.'

'I'm all right now, girl. I'm in time with meself.'

Molly had turned her head to put a cup back in the saucer, and she almost dropped it with fright when Nellie's hip hit the table at the same time as her voice belted out:

'I'm a high-falutin' rootin' tootin'
Son of a gun from Arizona
Ragtime Cowboy Joe.'

There was a childlike look of excitement on Nellie's face when she asked, 'Ay, girl, wasn't that good? I'm going to add that to me repertoire, for our parties. What did yer think of me performance?'

'I'm almost lost for words, Nellie. Almost, but not quite. And I think yer'll understand why, when I tell yer that yer knocked a handle off one of me cups, and spilt tea all over me tablecloth. On top of that yer weren't singing any of the words I made up! Yer just belted out "Ragtime Cowboy Joe". Everybody knows that song, even next door's cat!'

'Well, I forgot the other words, girl. But I got the music right, so yer can't ask for anything more. Not until I know the proper words. I can't be expected to remember everything! Tell me the words and I'll do it proper for yer.'

'What!' Molly wasn't half as mad as she pretended. In fact she thought it was dead funny. 'You do that again, Nellie McDonough, and I won't have a decent cup in the house. And if this table could speak it would give yer the length of its tongue. Yer knock it around and don't even say ye're sorry.'

Nellie's eyes rolled to the ceiling before coming to rest on the table. 'I am so sorry, Mr Table. I didn't mean to knock you around and I'll try not to let it happen again.' She jerked her head at Molly. 'Will that do, girl, or d'yer want me to get down on my knees to it?'

'No, that's fine, sunshine. When we get back from the shops, I'll give it a wipe over with a nice soft cloth, and that will cheer it up no end. It's given us good service over the years, so it deserves being looked after. We got our money's worth when we bought this suite. It was second hand all those years ago, and it's put up with four children knocking it around. I'm surprised it hasn't fallen to pieces before now.'

'This suite is not going to fall to pieces, girl, it

gets too well looked after. It's the same age as mine, but mine looks its age, where yours gets the whole works. A good rub with furniture polish, then another rub over with a clean cloth. This will last you out, girl, yer'll see.'

'In that case it's going to have a very long life, 'cos I have no intention of going anywhere until I'm at least eighty. In fact I may go on until I'm ninety, like Victoria.'

Nellie clicked her tongue on the roof of her mouth. 'No, girl, there's a big difference between you and Victoria. She didn't have no husband or children to put years on her. No, girl, yer can forget about living to ninety, you and me won't last that long.'

'D'yer know what, sunshine, yer certainly know how to cheer someone up. And just for spite, I'll make meself stay alive till I'm ninety.'

'Well, I suppose I'm going to have to do the same, girl, 'cos I've always said that you were my passport to heaven.' Nellie watched her mate walk into the hall for her coat, and decided it was time to follow suit. But not until she'd got something off her mind. 'Ay, girl, in case I do peg out before you, can I ask yer to make a promise for me? Just in case like?'

'This is a charming conversation, I must say.' Molly tutted. 'It's bad luck, yer know, Nellie, to be flippant about death. But if we're ever to get out today, I suppose I'll have to agree. What is it yer want me to promise, sunshine?'

'Well, it's like this, girl. I always like to know what yer get up to in this house, being mates like. And I've had a good idea on how I can keep track of the goings-on, even when I'm dead.'

'That's enough, Nellie. I don't want to hear no more. I'm not going to any spiritualist, even for you. They bring bad luck.'

'Not that, girl. I don't want to speak to yer through no spiritualist. Ye're miles out, 'cos I don't want to speak to yer at all.'

Molly could tell by the devilment in her mate's eyes that she was up to some mischief. But never in her wildest dreams would she have been prepared for what was to come. And apart from that, the time was marching on. 'Hurry up, Nellie, or I'm going out without yer. And I mean it.'

'Keep yer hair on, girl, I'm doing me best. It's the words what are stopping me from telling yer. The big words, you know, the ones I can't say. I know what I mean, but I don't know how to tell you what I mean. I can describe it, that would be easier.'

'And a darn sight quicker, I hope, sunshine.' Molly pointed to the clock on the mantelpiece. 'Have yer seen the time? We're usually back with our shopping at this time!'

'There yer go again, Molly Bennett, hexaggerating as usual.'

'Nellie, it's exaggerating, not hexaggerating.'

'I'm not even going to answer that, clever clogs. Let's see how clever yer are with what I'm going to ask yer.' Nellie's folded arms disappeared beneath her bosom. 'D'yer know the place where the pyramids are? Where some high up people, when they die, are not buried like what we do when people die, but get wrapped up in cloths and stood up, and they're called mummies. And

186

they never die. Now d'yer know what I mean?'

'It's as clear as mud, Nellie, but I think you mean Egypt. At least that's all I can make out. Egypt, pyramids, and dead people. Kings and those in high places, who are preserved by being embalmed. But what that has to do with anything I do not know.'

Nellie's arms appeared again, and a smile lit up her face. 'That's enough, girl! I want yer to do that to me when I pop me clogs, and stand me where me posh chair is now. I won't be able to talk to yer, with me being dead, like. But I'll be able to see and hear everything what goes on. I'll be in touch with all yer doings, girl, and know how ye're getting on.' Her cheeky grin was back in place. 'Ay, that's good, isn't it, girl?'

'A wonderful idea, sunshine! One of yer best. I can't wait to see Jack's face when he comes in tonight and I tell him. And Ruthie, she'll be over the moon. To think yer'll be standing by that wall, every day and night, for the rest of their lives. But what about George? What are yer going to say to him? He'll probably be upset that yer chose here as yer final resting place, and not with him.'

'Oh, sod George, girl, he's never got anything to talk about. If he wants to see me, he can always come in here. But he's not to sit in my chair. Nobody is to sit in my chair, girl, d'yer hear? I mean, what if I came back to life again, and someone had bagged my chair? I'd break their neck for them.'

'I think I can safely say that if you came back to life, and there were people in this room, yer wouldn't need to break their necks, 'cos they'd be out of the front door like lightning, and halfway to the Pier Head before yer could unwrap yerself.'

'It would be a good idea though, girl, wouldn't it? I'd know how yer were getting on. And I've heard yer ma saying that good friends should always keep in touch.'

'It's a well thought out idea, sunshine, I'll grant yer that. But it does have a drawback.'

'Oh, ay, girl, and what's that?'

'Well, every time Jack wanted a cigarette, he'd strike his match on you!'

The two mates burst out laughing. 'Ay, that was a good one, girl,' Nellie said. 'I'm going to have to keep me eye on yer, or yer'll be getting more laughs than me. And I can't have that, even though yer are me very best mate.'

'Put yer coat on, sunshine, and let's be on our way. We'll call over the road to tell Doreen and Victoria about Phoebe and Paul, but don't you say anything about dying, not in front of Victoria. At ninety years of age I don't believe she'd appreciate that sort of humour. So watch what ye're saying, Nellie.'

'Okay, girl. I'll be like one of those mummies we were talking about.'

Molly picked up her key, and with her basket over her arm she pushed her mate towards the door. 'Just be yerself, sunshine, for if ye're too quiet they'll think ye're ailing for something. And for heaven's sake, don't make a meal out of telling them about the wedding, or they'll get fed up with it. Keep it short and sweet.'

'Just like me, eh, girl? Yer can't say I'm not short and sweet.'

'I'll meet yer halfway on that, Nellie. You are

188

short, and one out of two isn't bad.'

Doreen heard that as she opened the door. 'Which one out of the two did Auntie Nellie get, Mam?'

'I'll tell yer, girl,' Nellie said, pushing herself ahead of Molly. 'Your mam said I'm little and sour.'

Doreen feigned surprise. You never knew when Auntie Nellie was being serious, or pulling your leg, so it was best to be neutral. 'I don't believe that, 'cos I know me mam wouldn't say that about yer.'

Victoria smiled when the two mates walked in, and Bobby, who was standing up by the couch, dropped on to his bottom and crawled towards them. The smile on his bonny face was a wonderful welcome. Although Molly was his blood grandmother, Nellie had been allowed to become his adopted grandmother, and he was always happy to see them.

Molly swept him up and gave him a hug and a kiss before lifting him over her head. 'Ye're not half getting big, sunshine, and bonny.' The baby gurgled as he tried to get hold of her nose. 'One of these days you'll be opening the front door to us.' She passed him over to Nellie who was waiting with open arms. 'Let yer grandma McDonough see what a ton weight yer are now.'

'He is big for his age,' Victoria said, pride in her voice. Being part of a big family, and well loved by them, had made a new woman of her. Five years ago, she was a lonely old lady with nothing to look forward to. And now, every night in bed she said a prayer to thank God for her blessing.

189

'And he's getting more like his father every day. Don't you think so, Molly?'

'I certainly do, Victoria.' Molly pulled a chair from the table and sat facing the old lady in her rocking chair. 'And he won't go far wrong if he takes after his dad.' She tilted her head. 'And it's all down to you, Victoria. We all told you not to take a stranger into your home; even Corker was against it. But you took Phil in, and proved we were all wrong. And what a blessing yer did, sunshine, for he turned out to be a jewel. A wonderful husband to Doreen, a son-in-law to be proud of, and a doting father to Bobby. Phil adores you, Victoria, and rightly so. You gave him a home when he was homeless, and he's given you a family when you were lonely.' She sniffed. 'I don't know what brought that on, I'll be crying in me tea when Doreen fetches it in. But your life, and Phil's, would make a marvellous story. If I knew how, I'd write it meself.'

Nellie walked into the kitchen with Bobby nestled against her soft bosom. 'When yer mam makes up her mind whether she can write a book or not, and we can sit down and have a natter, then we've got some news for you and Victoria.'

Doreen had the tray set and ready to carry in, but she was curious now. 'Ooh, what is it, Auntie Nellie? I hope it's something exciting, so I can tell Phil when he comes home. The first thing he asks when he's washing his hands is, "What have yer mam and Mrs Mac been up to today?"'

'Ah, that's nice of him, girl. It's good to know someone appreciates us. But I can't say what news we've got to tell yer, because my mate

190

would have me life if I told yer when she wasn't here. You carry the tray in, and I'll see if she's finished writing the book she was yapping about. I'll take the baby in.'

'I'll take Bobby once I've put the tray down, Auntie Nellie, and you can drink yer tea in comfort. Mam will do the honours and pour, won't yer, Mam? And I believe yer've got some news for us? Auntie Nellie was tight-lipped, she said yer'd go mad if she told me. So be an angel, Mam, and hand Aunt Vicky her tea, with two custard creams in the saucer. There's only two biscuits each for us; I'll have to buy some when I go to the shops later. Jill's coming down, with little Moll, and we're going for a walk.'

Molly placed the saucer in Victoria's hand and held it steady. 'Can yer manage if I put the biscuits in the saucer, sunshine? I don't want yer to spill any tea on yer dress.'

'I can manage fine, Molly. My hands are very steady.'

'We're all settled now, Mam, so let's be having the news.' Doreen pulled the baby's grasping fingers away from the table, where they could do no harm. He was into everything now, and she had to watch him like a hawk. 'I'm all ears, Mam.'

'I'm having second thoughts about telling yer, sunshine, because there's someone else who has the right to be the first to be told. And I don't want to cause any unpleasantness in the family.'

Nellie looked puzzled. 'What are yer talking about, girl? I'm the one what has more right than anyone, 'cos I'm family.'

'Doreen, and you, Victoria, I hope yer won't

191

think me rude, but I'd like to have a quiet word in the kitchen with Nellie. We won't be more than a couple of minutes. I just want to make sure we're not stepping on anyone's toes. Come on, sunshine, the biscuits will still be here when we come back.'

Nellie pulled a face and was muttering under her breath as she scraped her chair back. And in the kitchen she glared up at her mate. 'What the hell are yer playing at, girl? Yer were all for telling them before, and now yer've changed yer mind! But it's not up to you, Molly Bennett, 'cos it's my son's wedding.'

'I know that, sunshine, and I never gave a thought to whether we should leave Paul and Phoebe to break the news. After all, there are others who should be told. Like Steve, he should be the first, being Paul's brother. And from what we heard, he'll be asked to be best man. Plus your Lily should be one of the first to know as well, being Paul's older sister.'

'Is that all?' Nellie's face creased. 'Well, for your information, Steve and Lily already know. As soon as we'd left Corker's last night, Paul and Phoebe went over a few things with Ellen and Corker, then they went to tell Steve and Lily the news. Yer don't think our Paul would leave his brother and sister to be the last to hear, do yer? That would be the last thing Paul would do, 'cos my three children are very close. So yer don't need to worry about stepping on toes, girl, because all the family know. And Jill knows as well because she was there when Paul asked Steve if he'd be his best man.'

Molly breathed a sigh of relief and bent to hug

192

her mate. 'I wish yer'd told me before, sunshine, then we wouldn't both be standing in the kitchen letting our tea go cold.'

'You worry too much, girl, that's your trouble. Yer always try to please everyone, and do what yer think is right. Well, worrying is bad for yer health, girl, and if yer don't watch out, it'll be you what ends up like one of those mummy things, standing by the sideboard in my living room. But I won't let George strike a match on yer, girl, that's one thing yer won't have to worry about.'

In the living room, Victoria and Doreen exchanged glances when they heard laughter coming from the kitchen. 'That's your two grandmas yer can hear, Bobby, and that's how they always are.' Doreen smiled as Bobby bounced up and down on her knee, and silently told herself she was indeed a very lucky daughter, wife and mother. And more than lucky to have an adopted aunt like Victoria Clegg.

Nellie waddled back into the living room. 'Your mam will worry over anything, girl, even the tiniest thing. Just wait until I tell yer why she wanted a word in private.' She jerked her head back, and in agreement, her chins decided the tempo was right for a slow foxtrot. 'Come on in, Molly. There's no need to be embarrassed, even if yer are a silly nit.'

'I can't help being fussy, sunshine.' Molly gave a broad wink as she followed Nellie into the room. 'Better to be sure than sorry, and better to be slow than slapdash.' She sank on to her chair. 'I am the way I was made, and that's all there is to it.'

'I wasn't made like this, girl.' Nellie's grin was so wide her eyes and mouth completely disappeared for a few seconds. 'I was lovely and slim, with a face like Marilyn Monroe and legs like Betty Grable.' She gave an exaggerated sigh. 'What yer see before yer today is due to my liking for cream slices and biscuits. Not just a couple, like, 'cos this voluptuous body didn't come overnight. It took thousands of cream cakes and no willpower to get this way.'

'Now we've admitted to our failings, sunshine, I'll have to ask yer to tell your news, so we can get to the butcher's before they close for dinner. Go ahead, sunshine, we're all ears.'

Nellie shuffled on her chair until she felt comfortable, then reached for a custard cream which she devoured in two seconds flat. 'I'll just have a mouthful of tea to wash that down.' She licked her lips, lifted her bosom on to the table, then asked, 'Yer know our Paul, don't yer?'

Doreen chuckled. 'I think so, Auntie Nellie. Isn't he the boy I used to play with when I was a kid? Black hair, brown eyes and dimples. That's the one, isn't it?'

'Right on the nose, girl, right on the nose!' Nellie very seldom took offence, and she didn't now. 'Well, he's getting married in a few months' time.' A kick on the shin from her mate had her quickly adding, 'Him and Phoebe are getting wed.'

'Oh, that's wonderful news, Nellie.' Victoria set her rocking chair in motion. 'I'm really delighted, for they make a lovely couple.'

Doreen danced the baby up and down on her

knee. 'At last, Auntie Nellie. We've waited a long time to hear that. I am so happy for both of them. When is the big day to be?'

'It's going to be on Phoebe's birthday, which is on the eighteenth of September. It's a Friday, but the men all said they can get the day off. Steve's going to be best man, but that's all I know for now. Your Jill may be able to tell yer more, because she was in last night when Paul and Phoebe went up there. Our Paul said Steve was very happy for them, and he's over the moon at being asked to be best man. But that's all I know, girl, 'cos they haven't had time to sort bridesmaids out or anything. Everyone was too excited last night to be able to think straight, but they'll calm down in a few days and go and see Father Kelly to book a time for the wedding.'

Doreen, who was thrilled for the engaged couple she'd known all her life, asked, 'This calls for a new mother of the groom hat, eh, Auntie Nellie? Or are yer making use of the one yer had for Lily's wedding? That is a real humdinger of a hat.'

'Am I hell wearing the same hat!' Nellie was quite adamant about that. Hadn't she lain awake for hours last night, too excited to sleep? And hadn't the main issue on her mind been, not the bride's dress, but her own hat! After all, this would be the fourth wedding in the Bennett and McDonough clan, and hadn't her hats been the talk of the whole neighbourhood for weeks? She had no intention of lowering her standards now, and letting the side down. 'Me and yer mam will be going hat hunting soon. And for the other things, like dress, shoes and handbag. Oh, and I can't forget gloves. We mustn't give the neighbours room to say we are as common as muck.' The chins anticipated the sharp nods, and immediately went into a quickstep. 'Paul will be the last of my children to get married, and I intend it to be a wedding the whole neighbourhood will still be talking about in years to come. Only the best will do.' She turned to Molly. 'Don't you agree with me, girl?' Then the devil in her surfaced. 'I've already told yer mam she can't wear her red beret, even though they are the height of fashion in France.'

Doreen let it be known she wasn't without humour. 'Oh, I don't know, Auntie Nellie, I think me mam would really look nice in a beret. Especially a bright red one. Just think how the red would show off her long blonde hair. She'd really stand out.'

'Oh, she'd stand out, girl, I'll agree with yer on that. Outside the church is where she'd stand! And she wouldn't be there long before the police moved her on. They'd think she was a lady of the night.'

Victoria tittered before saying, 'But it wouldn't be night, would it, Nellie? Surely the wedding will be in the morning or afternoon? Father Kelly would never perform a wedding ceremony at night.'

'I don't care what nobody says, she's not coming to my son's wedding in a red beret. Even if she is me best mate, she not making a laughing stock of the McDonough family. And that's me last word on it, so there!'

Molly asked, 'Even if I promise to sit on me own in the back pew?'

'Yer can wear a black veil over your face, girl, as long as there's no red beret on top of it.'

Doreen was tickled. 'Ye're not helping French fashion, Auntie Nellie, and the French are very fashion conscious. I don't know what they'd say if they heard you.'

'Well, d'yer know what I say, girl? I say sod the French, and their knickers. Have yer seen those knickers? There's nothing of them! The price they charge for a bit of satin and lace what wouldn't even keep the draught out! Indecent, that's what they are. Those French people must all be heathens. Cold ones at that, if all they wear are those ruddy knickers. Give me the old fleecy-lined bloomers any day. Yer know where yer are with them.'

'Nellie, bloomers went out of fashion before the war,' Molly said. 'You're probably the only woman under eighty years of age wearing them. These days, that part of the anatomy is covered by knickers or briefs.'

'Yer don't need to tell me that, girl, 'cos since Blacklers closed down, the only place what sells bloomers is Paddy's Market. And they only have them in blue and pink, no variety.'

'Why, what colour would yer like, Auntie Nellie?' Doreen asked. 'A nice bright orange, or red?'

'Ay, red would be nice, Nellie. Yer could wear them when ye're doing the flamenco.' Tongue in cheek, Molly added, 'Mind you, yer couldn't wear them for the wedding. Yer'd have to stand outside the church with me in me red beret.'

'No I wouldn't, clever clogs, 'cos no one would see me knickers. And what is the flameco when it's out?'

'It's called the flamenco, Auntie Nellie,' Doreen told her, 'and they do it in Spain. Yer must have seen it in a film at some time. The senoritas have those maracas in their hands and they click them while they stamp their feet and swish their full skirts around.'

'Ooh, I know what yer mean, girl, 'cos I think me and yer mam did see a film with dancers like that in. The woman were showing their legs off, and dancing round this man.' She gave Molly a none too gentle dig. 'Ay, girl, what was that film star's name? The one with black hair and flashing white teeth. Dead handsome, he was. I wouldn't have minded dancing round him meself.'

'I can see the man in me head, sunshine, but for the life of me I can't remember his name. It's on the tip of me tongue, but won't come out. Ye're right about him being handsome, and he really looked Spanish.' Then Molly thumped the table with a clenched fist. 'I've got it, Nellie. His name's Anthony Quinn.'

'Oh, yeah, I remember now,' Nellie said. 'Ay, if he ever asked me to dance, I'd definitely buy a pair of those French knickers. And I'd be swishing me skirt around so he could see them. He wouldn't half get his money's worth.'

'And an eyeful.' Molly tutted. 'Is there anything you wouldn't do to get attention, sunshine?'

'Yeah, of course there is, moaning Minnie. I wouldn't give up eating me cream slices and custard creams. And another thing I wouldn't do is

198

to cut me throat.'

'Oh, dear, oh dear.' Molly shook her head several times. 'If yer did the latter, sunshine, then yer'd have to give up the former.'

Nellie's face was like rubber, bending into every shape. Then, when she couldn't figure out what Molly had said, she turned to Doreen. 'I'm sure your mam makes up words what aren't real, just to get me mad. Can you tell me in plain English what she's just said about me?'

'She wasn't trying to be funny, Auntie Nellie, but to tell yer the truth I thought it was hilarious meself. Anyway, if yer go back to what yer said, yer'd know what me mam was getting at. If yer cut yer throat, then yer wouldn't have no need to buy cream slices, would yer? On the other hand, if yer gave up yer cakes and biscuits then yer wouldn't have any reason to cut yer throat. Is that more clear to yer now?'

'Clear as mud, girl, clear as mud. But thank you. Yer did yer best and no one can ask for no more.'

'Will you do yer best and finish that last custard cream, sunshine,' Molly said, 'so we can try and make the butcher's in time. I don't know what to get in for the dinner, but I'll think of something by the time we've walked there.'

'I'm just doing mashed potatoes for our meal,' Doreen said. 'Mashed potatoes with butter in, and two runny eggs on top. Phil loves that. He'd have it every night if I let him.'

Molly and Nellie looked at each other and grinned. 'There yer are, girl,' Nellie said, 'problem solved.'

Molly nodded. 'Thanks, Doreen, we'll have the same, save us racking our brains. It's an easy meal, and we all like it.'

Nellie added another reason for egg and mash. 'And it's cheap, girl, two bob at the most.'

'I bet yer won't tell George that the dinner for three of yer only cost two shillings.'

'I might act daft, Molly Bennett, but where George is concerned I'm not that daft. If I told him, when he was halfway through his dinner, that it only cost two bob, he'd lower me housekeeping money.'

'I won't snitch on yer, sunshine, if yer'll say farewell to our hosts and we can be on our merry way.'

Having duly kissed the baby and Doreen, Nellie bent to kiss Victoria and whispered, 'See what I mean about me mate? I mean, ye're not our friends or neighbours, ye're our hosts!' She tapped her temple. 'Don't forget now. And don't worry if we give a little curtsy next time we come, just put it down to Molly's age and go along with anything she says or does. Spring is in the air, yer see, and I've heard it does affect some people.'

'Spring had better be in your steps, Nellie Mc-Donough, as well as in the air. And don't be making a beeline for the butcher's so yer can have a good natter to Ellen about the wedding, because we don't need to go to the butcher's seeing as we're having egg and mashed spuds for our dinner.'

Molly was opening the front door when she heard Nellie saying to Doreen, 'See what yer've done now? Because of you, we are not going to the butcher's, which means I don't get to speak to Ellen. The mother of the bride and the mother of the groom are being kept apart because you are having egg and mash. So in future, girl, don't bother telling us what you eat, but keep it to yerself.'

'I'll do that, Auntie Nellie. I was going to tell yer I'd make a mince pie for you and me mam tomorrow, with thick onion gravy inside. But I won't tell yer now, 'cos yer've told me to keep me mouth shut.'

Molly had stepped down on to the pavement and she was chuckling. It would be interesting to see how her mate got out of the mess she'd got herself into. Oh, she'd get out of it, of that there was no doubt. But seeing her facial contortions, and hearing her coaxing voice, well, it was worth waiting for. And there was no hurry now, seeing as they were having an easy meal.

'I didn't mean no harm, girl. Yer should know me well enough by now to know when I'm joking.'

Doreen, like her mother, had to bite on the inside of her mouth to stop herself from laughing. 'It's all right, Auntie Nellie, we're all entitled to say what we think. Don't you worry now, because it's easier for me to just make one extra mince pie for me mam. So then you can buy whatever takes yer fancy.'

Molly called, 'Come on, Nellie, Hanley's will sell our bread if we leave it any longer. Besides which, me corn is playing me up.'

'Stop yer moaning, Molly Bennett, I'm having a serious conversation with yer daughter. And

201

ye're always telling me it's rude to interrupt a conversation, so put a sock in it.'

'I think yer'd better do as me mam says, Auntie Nellie.' Doreen was sorry she'd started now. 'Otherwise Hanley's will sell yer bread.'

'Sod the bread and sod yer mam's bleeding corn. I'm not moving until you agree to make two extra mince pies tomorrow instead of one. I haven't been yer Auntie Nellie since the day yer were born for nothing, yer know. Just think of all those years I've wasted, treating yer like me own flesh and blood, if yer turn yer back on me now.'

Molly waved a hand to attract Doreen's attention. 'Make that two pies tomorrow, will yer, sunshine?'

Doreen nodded. 'I've made a note of it in me head, Mam. Two pies it will be.'

Nellie's face was transformed. 'I knew yer wouldn't let me down, girl, yer wouldn't leave yer Auntie Nellie out.' She stepped down on to the pavement, and linked Molly's arm. With a cheeky grin, she told Doreen, 'By the way, girl, my feller likes plenty of salt, so don't be mean with it.'

'Don't push yer luck, sunshine,' Molly said, 'quit while ye're ahead.' She waved a hand to her daughter and winked. 'It's the luck of the Irish she's got, sunshine. Always comes out on top because suckers like us give in to her. And I'll give yer a warning for tomorrow. Make sure the pies are exactly the same, because Tilly Mint here will bring a tape measure and scales with her.'

Doreen roared with laughter when she heard Nellie saying, 'Yer'll have to lend me yer tape measure, girl, 'cos I haven't got one.'

Chapter Eight

There was no desperate hurry now that they only needed potatoes and eggs for their dinner, and their tin loaves from Hanley's, so the two friends walked at an easy pace. 'Ay, girl.' Nellie tugged on Molly's arm. 'Your Doreen didn't think I was serious about the pie, did she? I was only joking, but the trouble with me is that I'm so good at it, people think I mean it.'

'Oh, I imagine Doreen and Victoria are having a good laugh about it right now, sunshine. My family, and all our mates, are well used to yer shenanigans, and they don't take what yer say to heart. Which is just as well, Nellie, because if they did, yer wouldn't have a friend in the world.'

'Yes, I would, girl, I'd always have you, and St Peter.' They weren't far from Hanley's now, and Nellie was walking on the outside. This was the way she liked it, because she had more space to allow her hips to sway. 'And my feller always said he would stick to me through thick and thin. Mind you, that was on the day we got married, and I was as thin as a rake.' Then Nellie's attention was distracted, and the words she was about to utter were left unspoken as she pulled Molly to a halt. 'Look at that, girl! It's old Mrs Reagan standing on the edge of the pavement waiting to cross the road. And look at the way she's swaying. She's going to fall in the road if she's not careful, she's very unsteady on her feet.' As she said that, Nellie saw a bus coming towards them, and pulling her arm from Molly's she dashed forward.

Molly stood with a look of bewilderment on her face. It was a couple of seconds before she realized why Nellie had panicked, and with her hand covering her mouth, she watched the scene with mounting horror. The bus driver hadn't seen the old lady step off the pavement until he was almost on top of her, and then he slammed on his brakes. But it would have been too late if it hadn't been for Nellie pulling the old lady back, and he would surely have knocked her down. He wouldn't have been able to avoid her, for she was right in his path. He climbed out of the cab, and with fear in his heart walked round the bus to find the elderly lady lying on the pavement, and a stout lady bending over her. 'Is she all right?'

'I think she banged her head when I pulled her out of the road. It's a good job I did, or she'd have been under the wheels of yer bus,' Nellie said.

'I couldn't help it, missus, she just stepped out in front of me. There was no way I could stop the bus in time. I can't be blamed for it; she should be more careful.'

'She's an old lady, yer stupid sod. Wait until ye're her age, and then perhaps yer'll understand.'

Molly knelt down next to Nellie. 'Is she all right, sunshine?'

'She banged her head, girl, but I think she'll be all right. Her eyes are open, and she tried to cover her legs up, so that's a good sign. I couldn't help her banging her head, 'cos all I was thinking about was getting her out of the way of the bus.'

The bus driver was shaking inside with the shock. 'It's a good job yer were so quick-thinking, missus, or she would have been a goner. And although I know it wasn't my fault, I'd have had to live with a nightmare all me life. I've got a mother of me own about her age. I'd like to know if she's all right before I get back in me bus. Or do yer want me to ring for an ambulance?'

Molly saw the old lady's pleading expression, and the fear in her eyes. 'She's going to be all right. You go back to yer work. It wasn't your fault, so don't let it worry yer. Yer need yer wits about you, especially after the fright yer've had. Yer can thank my mate that the worst didn't happen. Without her quick reaction there could have been a very different outcome.'

'Don't I know it!' The driver tapped Nellie on the shoulder. 'Thanks, missus, yer saved the day all right! I hope the old lady gets over it. But tell her to be more careful in future.'

Nellie had her hand on Mrs Reagan's forehead. 'She'll be all right now, lad. We'll just give her a few more minutes to settle her nerves, then me and me mate will take her home. She lives near us, so we'll keep an eye on her for a few days.'

Word had spread to Hanley's shop, and the bus driver had only been gone a few minutes when Edna Hanley appeared. 'In the name of God, what happened to Mrs Reagan? Is she all right?'

'Thanks to Nellie she is, Edna,' Molly felt like giving her mate a bear hug, but she couldn't because Nellie was kneeling on the ground stroking the old lady's silver hair. 'I'm really proud of my mate, Edna, 'cos she definitely saved Mrs

Reagan's life. While I was standing with me mouth open, trying to take in what was going on, Nellie was pulling the poor soul out of the way of the bus. Yer've just missed the bus – it's just gone. The driver is as white as a sheet. It was a terrible shock to him, but it wasn't his fault. And the passengers must have got the fright of their lives because he didn't half slam his brakes on.'

Edna, who had left several customers in the shop, bent down. 'How is she, Nellie?'

'She coming round now, but I'll let her do it in her own time. The shock was enough to give her a heart attack.'

'Would yer like to bring her in the shop? My feller would carry her, and a cup of weak, sweet tea would do her good.'

Nellie looked up at Molly. 'What d'yer think, girl?'

'Yer'd better ask Mrs Reagan, sunshine. But I think the best thing would be to take her home, where she can lie down on the couch. We could stay with her until she's got over the worst of the shock, and make her a drink in her house.'

'Would yer like to go home, Mrs Reagan?' Nellie asked. 'If yer wanted some shopping, we'd see to it for yer.' When the old lady nodded her head, Nellie said, 'Let's try and sit yer up. Molly will give me a hand and we'll do it nice and slow.'

'If yer don't need me, I'll get back to the shop,' Edna Hanley said. 'I left the customers standing there. They must have thought I'd gone mad the way I dashed out.'

'You go, Edna, we'll manage,' Molly said. 'But don't forget to keep our bread for us.'

A man was standing at the back of the group that had formed, and he offered, 'I'll give you a hand to take her home if you wish. I'd be very happy to be of assistance.'

But the two mates had never seen the man before, and they were reluctant to trust him, even though he was quite well dressed. For all they knew, he could be someone who would take advantage of the situation. He'd have the address of an elderly woman who lived on her own, and if he was less than honest, he could pass the information on. 'Thank you for offering, we appreciate it,' Molly told him. 'But she lives near my friend and me, and we'll see she gets home safely to her family.' It was a lie in a good cause, Molly thought, for they didn't know the man from Adam.

The few people who had gathered around, concerned for Mrs Reagan, began to disperse when they were satisfied she was not seriously injured, and Molly and Nellie began the task of raising the frail old lady to a sitting position. She was confused and disorientated, and the two mates held her steady so she wouldn't fall. They were talking to her softly, comforting words to reassure her she would soon be feeling better and they would take her home. She was very distressed, because sitting on a pavement being stared at by passers-by was not something she was used to. Her loss of dignity would be an enormous embarrassment to an old lady who still lived in an age where clothes were never shorter than ankle length. And Molly was aware of her predicament.

'When yer feel fit enough to stand on yer feet, sunshine, just say the word and me and Nellie will take yer home. But do it in yer own time, 'cos we're not in any hurry.'

Mrs Reagan licked her lips, which were dry with shock and fear. She just wanted to be in her own little house, where she could lie down until the shaking and dizziness wore off. 'I'll try now, Molly, if you and Nellie will help me. I'm sorry to be such a nuisance; you are very kind. And I owe my life to Nellie. I'll never be able to repay her for what she did.'

'Ay, girl,' Nellie said, 'if someone pulled me over, I wouldn't be thanking them, I'd be knocking their block off. I bet when ye're feeling better, yer'll be round to my house to give me the length of yer tongue, wanting to know what I was playing at.'

The two mates kept the chatter up as they raised the old lady to her feet. She was shaking badly, and wouldn't have been able to stand if they hadn't held her tight. 'Take yer time, sunshine,' Molly told her. 'Stand here until yer feel you've got the strength to walk. I don't want to make yer feel any worse than yer do already, but you'll probably be very bruised at the bottom of yer back, and the back of yer head where it hit the pavement. So you'll have to rest for a least a week. Which means you'll be confined to the house and not able to go to the shops. I suggest yer get enough shopping in to last a few days because yer need to get some nourishment down yer after the shock yer've had.'

'My mate is right, girl,' Nellie said, feeling very proud of herself. Just wait until she told George and Paul she'd saved someone's life, they wouldn't half be proud of her. That's if they didn't think she was pulling their legs. 'We'll get yer shopping in this afternoon, when we're doing our own.'

'If yer give me an arm each to lean on, then I'll try and walk.' Rita Reagan leaned heavily on their arms until she felt safe to put a foot forward. She was a very independent lady who had lived alone since her husband was killed in the First World War. They'd only been married a few months when he was killed, not even long enough to have started a family, so she'd had to fend for herself ever since. She'd known mental pain and heart-break, but never physical pain. Not until she put her foot forward and a pain so fierce shot up from her spine that it caused a cry to leave her lips.

'Oh, sunshine,' Molly said, 'if it's so bad, don't attempt any more walking for a while.'

'We've got to get her home, girl, one way or another. She can't stand here all afternoon. The only other way is a wheelchair, and I don't know anyone who's got one.'

'Oh, no, please don't do that!' The old lady was wishing the ground would swallow her up. 'We aren't far from my home; I can make it if you help me. I'll be fine when I'm in my own home, honestly I will. I can go at my own speed then.'

'Whatever you say, sunshine.' Molly could see that the more they tried to help, the more flustered Mrs Reagan got. And she agreed with herself that it was understandable, she'd feel the same if she was over eighty and two clever clogs were telling her what she should or shouldn't do.

'I've got an idea what might help,' Nellie said. 'Don't laugh when I tell yer where I got the idea from, 'cos if it worked when I was a kid, there's no reason why it won't work now.'

'Tell us what the idea is, sunshine, and see what we think. After all, any idea that will help is better than none.'

'Well, it's like this, girl.' Nellie let go of the old lady's arm and reached for her hand instead. 'Now what me and me mates used to do is this.' She bent the frail arm until it was flat against Mrs Reagan's chest, then cupped her elbow. 'If you do the same, Molly, I bet we could carry Rita. Lift her off the ground by her elbows and she might not feel any pain then.'

Molly didn't know what to think. It was all right doing that as a kid, 'cos she remembered doing it herself in the school playground. 'It's worth a try, I suppose.' She did the same as Nellie had done with the left arm. 'If it hurts at all, sunshine, just shout out and we'll stop.'

With the two mates cupping an elbow each, Nellie called, 'Are yer ready, girl?'

'Ready when you are, sunshine. But take it easy, one step at a time. Don't forget ye're not still a schoolgirl, and go charging hell for leather.'

'Oh, stop yer moaning, and when I say "go", then lift Rita and walk a few steps until she tells us to stop.'

'Stop calling her Rita, Nellie. Don't be so forward.'

The old lady was so busy listening to the couple, she didn't realize she was walking through the air. And when Molly called Nellie to stop for a moment, to ask if she had felt any pain, Mrs Reagan had to admit she hadn't felt any

210

sensation at all.

'Ye're a genius, sunshine.' Molly looked across at her mate. 'I'd never have thought of that in a million years.'

'I keep telling yer how clever I am,' Nellie grinned, 'but yer don't believe me. Now let's walk to the corner of the next street, which is where Rita lives.'

'Are yer sure it didn't hurt yer, sunshine?' Molly had to be sure for her peace of mind. 'Don't suffer in silence.'

'I'll be fine, Molly. I just want to get home.'

When they turned the corner of the street, Molly called for a halt while she flexed her hands and fingers. 'Thanks to Nellie, we're now in your street, Mrs Reagan, so it won't be long before ye're home.' She was just about to cup the woman's elbow again when out of the corner of her eye she sensed a movement. She turned her head quickly, and caught sight of a figure standing just round the corner, on the main road. She stepped a pace back, and saw the man who had offered to take Mrs Reagan home. He had flattened himself against the shop front, and his trilby was pulled down over his forehead to hide his face. The sight of him disturbed Molly, who couldn't help wondering what he was up to. He looked respectable enough, but why was he trying to hide himself? He'd left the scene of the incident fifteen or twenty minutes ago, so he should be well away by now. This all flashed through Molly's mind within seconds, and she came to the conclusion he had been following them. And the only reason he would do that was to find out where Mrs Reagan lived. Because he looked respectable, it didn't mean that he was. He could be a rotter who preyed on elderly people who lived alone. He would have seen how frail and vulnerable she was when she was lying on the ground, and if he was a thief, then he would consider her to be easy pickings.

'Ay, come on, girl, what the hell are yer doing?' Nellie asked. 'Yer'd better hurry up, 'cos I'm dying to go to the lavvy.'

'I'm ready now, sunshine, keep yer hair on.' Molly didn't want to mention her fears, for the old lady had had enough frights for one day. But she needed to try to put the man off any nefarious plan he had in mind. If she was wrong about him, then she was sorry but as her ma always said, it was best to be sure. 'We'll make a nice pot of tea when we get to your house, Mrs Reagan.' Molly spoke loud enough for anyone close by to hear. 'And then there's the meal to see to for George and Jack, when they get in from work.'

'What have...' Nellie's words were cut off when she saw the message in her mate's eyes. 'It doesn't matter, girl, I've forgotten what I was going to say. So let's make haste and get Rita back home. She'll soon feel better when she sees her familiar rooms again. There's no place like home, girl, and we'll have yer there in less than five minutes. So hold on tight.'

The front door key was in the old-fashioned purse, which was still intact, and Molly opened the front door before putting the key back in the purse and handing both to Mrs Reagan. 'I'm going to give yer a piggy back, sunshine, so put yer arms round me neck.'

There were tears in the faded blue eyes when Molly set the old lady down by her couch. 'You put yer feet up, sunshine, while I put the kettle on.' She saw the tears glisten, and put her arm round the bowed shoulder. 'Yer'll soon be feeling better now ye're in yer own surroundings, sunshine.'

'I never thought I'd see them again, Molly. There's nothing here of any value to anyone but me. All me memories are in this room.'

'Sit yerself down, sunshine, while I make a drink. I didn't hear Nellie asking if she could use yer lavatory, but that's where she is. My mate doesn't stand on ceremony, yer see.'

'She saved my life, did Nellie, and I'll never forget that.'

'Then when she comes in, sunshine, tell her she doesn't need to pay a penny. Yer'll let her off on account of her saving your life.' Molly chuckled. 'Here she is, coming up the yard now, with a very relieved expression on her face.'

Nellie pushed the door closed, then came into the living room with a beaming smile and rubbing her hands together. 'Oh, boy, did I need that! I'd been keeping me legs crossed until I could stand it no longer.'

'Yer might have asked Mrs Reagan if she minded yer using her lavatory, sunshine, because a lot of people are fussy about that. They don't like strangers using their toilet. She would have been within her rights to refuse.'

'It might well have been within her rights, girl, but it wouldn't have done her no good. Yer see, I'd had me legs crossed for as long as I could, but

213

in the end I couldn't hang on any longer. I only just made it in time, so she's been lucky. Think what would have happened if I hadn't made it in time. It would have been red faces all round, and you and me with a mop and bucket.'

Molly could picture the scene in her mind, and the only thing that stopped her from laughing out loud was the thought that the idea might not have gone down well with Mrs Reagan. 'You'll have to excuse Nellie, I'm afraid, sunshine. She's apt to be a little outspoken at times.'

The old lady lowered her head, but not before Molly had seen the trace of a smile on the wrinkled face. 'That's all right, Molly. I thought it was rather funny.'

'Oh, don't encourage her, sunshine, yer'll only make her worse.'

Nellie followed Molly into the kitchen. 'Haven't yer made a pot of tea yet, girl? Ye're too slow to catch cold you are. Poor Rita must be gasping.'

'I put the kettle on a low light, because I didn't know how long yer'd be. Now ye're here, yer can help get the cups ready while I see to the tea. Won't be long now, sunshine, five minutes and yer'll be sitting pretty with a drink in yer hand.'

As soon as they were in the kitchen, Nellie asked a question that had been puzzling her. Keeping her voice to a whisper, she asked, 'Ay, girl, why did yer tell Rita that Jack and George would be home for their dinner? They won't be coming round here.'

'That's why I asked yer to come and help me out here, 'cos I don't want Mrs Reagan to hear, in case it worries her.'

214

'Why, what's happened?' Nellie looked concerned. 'Rita is going to be all right, isn't she? I know she's had a terrible shock for a woman of her age, but she does seem to be a bit brighter now. I was a bit worried meself for a while, girl, but I really think she'll get over it, and be as right as rain in a few days.'

'That isn't what's on me mind, sunshine.' Molly glanced through to the living room to make sure her words weren't carrying. 'D'yer know the bloke that offered to bring Mrs Reagan home? He was standing at the back of the crowd, then pushed his way forward?'

'Oh, I know the one yer mean, girl, he had a trilby on.'

Molly nodded. 'That's the one. Well, he followed us. When we turned into this street, and we stopped for a while because me fingers were getting numb, I just happened to see him out of the corner of me eye. So I took a step back, just to satisfy meself, and sure enough he was pressed against the corner shop, and he'd pulled his hat down over his forehead, thinking he wouldn't be recognized. He'd followed us, I'm sure of that, 'cos he was acting shifty.'

'What d'yer think he's up to, girl?' Nellie's brow was furrowed. 'It could be coincidence.'

'I've got a gut feeling it wasn't coincidence, sunshine. I think he's one of the rotters who prey on old people who live on their own. I know he was dressed well, and seemed respectable, but that could be all show. I mean, if a crook looked like one, he wouldn't make much of a living, would he?'

Nellie watched her mate pour the tea into a nice china cup, which Molly had found in the larder. 'You take that in to Rita, girl, 'cos yer know how clumsy I am. Sure as eggs I'd break that cup if I got hold of it.'

'I've made enough for three cups, sunshine, so you can pour ours out while I take this through. Then we can sit with Mrs Reagan for half an hour, to make sure it's safe to leave her. Then we'll do the shopping.'

'What if ye're right about the bloke?' Nellie was thinking that she wasn't going to save a person's life, just to have a thief come and rob them. 'Will we tackle him if he's still hanging about?'

Molly put a finger to her lips. 'We'll take things as they come, sunshine, but for now we'll have a drink and a chat with Mrs Reagan. We can discuss the situation later.'

As Molly handed the old lady her tea, she was told to keep hold of it until Rita moved to her fireside chair. 'It'll be more comfortable for me back, you see, 'cos the couch is a bit hard. That's because it never gets sat on. There's only me here, and I like me chair the best.'

'I'm the same over my chair,' Molly said, when they were all seated. 'It's like an old friend, fits lovely into me back.'

After half an hour's chatting, and a second cup of tea, Rita seemed a lot brighter, and appeared to be happy having company to talk to. Without sounding sorry for herself, she said it was a long time since she'd had a visitor. 'Hilda next door, she comes in now and again, or I'll pop into hers for a cuppa, but we don't live in each other's pocket.'

'No, but ye're here for each other if help is needed, that's the main thing,' Molly said. Then she had an idea, 'Does Hilda live on her own?'

'Yes.' Rita nodded. 'She has a son, but he married a girl from Kent, and only comes up once every six months. Which is understandable, because he's in his late fifties now and has children and grandchildren of his own.'

'I wonder if she could keep yer company tonight, sunshine?' Molly asked. 'It would be nice for yer to have someone to talk to, take yer mind off the fright and shock yer've had. If yer're on yer own, yer'll keep dwelling on it, and yer wouldn't get any sleep.'

Nellie pursed her lips, as she and her chins agreed that Molly was a very caring and clever woman, to have thought of a way of helping Rita, and kept her safety in mind.

'Oh, I wouldn't like to suggest it,' Rita said, 'it's a bit much to ask of her. Actually I'm surprised she hasn't been in, for yer know how news spreads in these little streets. It goes around like wildfire.'

'I'll tell yer what, sunshine.' Molly was determined not to be put off. 'I'll give her a knock and tell her what's happened, and perhaps she'll come back with me. Is she an easy person to get on with?'

The old lady had a smile on her face when she answered. 'Oh, yes, she's very easy-going. If Nellie won't mind me saying so, Hilda is very much like her.'

'Ay, is that a compliment, or an insult?' Nellie pretended to get on her high horse. 'And does she have a voluptuous body like mine, what men

217

crave for?'

'I wouldn't know about that, Nellie, but she is full of life for a woman of her age.'

'She sounds friendly enough, so I don't think she'll mind me giving her a knock. She might not have heard what happened, so we can fill her in with the drama.' Molly gave a broad wink. 'Tell yer what, sunshine, we'll let Nellie tell her. She'll put more heart into it seeing as she was the main one involved.'

'If she's busy, yer will tell her it's not so important it can't wait until later, won't yer? I don't want her to break off her work if she's busy.'

'Not to worry, sunshine,' Molly said. 'I'll not interrupt her if she's in the middle of doing something. And I'll be very polite and friendly. I'll not be long, and Nellie can keep yer company while I'm gone.'

When Nellie heard the front door opening, she nodded her head in a knowing manner. 'Yer don't have to worry about my mate, Rita, 'cos Molly never swears, and she can talk proper. Yer should hear some of the long words she comes out with; she leaves me flabbergasted. I pretend to know what she's talking about, but half the time I'm nodding me head when it should be shaking, and shaking when it should be nodding. But we can't all be clever clogs, can we, girl? Life would be bloody miserable if we were!'

While Nellie was singing her praises, Molly was knocking on the house next door. She'd have to watch her words carefully, for she didn't want Rita, or her neighbour, to know of her fears regarding the man in a trilby. It wouldn't be fair to frighten two elderly people when it could turn out to be her imagination. On the other hand, it was possible her instinct was right, and then she'd never forgive herself if any harm came to them.

When there was no answer to Molly's first knock, she tried again, in case the woman was in the kitchen or upstairs. And when the door was opened, Molly was delighted to be greeted with a broad smile, on a round chubby face. Her first thought was that Rita's neighbour looked as jolly as her mate Nellie. 'I'm sorry to bother you, sunshine, I hope I haven't brought you away from your work?'

Again the chubby face beamed. 'No, I was sitting down talking to meself, and I was getting fed up with the sound of me own voice.' Folding her arms, Hilda stood on the step. 'It's Molly Bennett, isn't it? I've often seen yer at the shops with Nellie Mac, but never had the opportunity to speak to yer. Anyway, what can I do for yer now?'

'It's about your neighbour, Mrs Reagan. Haven't yer heard what happened to her today?'

'I haven't been out this morning, queen, and I haven't spoken to no one. Why, what happened to Rita?'

Molly only got as far as Nellie seeing Rita standing on the edge of the pavement when Hilda stood to one side and jerked her head. 'Come in, queen, and yer can sit down while ye're telling me. As me old ma used to say, it's bad manners to keep someone standing at the door.'

Molly glanced around the living room with approval. 'Yer house is a credit to yer, sunshine,

219

it's like a little palace. You and Rita put us younger women to shame.'

'The name is Hilda, queen, and I don't believe in standing on formality, so park yer bottom and take the weight off yer feet. I do keep me place nice, but that's only because I've nothing else to do. I get bored stiff sometimes, and find meself counting the leaves on the wallpaper.' She nodded to the wall behind the sideboard. 'There's a hundred and twenty-seven on that wall.' Then her next action reminded Molly of something Nellie did every day without fail. She lifted her bosom and rested it on the table before circling it with her arms.

'Now, what were yer saying about Rita standing on the pavement? Yer'll have to forgive me for interrupting yer so rudely, but that's only because I don't get much chance of talking to people. So go on, and I promise I'll keep me trap shut.'

However, while Molly was telling of Rita's plight, although Hilda did keep her promise to be quiet, she couldn't keep her trap shut, and her mouth remained open throughout Molly's version of events.

'There yer have it, sunshine,' Molly said. 'She's had a bad shock and I'm here to ask if yer could keep an eye on her, just for today, to make sure there are no lasting effects. It would have been a bad experience for a young person, never mind someone of Mrs Reagan's age. Would yer mind watching out for her?'

Hilda scraped back her chair. 'I'm surprised none of the neighbours have called to tell me.

Unless the word hasn't got around yet.' She used the table to push herself to her feet. 'I'll see Rita's all right, yer've no need to worry about that, Molly. We've been neighbours for longer than I care to remember, and there's never been a cross word between us. I'll come in with yer now, and see how the land lies. As yer say, it's a nasty experience for someone in their eighties.'

'Oh, that's taken a load off me mind, sunshine. Otherwise, I'd never have got a wink of sleep tonight. I probably won't anyway.' Molly was keeping her fingers crossed, and hoping Nellie's mate, St Peter, was listening, and willing to give a helping hand. 'I'll be thinking of her all night, hoping she doesn't have a bad turn.'

'We'll sort something out, don't you worry.' As they walked towards the front door, Molly noticed that Hilda waddled like Nellie, and her hips touched the wall on each side. Yes, just like Nellie.

Chapter Nine

Molly had left Mrs Reagan's door ajar, and when she pushed it open she could hear Nellie's voice. Putting a finger to her lips, she winked at Hilda. 'Just listen to my mate.'

'What the hell is my mate doing all this time?' Nellie was saying. 'I bet she's talking the ear off yer neighbour, saying she was the one what pulled you out of harm's way and saved yer life.'

Molly turned her head and winked again at Hilda. 'Just listen.'

'I'll put yer neighbour wise when she comes in.' Nellie was in full flow. 'I'm not taking a back seat while me mate basks in the glory. Sod that for a lark!'

Molly coughed before pushing the living room door open, and she walked in with Hilda close behind. 'What was that yer were saying about me, sunshine? It sounded like yer were blaming me for leaving baskets in the 'allway.'

Nellie didn't even blush. 'The wanderer's returned, eh? Yer took yer bleeding time about it. And I don't know nothing about no baskets, either, so yer must be hearing things.' Her chubby face lit up when she spotted Hilda. 'Ay, I've seen you many times at the shops, but I never knew yer were Rita's neighbour. It's a small world, isn't it, girl?'

'It is that, queen! And the older yer get, the smaller it gets.' Hilda sat down on the couch next to Rita, and patted her arm. 'What's all this about you nearly getting run over, queen? From the sound of things, yer could have been killed.'

'I would have been a goner if it hadn't been for Nellie. She pulled me out of the way of a bus. Me thoughts must have been miles away, 'cos I didn't see the bus coming.'

'Ye're lucky to be alive, queen, from the sound of things. It must have given yer a shock. How d'yer feel now?'

'A bit shaky inside, Hilda, and I've got a bruise on the bottom of me back, and a lump on the back of me head.'

Hilda chuckled. 'That's the top and the bottom of it, then, eh?'

'Ay, that's a good one, that, Hilda,' Nellie said. 'I wish I'd thought of that meself.'

Molly looked from one chubby face to the other. 'I've always said there could only be one Nellie McDonough, but you two are as alike as two peas in a pod. The names are different, but that's about all. I'm glad yer don't live in our street, Hilda. It's no reflection on you, but I couldn't do with two of yer.'

'Well, that's nice, I must say.' Nellie's hands went on her hips. 'Am I the only one what thinks I'm a hero? Some people get medals for bravery, yer know. Patted on the back, and have their hands shaken.' Then she had what she thought was a marvellous idea. 'And what about them what are carried around the streets shoulder high, followed by a crowd of people what are clapping and cheering?'

'Is that what you'd like, sunshine, to be carried through the streets on a man's shoulder?'

'Ooh, yeah, I'd love that! You could walk next to the feller carrying me, girl. Seeing as ye're me best mate I'd make sure yer got a good speck.'

While Rita and Hilda looked from one mate to the other, rather like spectators at a tennis match, Molly asked, 'Have yer given any thought to this hero worship, sunshine? Such as who yer'll ask to carry you on his shoulders? Don't forget it would have to be a real he-man, because ye're not exactly small and slim, yer must admit. Unless yer find Tarzan's visiting the area, then that would be a sight to behold. Any man less than

223

Tarzan would spoil yer parade. He'd end up on the ground, no breath left in his lungs and a few of his bones broken. It would be a real turn-around, with him the hero, and you carrying him across your shoulders.'

'Just listen to misery guts.' Nellie sighed. 'She is me best mate, and I do love the bones of her, but, honest to God, she can be a heavy burden at times.'

'Can we move on from your bravery, sunshine, and me being such a burden to yer? Mrs Reagan is our main concern now. She will want us to do some shopping for her, while we're getting our own. So we need a piece of paper and a pen to make a list out.'

'I'll get Rita's shopping for her,' Hilda said. 'In fact, if she feels up to it, I'll walk her down with me.'

'I don't think that's a good idea, sunshine,' Molly told her. 'She's acting as though she's as right as rain, but I think that's just bravado. I bet her inside is still in a state of shock. It'll take a damn sight longer to get over an ordeal like that than she's making out.'

'Molly is right,' Rita admitted. 'I'm shaking inside. Me heart is pounding so hard it's a wonder yer can't hear it. And me head is splitting, me tummy is upset, and I feel like being sick.'

'That's only what yer can expect, girl.' This was Nellie's opinion. 'It'll be a week at least before yer feel yer old self again.'

'Hilda's going to keep an eye on yer, sunshine, so yer won't come to any harm. Isn't that right, Hilda?'

'I'll do better than that,' Rita's neighbour said. 'I'll take her home with me now, and she can stay overnight. She'll get a good night's sleep and feel much better in the morning.'

Rita's head was shaking before her neighbour had finished speaking. 'Oh, I couldn't impose on yer like that, Hilda. I'll be all right here, I can bed down on the couch.'

'Yer'll do no such thing!' Hilda said. 'The very idea! What sort of neighbour would I be to leave yer on yer own all night, after what yer've been through? Oh, no, Rita Reagan, yer can argue as much as yer like, but ye're staying in my house tonight. I've got a bed in the back bedroom, which I keep aired off in case any of me grandchildren come. The bed is made up, so you've no excuse. And yer'd have yer privacy.'

'Oh, ay, Rita, yer can't refuse an offer like that,' Molly said. 'It's just what the doctor ordered. A bed of yer own, and help at hand if yer need it. What more could yer ask for?'

'Yer'd be daft to refuse, girl,' Nellie said. It was slowly dawning on her that Molly had brought this about, so the old lady wouldn't be in the house on her own tonight if the man in a trilby was a burglar and paid her a visit. 'My old ma used to say that yer should never bite the hand that feeds yer.'

Hilda chuckled, and her whole body shook. 'Ay, queen, I never said I was going to feed her. She won't starve, that's for sure, but it'll be whatever I'm having, nothing fancy.'

'It sounds like a good offer to me, sunshine,' Molly said. 'Too good to turn yer nose up at. So

225

if yer tell me what shopping yer need, me and Nellie will go to the shops. We'll get your bits in, then go back for our shopping. I feel a lot better now I know ye're going to have company to keep an eye on yer. Ye're lucky having such a good neighbour.'

'It's not all one-sided, Molly,' Hilda told her. 'Rita's helped me out over the years. We don't live in each other's pockets, but we're there for each other when we need help. Times like now, when one of us needs support.'

'That's like me and Molly,' Nellie said. 'We're always there for each other, aren't we, girl?'

Molly took her mate's chin in her hand. 'There is one difference, sunshine, and d'yer know what that is?'

Nellie couldn't shake her head with her chin held fast, so she said, 'There is no difference, girl, what I can think of.'

'I'll tell yer then. We do live in each other's pockets. We're practically joined at the hips.'

The little woman had a vision which brought a smile to the chubby face. 'Ay, it wouldn't half be painful for yer, girl, if we were. It wouldn't worry me, but I'd feel dead sorry for you.' Nellie began to roar with laughter, causing the floorboards to creak in protest. They were only used to Rita's weight walking across them, so Nellie's eighteen stone was something of a shock. And it took a while for her laughter to die down long enough for her to splutter, 'Yer'd have to buy yerself a new pair of shoes every week.'

Three faces looked at the mountainous bosom rising and falling, and the tears running down the creases in her face. 'Oh, dear, I haven't laughed so much since me knicker elastic snapped when I was bending down to fasten me shoelace in the butcher's.'

Molly's head was shaking slowly as she told Rita and Hilda, 'She often has a funny turn, so don't let it worry yer. She'll be as right as rain in a minute, and then we'll find out what brought it on. We probably won't find it as funny as she has, but at least we'll be put in the picture.'

Nellie closed her eyes tight, and with her two hands flat on her tummy she took a really deep breath, held it for a few seconds, then let it out slowly. 'Ooh, that's better. I was nearly choking with laughing so much. But I'm better now, girl, yer'll be glad to know.'

'We'd also be interested to know what yer found so funny.' Molly told her. 'And we'd like to be told in as few words as possible, otherwise we'll miss the shops and it'll be fresh air sandwiches for dinner tonight.'

'Okay, girl, I'll be as quick as I can.' Nellie beckoned her mate over. 'Come and stand next to me, girl, and it'll make it easier to explain. Come on, slowcoach, don't be standing there looking gormless. Stand at the side of me, so Rita and Hilda will have a good view.'

Molly tutted. 'Anything for a quiet life, sunshine, but make it snappy, please.'

When they were standing side by side, Nellie spoke to the two older women. 'Now, see where my hip is, down here?' After seeing the two heads nod in agreement, Nellie put her hand on Molly's hip. 'Now see where me mate's is, about

227

six inches above mine. Well, that's what brought on me bout of laughter. If we were joined at the hip like me mate said, well, one of us would have to suffer. Molly couldn't carry my weight, so she'd have to come down to my size. Which means she'd have to chop her feet and ankles off, or drag them along the ground. And no shoes could take that treatment for long, so, as I said, she'd be going through shoes like nobody's business. Every two weeks I reckon.'

Molly looked down at her. 'Nellie McDonough, it doesn't take much to make you laugh, does it? Yer've wasted all that time, when we could have been to the shops and back by now.'

Nellie tilted her head and viewed her mate through narrowed eyes. 'What's wrong with yer, girl, have yer swallowed yer sense of humour? If you can't see the funny side of us being joined at the hip, which were your own words, by the way, then I feel sorry for yer.' She moved closer to Molly. 'I'm down here, girl, and you're up there. We'd look well walking in the butcher's like Pegleg Pete.'

Molly couldn't keep the laughter back any longer, and she doubled up with mirth. This was a relief for Rita and Hilda, who had been afraid to laugh in case they upset one of the mates. But when they heard the roars of laughter from them, they joined in, until the tears rolled down their cheeks. 'They're as good as a tonic, aren't they?' Rita said. 'I was feeling sorry for meself, all aches and pains a few minutes ago. Now I haven't even got a headache.'

Hilda was wiping away the tears with the back

of a hand. 'Did yer hear that, Nellie? Rita would like to thank the driver of that bus for coming along when it did. She's never laughed so much in years.'

Nellie tried to look indignant. She wouldn't be able to spell it, of course, but she knew what it meant. 'Ay, girl, sod the bleeding bus driver, it was me what saved yer life. And as I won't always be on hand when you're standing on the pavement and there's a ruddy big bus coming towards yer, then keep telling yerself to take a step back, not forward.'

'I can go to the shops the same time as her, queen, and I'll remind her. We both go out every day, so we may as well go together.'

Molly still had a picture in her mind of the man in a trilby, and didn't want Rita to feel she was well enough now to be left alone. 'I wouldn't be too quick about going out again, sunshine. Yer've got company now, and we've all had a laugh, but it doesn't mean there'll be no after-effects. I hope yer'll be sensible and take up Hilda's offer of a bed for the night.'

'Of course she will,' Nellie said. 'She's not soft enough to pass up an offer like that.'

'Tell me what shopping yer need, and me and Nellie will go for it now. And we can get yours as well, Hilda, save yer a journey. We can be there and back in no time.'

'If ye're going to Hanley's, yer can get me a small loaf, if yer don't mind,' Hilda said. 'We've both got milk because the milkman leaves us a pint every other day, and he left it this morning. He left me half a dozen eggs as well, so if you get

229

a loaf, I've got enough to feed me and Rita for today. If she's up to it tomorrow, we'll walk down and get what we need. And the fresh air will do us both good.'

'Are yer sure, sunshine?' Molly asked. 'Me and Nellie will give yer a knock tomorrow if yer like? We've got to go to the shops, so we wouldn't be putting ourselves out.'

Rita shook her head. 'Yer've both done enough for me. I've wasted a couple of hours of yer time this morning. If yer can get us a loaf from Hanley's, me and Hilda will be fine. I can't thank yer enough, yer've been kindness itself.'

'What are yer looking at me mate for?' Nellie's hands went to her hips. 'It was me what saved yer life, not slowcoach Molly. She didn't even see the bus, and God knows, it was big enough.'

'Oh, dear,' Molly said. 'I think you're not going to be allowed to forget what happened this morning, sunshine. So I'll give yer a little bit of advice. In future, if yer see Nellie before she sees you, then do an about turn and run like hell. For my mate will expect nothing less than a curtsy from yer, or a tug on yer forelock.'

Nellie's face screwed up as her mind started ticking over. She knew what a curtsy was because she'd tried it herself once, in practice in case she ever met the Queen. However, her valiant effort turned out to be a disaster, for her foot got caught in the hem of her dress and she toppled over sideways. So she had good reason to know what a curtsy was. But forelock, no, she'd never heard that before. 'What was it yer told Rita she should do if she ever sees me in the street? Oh, I

230

know yer said to run like hell, and I know yer said curtsy.' A crafty expression came to her face. 'But I didn't quite catch the other word. I think I was coughing, and missed it.'

'What word was that, sunshine?'

Nellie made a hissing sound before grinding her teeth. 'If I knew what the bleeding word was, yer daft article, then I wouldn't be asking yer, would I?'

'I've said a lot of words since I came in here, sunshine, yer can't expect me to remember every one.'

'I think she means forelock, queen,' Hilda said. 'That was the word yer used after curtsy.'

'That's the word, Hilda.' Nellie beamed. 'Thank the Lord for someone with a bit of sense. Now tell me what it means.'

'Well, all I know is that in the old days, the peasants had to pull it whenever their lordships were around. As a mark of respect, like.'

Molly was intrigued as she listened. She was dying to laugh but held it back, for she wouldn't upset Hilda for all the world. But wait until the family were having dinner tonight, and she told Jack and Ruthie about the peasants pulling their forelocks when their lordships were around. And Nellie standing listening with her mouth open, taking it very seriously. Heaven alone knew what tale Nellie would be telling George tonight. She'd be getting her forelocks mixed up with her curtsy and their lordships.

'Yes, I know all that now, girl,' Nellie said, getting herself all wound up. 'But what was it they pulled?'

Molly decided that if she didn't step in, no one would be getting dinner that night, so she leaned over and gently pulled a handful of Nellie's hair down over her forehead. 'Get hold of that, sunshine, and pull on it. Not hard, just gentle.'

'Oh, sod off, Molly Bennett, yer must think I want me bumps feeling! If yer want to play silly buggers, then pull yer own hair out.'

Rita hadn't said a word while all this was going on, but now she couldn't keep quiet any longer. After all, hadn't Nellie saved her from being run over by a bus? 'Nellie, that lock of hair Molly told yer to get hold of, well, that is what they call a forelock. And like Hilda said, in days gone by, the poor people had to pull on it as a sign of respect.'

Nellie turned to Molly. 'Are you all having me on, or in days gone by were the poor people daft enough to pull their own hair?'

'It was a case of having to, sunshine, or they'd be whipped with a thick leather belt.'

'Well, I wouldn't let no one whip me with a leather belt. I'd have snatched it off them, clouted them with it, then used it as a garter. But I've got a feeling you lot are having me on, 'cos I don't remember that ever happening when I was a kid.'

'Of course you wouldn't remember it, sunshine,' Molly said. 'It was hundreds of years ago when that was going on.'

'Hundreds of years ago?' Nellie's voice was a high squeak. 'Ten minutes ago we were going to Hanley's for a small loaf, and now you're talking about hundreds of years ago! Yer all want yer heads testing!' Then she brought a smile to all their faces by saying, 'I'm the only bleeding sensible person in this room, and it's a good job I've got me wits about me or they'd have me as daft as themselves.'

Molly put her arm across her mate's shoulder and squeezed. 'I could remind yer that it was you that started it all by asking what the word fore-lock means. But I won't do that 'cos yer are me best mate and I'd be lost without yer. So can we come down to earth now, and go to Hanley's for the loaf? Or if yer like, you can stay and talk to Rita and Hilda, and I'll run down there meself. I'd be there and back in ten minutes.'

'Go on then, and I'll stay here.' Nellie was about to plant her bottom on a chair when she thought of something, and her bottom remained in mid-air while she added, 'Don't you dare come back here with a blob of cream on yer nose, or I'll pulverize yer. And tell Edna Hanley to put two cream slices away, and to make sure they're the ones with the most cream in.'

Molly stood to attention, clicked her heels to-gether and saluted. 'Aye, aye, sir. Message received and understood.' Then she hurried from the room before her mate came out with more of her pearls of wisdom.

Dinnertime was always lively in the Bennetts' house, with Jack and Ruthie exchanging incidents that had happened in work. Usually they were comic incidents, enlarged by father and daughter to bring laughter to the dinner table, and it was a time of closeness, warmth and affection. And of course Molly always added to the laughter by telling of the antics of her mate Nellie.

But that night it was different. For, although

233

Molly had made up her mind not to mention the events of the day until the meal was over, she found it wasn't possible to hold her tongue. 'I've got something to tell yer, and although I was going to wait until yer'd finished eating, I'll burst a blood vessel if I don't get it off me chest.'

'What's Nellie been up to now?' Jack asked. 'It must be something outrageous if ye're nearly bursting a blood vessel.'

'No, ye're in for a surprise, as it happens, for my mate was a hero today. She saved an elderly lady from being run over by a bus.'

While Jack laid his knife and fork down, Ruthie's eyes and mouth opened wide. She licked her lips before asking, 'Are yer pulling our legs, Mam?'

'No, sunshine, I wouldn't pull yer legs over something so serious. Just finish yer dinner and I'll tell yer what happened from the very beginning. I don't want to go through it in dribs and drabs.'

The plates had never been cleared as quickly, for, like her dad, Ruthie knew her mam had something of importance to tell them. 'I'll take the plates out, Mam, then we can lean on the table. Pass yours over, Dad, and neither of yer are to say one word until I come back. I'll help yer with the dishes before I go out, Mam.'

'It's a long story, sunshine, so don't expect me to rush it because yer're going out.' Molly smoothed the tablecloth down before resting her elbows on it. 'Me and Nellie went over to Doreen's after we'd had our usual mid-morning cup of tea, and although I always intend to make it a short visit, it never works out that way with Nellie. She expects tea and biscuits in every house we go

234

in. And she gets them too! But where she goes, laughter follows, and she cheers everyone up.' Molly brought guffaws from Jack, and chuckles from Ruthie, when she told them in detail about the pies Doreen had promised to make, and the request from Nellie for the loan of her tape measure.

'We were just walking towards Hanley's, taking it easy because we'd sorted out what we were having for dinner, when Nellie suddenly stopped. And from then everything happened so fast it was just a blur. All I could see was Nellie moving faster than I've ever seen her move, then she pulled this elderly lady down on to the pavement, just as a bus came along.'

Molly went on to tell them in detail about the driver of the bus, the crowd of people that gathered, Edna Hanley's appearance, and the man in the trilby who offered to take Rita home.

'So, Nellie saved the old lady's life?' Jack shook his head. 'How is this Mrs Reagan? Will she be all right?'

'We got her home somehow, because she was in agony, and we stayed with her for a while. Then I went to see the woman next door, and she was really good. She's taken Rita in her house, and she's keeping her there until tomorrow. I was relieved, because I didn't like the thought of a woman of her age being left alone after the shock she'd had. It was enough to bring on a stroke.'

'Yer've had quite a day, then, love?' Jack reached for Molly's hand. 'No one can say you and Nellie lead dull lives.'

'I'd be lost without me mate, sunshine. No

matter how bad a situation is, she always ends up making everyone laugh. Take today for example. Who would have thought that after the drama and shock of nearly being run over by a bus, Mrs Reagan would be shedding tears of laughter? Only Nellie could bring that about. She was making fun of being a hero, but she was a real hero today. That old lady would have been under the wheels of the bus only for her quick thinking. I was useless – I didn't see the old lady, or the bus, until it was too late. I made up for it later, making sure Mrs Reagan is being looked after, but I couldn't compete with Nellie today. She was the tonic that was needed.'

'Auntie Nellie is really funny, isn't she, Mam?' Ruthie's hands were cupping her chin. 'She's been a good mate to you. Like me and Bella are good mates.'

'Yer'll go a long way to find a mate as funny as yer Auntie Nellie, sunshine, because they broke the mould after she was born.'

Now Ruthie loved her Auntie Nellie, but she loved her mother more. 'Mam, you're just as funny as she is, because if you weren't there to encourage her, she wouldn't be so comical. You feed her the lines, and it's like a partnership. Like Laurel and Hardy! Now they were funny as a team, but I bet they couldn't have done it without each other.'

'I may set her up and lead her on, but I couldn't think up half the things she comes out with. Now I've told yer the serious side of our day, I'll give as good an impersonation of my mate as I can. And I'll try to do her justice.' Molly looked across at her daughter. 'If you've made arrangements to go out with Bella, sunshine, then perhaps yer should go now, before I start. Yer can't let Bella down.'

'We're not going anywhere tonight, Mam, so I'm not in any hurry. I'd rather have a laugh with you and me dad, and Bella won't mind if I'm later than usual.'

Molly stood behind her chair, hoping she remembered all the words. 'I'm with Mrs Reagan's neighbour, whose name is Hilda, and she's walking behind me. The front door is ajar, so we just walk in. I could hear Nellie talking, and made a sign to Hilda to be quiet and listen. And this is what we heard.'

Molly folded her arms across her bosom, and began to pace the room, ranting, '"What the hell is my mate doing all this time? I bet she's talking the ear off yer neighbour, saying she was the one what pulled yer out of harm's way and saved yer life. Well, I'll put yer neighbour wise when she comes in. I'm not taking a back seat while me mate basks in the glory. Sod that for a lark!"'

With her eyes narrowed, her head moving from side to side, and the hoisting of her bosom, Molly had all of Nellie's mannerisms off to perfection, causing howls of laughter from her husband and daughter. And then she went on about being a hero and being carried through the streets shoulder high. Then came the part about the two mates being joined at the hips, and Nellie's 'I haven't laughed so much since me knicker elastic snapped when I was bending down in the butcher's'.

Molly stopped for a while and dropped the pose, for, like Jack and Ruthie, she had tears of laughter rolling down her cheeks. 'I'm going to have to stop, I feel sick with laughing.'

'Oh, don't stop now, Mam,' Ruthie pleaded. 'It's dead funny.'

'Well, just give me a minute to compose meself. There's not much more, anyway. Ye're getting a very shortened version of events.'

After taking a deep breath, Molly once again struck up the pose and began with her mate's reaction to the word forelock. How she wouldn't be pulling her hair for no one, and she'd never heard of it when she was young. 'Well, yer wouldn't, would yer, sunshine,' Molly said as herself. 'It was hundreds of years ago.'

Then Nellie's high squeak. '"Hundreds of years ago? Ten minutes ago we were going to Hanley's for a small loaf, and now ye're talking about hundreds of years ago! I'm the only bleeding sensible person in this room, and it's a good job I've got me wits about me or they'd have me as daft as themselves."'

The loud rat-tat on the doorknocker brought silence for a mere two seconds before Molly reverted back to herself. 'Oh, my God, who can this be? Ruthie, take the tablecloth out and shake it in the yard, while I put the chenille cloth on. Jack, you open the door.'

Jack got to his feet. 'Molly, what's all the panic for?'

'Because it's been that sort of day, that's why. Open the door, and if it's Nellie, tell her I packed me bag and have left home. Tell her I've emigrated to Australia and will drop her a line when I'm settled.'

Chapter Ten

Molly was running a comb through her hair when she heard Jack say, 'Come in, Ellen, this is a surprise.' Then she heard his chuckle. 'My wife can relax now. She heard the knock and started running around clearing up. I can never understand why women are so fussy. We men don't even notice whether there's dust on the sideboard or crumbs on the floor.'

'Will yer stop talking, and let the woman in,' Molly called. 'And be careful yer don't trip over the mat, because I've brushed all the dirt under it, out of the way.'

Ellen came in smiling. 'Men haven't got a clue, have they, Molly? If they stayed at home while the women went to work, the dirt would be meeting us at the front door.'

'Sit down, Ellen.' Molly pulled out a chair. 'We don't charge.'

'I won't sit down, because if I get too comfortable I'll be here for ages. All I've come for, Molly, is to ask how Mrs Reagan is. Me and Tony knew nothing about her accident until late this afternoon, when the customers were talking about it. I believe she nearly got run over by a bus, and if I'm to believe everything I've been told, it was Nellie who saved her.'

Molly nodded. 'It's true, sunshine. It all happened so fast it was like watching a movie, and I didn't take it all in. I remember me and Nellie were on our way to Hanley's, talking fifteen to the dozen as usual, when Nellie said something about Mrs Reagan, and then she took off like a bat out of hell. Then I saw the bus coming, the old lady stepping off the pavement, and for a few seconds I just froze. The next thing I saw was Nellie pulling Mrs Reagan backward just as the bus came level with them, and I can still hear the screech of brakes. It wasn't the driver's fault; I felt really sorry for him. He didn't stand a chance, with Mrs Reagan stepping off the pavement without looking. But it was Nellie's quick thinking that saved the day. She saved Mrs Reagan's life, and she saved the bus driver from having nightmares for the rest of his life.'

'It must have been a terrible shock to Mrs Reagan,' Ellen said. 'She's a very gentle person, wouldn't say boo to a goose. Is she going to be all right, or did she have to go to the hospital at all?'

'No, me and Nellie got her home. God knows how we did, but we managed. The bus driver mentioned her going to hospital, but the poor soul looked so frightened it would have done her more harm than good.'

Ruthie came through from the kitchen, where she'd washed the dishes and put them away. She'd got herself ready to go out. 'Hello, Auntie Ellen. Hearing about all the excitement?'

'It's the kind of excitement we could do without, love,' Ellen said. 'I'm glad I wasn't there, I'd have been a nervous wreck, neither use nor ornament.'

'You get over to Bella's, sunshine, she'll be wondering what's keeping yer. And don't make a drama out of what happened to Mrs Reagan, there's a good girl. If Mary mentions it, just give her the bare facts.'

Ruthie gave her a kiss. 'Okay, Mam, just the bare facts.' She dropped a kiss on to Jack's forehead, then made for the door. 'See yer later. Ta-ra, Auntie Ellen.'

Molly waited until she heard the front door close, then said, 'I didn't want to say anything in front of Ruthie, but there's something I haven't mentioned to Rita, her neighbour Hilda, or you, Jack. It might be my bad mind, but better to be sure than sorry. So stay until I get it off me chest, Ellen, and you and Jack can tell me if I'm making a mountain out of a molehill, or whether yer think I'm right to be concerned.'

Molly explained about the man in the trilby offering to take Mrs Reagan home, and how they'd thanked him, but said they could manage to get her there. 'I'd forgotten about him by the time we'd managed to get to her street, 'cos it took us ages. And it was pure chance I happened to see the bloke again. The three of us had just turned the corner of the street, and I asked Nellie to stop because me hand had gone numb. And out of the corner of me eye, I saw a movement, and I peeped round the corner to see this bloke flatten himself against the wall so we wouldn't see him. He'd been following us, I know he had. It was half an hour after the people who had gathered around when Mrs Reagan was on the ground had gone about their business. I believe he was following us to find out where the old lady lived. It was no coincidence, because he was

241

definitely hiding from us.'

'I'd trust your intuition, Molly,' Ellen said. 'I've never known yer to be wrong yet.'

'I thought you'd fixed it for Mrs Reagan to sleep in her neighbour's house for the night,' Jack said. 'She'll be safe enough there.'

'If he is a burglar, he won't worry whether she's in or out. She's too frail to stop anyone stealing from her. If he does break in, think what that would do to her. Walking into the house she keeps like a little palace, to find some of her possessions have been stolen. That a thief has been touching her things and going through her drawers. It's enough to finish her off after the shock she's had today.'

Ellen was nodding in agreement. 'Does she have many things of any value? Would there be anything worth stealing?' Then she chastised herself. 'What am I talking about! Everything in that house is valuable to her. Everything is precious.'

'You've got me thinking now, love,' Jack said. 'I'd go round meself, but what could I do? I mean, I could do plenty if I caught anyone breaking in, but I might stand there all night and nothing happen.'

'I didn't tell Hilda about the bloke, because she's as old as Rita, and she'd worry herself sick. So they don't know anything.'

Ellen scraped her chair back. 'I'll go and get Corker, and see what he thinks. He's only reading the paper, I'll be back with him in five minutes. An extra head won't go amiss.'

True to her word, Ellen was back within minutes, with Corker in tow. The giant of a man, as always, had a smile on his face and in his blue eyes. 'You and Nellie don't lead a dull life, do yer, me darlin'? It seems ye're always there when help is needed.'

'Nellie is the hero this time, Corker, as she'll tell yer when she sees yer. In fact, when we go shopping tomorrow she'll stop everyone she sees, even complete strangers. But I'll not be pulling her away, like I usually do, for she deserves all the praise she gets. And d'yer know what, Corker? After the horror and shock, which would have caused most people to take to their bed, especially an eighty-year-old, Nellie had the old lady laughing at her antics. She's a treasure, is my mate Nellie.'

'It's a good team you are, me darlin'. Mates like you two don't come along very often. I know briefly what happened, and Ellen just had time to tell me that you arranged for Mrs Reagan to sleep with a neighbour tonight, in case the old dear suffers from a delayed reaction. But apparently there's something else on yer mind, and ye're concerned about it. If it's anything I can help with, Molly, then yer know yer only have to ask.'

'I didn't have time to tell him, Molly,' Ellen said. 'I thought it would be best coming from you.'

So once again Molly repeated the tale of the man in a trilby, and why she was concerned. 'I'm not going to say I might not be imagining things, and there's probably nothing to it. I'm not going to say the man in the trilby could be an honest and respectable man either, because I've got it fixed in me mind that he is not. I didn't give any thought to him when he offered to take Rita home, because there was a swarm of people around wanting to help. But most of them were women, out doing their shopping; he was the only man. Even then I wouldn't have given him another thought. But to catch him following us half an hour later, and hiding from us, well, that set the alarm bells ringing. And I'll lay odds that he's up to no good. However, I can't see what we can do about it. I should have kept me worries to meself, instead of passing them on to you.'

'A woman's intuition is seldom wrong, me darlin',' Corker said, stroking his beard. 'And from what yer've told us, yer have reason to be concerned. In fact, because it's a woman in her eighties we're talking about, we should all give it some thought. Because she's safe in a neighbour's house tonight shouldn't make us complacent. Imagine her walking into her house tomorrow and finding it ransacked. She'd lose heart, feel that life wasn't worth living.'

'That's what has been running through me head for the last few hours,' Molly admitted. 'I've thought of going round there and sitting there meself all night, but I'd have to ask Mrs Reagan for her key and she'd want to know why I wanted it.'

Jack snorted. 'Yer don't think for one moment that I'd let yer go and sit round there on yer own! If you go, I go! But there'd be no point in either of us going and sitting in the dark, we'd be bumping into everything. Let's face it, love, neither of us come up to the standard of Sherlock Holmes.'

Corker's guffaw filled the room. 'I can see it in me head, the two of you bumping into each other. Yer'd do more damage than the burglar. I think it would be better if Jack and I take a walk round there and see how the land lies. If the bloke is a burglar, then he'll try and get in through the back. And he won't do that until all the pubs are shut and the streets empty. He'll expect the old lady to be in bed by then, and the house to be in darkness.'

'There's not much point in us walking round there now then, is there? If you say he won't try to break in until the pubs are shut and the streets empty,' Jack said. 'That's if he is a burglar, and we can't be sure of that.'

'As yer know, I've got a few mates in the police force, and when we were chatting one day they said most burglaries take place between one and three in the morning. That's the time when most people are in a deep sleep. Now we're not sure about this man, but presuming he is up to no good, then he would most likely make it earlier than that, with Mrs Reagan being so old she probably goes to bed about nine o'clock. And this bloke will have that in mind. They're crafty buggers, these robbers, they have everything worked out. It's how they make their living, and they know all the tricks of the trade.'

Molly let out a sigh. 'From the sound of it, there's not much we can do, Corker. I wish I had Mrs Reagan's key, then me and Nellie could have spent the night there. Not that I'd like the idea, but Nellie would, she'd be over the moon. And it would be God help anyone that did break in, 'cos she'd flatten them with one blow. They'd have more than one black eye, believe me.'

Corker, who had a keen imagination and sense of humour, shook with mirth. 'Oh, that is something I'd like to see, Molly, it would be a sight for sore eyes. Nellie in action would be like a whirlwind; the man wouldn't know what had hit him. But it might be better to leave you ladies out of it. I'll walk round there now, just to familiarize meself with the entry and Mrs Reagan's door. Then I'll come home again and spend a few hours with Ellen before going back around midnight. I don't need much sleep, as my dear wife will tell you, so it won't interfere with me going to work at my usual time in the morning.'

Jack was quick to offer his services. 'I'll come with yer, Corker, to keep yer company. What time shall I call for yer?'

'A quarter to twelve should be about right, Jack, because some people don't go to bed before then, and there'll be lights on in some houses.' Corker pushed himself off the couch and stretched to his full height of six foot five inches. 'Have a couple of hours' kip, Jack, or yer'll be dead on yer feet in work tomorrow.'

'I feel terrible now, causing all this trouble,' Molly said, her hands clasped tight. 'I shouldn't have said anything, because I might be completely wrong.'

'Not to worry, me darlin',' Corker told her. 'It'll break the monotony if nothing else. And think how bad we'd all feel if we sat on our backsides and did nothing, only to be told tomorrow that the old lady's house had been ransacked. I'd rather waste a couple of hours than live with that guilt. From what you told us about the man in the trilby still following you half an hour after the incident, I would agree it seems more than mere coincidence. And I'm sure Jack would rather be involved in doing something than sitting at home wondering.'

Jack nodded. 'I'll give yer a knock at a quarter to twelve, Corker, but I won't have a kip, I'll keep Molly company and listen to the wireless. If it's a comedy we'll laugh, if it's a romance we'll hold hands, and if it's a murder mystery we'll switch off.'

Ellen reached up and pulled on the big man's beard. 'And what will my husband be doing until a quarter to twelve? Listening to the wireless, like Jack and Molly?'

'I believe a little lubrication is called for, my darlin'. A pint or two of the landlord's best bitter to wet me whistle and waken me brain cells. Yer have to be alert to apprehend a burglar, and two pints should see me in peak condition and ready for any eventuality.'

Molly giggled. 'Oh, if only Nellie was here! I can see the look on her face when yer came out with words like lubrication, apprehend and eventuality. I'll write them down when yer've gone, and somehow I'll fit them into a sentence tomorrow. I wish I had a camera to take a photo of the different expressions on her face.'

'Yer may have more interesting news for her than my choice of words, Molly. Somehow I believe, or have an intuition, that the man in a trilby will show himself tonight.'

'I don't know, Corker. I'll feel a right fool if he doesn't, and you and Jack losing a night's sleep because of me.'

'Not to worry, me darlin', whichever way it goes.' He winked at Jack. 'I'll bring me hip flask for a little drink, but not too much or we'll waken the neighbours.'

'What time is it now, Corker?' Jack asked in a whisper. 'I'll have to buy meself a cheap watch. I'm always having to ask the time, even in work.'

The two men were standing pressed against the wall in the entry, about six doors higher up than Mrs Reagan's house. It was pitch dark as there were no lamps lit, and there was no light from any window. Corker had an illuminated face on his watch, and he said, 'It's twenty past twelve. We'll give it another hour.'

'I'm gasping for a smoke,' Jack said. 'I've no willpower when it comes to smoking. Molly hates me lighting up, says I'm weak. And I know she's got a point when she reckons that what I spend on fags in a year would pay for new furniture for the living room.'

'Yes, like Ellen, Molly does have a point. But I'm in a better position than you, in as much as there are six working in our house, against two in yours. Not that the two lads contribute much to the housekeeping, being apprentices, but at least they pay for their keep, and their pocket money.'

Jack suddenly heard a faint sound like a pebble's being kicked, and he nudged Corker while cocking an ear. Both men pushed themselves back against the entry door, which was inset a brick's thickness away from the wall. Not enough space to hide in daylight, but enough to be missed in pitch darkness. The footsteps were very faint, signs that whoever it was, the newcomer was wearing plimsolls rather than shoes. Seconds passed without another sound, then the two men heard a voice counting softly, 'Twenty-two, twenty-four, this must be twenty-six.' Corker grabbed Jack's arm and held it tight, a sign to be still, but alert. The next sound was one they recognized as scraping, and panting, as the burglar tried to get a hold on the top of the wall, but his shoes couldn't get a grip.

Corker could reach the top of the wall without even stretching, and at six foot, so could Jack. So the heavy breathing indicated a small man having difficulty carrying out his plan. While Jack was apprehensive, never having been in a situation like this before, Corker was feeling justified in taking Molly's fears seriously and saving an old lady from fear and heartache. 'Get ready, Jack,' he whispered. 'We don't want to lose him.' Then on second thoughts he added, 'No, you stay here in case he sees us and makes a run for it. Count to ten, then come after me.'

The would-be burglar, one Fred Griffin, dressed well during daylight to look respectable, and he had spent time getting rid of his thick Liverpool accent. But when he was not fooling the public, his speech was a different kettle of fish. His language was coarse and every other word a profanity. He was married to a woman as common as himself, and they had three children who had been taught from an early age that if they wanted anything they could get it by stealing. Fred Griffin made his living by stealing from those whose houses he broke into, specializing in elderly people who lived alone. He never worked on his home patch, for he was well known to the local police because of his method of operation. The house he lived in was a hovel, but there was one thing he insisted on, and his slovenly wife had learned to her cost: that while her house could be rotten from top to bottom, his suit, shirt, tie and trilby had to be kept in tiptop condition. For, dressed in those, he looked like a respectable businessman, and no one would be suspicious of his innocent-sounding questions. When he strode down the streets, his trilby at just the right angle, his shirt and tie spotless and the crease in his suit trousers ironed to perfection, he thought he was as good as anyone, and better than most. Even several short spells in prison for robbery hadn't dimmed the enthusiasm he felt for what he called his profession. He was never without money for his fags and beer, and he didn't have a boss ordering him around. Plus, he didn't have to get up early every morning; he could please himself what he did and when. He made enough money by stealing from the houses he broke into to satisfy his needs. What he took tonight would be sold in the pub tomorrow, and the money he made would last until he had another target lined up.

Fred Griffin wasn't in the best of moods that night though, as he jumped up to try to reach the top of the wall so he could haul himself up. He was just inches short, and cursed himself for not bringing a brick to stand on. All he needed was a couple of inches and he'd be over the wall in no time. Kicking the entry door in wasn't an option, for if he didn't wake the old lady, he'd wake one of the neighbours.

Determined not to be beaten, or go away empty-handed, Fred took a deep breath, bent his knees and put everything he had into a jump. He found his hands gripping the top of the wall all right, but only because he'd had help. His first feeling was one of elation, but it only lasted a matter of seconds before he realized he was being held up by a pair of hands as big as shovels spanning his waist. In panic he tried to pull himself over the wall, but he was being held in a vicelike grip. And when he glanced down he froze with fright. It was too dark to see clearly, but he sensed the person holding him was the size of a giant. Now Fred Griffin had been called many things in the past that most people would be ashamed of, but one thing he could never be accused of was being a hero. He was far from that. A coward, yes, a hero, no!

'I don't know who yer are, but could yer put me down?'

'I'll put yer down when yer've explained what ye're doing trying to climb over the wall at this time of night.' Corker said. 'Yer wouldn't be intending to break into the house, would yer?'

'No, I wasn't. Yer got me wrong, mate.' Fred's mind was working overtime. 'I live here! But yer see, I went out with a few mates for a bevvy, and I forgot to take me front door key with me. I daren't wake the wife up, she'd have me life for getting her out of bed this time of night. I told her I was only going for a couple of pints, but I ended

251

up going home with one of me mates and we've been playing cards. We didn't notice the time passing, and I got a shock when I looked at the clock.'

'A likely story, eh, Jack?' Corker said, putting more fear into Fred, who now knew he'd been caught by two men. 'I'll let him down and he might be more inclined to tell the truth if he's standing on his feet.' He lowered the now terrified man to the ground. 'Now, you tell me and my mate what ye're up to, 'cos we're very interested.'

That was when Fred had a brainwave, or thought he had. 'Oh, I get it, this is your patch! Oh, ay, I'm sorry lads, I didn't know I was treading on someone else's toes.' Feeling weak with relief, he squared his shoulders and attempted to walk between the two men. 'I'll leave yer to go about yer business.'

Corker barred his way. 'You ain't going anywhere, mate. And what business would my friend and meself be about?'

Fred thought he couldn't go wrong, because why would these two blokes be hiding in an entry at this time of night, if they weren't there for the same reason as himself? 'Look, I'll leave yer to it. Yer should have no trouble seeing as there's two of yer. And it should be an easy job, 'cos there's only an old lady lives there. She won't give yer no trouble.'

It was Jack who grabbed Fred by the scruff of his neck. He was furious that anyone should talk about its being easy to rob an old lady. Surely to God, any decent man would want to protect the elderly, not rob them and ruin their lives. 'Oh, ye're way off the beaten track, mate.' Jack's teeth were ground together. 'Me and me brother live here, with me mam. Tell him, Jim, that he's picked the wrong house when he picked ours.'

'It's just as well we came along when we did,' Corker said, mentally giving Jack ten out of ten for being so quick at thinking up that tale. 'He'd have frightened the life out of me ma, and I think he deserves a good hiding to teach him a lesson.'

By this time Fred Griffin was wishing he was miles away. But he still tried to bluff his way out of getting a hiding. One punch off these two would see him in hospital. 'I think yer've got the wrong entry and the wrong house, lads, 'cos there's definitely an old lady living in this house on her own. I know because I've seen her.'

'Oh, is that what your job of work is?' Corker asked. 'You find out where elderly people live on their own, and you break into their homes and steal from them? What a brave man you are, picking on people who can't defend themselves. Well, I'm going to give you a chance to defend yerself, which yer don't deserve but which I'm going to give yer because I think even an animal has the right to defend itself. And you are an animal.'

Jack took hold of Corker's arm. 'Don't make a noise or yer might wake me mam.' He was keen to stick to the lie that they were brothers for that was one way of making sure this robber never troubled Mrs Reagan again.

Corker nodded. 'I've had second thoughts on that. I now think our best bet is to take him along to the police station. There's a sergeant on duty all night, so he can put this blighter in a cell and keep him there until they interview him tomorrow. He'll be charged with attempted robbery, and you and meself will be witnesses.'

Fred struggled to free himself from Corker's grip, but he didn't stand a chance. 'Yer can't say I was breaking and entering because I was in the entry with you and yer brother all the time.'

'But you admitted yer were going to break in, and that's what the police call "intent".' Corker didn't fancy the long walk to the police station, nor did he fancy having to repeat the tale that he and Jack were brothers and making up a cock and bull story about their being in the entry after midnight. 'Do yer live round here?'

'No, I live miles from here. Four stops on the bus, it is.'

'If me and me brother let yer go, will yer give us yer word yer'll stay those four stops away?'

'I promise. Yer'll never set eyes on me again.'

Corker looked across to Jack. 'What d'yer think, brother? Shall we give him a chance?'

'It's up to you, Jim, but I'll be honest and tell yer that if I even set eyes on him again, I'll give him the hiding of his life. He'll rue the day he was born.'

'Yer won't see me no more, and that's a promise.' Fred looked from one to the other. They'd given him a fright, these two brothers, especially the one built like a battleship. And he'd definitely be staying well away from this neck of the woods in future. 'Can I go now, because the wife will be worrying about me?'

Corker clipped his ear. 'Go on, scarper. Con-

254

sider yerself lucky and never forget that if we ever see yer again, yer might not be so lucky.'

As they stood and watched the would-be burglar running as though his life depended on it, Corker said, 'There goes a man without a brain in his head. If he robs people for a living, then he and his family don't know what life is all about. He's the most stupid burglar I've ever heard of, and I've heard of plenty from my pals in the police. But I'll tell yer about that some other time. We better get home or the wives will be worried. And talking of wives, you can tell Molly from me that with her intuition she'd make a wonderful detective.' Corker chortled. 'On second thoughts I'll tell her meself tomorrow night. Right now, let's head for home and bed.'

'I hate to think we caught a burglar, and he got off with it,' Jack said as they neared their street. 'He should be behind bars.'

'There wasn't anything we could do, Jack, because he didn't commit any offence. And Mrs Reagan is best not knowing anything about the man Molly calls the man in a trilby. The old lady would worry herself sick. And one thing we can be sure of, she'll go back to her little house tomorrow and find everything just as she left it. And she must never be told how close she came to losing her treasures. At least we've stopped one robber from coming in this area again.'

They reached Jack's front door and he took a key from his pocket. 'All the lights are out here, and in your house. I hope I don't bump into anything, so I'll take me shoes off and creep up the stairs.'

'I'll bid yer goodnight, Jack, and I believe we can both be happy with the turn of events.' Corker moved to his own front door. 'See yer tomorrow night, Jack. Goodnight.'

'Yeah. Goodnight, Corker. See yer tomorrow.'

Chapter Eleven

Nellie received such a warm welcome when she arrived at her usual time of ten thirty that she looked at her mate with suspicion. 'Ye're in a very good mood, aren't yer, girl? What have I done to deserve that smile yer've got on yer clock? Not that I'm complaining, like, 'cos it's better than seeing yer with a face as long as a fiddle.'

'I've got news for yer, sunshine, so you sit yerself down and I'll bring the tray in. I've got it all ready and waiting for yer.'

Nellie's eyes were narrowed when she said, 'It's not my birthday, is it, girl, and I've forgot?'

Molly shook her head and turned towards the kitchen. 'No, it's more exciting than a birthday. But don't ask me to tell yer until we're settled down with our cup of tea.'

'And a custard cream, I hope, girl! In fact, seeing as yer look so happy, could yer make that two biscuits?'

'Don't push yer luck, sunshine.' Molly was grinning when she picked up the tray from the draining board. They say God loves a trier, and her mate was certainly good when it came to trying to get the most out of life. 'However, it just so happens that there were four biscuits in the tin, so we've got two each.' She put the tray down in the middle of the table. 'Tea is poured out, and sugared and milked, so all yer have to do is drink it. And remind me to get biscuits while we're out.'

Nellie dunked one of her biscuits in the tea, ate it in one go, then asked, 'What's the news, girl?' Her eyes warned of mischief. 'Ye're not pregnant again, are yer?'

'I said the news was exciting, sunshine, and I wouldn't find being pregnant at my age exciting. More like a miracle.'

'I don't know so much, girl, there's women older than you what have got themselves in the family way. What about Mrs Higgins from the next street, she was fifty when she had her last baby.'

Molly was getting impatient. 'For heaven's sake, Nellie, what are yer bringing Mrs Higgins into the conversation for? We hardly know the woman, and it's none of our business if she has a baby at fifty.'

'Keep yer hair on, girl, don't be getting all hot and bothered, it's not good for yer at your age.' Reaching for her second custard cream, Nellie muttered, 'I knew that smile wouldn't last long, it was too good to be true. It's being taken over by misery guts, the look what turns milk sour.'

Molly decided the only way to shut Nellie up was to ignore her. So, feigning a yawn, she sat back in her chair, folded her arms, and began to count the seconds ticking away on the clock. She had counted up to twenty-five when her mate broke the silence.

'What's up with yer, girl? Yer were full of smiles when I came in, now yer look as miserable as sin! Surely I don't have that effect on yer?'

'I've been waiting for yer to stop trying to be funny, sunshine, that's why I'm not grinning like a clown. I did have some news for yer, but as ye're not interested I won't bother. We'll finish our tea, and then be on our way.' Molly knew her mate so well, she could predict what was going to happen next. First would come the narrowing of the eyes, then the face contortions, and finally the question. And as usual she was right.

'Aren't yer going to tell me what yer news is? I want to know, I'm eager to know, and I'm all ears. So come on, let's have it.'

Molly shook her head. 'No, I'm not in the mood now, sunshine, so let's skip it. But if yer happen to see Jack or Corker in the street, they might tell yer. That's if ye're interested, of course, and they've got the time.'

'Corker and Jack!' Nellie's voice was shrill. 'What have they got to do with anything? Yer've got me going now, girl, and I ain't leaving this house until yer tell me what yer've been up to with Corker and your Jack. So yer can just plonk yerself down again, girl, and spill the beans.'

'Well, don't blame me if I keep yawning, sunshine, because I didn't get to bed until just on one o'clock this morning and I'm dead beat. I could do with another cup of tea to liven me up, but I haven't got the energy to put the kettle on.'

Nellie was off her chair like a shot. 'You just stay where yer are, girl, and I'll make us a nice pot of fresh tea. I wouldn't be much of a best mate if I couldn't make yer a drink when ye're feeling weak.'

While Nellie was filling the kettle, Molly was sitting back in her chair with a smile of satisfaction on her face. 'Don't make the tea too strong, sunshine. I can't stand tea that is strong enough to stand the spoon up in.'

Nellie could hear the laughter hidden in her mate's voice, and she popped her head round the door. 'Sod off, Molly Bennett, I'm not a ruddy slave. Yer'll have the tea just as it comes out of the spout, and yer can like it or lump it. What's good enough for me is good enough for you.'

'All right, sunshine, it'll be all joking aside when we're sitting at the table. We'll start all over again, as if yer've only just arrived. No messing around, because when I tell yer why I didn't go to bed until one o'clock this morning, yer'll realize there was a very good reason for it.' Molly took the cup and saucer handed to her, and after taking a sip she said, 'This is what I call a nice cup of tea, sunshine, just the way I like it.'

The poor chair that Nellie was sitting on was having a hard time trying to stop its legs from breaking under the strain as she shuffled her bottom until she felt comfortable, and then the chair sighed with relief. It wasn't that it didn't like Nellie, because it had enjoyed many a laugh when she told her tales. If only her voluptuous body wasn't so voluptuous, though, for she really did put a strain on it. And it wasn't getting any younger.

'Go on, girl, tell me what the news is! Don't be sitting there like Lady Muck with a soppy grin on yer face. I made the tea for yer, just as yer bleeding well like it, and now I'm waiting for you to repay my kindness. And I warn yer, it had better be good after all this palaver.'

Molly drained her cup, put it back in the saucer and wiped the back of her hand across her mouth. 'I can honestly say, sunshine, without fear of contradiction, that that is the best cup of tea I've had in a long time.'

'I don't want flattery, Molly Bennett, I want to know what happened last night. And I want it right now, or so help me I'll throttle yer.'

Molly leaned her two elbows on the table. 'And you shall have it, in chapter and verse. Now, d'yer remember the man in a trilby who offered to take Mrs Reagan home yesterday, when she was lying on the pavement?'

Nellie huffed with frustration. 'Of course I remember him, girl, I'm not in me dotage yet. I also remember yer saying yer thought he'd followed us home to Rita's! So, now tell me something I don't know.'

Molly didn't waste any time. 'Well, at half past twelve last night he was trying to burgle her house.'

Nellie's jaw dropped, and it took her a few seconds to recover. 'How d'yer know that?' Her eyes narrowed and she leaned across the table. 'Ye're pulling me leg, aren't yer? Well, I don't think it's bleeding funny.'

'I am not pulling yer leg, sunshine, it's the God's honest truth. He didn't get in, thank goodness, because Corker and Jack were there to stop him.'

This was all getting too much for Nellie to take in. Head going from side to side, mouth wide and eyes narrowed, she was lost for words and understanding. Then, after telling herself to calm down, she lifted her bosom, placed it on the table and leaned towards Molly. 'I'm not going to lose me temper, girl, and I am trying very hard to understand what ye're telling me. But I just can't make sense of why Corker and Jack would just happen to be in the entry at half past twelve in the morning when the queer feller was trying to burgle Rita's house! I think ye're making it up, 'cos it's too far-fetched to be true.' She gave a sharp nod of her head sat back in her chair putting an expression on her face that told her mate to put that in her pipe and smoke it.

'Let me spell it out for yer, sunshine, and all will become clear.' Molly was feeling a little guilty about giving her mate the runaround, for it would be hard for anyone to believe what had happened unless they were there. 'I told yer I was worried about that bloke following us, and how I thought he had designs on breaking into Rita's. That's why I got round Hilda to let her sleep in her house last night. Anyway, Ellen called in last night because some of their customers had told her and Tony about Rita, and Ellen came to see how she was. I mentioned the man in the trilby, and how I didn't trust him, and she passed on what I'd said to Corker. Now yer know what Corker's like when it comes to old people being robbed, he's dead set against it. So it ended up with him and Jack going out at a quarter to twelve, just on spec, like, in case the bloke did have robbery in mind. They stood in Rita's entry, and lo and behold, at half past twelve, doesn't the bold man turn up and try to scale Rita's wall!'

Nellie had been leaning closer as the tale was unfolding, and no one could have asked for a more appreciative audience. For the little woman's chubby face went through every emotion known to man. Her hand clenched into a fist, and she shook it, muttering, 'The bleeding robber. Just let me get me hands on him, and I'll show him what for.'

'Anyway, he didn't get away with it, sunshine, for the men caught him red-handed. But what a blessing, eh, that I mentioned my suspicion to Ellen? He wouldn't have got to Rita, with her being next door, but imagine if she'd walked in this morning to find the place ransacked. The shock would have been enough to kill her.'

'What did Jack and Corker do with the bloke?' Nellie asked. 'Did they give him a good hiding, and take him to the police station?'

'I don't know any more than I've told yer, sunshine, because the men were eager to get a few hours' sleep. And Jack didn't have time to tell me this morning, because Ruthie was having her breakfast with us, and I'd warned him not to mention anything while she was there. The least she knows the better, for we don't want Rita to find out. Anyway, that's it for now, sunshine, yer know as much as I do. Corker is coming here tonight, and him and Jack will give us the full story.'

'What time are they coming, girl?' Nellie asked. 'I want to be here before they arrive, 'cos I don't want to miss anything.'

'It'll be about eight o'clock, Nellie, so don't you come too early. I want to wait until Ruthie is out of the way, and also I don't want you asking Jack questions until Corker gets here.'

'Okay, girl, I won't come too early. I'll wait until I see Ruthie going over to Bella's.'

'Oh, no, you don't, Nellie McDonough. How crafty you are! Yer know Ruthie goes out at half seven. I don't want you coming here too early. If yer do, I won't let yer in.'

Crafty was the word for the look in Nellie's eyes. 'Jack would open the door for me. He's a gentleman, is Jack, and he wouldn't leave a woman standing on the doorstep.'

'Listen to me, sunshine, even your voluptuous body wouldn't tempt Jack to go against my wishes. Yer see, he's very happy with my not so voluptuous body.'

Her eyes down, Nellie muttered, 'Some men are bleeding easy to please. They don't know what they're missing.'

'Lift yer head up, sunshine, I can't hear what ye're saying.'

'I just noticed, girl, and told meself a button on me coat was missing.'

Molly, of course, had heard the muttered words, and gave her mate credit for fast thinking. And she decided she'd do some fast thinking herself, even though she would not be given any credit. 'Oh, well, that settles it, sunshine, yer can't come here tonight after all. We'll be having an intelligent conversation, and anyone with a button missing from her coat would spoil it. Yer'd stick out like a sore thumb.'

'Sod off, Molly Bennett! And don't be trying to belittle me, either, saying I'd stick out like a sore thumb. Besides, yer can easy hide a sore thumb, but yer can't hide a broken nose. And that's what you'll be sporting tonight if yer keep having a go at me. To hear yer talk, anyone would think yer owned the bleeding house!'

'I know I don't own the house, sunshine, but I am the tenant and pay me rent every week. Which means I can have who I like in the house, and keep out those I don't like.'

'Oh, Miss Hoity-toity, eh? Think ye're better than anyone else, just because yer know a lot of big words what nobody else knows. Well, ye're not the only one who is a tenant and pays their rent every week, 'cos I do as well. And I can have who I like in me house, and keep out those what I don't like. So there, clever clogs!'

'Oh, I agree with yer, sunshine, a hundred per cent.' Molly kept a straight face. 'But we're not having the meeting in your house tonight, are we? Unless yer'd like to have it in yours? That would suit me and Jack, and Corker wouldn't mind.' Molly knew she was on safe ground because Nellie didn't like having to tidy up for visitors. She much preferred to visit than be visited. 'In fact it would be a break for me, not having to make pots of tea. So, if you're game, sunshine, I'd be delighted if we met in yours for a change.'

Nellie couldn't think of an excuse right away, so there was silence until a victim came to mind in the shape of her husband. 'I'd like to accommodate yer, girl, but I can't. It's George, yer see.

264

Yer wouldn't be able to hear yerselves talk with the noise.'

Molly's brow furrowed. 'What's George got to do with anything? And why wouldn't we be able to hear ourselves talk?'

'The noise, girl, the noise! It's chronic!'

'Yer've lost me now, sunshine. What noise are yer worried about? There's no children in yer house, and I know Corker has a loud voice, but not loud enough to deafen us.'

'It's the snoring, girl, it's something wicked. Yer wouldn't believe it, but sometimes I can feel the floorboards creaking, he snores so loud.'

'I thought George spent the night reading the paper, sunshine. Ye're always saying yer can't get a word out of him. In fact yer call yer poor husband fit to burn 'cos he's so quiet. Now yer say he makes so much noise the house shakes! I think ye're telling fibs, Nellie, 'cos ye're too blinking lazy to make a pot of tea for yer neighbours and friends.'

Her lips pouting, Nellie gave in and nodded. And her chins felt sorry for her as well, so to show they were on her side they swayed very gently. 'Ye're right, girl, as usual. I'm no flaming good at being a hostess without you. I never know what to say, and another thing, I always spill tea in the saucers, what you never do. So can we be best mates again, and let me come here tonight? I'll be as good as gold, I promise.'

'I will, sunshine, as long as yer come clean over George. Admit that he doesn't snore, and that he's a smashing husband.'

Nellie had to think about that for a few seconds.

'That's not something I can easy answer, girl, 'cos it's half and half. George doesn't snore, but when we're in bed he does breathe very heavy, if yer know what I mean.'

Molly waved a hand in the air. 'Yer don't need to give me chapter and verse, Nellie, I get yer drift.'

A cheeky grin covered the chubby face. 'I thought yer would, girl, 'cos ye're quick on the uptake, you are. And George is a smashing husband, and I do love the bones of him. I wouldn't swap him even for Clark Gable.' She ran her finger along the tablecloth. 'I might have to think twice if Cary Grant came on the scene, though, 'cos he's not half handsome. And he's funny with it, so me and him would get on like a house on fire.'

Molly let out an exaggerated sigh. 'I feel sorry for your feller, he can't win. He should have married a girl who appreciated him.'

'I don't know so much, girl, 'cos he did well for himself when he picked me. I mean, how many other women have got a voluptuous body like mine? I think he did very well for himself. He doesn't need a hot water bottle in bed in the winter, not when he's sleeping next to me. He'll tell yer himself I'm better than an eiderdown and two blankets any day.'

'I don't think that subject will come up in any conversation I have with George, sunshine, for neither of us would want to embarrass the other.' Molly watched her mate's face changing expressions, and she could almost read her mind. She couldn't put her finger on it, but if she was a betting person, she'd put a tanner on at ten to

266

one that Nellie was holding something back. But her mate couldn't keep a secret if her life depended on it, so it wouldn't be long before Molly was let into the secret. At least that's what Molly thought. But when the mates left the house to go to the shops, whatever the secret was, it stayed in Nellie's head.

When Corker called that night at eight o'clock, Nellie was already seated at the table in her carver chair. And when Corker greeted her with the words, 'Nellie, me darlin', it's a hero yer are,' well, her bosom rose to the occasion and stood firm and proud, while she gave Molly a sly look which said that she was being treated by the big man as though she was special, and her mate wasn't in the meg specks.

'Sit down, Corker,' Molly said. 'I've got the kettle on, tea won't be a couple of minutes.' On her way to the kitchen, she had to pass Nellie's chair and she bent down and whispered, 'Don't push yer luck, sunshine, 'cos sometimes it runs out.'

But Nellie's Cheshire cat grin stayed put. She wasn't going to allow anyone to steal her spotlight, not even her best mate. 'Did yer hear that, girl?' she asked, trying to rub salt in the wound. 'Corker said I'm a hero.'

Molly resisted the temptation to cup the chubby face in her hands and kiss it. 'No, yer can't be a hero, sunshine, I'm sorry.'

'Ye're only jealous, Molly Bennett, because it was me what saved Rita from being run over. My George said I might get a medal for it, seeing as

I'm a hero.'

After giving Corker and Jack a huge, exaggerated wink, Molly stood her ground. With her hands on her hips, she looked down at her mate. 'I'm sorry, sunshine, but there's no way you can be a hero.'

The little woman was getting her dander up now. Her nostrils were flared and her cheeks red. She glanced up to the ceiling, but her friend St Peter wasn't offering any help. So she turned to the man who had started this confrontation. 'Corker, will yer put Molly straight, before I clock her one.'

Corker, however, had guessed what Molly had in mind, and he shrugged his shoulders. 'I don't like to take sides with one mate against another, Nellie, but in this instance, to save any more argument, I'll have to take Molly's side. For she is right when she says you can't be a hero.'

Nellie looked so let down and disheartened, Molly couldn't bear to keep it up. 'What yer can be, sunshine, and you are, is a heroine.'

Suspicion was in Nellie's eyes. 'Don't you try and kid me, girl. I might be cabbage-looking but I'm not green. What's a bleeding heroine when it's out?'

'It's a lady hero, Nellie,' Corker told her. 'A hero is a man, and a heroine is a female. And yer should be very proud of yerself.'

Nellie appealed to her mate. 'I've never heard that word, girl, so why can't I just be a hero? Everyone knows what that means.'

'Nellie, yer should be very proud because as a heroine ye're in very exclusive company. Florence Nightingale was a heroine, and yer know

268

who she was, and the good work she did for the sick when there were no hospitals like the ones we're lucky to have today. She had to work in dreadful conditions.'

Nellie's head and chins were nodding knowingly. 'I know her 'cos I've seen her on the pictures, and she's always carrying a lamp.' With a look of innocence on her face, she asked Corker, 'Ay, does Florence live round here, lad? I mean if I'm a heroine, like what she is, then we should be mates, shouldn't we? Molly could invite her here for a cup of tea, and I'd let her sit in me chair. D'yer think yer could arrange that, Corker? I'd like to meet her, to see if she was as brave as what I was.'

There was a ten second silence, then laughter filled the room, causing the little woman to wonder what she had said that was funny. 'Ay, what is funny about me and Florence meeting up? I mean, if she couldn't come here, I'd go to her house, as long as it wasn't too many tram stops away.'

'Oh, dear, oh, dear.' Molly wiped the tears from her eyes. 'I'm afraid even Corker can't bring about a miracle, sunshine. Unfortunately ye're doomed never to see Florence Nightingale, to see whether she was as brave as you were.'

'That's all your fault, Molly Bennett, 'cos ye're jealous, that's why. I saw the way yer looked at Corker, telling him to put me off. Well, I'm not soft yer know, I'm up to yer tricks.'

Molly attracted her husband's attention. 'Jack, be an angel and see to the tea, please. There'll be no backside left in the kettle if it's not taken off the stove. I'll be out in a minute, I just want to explain to Nellie why she can't meet Florence Nightingale.'

'Oh, yer don't need to explain anything to me, girl, 'cos I know without yer telling me why I can't meet Florence. It's because ye're eaten up with jealousy, that's why.'

'Nellie, will yer watch my lips, please?' Molly leaned closer. 'I don't want yer to meet Florence, because I'd have to lose a mate to let yer do that. Yer see, sunshine, Florence Nightingale has been dead for about fifty years.'

'Go 'way, fancy that, now! Nobody told me she died.' Then Nellie saw a bright light in the darkness. 'Well, it's an ill wind that doesn't blow somebody some good.' She narrowed her eyes. 'Did I say that right, girl, or did I get it back to front?'

'Yer got it right, Nellie, and now we've cleared the air and yer know ye're a heroine, I'll give Jack a hand in the kitchen.'

As Molly turned away, Nellie winked at Corker before calling, 'You come and sit down, girl, and I'll give Jack a hand in the kitchen.'

Molly was back like a shot. 'I've got every faith in my husband, Nellie Mac, but I wouldn't trust you as far as I could throw yer. So stay where yer are, and keep reminding yerself that ye're very lucky not to be on yer way to having tea with Florence Nightingale.'

Nellie wagged a finger, inviting her friend to come nearer so she could whisper in her ear. 'Life's a bugger, isn't it, girl?'

While Molly patted her mate's cheek, Corker's

loud guffaw filled the room, and the living rooms of neighbours in the nearest six houses. 'Nellie, me darlin', it's a treasure yer are, as well as a heroine. You and Molly make a good pair, and yer've filled our lives with laughter for the last twenty years. Mates like you two don't come along very often.'

'It's just as well, Corker.' Jack came through carrying the wooden tray. 'I can't keep up with these two, so I'd be lost with two more added on. Me heart wouldn't stand the excitement.'

'I'm still waiting to be told about the excitement you and Corker had last night, lad,' Nellie told him. 'Your wife said she couldn't tell me what happened because she didn't know, but I find that hard to believe. If yer were my husband, I'd have found a way of wheedling it out of yer in bed. My George is a sucker for wheedling, he gives in every time.'

Molly was putting Corker's tea down in front of him when she told her mate, 'That's nothing to brag about, Nellie! The poor man probably gives in for the sake of peace.'

Nellie's sly grin told Molly she'd been too hasty to criticize, and should have kept her mouth shut. It was too late now, and she had no way of stopping the words that came from her mate's lips, or the laughter in her voice. 'Oh, my George doesn't give in for the sake of peace, girl. He knows which side his bread is buttered on, and he gives in for pleasure. I mean, why would anyone go to the trouble of inventing beds if they weren't to serve a purpose? And if someone did go to the trouble, then it's only right we should

271

use them for what they were intended. That's the way I look at it, anyway. I wouldn't want the poor man to think he'd wasted his time.'

Corker thought Nellie was hilarious, but then Corker had spent most of his life going to sea, and sailors did have very open minds. So to spare Molly's blushes, he turned the conversation away from beds and bedrooms. 'Do yer want to know what Jack and I were up to last night, Nellie, and how it came about?'

Nellie leaned forward so fast, she bumped her bosom on the edge of the table and grimaced. 'Bloody things, always in the way. If God had given a little more thought when he was making us, He'd have put them on our backs, out of the way.' Then she changed her mind. 'No, God was right. We couldn't have fed the babies if they'd been at the back.' She grinned across the table. 'Go on, Corker, lad, what are yer waiting for? Ye're not half slow for the size of yer.'

'It's been hard to get a word in edgeways, Nellie, but I have to admit it's been interesting in a strange sort of way. I'd never given much thought to Florence Nightingale before, or to the man who invented beds, but I'll be passing all I've learned on to Ellen. I'm sure she'll be very interested.' Corker was being very tactful. For if he told his wife half of the things Nellie had come out with, she'd either say he was making it up, or laugh herself sick. 'Anyway, let me tell you what happened last night. Jack can add things as we go along.'

The tale took half an hour in the telling, and for the first time in living memory, Nellie never uttered one word. She was as quiet as a mouse. But her expressions and gestures spoke volumes. When Corker talked about how he pulled the robber down off the wall, Nellie's arms did a pulling down movement, and she curled her hand into a fist and punched the air as though belting the man. Her movements distracted Corker and Jack for a while, but they soon got used to it and thought it funny. In fact they found themselves waiting for her reaction to their words and gestures.

'Well, that's about it, ladies,' Jack said, putting a hand on his wife's arm. 'Due to my dear wife's intuition, me and Corker were able to prevent Mrs Reagan's house from being ransacked. Don't yer think that makes us heroes, Nellie? You, me and Corker, we should form a club.'

'Yer would have been a hero if yer'd done the job proper, lad, but yer didn't. Yer let the bugger go free, instead of taking him to the police. He'll be out robbing someone's house tonight, all because yer let him get off with it! He must be laughing his bleeding head off! If I'd have been there he wouldn't have got off scot free.'

'We couldn't take him to the police, Nellie, because the first thing they'd do would be to visit Mrs Reagan, check her entry door for any marks, or signs on the wall. And we didn't want the old lady to know anything about it. She's had a bad shock and we didn't want her to get another one. At least we put the fear of God into the bloke. He'll not come within a mile of here in the future.'

'Yer could have given him a black eye.' Nellie

273

was all for revenge. 'I would have done if I'd been there. In fact I'd be so mad with him, I'd have given him two black eyes and a broken nose. See how he likes being picked on.'

'Well it's over with now, sunshine, so all we have to worry about is Mrs Reagan. We'll call round in the morning to see if she's all right, and if she needs any shopping,' Molly said. 'Although I think Hilda will be keeping a watchful eye on her. They'll be good for each other. And who knows, sunshine, the accident may turn out to be a blessing in disguise. The two old ladies might spend more time together, go to the shops or for a walk in the park.'

'That's true, girl, they'll be company for each other. We could call there in the morning before we go to the shops, eh?'

Corker had been keeping his eye on the clock. He didn't want to look as though he was rushing away, but he'd been planning to take Jack for a pint or two. And he thought of a way of getting what he wanted without feeling selfish or guilty. He stood up to put a hand in his pocket, brought out a two shilling piece and placed it on the table. 'This is not blackmail, Molly, me darlin', it was a case of having two thoughts at once. I'd like, with your permission, to take Jack for a pint before the pub closes, and I'd like you to buy some cakes with that two bob, and take them with yer when yer go to Rita's. Have a cake and a cup of tea on me. There's enough there for a cake each, isn't there?'

It was a beaming Nellie who told him, 'Ay, Corker, I've just counted on me fingers, and we can buy eight cakes with two bob. That means two each for the four of us.'

Molly chuckled. 'It's a good job yer didn't give her five bob, Corker, 'cos she'd have run out of fingers.'

'Oh, aye, Mrs Sarcastic, have yer forgotten I've got toes as well? I don't see them very often, like, but I'm on wiggling terms with them. Except the little toe on me left foot. I don't get on with that at all because it's got a ruddy corn on it.'

Corker pushed Jack towards the door, 'Come on, or they'll be putting the towel over before we get there.' He turned to Molly. 'I'd give up if I were you, me darlin', 'cos yer'll never get the last word with Nellie.'

Molly hurried to the door after him. 'Corker, it's a bit late to ask, but why didn't Ellen come with yer?'

'Paul arrived just before I came out, and I left him sitting at the table with Phoebe and Ellen. I think they're sorting bridesmaids out, and making lists of things they have to do. I don't have to tell you what a lot has to be thought of when arranging a wedding, yer've done it often enough. Anyway, they'll have called time before me and Jack wet our whistle, so we're going to scarper. Ta-ra.'

Molly was walking back to the living room when Nellie confronted her. 'I'll go now, girl, 'cos I don't want to miss what's going on next door. Our Paul didn't tell me he was going to Phoebe's to make lists out. I'll have missed most of it now, and our Paul will only tell me bits and pieces, yer know what men are like.'

'Yes, I do, sunshine, they're not nosy like us women. But I think it's late for yer to be calling next door. Phoebe and Paul have been to see Father Kelly and got the date they wanted for the wedding, and they've booked Hanley's hall. They can't give guests numbers yet because they haven't had time to make a list. So why don't yer leave it for tonight? Ellen will be tired, 'cos yer know she works all day. So have another cup of tea with me, and yer'll find out what arrangements they've made when they've made them.'

Nellie was very reluctant, for she hated to miss anything, but she walked back into the living room under Molly's gentle persuasion. 'Our Paul's a dark horse, girl. He never mentioned he was going next door.'

Molly pressed her down on to her carver chair. 'He didn't go next door, as yer put it, sunshine, he went to the home of his girlfriend. Phoebe, his future wife.'

'Well, that's next door, isn't it?' Nellie failed to see the difference. 'He could have told me.'

'Then what a predicament yer'd have been in, sunshine. Yer'd have had to make a choice. Here or next door!'

'Oh, what's the use, I can't win! Go and put the bleeding kettle on, girl, before I cut me throat.'

Molly burst out laughing. 'Yer'd have to go home to do that, sunshine, 'cos I haven't got a sharp knife.'

Chapter Twelve

When Nellie called the next morning, she moved her carver chair to the table and plonked herself down. Molly had walked through to the kitchen and was striking a match under the kettle when Nellie shouted through. 'We all slept in this morning, girl, the ruddy alarm clock didn't go off. I've never seen George in such a bad temper as when he was struggling to get into his trousers. He doesn't swear, as yer know, but the air was blue this morning. He called me all the names under the sun for not setting the clock. Him and Paul only had a mouthful of tea and a jam butty, and I didn't have time to do their carry-out.'

Molly popped her head in. 'Oh, dear, they wouldn't be very happy with a jam butty, would they? It's not much to start a day's work on.'

'They'll manage, girl, don't worry about that. Both of them are good eaters, they love their tummies. They'll cadge off their mates until dinnertime, and then they'll get something from the canteen. It won't kill them for once.'

The kettle began to whistle and Molly disappeared to switch the gas off and pour the water into the teapot. 'I'll let it stand for a few minutes, sunshine.' She stood inside the living room and looked down at the glum face on her mate. 'What made yer forget to set the alarm, Nellie? That's not like you. I know yer've done it before, but that was ages ago.'

'Well, I was tired when I left here last night and it slipped me mind.' Nellie jerked her head in disgust, sending her chins in all directions. 'Anyway, George should have made sure, for it's him what has to go to work.'

'Yes, sunshine, it's him what's got to go to work, and it's him what brings the wages home. Yer can't have it both ways, yer have to share, give and take. Anyway, I'll bring the tea in and that might cheer yer up a bit. Yer look down in the dumps.'

'A cup of tea will cheer me up, girl, ye're right. And if there's two custard creams in the saucer, I'll be twice cheered up.' Nellie frowned. 'That doesn't sound right, girl, does it? Twice cheered up? Nah, I'll stick to saying I'll be very happy and yer'll know what I mean.'

'Yer getting all tongue-twisted now, sunshine, so why don't yer skip how yer feel and enjoy the tea when it comes. And I'm pretty sure I can run to two biscuits each.'

Nellie sighed. 'Like I said to yer the other day, girl, life can be a bugger sometimes.'

Molly came through with a cup and saucer in each hand, and the steam was rising from the cups. 'I couldn't be bothered setting the tray, it just makes more work for meself. And as for life, Nellie, well it's better than having no life. It's up to us to do the best we can with it.'

Nellie's chins weren't expecting her head to give a sharp shake, and they weren't very happy with her. If she'd only given them notice they could have been prepared. 'I can't agree with yer today, girl, I'm not in the best of moods. You wouldn't be, either, if yer'd heard the way George carried on. And if he starts off when he comes in from work, he'll get the dinner thrown at him.'

'That's a bit drastic, sunshine, and a waste of good food,' Molly said. 'What about Paul, was he in a temper?'

'No, girl, our Paul never gets in a temper. He just took things in his stride. He even gave me a kiss when he was going out of the door, like he always does. And d'yer know what, Molly? He even whispered in me ear that the day could only get better. It was on the tip of me tongue to say that it couldn't get any bleeding worse, but I didn't because he was only trying to cheer me up.'

'He's a good lad is your Paul, always happy and smiling. He's settled down a lot now, and he'll make Phoebe a good husband. One thing she can be sure of, she'll never be short of laughter 'cos he takes after you for cracking jokes.' Molly leaned forward. 'And yer've got a good husband in George. Yer can't blame him for being a bit bad-tempered this morning, because like Jack, he doesn't like being late for work. So bear that in mind, and when he comes in tonight put yer arms round him and give him a big hug and kiss. He'd like that, and it would clear the air.'

Nellie huffed and puffed. 'Oh, he'd like it all right, girl, but he ain't going to get it. It's him what should hug and kiss me, and say he's sorry for being so bad-tempered.'

'Ye're not going to like me for saying this, sunshine, but yer can be a bit childish at times.

Yer can't have everything yer own way, and George has spoilt yer by being too lenient with yer. Me and Jack never argue or fall out, because we share and share alike. I know how much is in his wage packet every week, and how much I get from him to buy all the food for the week. I put me rent away first, that's the most important, having a roof over our head. Then money gets put by for gas and electric. And Jack is quite happy to have a couple of bob in his pocket for his ciggies and the odd pint of beer he has during the week. Me and him are quite happy with our lot. We love each other, adore our children, and I thank God I've still got me ma and da.'

'Don't be bragging, girl! Anyone would think yer were the only one with a loving husband, and kids that are adored. I love my kids as much as you do, and there are times when my husband is very loving. I bet he beats your Jack hands down when it comes to love and passion.'

Molly grinned. 'That's better, sunshine, more like yer old self. And I'll let yer off bringing yer bedroom into the conversation 'cos yer haven't mentioned it much lately. Which I have appreciated.' She reached over for Nellie's empty cup and saucer. 'And now ye're looking a bit more like yer old self, I think it's time we were on our way. I'd like to call to Rita's first, make sure she's all right, and then come back and call in on Doreen and Jill before we go shopping. Does that arrangement suit you, sunshine?'

'Down to the ground, girl, down to the ground.'

'Right, well, I'll stick these in the sink and we'll

280

be on our way. And keep our fingers crossed that Rita's had a good night's sleep, and is none the worse for her ordeal.'

The two mates cut through two side streets to save time, and just over five minutes after closing Molly's door they were knocking on Rita's. There was no answer to the first knock, and Molly shrugged her shoulders. 'Perhaps she's in the back and can't hear us.'

'I'd think it's a safe bet she's next door.' Nellie didn't like hanging around and she rapped on Hilda's window. As usual it wasn't a light rap; it shook the windowpane. And Hilda came out of the door shaking a fist, thinking a youngster was playing tricks.

'Where did he go?' Hilda, her lips tight and her eyes narrowed to slits, looked up and down the street. 'Which way did he go? I'll have his ruddy guts for garters.'

As innocent as a child, Nellie asked, 'Where did who go, girl?'

'Whoever banged on me window and nearly broke it, that's who. Gave me and Rita the fright of our lives. Yer must have seen him, he's probably run down one of the entries. I don't know how you two could miss him, he must have only been inches from yer.'

'Yer keep saying "he", Hilda,' Molly said, wondering how her mate was going to talk her way out of this. 'What makes yer think it was a lad?'

'Because there's a couple of scallywags in the street what bunk off school, queen, that's why. The mothers let them run wild.'

Nellie's brain was working overtime. 'It was

probably a gust of wind, girl, and it rattled the pane of glass. My window often does the same thing.'

Molly couldn't get over the likeness between the two women. They'd pass for twins. Equal in height and weight, if it came to a fight with blows exchanged, they'd knock each other out with the first punch. The only difference Molly could see between the two women was that Hilda wasn't crafty like Nellie. For her mate's face was really angelic when she blamed the wind for the window's rattling.

'There's no ruddy wind out!' Hilda glared at Nellie, thinking she was having her leg pulled. 'There's not even a breeze!' She looked at Molly. 'Did you see any lads, Molly?'

Thanking her lucky stars that the question had been asked in such a way that she didn't need to tell a lie, Molly shook her head. 'There's been no lads here, Hilda, not that I saw. The street's been empty while we've been here, not a soul in sight.' She looked at Nellie, willing her to tell the truth and save a lot of bother, but her mate was quite unperturbed. After all, what was the point of asking for trouble? 'Not a soul, sunshine, not a soul.'

Hilda's arms dropped to her sides. 'Well, queen, it's a blinking mystery, that's all I can say.'

Changing the conversation completely, Molly asked, 'Is Rita still with yer, sunshine? We have knocked but didn't get an answer.'

'Well, yer wouldn't, queen, because she's sitting at me table finishing her breakfast off. She slept like a log all night. Went to bed at half past eight last night because it had been a hard day for her and she was worn out. And she slept right through until half past ten this morning.'

'Oh, that's marvellous news, Hilda,' Molly said. 'Thank God she's got a neighbour like you.'

Hilda jerked her head, and as her chins swayed they said 'Hello' to Nellie's chins, making friends, like. 'Come on in and see her for yerselves. She's probably finished her breakfast now, and she'd be delighted to see yer. She spent most of yesterday singing yer praises. Go on, get in, I don't stand on ceremony.'

Rita was really pleased to see them, and she made such a fuss, the window incident was forgotten. She waited until they were seated, then said, 'I have never slept so long in all my life. I couldn't believe it when Hilda woke me and said it was half past ten! When I'm in me own house next door, I toss and turn for ages before I drop off, and then I only sleep in fits and starts. Hilda has been really kind. I can't thank her enough. That long sleep has done me good; I feel much better and more light-hearted.'

'That's with having company, sunshine, someone to talk to,' Molly said. 'And you look fine to me, which has set my mind at rest.'

'Yes, yer look ten years younger, girl,' Nellie said, trying to make up for the window episode. She knew she would get a lecture off Molly as soon as they got outside, and she was trying hard to butter her mate up. Not that she thought she'd done anything bad enough to warrant the fuss that Hilda made. It was only a ruddy window, after all, and no real harm was done. But she wasn't going to say that to Molly, she was going to be very diplomatic and watch her words. 'Don't yer think Rita looks a lot younger, girl?'

Molly was aware of Nellie's tactics, but this wasn't the place to say so. She'd wait until they were on their own. 'Yes, she looks very well. Thanks to Hilda for having a spare bed – it certainly came in handy last night.'

Hilda was leaning back against the sideboard, a chubby finger making circles in the fat on her elbows. 'She's staying here tonight as well. Rita was against it when I suggested she stay, because she thinks she's being a nuisance, but I enjoyed having her company. It was a change from talking to the wallpaper. So I'm glad she's agreed to stay, for my sake and her own. Another decent night's sleep will do her the world of good.'

'Me and Molly are going to the shops,' Nellie told her, for the sake of getting in her mate's good books. 'We can get yer shopping for yer if yer like?'

Hilda shook her head. 'Thanks all the same, queen, but me and Rita were talking while we were having our breakfast, and we decided we'd go to Walton Park and have a walk around. Just for half an hour, like, I don't want her tiring herself out. On the way back we'll call at the shops.' She leaned over the table and patted Rita on the shoulder. 'We haven't decided what to have for our dinner yet, queen, have we? We've considered making a stew with mince and vegetables, or perhaps buying a nice piece of fish for a change.'

'Oh, it's nice to hear that,' Molly said. Then, forgetting she was angry with Nellie, she said,

'I'm really pleased for the pair of yer, aren't you, Nellie?'

Her mate's face was a joy to behold, and she hastened to agree. 'Ye're right, girl, I think it's smashing. And just think, if they make a stew for the two of them, it'll only cost them half the price it would if they made one each.'

Hilda and Rita looked at each other with surprise, until Molly enlightened them. 'Nellie often comes out with her pearls of wisdom, ladies, and although they don't always make sense, she means well. And it's not a bad idea anyway, when yer come to think of it.'

'I think it's a good idea, Hilda,' Rita said. 'We could share a pan of stew, rather than me making one in my house and you making one here. Think of the gas it would save, and the washing up.'

Nellie's rising bosom told Molly her mate was getting excited about something she was cooking up in her head. 'Ay, Rita, you and Hilda could be another Molly and Nellie! Mates what do everything together and share things! Ooh, ay, wouldn't that be good?'

It was Hilda's bosom that rose now, but it was with laughter. 'In case yer haven't noticed, queen, me and Rita are twice your age. Ye're only youngsters compared to us.'

'Not quite twice our age, Hilda,' Molly said, 'although I admit there is quite a difference. But that doesn't count if ye're still young at heart. I wouldn't expect the pair of yer to do cartwheels down the street, mind you, or run after a bus. But ye're both lively and could get a lot out of life if yer did it at yer own speed.' Molly was warming to the idea of the two elderly women enjoying each other's company instead of knowing only loneliness. 'I'm not trying to push you into anything, for yer've got minds of yer own that are far more intelligent than mine.'

'I wouldn't say that, queen, not about meself. I think Rita's got a good head on her shoulders, though. She had a better education than me.'

Nellie snorted, 'Yer don't have to be clever to be friends. Look at me and Molly! I'm as thick as two short planks, and she's a right clever clogs. Yer should hear some of the words she comes out with! Yer'd think she was talking in a foreign language. But for all that she's clever, and I'm as soft as a brush, we've been mates for nearly twenty-five years. And when we get to your age, we'll still be best mates.'

'Don't tempt fate, sunshine,' Molly chuckled. 'I think by the time I'm eighty, you'll have worn me out.'

Hilda suddenly remembered her manners. 'What am I thinking of, leaving yer sitting there! I'll make a fresh pot of tea. Yer must think me very inhospitable not asking yer as soon as yer came. But we've done that much talking it took me mind off me manners.'

Molly caught hold of Hilda's arm as she bustled towards the kitchen. 'Don't make any tea for us, sunshine, because we had two cups before we came out, and we're going to me daughter's from here, where we'll be getting more!'

Nellie's chins were the first to agree, and they were swaying when she said, 'After that we're going on to yer other daughter's, girl, don't forget, and that means another drink! I'll be wanting to go to the lavvy every five minutes.'

'Are yer sure yer won't have a cup?' Rita asked. 'Ye're more than welcome.'

'No thank you, sunshine. We only came round to make sure you were all right, and we can see ye're being well looked after by Hilda. So we'll love yer and leave yer. We'll call in and see yer again in a couple of days, but yer know where we live if yer need anything.' Molly stood behind Rita's chair and hugged her gently before kissing her on the cheek. 'I hope you and Hilda have a nice walk in the park, but don't overdo it.'

While Nellie was saying goodbye to Rita, Hilda followed Molly out to the door. 'Yer don't need to worry about anything, queen, 'cos I'll make sure Rita's all right. I know she'll want to go back to her house tomorrow, and I can understand that, 'cos there's no place like home. But she can sleep here any time she likes, and from now on we'll see more of each other than we have done in the past.'

Molly looked down into the chubby face and cupped it in her hands. 'Ye're a lovely, kind woman, sunshine, and I'm glad I made your acquaintance. Thank you for looking after Rita, and make sure yer take care of yerself 'cos good people are hard to come by.'

Nellie's head appeared over Hilda's shoulder, and what happened next had Molly doubled up with laughter. For Nellie tried to get past Hilda, and the two eighteen-stone women got stuck in the door frame. Their bosoms and their tummies were the sticking point, and both women struggled till they were red in the face. And while Molly was holding the stitch in her side, she was wishing she had a camera, for Jack and Ruthie would never believe this, and it was the one time she couldn't impersonate her mate.

'My God, Hilda,' Nellie puffed, 'yer haven't half got a big tummy. It sticks out a mile!'

Hilda's mouth gaped. 'Ye're a fine one to talk, queen, 'cos yours is twice the size of mine! The very cheek of yer! And why did yer have to try and pass me? Why didn't yer ask me to move out of the way?'

'Because me mate is waiting for me, that's why!' Nellie was sweating now. 'And she doesn't like to be kept waiting, especially when we've got calls to go on.'

Molly wiped the tears of laughter away before suggesting, 'If yer would both keep calm it would make it a lot easier. Just cool down and give it some thought, instead of getting yerselves all het up.'

'It's all right for you to talk, queen,' Hilda said. 'If I was standing where you are I'd be as cool as a cucumber. It's Nellie's bust what's in the way, it's squashing mine and it doesn't feel very pleasant.'

This didn't help matters because Nellie got on her high horse and took her tummy and bosom with her. 'Well, that's very nice I must say! Ye're not the only one getting squashed, girl, so don't be feeling sorry for yerself.'

Molly raised her voice when she called, 'That's it, enough is enough. I know ye're very fond of yer voluptuous body, Nellie, but will yer try and put it to good use for once, instead of bragging about it. And as ye're younger than Hilda, I suggest yer show her the respect she deserves. So, while she stands still, will you put both of yer hands flat on yer tummy and press it in. With a bit of luck and the right actions, it should be enough to separate the pair of yer. And Hilda, will yer use your hands to flatten yer bosom, please, 'cos every little helps.' Molly tried very hard to keep her face straight, as the neighbours walking past were giving the two women some funny looks. After all, it would take some believing that two women could get stuck in a doorway. Molly wouldn't have believed it herself if she hadn't seen it with her own eyes.

'Thank God for that.' Nellie blew out a sigh of relief. 'I can breathe now.'

'It's you what caused the trouble,' Hilda told her, 'so don't expect any sympathy from me.'

'Yer should have got out of me way,' Nellie said, 'so yer were as much to blame as me. Don't you go saying it was all my fault, 'cos it wasn't.' She ran a hand over her breasts. 'I'm sore now.'

'Serves yer right.' Hilda wasn't going to sympathize, not when she was feeling embarrassed that some of the neighbours had witnessed the indignity. 'Perhaps yer'll be more careful in future, and not throw yer weight around.'

Molly decided to call a truce. 'Excuse me, ladies, for butting in, but I have work to do, and calls to make, even if you haven't. And because ye're both looking as though yer want to throttle each other, I'm going to say something I think is very funny. If yer don't laugh, I'll think ye're both past redemption and I'll give up on yer.'

'Oh, I'll laugh, girl, 'cos I like to hear a good joke.' Nellie had a horrible feeling she was in for a lecture as soon as they left Hilda's, and if it meant crawling to get back in her mate's good books, then crawl she would. 'I don't know about Hilda, but I'll laugh.'

'Yer haven't heard what Molly's got to say, queen, so how d'yer know it'll make yer laugh? I'll wait until I hear it before I say anything.' Hilda nodded to Molly. 'Go on, queen, I could do with a good laugh.'

'It came to me when I saw the two of yer stuck together,' Molly said. 'And I thought I'd ask yer if yer'd ever consider being bosom pals?'

It was Hilda who got the joke first, and she gave Nellie a dig. 'Oh, ay, queen, I think that's very funny.' Her eyes disappeared as her well-endowed body shook with laughter. 'Where's yer sense of humour, Nellie? Don't yer get it? Bosom pals, that's you and me. But I still say yours are bigger than mine.'

It was then the penny dropped, and Molly was delighted when the two women clung to each other, their laughter loud and contagious. It brought Rita out from the living room to see what the hilarity was about. 'What's going on? Will yer let me in on the joke, please?'

'Oh, Rita, queen, I'm sorry but yer haven't got the right figure to be a bosom pal. Yer have to be fat and dumpy.'

'Ay, you speak for yerself.' Nellie pretended to be indignant. 'I'm not fat and dumpy. Yer can ask my husband, and he'll tell yer I'm just right. He doesn't like skinny women, he likes them with plenty of flesh to get hold of.'

Rita tutted. 'There's nothing down for me, then. I was always thin, right from being a child. Still, it never did me any harm. I'm still alive and kicking, thanks to Nellie.'

'Oh, don't start her off on that, Mrs Reagan,' Molly said, 'or I'll have to listen to her bragging all day. She's not one of those people who does someone a good turn and then walks away before the person has a chance to thank them. Not my mate, no, she's not like that. She is most definitely not a shy heroine.'

'I might not be shy, Molly Bennett, but I am a heroine, what you will never be. And yer better watch what yer say to me in future, as well, 'cos I've got another mate now, and that's my bosom pal, what has a bigger tummy than I have, but not such a voluptuous body.'

'To each his own, queen,' Hilda said. 'Some men like their women thin, others like them fat. Then yer have the men who like them just right, like Molly is.'

Nellie glared at her. 'Ay, ye're supposed to be my bosom pal, so don't be trying to get pally with Molly.'

'Let's say we're all good friends, sunshine, with no favourites, and then we can be on our way. We only came round to see how Rita is, and that must be at least three-quarters of an hour ago. At this rate, it'll be time to go to bed before we've got our shopping in.' Molly stepped forward and kissed the two elderly women. 'You two get yerselves out for some fresh air. And take care of each other.'

291

'We will, queen, don't worry.' Hilda linked Rita's arm as they stood on the step. 'Ye're welcome any time.'

Molly nodded. 'Oh, yer haven't seen the last of us, but it's ta-ra for now.'

Nellie put her arm through Molly's. 'Ay, that bosom pals was good, girl. Where did yer get that from? It just suited me and Hilda down to the ground.'

'Yeah, but the point is, sunshine, yer never tell lies to yer bosom pal. Well, most people don't, anyway.'

'I didn't tell no lies, Molly Bennett, and yer can't say I did!'

'Yer might not have told a lie, sunshine, but yer acted one and that's just the same.'

'How can yer act a lie, girl?'

'You should know that better than me, because I've never acted a lie, but you have.'

'When did I do that, Molly Bennett? If ye're trying to pull me leg, I don't think it's very funny.'

'Hilda didn't think it was very funny when her window nearly went in. And instead of telling her the truth, that it was you who banged on it, yer kept quiet. And that is what I mean by acting a lie! Instead of letting her think it was a lad in the street, yer should have come out right away and told her it was you.'

'Ooh, I couldn't do that 'cos she was in a right temper and she'd have clocked me one.'

'No, she wouldn't, because unlike you she isn't the fighting type. She wouldn't have been pleased with yer for giving her a fright and nearly breaking her window, but she'd have got over it in a few minutes. That would have been the honest thing to do.'

They were turning into their Street when Nellie spoke again. 'Shall we go back, girl, and I'll tell her the truth?'

'You're not soft, sunshine, I'll say that for yer. Yer may be many things, like sly and crafty, but never soft. Yer know damn well I'll say we can't go all the way back there because we're late as it is. The girls will think we're not coming, and I want to see the babies before they take them for a walk.' Molly looked down at her mate. 'It was a good try though, sunshine. But what yer could do to make up for it is have a word tonight with your friend St Peter. Tell him what yer did, and see if he'll forgive yer.'

'Oh, he will, girl, I know he will. After all, that's what friends are for, isn't it? But I won't tell him about being bosom pals with Hilda, 'cos he might not understand, him being a saint. D'yer know what I mean, like?'

'Oh, I think so, sunshine, I think so. But we're near Doreen's now, and I don't think Victoria would understand either. D'yer know what I mean, like?'

Chapter Thirteen

'Ye're late, Mam,' Doreen said when she opened the door. 'Me and Jill have waited, wondering where yer'd got to.' She grinned at Nellie. 'What have you and me mam been up to, Auntie Nellie? Been leading her astray, have yer?'

'The days of me going astray are long gone, girl, worse luck.' Nellie brushed past her and made for the living room. 'The only excitement I get is when yer mam tells me off for making a show of her.'

'I don't see Jill's pram outside,' Molly said, kissing her daughter's cheek. 'Is she not going out with yer?'

'Come in so I can close the door.' Doreen pushed Molly into the living room, where Jill was sitting on the couch nursing little Moll. 'We're only taking the one pram with us. Bobby is big enough to sit up now, so Moll can lie on the pillows and it saves taking both prams to the shops.'

'Hello, sunshine.' Molly hugged her eldest daughter, but was careful not to crush the baby, who tugged on her heartstrings every time she saw her, for she was the image of the three Bennett girls when they were her age. Sparse blonde hair, and eyes as blue as the sky on a summer's day. She was very dainty, but all there when it came to knowing who her grandma Bennett was, and her grandma Nellie. She was gurgling now, her arms flailing to be lifted up. 'Wait until I put me bag down, sunshine, and take me coat off. Then we can have a big cuddle.'

Molly was draping her coat over the arm of the couch when she asked, 'Where's Bobby?'

'He's in the pram in the yard,' Doreen told her. 'Now he's walking around the furniture, he won't leave little Moll alone. As quick as I take him away from her, he crawls back and pulls himself up by the chairs.'

Molly smiled down at the baby who was trying to free herself from Jill's arms. 'Wait until I've said hello to Victoria, then I'll give yer a big cuddle and a swing.'

'We've been watching out of the window for yer, Molly.' Victoria Clegg was loved by everyone, old and young alike, and was always treated with respect because she was a real lady. She accepted Molly's kiss with a smile. 'Are yer not going to tell us what you and Nellie have been up to? We could do with a laugh.'

'We went round to see how Mrs Reagan was, and I'm happy to say she's fine. It would take too long to tell yer the whole tale, except that Nellie has a new bosom pal. And when I say bosom, I really mean it. For although Mrs Reagan's neighbour, Hilda, is an elderly lady, she still has a bosom as big as Nellie's. In fact she is so like my mate they could be twins, except for the difference in their ages.'

Nellie's eyes were shooting daggers. 'Are you hinsinuating that a woman of eighty has the same voluptuous body as what I've got? Yer must need yer eyes testing if yer didn't see the difference between me and Hilda. How can she look as good as me when she's thirty years older?' Nellie saw Molly's lips move, and she held up a hand to silence her mate. 'Oh, I know she's a very nice lady and all that, but she's not a patch on me. You put her in bed with my George, and he'd soon tell yer the difference.'

'I'm sure he could, sunshine, but that sort of conversation between me and your husband will never arise, so yer can forget it.'

Nellie looked down at Victoria, her hands spread out, and in an appealing voice she asked, 'What would yer do if yer had a mate what didn't stick up for yer, Victoria? Would yer tell her she should support her mate, or tell her to sod off, 'cos yer've found another pal? One what is a bosom pal?'

Victoria tried not to smile, but she couldn't stop her mouth twitching. 'If yer have a good mate, Nellie, then ye're very lucky and should appreciate her. Not everyone is blessed with a true friend; they are hard to come by, and should be treasured. It's better the devil that yer know, than the devil you don't know.'

'Now I didn't say nothing about no devil, Victoria, so don't be making things more comycated than what they are.'

Doreen had brought Bobby in from his pram, and she was seated at the table with him on her knee, next to Jill and little Moll. Both babies were eager to escape and they were making it plain by lashing out and gurgling. They could see and hear their grannies, and wanted to be picked up and cuddled and tickled. So Jill and Doreen were trying to keep them quiet, for the sisters didn't want to miss Auntie Nellie when she was in full flow.

'Now you're a clever woman, Victoria, and I'd like some advice from yer. And don't take no notice of the looks I'm getting off Molly Bennett, 'cos I don't want her giving you signals.'

'All right, Nellie,' Victoria said, 'I won't look at Molly. I'll keep my eyes averted.'

'Oh, there's no need to do that, Victoria.' Nellie patted a frail hand. 'Just don't look at her.' When there was a burst of laughter, the little woman tutted. 'They haven't got no manners they haven't, so don't take no notice of them.'

Oh, how Victoria Clegg loved it when Molly and Nellie called, for they really brightened up her days. 'Now, how can I help you with your dilemma, Nellie?'

Nellie blinked several times, wondering why Victoria had used that word what sounded foreign. Why couldn't she use English, what everyone understood? Never mind, she could pretend she did understand and no one would know any difference. 'Well, it's like this, yer see, girl. If you were in my shoes, which I know ye're not, like, but pretend yer are. Well, what I want you to tell me is, if yer had to choose between two mates, one what used big words, and one what had a big bosom, which one would yer choose?'

Doreen and Jill decided they'd be better in the kitchen if they wanted to release their laughter. So holding their babies close to their chests, they made themselves scarce. But Bobby and little

Moll didn't approve, so mothers and children ended up in the yard and they missed Victoria's reply. They'd have to wait and ask their mother later.

'That decision would be an easy one for me, sweetheart,' Victoria told Nellie, 'because I would choose the one I believed would be a true and loyal friend for life.' A soft laugh left her mouth before she went on, 'I wouldn't choose a friend by the size of their vocabulary, or their breasts.'

Nellie nodded after a short deliberation. 'That's just what I thought meself, Victoria, and Molly is always telling me that great minds think alike.' She pushed herself up, squared her back, stood her bosom to attention, and gave her head three quick shakes, waking her sleeping chins. Walking to the window, which looked out on the yard, she rapped on the pane and wagged a finger, asking Doreen and Jill to come back into the house.

Molly had been sitting at the table through all this, leaning on her elbows and telling herself they'd miss the butcher's the way things were going. Still, Nellie was enjoying herself so why worry? She smiled when she remembered the old saying that you die if you worry, you die if you don't, so why worry at all?

'What is it, Auntie Nellie?' Jill asked. 'Is it anything to do with the wedding?'

Doreen chipped in, her face aglow with excitement. 'Ay, it's not half going to be some wedding from the sound of things. Phoebe and your Paul are really going to make it the wedding of the year.'

'With Uncle Corker's help,' Jill reminded her. 'They both said he's going the whole hog on it,

298

no expense spared.'

'Don't you two start!' Nellie glared at the sisters. 'I've had me leg pulled enough for one day. And just because ye're married to our Steve, Jill Bennett, doesn't mean I can't clock yer one.'

'Jill McDonough, she is now, Nellie, seeing as she married into yer family,' Molly said. 'And if I were you I wouldn't dream of clocking her one, because I wouldn't take kindly to it. In fact I'd be forced to clock yer one back.'

'No yer wouldn't, girl, not when I tell yer I've made up me mind that I don't want no one else for me best friend, I want to stay best mates with you. I know yer haven't got big breasts, but mine are big enough for both of us.'

'Oh, that's taken a load off my mind, sunshine. For a while there I thought yer were going to drop me as yer best mate. And while at first I didn't know whether to be glad or sorry, I finally told meself I've put up with yer for half of me lifetime, so I may as well stay the course to the bitter end, even if it's only out of curiosity.'

'I knew it would end up like this, girl, 'cos yer'd miss me too much. I mean, like, what would yer do at half past ten every morning if I didn't call to yours?'

'Sit with me feet up on the couch, sunshine, with a cup and saucer in me hand and four biscuits on the saucer.' Molly grinned at Nellie's expression. 'Yes, sunshine, with you not expected I could take life easy, eat your share of the biscuits, and I wouldn't call the King me aunt!'

'The King couldn't be yer aunt, girl, 'cos he's a man.'

'Oh, of course he is, sunshine, aren't I silly. That's a very useful piece of information, Nellie, and I'll bear it in mind.'

Molly turned to her two daughters. 'Now me and Nellie have got our relationship sorted out, can we go back to what yer were saying about the wedding?'

The sisters exchanged glances. 'You go first, Doreen,' Jill said, 'but leave me a little bit to tell them, 'cos I'm as excited as you.'

'Let me take the baby off yer, sunshine, give you a little break, and me a chance to cuddle me granddaughter.'

Not to be outdone, Nellie held her arms out for Bobby. 'Come on, lad, come to yer grandma McDonough.'

The two children were delighted and shrieked with excitement. 'Oh, we'll not be able to hear ourselves think,' Molly said, hugging little Moll close. 'I suggest giving her a dummy for a while to keep her quiet, while you bring us up to date on what yer know about the wedding plans.'

'I've got a better idea,' Doreen told her. 'They're both due for a bottle, so that will keep them quiet. The bottles are made up already, 'cos we were going to feed them before we went out to the shops.'

'Won't they be cold by now?' Molly asked. 'Yer don't want them getting colds in their tummies.'

Doreen put her hands on the table, but before pushing herself up she grinned at her mother. 'Mam, I remember yer once told me to "Go and teach yer grandma how to milk ducks". Well, you saying that Bobby would get a cold in his tummy brought it to mind. I do know how to look after my baby, Mam. I'm a wife and mother now, not the selfish, mouthy tearaway I was years ago.'

Nellie pursed her lips and nodded her head. 'That's telling her, girl! My mate forgets you and Jill have yer own families now, and ye're both doing a good job.'

'I haven't forgotten, sunshine, it's just that I haven't the heart to cut the strings that bind. And I don't think I ever will, so ye're going to have to put up with me meddling in your lives.'

Doreen leaned across the table and kissed her. 'Mam, the day you stop meddling in my life will be a very sad day for me.'

Jill was quick to agree. 'And me! Yer can interfere as much as yer like, Mam, because I know you only want what's best for us.' She had always been the most gentle of Molly's three daughters, and she still was. And now her pretty face shone with the love she felt for her mother. 'Like now, you are right about the babies' bottles being cold. We need to stand them in pans of hot water to warm them up.'

'I'll do it, Jill, you stay there,' Doreen said before looking at Nellie, who had been listening with interest. 'I suppose yer know it's your fault that the babies' feed has gone cold, don't yer? If yer hadn't spent so much time making up yer mind about who to have for a best mate, they would have been fed by now, and we'd be discussing the news about the wedding.'

Nellie's shoulders were squared before she faced Molly. 'Are you going to sit there and let yer daughter talk to me like that?'

'Well, I'm not going to stand and let her talk to yer like that, Nellie. And neither am I going to say she shouldn't have said what she did, because it's the truth! No one could get a word in edgeways 'cos yer didn't even stop for breath.'

'Oh, I must have stopped for breath, girl, otherwise I wouldn't be alive to tell the tale. I'd be flat out on the floor, making the place look untidy.'

Doreen slipped out to stand the bottles in a pan of water on the stove, and she chuckled when she heard her mam say, 'Not another tale, sunshine, for heaven's sake! Where do yer get them all from? It wouldn't be so bad if yer were a donkey, we could cut yer tale off.'

Nellie appealed to Victoria, who was rocking gently as she listened to the exchanges. 'Now was that a nice thing to say about a mate, Victoria? I'm cut to the quick, I really am.'

'I'll not get involved, Nellie, but I have to say I am enjoying listening to the various conversations,' Victoria told her. 'It is the spice of life for me, seeing as I seldom go over the threshold these days.'

Doreen came in carrying a feeding bottle in each hand. 'These are just the right temperature, so we should have about twenty minutes of peace.' She passed one over to Jill, then asked Nellie, 'D'yer want to feed Bobby, Auntie Nellie?'

The little women looked horrified. 'Not on yer life, girl! He's a handful now, and I don't want to be deactive when we're discussing my son's wedding.'

Molly bit back a chuckle before asking. 'What don't yer want to be while we're talking? I didn't quite catch it.'

'Deactive, girl, deactive! Sometimes I think yer've either got cloth ears, or yer don't listen proper.'

'Nellie, it isn't that I don't listen, or that there's anything wrong with my hearing. The problem I have is the way yer've changed the English dictionary. Or changed the words in the dictionary to suit yerself.'

Indignant, Nellie balled a fist. 'I haven't changed no words to suit meself, so don't be telling fibs.'

'All right, I give in, but only because if I don't Jack and Ruthie won't be getting a meal when they come home after a hard day's work. Hopefully the news of the wedding won't take too long, and we'll make it to the shops before they put the bolts on the doors! And now, while Bobby and Moll are quiet, there'll be no distractions.'

The table wobbled as Nellie shuffled her bottom to a more comfortable position. 'I know about the wedding, girl, so I can tell yer what yer want to know.'

Doreen exchanged glances with her sister, who raised her brow in surprise. 'So yer knew Phoebe was having four maids of honour and two bridesmaids, did yer, Auntie Nellie?'

Nellie nearly fell off the chair. Speaking in a croaky voice, she said, 'How many bridesmaids?' And without giving Doreen a chance to answer, Nellie jerked her head at her daughter-in-law. 'If this isn't a leg-pull, and I'll throttle yer if it is, then how come you know about it and I don't? After all, I'm only the mother of the bridegroom.'

'Paul came up to our house last night, Auntie

Nellie.' Jill moved the baby over to her other arm for comfort. 'He asked if I would honour him and Phoebe by being a maid of honour, along with Lily, Doreen and Rosie. He'd already been to see Lily, and from ours he was coming down here to ask Doreen.' Jill's smile for her mother-in-law was an affectionate one, for she was really fond of her. 'I said at first that Phoebe wouldn't want so many of us because of the expense, but I thought it was really nice of them to ask. Anyway, Steve was delighted and he talked me into it. Not that I needed much coaxing because I'm thrilled to bits. It was the money that put me off at first, if I'm truthful, but Paul said Uncle Corker insists on buying the dresses. According to Paul, he intends Phoebe to have a wedding day she'll remember for the rest of her life. He also said it wouldn't be a proper wedding without the Bennett girls, all three of us. Not to mention Lily, Rosie and Dorothy, of course.'

Molly gasped. 'All of yer? It'll cost Corker a fortune!'

'I offered to make our dresses, Mam,' Doreen said, ''cos I was thinking of what a lot of money it would cost to buy six bridesmaids' dresses, but Paul insisted.'

Nellie's narrowed eyes went round the table. 'Pardon me for breathing, like, but how come you know all this when I haven't been told? Just wait until I get me hands on our Paul, I'll bleeding pulverize him. I'm only his mother, like, but he hasn't told me nothing. It comes to something when I have to hear his plans from somebody else.'

'Ay, hold yer horses, sunshine, don't be getting yerself all het up until yer've heard everything,' Molly said. 'Paul only told the girls last night, and where were you last night? Sitting in our house until half past ten.' She saw Nellie's mouth open, and was quick to put a hand over it. 'Before yer say he could have told yer this morning before he went to work, remember the alarm didn't go off, and Paul and George went out without breakfast because they were afraid of being late for work.' She gave a sharp nod. 'So think on, sunshine, before yer shout yer mouth off.'

Nellie's manner changed completely after a few thoughts ran through her mind. 'Yeah, ye're right, girl, it's not worth getting meself in a lather over. The best thing you and me can do is get all dolled up for this wedding, and put everyone else in the shade.'

'Ay, sunshine, I'm too old, and too skint, to try and outshine a bride with six bridesmaids! I'll settle for a nice dress and hat that don't cost the earth.'

'Blimey, girl, ye're not going to have that long face on yer all the time, are yer? Right up to the wedding?'

'I haven't got a long face on me, I'm just being practical, which is something you don't know the meaning of.'

'Listen to me, girl, and if yer don't believe me, then take a good look in the mirror. Right now yer've got a face on yer like a wet week. But don't look in this mirror, wait until yer get home. I don't see why Doreen should have seven years' bad luck and glass all over the floor, when she

305

hasn't done anything to deserve it.'

'Nellie, I'm pulling yer leg, sunshine! I thought yer'd have twigged it, seeing as yer know me so well. Of course I'm going to titivate meself up for yer son's wedding! I wouldn't let the side down. You and me will be dolled up to the nines, there'll be no flies on us! A few bluebottles, perhaps, but no flies.'

Nellie's smile was growing wider and wider, and her eyes were shining. 'Ooh, yer've got me going now, girl, I can't wait. Shall we go into town tomorrow and look for our wedding hats?' The chair Nellie was sitting on was groaning with the strain. If it was able to speak it would have given its notice in.

The retort on Molly's lips stayed there, for she couldn't bring herself to take that look of eagerness off the chubby face. Nellie was almost like a child at times, but it was too late now to try to make her grow up. And anyway, she was probably better off than any of them. She didn't worry about housework or cooking, and now Lily wasn't at home to do the washing and ironing, it was done in a haphazard way when Nellie felt like it.

Molly nodded. 'We'll only go to look around, Nellie, don't forget. I won't have any money to spend, so get that into yer head now, save any argument tomorrow.'

Nothing could quell Nellie's delight. 'Ay, I've had another idea, girl, what yer will like.' The poor chair was put through another bout of agony from Nellie's bottom as she twisted this way and that. 'We could call into the market and see Sadie and Mary Ann. Isn't that a good idea? And wait until they hear about our Paul getting married with six bridesmaids. That'll be a big surprise to them.'

Molly chuckled. 'Don't yer think yer should mention that the six bridesmaids are Phoebe's? I mean, sunshine, it's her big day, yer can't keep leaving her out of the wedding plans. Tell Sadie and Mary Ann what yer want about the wedding, true or untrue, but bring Phoebe's name into it for heaven's sake, 'cos she's the main one on the day. The one all eyes will be on. And I bet she'll look like a million dollars.'

Nellie's eyes rolled. She wasn't going to let that pass without a comment. 'And my Paul will look like Clark Gable in *Gone With The Wind*. Tall, dark and handsome.'

'Well, that's what Paul is, sunshine. Tall, dark and very, very handsome.'

That pleased the little woman very much, and to groans and creaks from the chair, she began to swing her legs. There was only one blot on Nellie's horizon now, and that was the absence of tea and biscuits. 'Doreen, I'll take Bobby off yer now, to give yer a break. He's a ton weight these days, yer arms must be tired.'

Doreen wasn't going to argue, for her son wouldn't keep still for a second. 'With pleasure, Auntie Nellie, he does tire me out.' She handed the baby over. 'He'll be going down for his nap soon, and it'll give me a breather.'

Nellie sat Bobby on her knee, then moved her head quickly when he made a grab for her nose. 'Now you behave yerself, lad, be a good boy for yer grandma Nellie. And when yer mam has made me and Grandma Molly a pot of tea, I'll

307

give yer half of one of me biscuits.'

Molly gasped. 'Have yer no shame, Nellie McDonough! Yer put me to the blush, yer really do! It's manners to wait until ye're asked if you'd like a cup of tea, yer don't take it for granted that people are going to wait on yer.'

'But I'm thirsty, girl, 'cos we didn't have a drink in Hilda's, and me mouth is as dry as sawdust. Your Doreen doesn't mind, I'm like one of the family.'

'Not only do I not mind, Auntie Nellie, I'd be delighted, because I'm dying of thirst meself. And Aunt Vicky must be wanting a cuppa, so it's tea and biscuits all round.'

Jill pushed her sister back in the chair. 'I'll see to it, you relax while yer've got the chance. Bobby's enjoying himself with Auntie Nellie. And Moll's quite content with me mam. I know where everything is, and refreshments will be on the table in ten minutes.'

During that ten minutes, little Moll had dropped off to sleep in Molly's arms, and Bobby was having trouble keeping his eyes open. 'I'll take Bobby now, Auntie Nellie, and I'll put him in his pram,' Doreen said. 'And Moll can go down on the couch, Mam, and they'll both sleep for an hour.'

With the children settled, the grown-ups sat back to enjoy their tea and biscuits. 'What are yer having for dinner tonight, Mam?' Jill asked. 'Anything exciting?'

'Everything has gone to pot this morning, what with staying longer round at Rita's and Hilda's. So it's going to be an easy meal, and I quite fancy bacon, egg, soft tomatoes if the greengrocer's got any, and fried bread. Cheap and easy, and a favourite with Jack and Ruthie.'

Nellie's head was nodding. 'Sounds good to me, girl, so I'll have the same. As yer say, it's quick and easy, and tasty into the bargain.'

Victoria leaned forward in her chair. 'I rather fancy the same myself. Doreen, what do you think?'

Doreen nodded. 'It's fine by me 'cos Phil is very partial to bacon and eggs. So that's us sorted as well.'

'It's Steve's favourite,' Jill said, 'so it looks as though the whole family are sorted out.'

They talked about things in general for a while, then Molly said it was time to leave. 'We'll just catch the shops before they close for dinner if we put a move on. I don't like shopping in the afternoon. So finish yer tea, Nellie, and we'll be off.'

Replenished now, Nellie was quite happy to be on their way. So after hugs and kisses, and a peep at the sleeping babies, the two mates set off for the shops.

'Ay, I've enjoyed meself, girl,' Nellie said, looking up at Molly. 'It's been a nice morning, don't yer think?'

'It's been a long one, sunshine, interesting and funny in part. And to think the day started for you when the alarm didn't go off. It's a funny old world.'

Chapter Fourteen

The mirror over the mantelpiece in the McDonough house was far too high up for Nellie to see herself in. She jumped up and down in an effort to see her reflection, but all she could see was the top of her head. She did think about standing on a chair, but she dismissed that idea very quickly, 'cos it was only a couple of weeks since she'd had trouble with a chair and she didn't fancy going through that again. She wasn't a vain woman, and usually she didn't really care what she looked like, but today was different. She was going to take her mate's suggestion and make a fuss of her husband when he came in from work, to make up for forgetting to switch the alarm clock on for this morning. He'd been in a right temper over it, for he'd had no time for breakfast and would be late for work.

However, it wasn't Molly's words that were causing Nellie to want to look her best, and to practise what she was going to say to George when she was hugging and kissing him as he came in the front door. Oh, no, Nellie had an ulterior motive, being her usual crafty self. For she was going into town with her mate tomorrow, to look at wedding hats. Not to buy one, just to find out which shop had the most eye-catching creations, and how much they were likely to cost. It was a long way off the wedding yer, but it wouldn't hurt to shop around, looking at dresses as well as hats. It gave her something to look forward to. And this is where being nice to George would come in handy. For when he was in a good mood she could coax him into giving her extra house-keeping money, which, of course, wouldn't be spent on food, but on her wedding outfit.

Nellie decided to try to see herself in the mirror in the kitchen, which was used by George and Paul when they were shaving. So she waddled out to the kitchen and picked up the mirror which was donkey's years old, and pockmarked. She carried it through to the living room and stood in front of the window holding it up to her face. 'Oh, my God, I look as though I've got the bleeding measles. I'll buy a decent mirror when I go to the shops, I can get one for sixpence from Woolworth's. And I'd better start on the tea now, 'cos the men will be in soon.' Nellie was talking to the mirror as she walked back to the kitchen. 'Thank goodness it's an easy meal. And if George smells bacon frying as he opens the front door, that should put him in a good mood.'

However, it was Paul who came through the front door first, and called, 'That's a nice smell, Mam. It's made me realize how hungry I am.'

'Isn't yer dad with yer?' Nellie felt really let down. She'd dolled herself up for greeting George, with a loving welcome on her lips, and in walks Paul!

Her son kissed her cheek. 'He won't be long, he's talking to Uncle Corker.' His dimples appeared when he smiled down at her. 'And he's in a better temper than he was this morning.'

'It's to be hoped so, lad, because although I've told meself not to get in a state about it, I can't always trust meself. I say one thing and do another. But one thing I know for sure, I'm not going to be responsible for winding the alarm every night, he can do it himself. Anyway, lad, you wash yer hands and I'll put the dinner out. If yer dad stands gassing and his dinner goes cold, that's his lookout.'

'I've just heard him saying ta-ra to Uncle Corker so he's on his way now.'

Nellie touched his arm. 'Ay, lad, if yer hear me being two-faced, and gushing, don't say nothing 'cos I'm only trying to get round yer dad for a few bob.' At that moment George was closing the front door behind him, and when he walked into the living room to find Nellie smiling sweetly with her arms outstretched, he stood and gawped. 'Hello, love.' She lifted her face for a kiss. 'Yer dinner is ready, and it's yer favourite. Hang yer coat up, and while ye're washing yer hands I'll fetch it in.'

George watched her retreating back, astonishment written on his face. To be welcomed with open arms, a smile and a kiss was unheard of. Nellie must be feeling off colour, that's the only thing he could put it down to. Then his brain came to light, and told him not to be taken in, because there could be another reason for her being so mellow. She could be after something. And as he went to hang his coat up, there was a smile on his face. That was it, she was after something and trying to soften him up. And she'd been crafty knowing he wouldn't be able to refuse with the smell of bacon wafting up his nose. Well, he'd go along with her 'cos he had been hard on her this morning and it had played on his mind all day. Not that he was going to give her everything she asked for, but he'd meet her halfway.

While George was washing his hands at the sink, Nellie carried Paul's plate in and put it down in front of him. 'I want a few words with you, lad. How come the neighbours know more about the wedding than I do? Yer own mother and I'm left in the dark! But eat yer dinner while it's hot, and I'll tell yer off later.' Before making her way back to the kitchen, Nellie bent down and whispered in her son's ear, 'Just listen to this, lad.' She swayed her way out to the stove and turned over the slices of bacon, saying, 'Light of my life, would you like one slice of fried bread, or two?'

Oh, this wife of mine is up to something, George thought, but I'll get a little dig in. 'I'll have two slices, Nellie, to make up for not having any breakfast.'

Nellie didn't rise to the hint, which was very unusual, for normally she'd fly off the handle at the least thing. 'Then two slices you shall have, my love.' How she was laughing inside at the expression on George's face. She felt like kissing him, for she loved the bones of him even though she didn't show it. Except for when they were in the bedroom, but that went without saying. 'And I'll sprinkle some salt on, just as you like it.'

Seated at the dining table, Paul was chuckling quietly. It was more than a few bob his mam was after. From the performance she was giving, he'd say it was more like a few pound. And she'd get it

313

as well. For if his dad didn't cough up, he'd give it to her himself. Like Steve and Lily, he adored his mother for what she was. Loving, warm, a bit batty at times, but always full of fun. She had no idea about money matters, though, and if it weren't for Mrs Bennett she'd spend the week's housekeeping in one day. It was Mrs B. who kept her on the straight and narrow, and for that the McDonough family were all grateful.

George pulled a chair from under the table and sat facing his son. He put a finger to his lips and winked, just as Nellie carried his dinner through. 'There you are, beloved, heart of my heart. Just as yer like it. Fried bread crisp, and egg soft and runny. Yer couldn't be better served if yer were in the Adelphi.'

George picked up his knife and fork, stood them like sentinels either side of the plate, then said, 'Okay, Nellie, what is it ye're after? If it's a few bob, I'll give it to yer now, then I can enjoy me dinner.'

'Well, it's like this, George. Me and Molly are going into town tomorrow, and although we're only going to look around, I'd like to have some money in me purse, just in case I see something I fancy.'

'Is it a couple of bob yer want, Nellie? I don't know what yer need, I'm not a ruddy mind-reader.'

'Oh, skip it,' Nellie said, 'it's not worth the ruddy trouble. I've got enough for me bus fare, I'll make do with that.'

'Now don't be acting childish, Nellie, I only asked yer how much yer wanted! I didn't say I wouldn't give yer any money.'

Paul knew his mother inside out, and he now hit the nail on the head. 'You and Mrs B. wouldn't be going to look at wedding hats, would yer?'

Nellie didn't even blush. 'Not in particular, lad, but yeah, we'll probably look at some, along with dresses and other things. That's what women do, yer know. They go window shopping.'

'If I can interrupt for a minute,' George said, 'where's your dinner, Nellie?'

'Oh, I had mine earlier 'cos I was hungry.' Nellie couldn't look down her nose, her face wasn't arranged for her to do that. But if she could she would have done. Instead she had to make do with saying in a voice as posh as she could manage, 'But thank you for noticing.'

'Don't you or Mrs B. buy anything for the wedding, Mam,' Paul said, 'because yer really need to see what colour the bridesmaids are going to wear. Yer don't want the colours to clash, do yer?'

'Well can't yer ask Phoebe what colour the dresses are going to be? It should be easy for yer seeing as ye're the ruddy groom. And while we're on the subject, how come I'm the only one what doesn't know what's going on?'

'Mam, yer weren't here last night, so I couldn't tell yer. And yer were in bed when I got in, it was half eleven. And I don't think yer'd have been pleased if I'd woken yer up to tell yer what we've planned so far.'

Nellie chuckled and the table rose from the floor. 'Ye're right, lad, I'd have clocked yer one. But yer can tell me now, can't yer, so I'm up to date about what's going on?'

Paul pushed his empty plate away and turned to face his mother. His deep brown eyes were shining with happiness, and his dimples deep. 'Our Lily is chief maid of honour, and Jill, Doreen and Rosie are also maids of honour. The two bridesmaids are Dorothy Corkhill and Ruthie Bennett.'

Nellie's bottom was polishing the seat of her chair she was so excited.

'Ooh, er, it's going to be proper posh, isn't it? I won't half be swanking. Me and Molly will be dressed to the nines, and the neighbours won't know us. I'm going to get meself a hat what will put everyone else in the shade.' Nellie remembered her mate's words, and added, 'Except Phoebe, of course. All eyes will be on her, as she's the bride. And Molly said, she's going to make a beautiful bride.'

'Me heart goes fifteen to the dozen when I think about the wedding, Mam,' Paul said. 'I want everything to be perfect for Phoebe because she deserves it.'

'Yer've got a good girl in Phoebe,' George told him. 'She's one in a million. Everything you would want in a wife. Pretty as a picture, quiet, respectful, and her head screwed on the right way.'

Up went the table when Nellie burst out laughing. 'In other words, lad, ye're marrying someone exactly like yer mam.'

'Then I'll be doing well for meself if that's the case,' Paul said. 'You and me dad have had a good marriage. We've always been happy, Steve, Lily and me.'

'Ay, this wedding is going to cost a lot of money, lad. I hope ye're still saving up?'

'Uncle Corker is paying the bulk of it, Mam. I've offered to pay towards everything, but he flatly refuses. Even the reception, I wanted to pay for that, but he said he wants to do his own thing. But when it gets nearer the time, I'm going to have another go at him. According to him, the bride's father always pays for the wedding and reception. The groom pays for the flowers, buttonholes and presents for the bridesmaids.'

'That'll cost yer a fair bit, lad.' Nellie's chins agreed with her. 'Yer can't buy them cheap presents from Woolies.'

'I know that, Mam. Me and Phoebe were talking about it last night, and she thought they'd be delighted with a cross and chain.'

Nellie frowned. 'Didn't Archie buy cross and chains for the bridesmaids when our Lily got married?'

'I can't remember, Mam. I wasn't as interested in that wedding as I am in my own.' He pulled a face. 'That sounds terrible, and I didn't mean it to come out like that. Of course I was interested and happy for our Lily and Archie, but men don't think of asking what sort of presents the bridesmaids got. That's more women's talk. But I will find out from our Lily, because I wouldn't want to buy them the same.'

'When are yer getting measured for yer suit, lad?' Nellie asked. 'Don't leave it until the last minute 'cos some shops take ages, and yer have to go for fittings. Yer've got to look good, yer can't let the side down.'

'Nellie, he's old enough to know what he's doing,' George said, shaking his head. 'He'll be a

317

married man soon, he doesn't need you to hold his hand.'

Nellie wasn't going to argue, not until she had some money in her hand. 'I know that, love, but don't forget he is me youngest child.'

'He happens to be my youngest child, too, Nellie. I did have a hand in him being born.'

Even if it meant she couldn't cadge as much if she carried on and said what was in her mind, Nellie couldn't resist. 'Oh, I know ye're his father, light of my life, but yer hand had nothing to do with it.'

Paul was chuckling as he got to his feet. 'I'm going to get ready before yer've got me blushing.'

'I hope Phoebe's got an open mind and a sense of humour,' George said. 'She'll need both if she's coming to live here after yer get married. I've been married to yer mother for twenty-five years and she still makes me blush. So warn the lass, Paul.'

'Oh, I think Phoebe's got more than a vague idea of what she's in for, Dad, she's used to me mam. In fact she's looking forward to living here.' Paul put his hand in his trouser pocket and took out half a crown. 'Put this to what ye're able to cadge off me dad, and you and Mrs B. can buy yerselves a pot of tea in the Kardomah.'

Nellie grinned up at him. 'Thanks, lad, me and Molly will think of yer when we're drinking the tea, and eating the cakes yer dad is going to treat us to.'

Paul patted his father's shoulder as he passed. 'Pay up, Dad, and make life a lot easier for yerself.'

318

'Don't worry, son, I know I'm beaten before I start. I know yer mam inside out, and half a crown isn't much to pay for an evening of peace.'

When Paul had gone upstairs to get changed, Nellie began to collect the dinner plates. 'I'll be going to Molly's when I've washed up, so yer'll have the house to yerself. We're going round to see Bridie and Bob, and we'll probably end up playing cards. But I'll be home to make us a cup of tea before we go to bed.' She was at the kitchen door when she added, 'You set the alarm clock tonight to make sure. I don't want another performance like this morning. What a ruddy to-do that was.'

'Well, what did you expect, love? I can't sail into work when I feel like it. As it happens, one of me mates clocked on for me, and I was lucky the boss was in his office and didn't see me.'

'Set the clock yerself every night, then yer've only got yerself to rant and rave at.' Nellie put the plates in the kitchen then came back to stand at the door. 'Mind you, though, love, while I was hopping mad at the time, calling yer all the names under the sun, I had a few good laughs when I'd calmed down. The look of your struggling to get yer legs in yer trousers, and falling all over the place, well it's a long time since I've seen such a funny sight.'

George chuckled. 'I can see the funny side of it meself now, and I had me mates in stitches at our dinner break. I stretched the truth a bit, mind you, to make it funnier than it was.' Once again George chuckled. 'I said I was putting them on back to front, and then trying to get both feet in

319

one leg.'

'Ay, lad, I'm the comedian in this family, so don't be trying to put my nose out of joint.'

'I'll never be that good, love. There's no chance of me catching up with you because if I remember rightly, your mam told me that when yer were born the first sound yer made was a joke!'

'She was pulling yer leg, lad.' Nellie wasn't going to let him have the last laugh. 'I remember when I first saw the light of day, I told the midwife her hands were cold and she was too bleeding rough.'

'That I can believe.' George struck a match and lit his Woodbine. After a few puffs, and through a cloud of smoke, he squinted at his wife. 'Yer never did like the cold. I remember when we got married, it was the middle of winter, and yer couldn't get into bed quick enough to warm yer cold feet on me.'

'My God, you've got a good memory, George. Yer might be slow in other departments, but yer've got a good memory.' Nellie had turned round to go back into the kitchen when she had a thought and stepped back. 'And yer still keep me warm in bed, lad, I've no complaints there. Plus yer've got staying power.'

'I need it with you, Nellie. If I'd been a weakling, I'd be dead by now.'

'I'm not soft, lad, I know what I'm doing.' Nellie couldn't decide whether to cross the room and give George a kiss, or retreat to the kitchen and wash the dishes. In the end she did both. A quick kiss on the cheek of a very surprised George, then on her way to the dishes she called, 'I knew yer would stay the course, 'cos I could feel yer muscles while we were dancing, and I told meself you were the man for me! Fit as a fiddle.'

With water running in the kitchen, George had to shout to make himself heard. 'I'm glad yer didn't marry me for me looks or me money, Nellie, I wouldn't have appreciated that. I bet there's not many girls marry men for their muscles, so I'll take that as a compliment.'

Nellie hummed as she washed the few dishes, then put them on the shelf after she'd dried them. It was an effort for her to reach the shelf, her being so small, so she could only do it one plate at a time while standing on tiptoe. Then she gave her face a cat's lick and a promise, and patted her hair into place.

George looked up from his newspaper when Nellie came into the room. 'There's a half a crown on the table for yer, love. It'll be enough with what Paul gave yer, for tea and a cake each for you and Molly. I'd give yer more, but I'm putting money aside each week for the wedding.'

'You won't need no money for the wedding, George, 'cos Corker is paying for everything. The father of the bride always has to fork out, that's traditional.'

'I'll have to have a new suit, Nellie. It's my son getting wed, don't forget. I want to do him proud. We'd look well, me and you, if you were dressed to the nines and I looked like a rag and bone man. It'll only be a Burton's thirty bob ready made suit, but with a decent shirt and tie no one will know the difference.'

'Ay, we won't half open the neighbours' eyes,

lad. They'll think we've won the pools, or someone's died and left us a fortune in their will.'

There was a loud guffaw from George. 'Seeing
as we don't know anyone with money it's unlikely
we'll ever be left any. And as I don't do the pools,
that's not possible. Never mind, love, we may be
poor, but we're honest.'

Nellie reached for her coat. 'Yeah, there's plenty
of folk worse off than what we are. We're lucky
compared to some.' She fastened the only two
buttons left on her coat, and waddled towards the
front door. 'I won't be late getting back, but don't
do anything I wouldn't do while I'm away.'

George called after her, 'Seeing as there's nothing you wouldn't do, Nellie, then I've got a free
rein.'

Nellie was back within the blink of an eye.
'Yer'd only be wasting yer time, lad, 'cos where
would yer find another woman what has a
voluptuous body like mine? No, lad, you just sit
and smoke yer ciggie while yer read the paper.
That way yer won't get in any trouble.'

'Don't stay out too late, Nellie. Yer know the
old saying about the only ones out on the street
after midnight are cats and women of ill repute.'

'I'm not going to answer that, lad, 'cos I'm late
getting to Molly's, and she'll think I'm not
coming. Ta-ra.'

When Molly stepped down on to the pavement,
Nellie linked her arm. 'How about calling in to
see our Lily and Archie, girl? We don't see them
as much as we see your Jill and Doreen.'

'Yes, we'll call there, if that's what yer want, sun-

322

shine. And you are right, we don't see as much of them as we do my family. Which isn't right. So we'll give them a call before we go to me ma's.'

It was Archie who opened the door, and his pleasure at seeing them made Molly feel ashamed. She vowed she'd come and visit him and Lily more often. He was a lovely man, was Archie, in looks and in nature. And a war hero, although he never mentioned it. He was given a medal for bravery, after leading a group of soldiers through a minefield when the war was coming to an end. The Germans had set mines as they were fleeing, and many soldiers were killed. Archie walked ahead of his group, at the risk of his own life, and he'd guided them to safety. And one of those young soldiers was Molly's son, Tommy, who was the one who told his family and friends that Archie had saved his life. Archie himself never spoke of it. But Tommy never forgot, and looked up to Archie as the bravest man he'd ever known.

Molly was thinking of the debt she owed the man who was inviting them in, his face showing how welcome they were. 'Hello, Archie, sunshine, it's lovely to see yer. We don't see yer often enough, but that's because my family is getting so big it's hard to keep up with them.'

Lily welcomed her mother and Molly with a hug and a kiss. 'Sit down and I'll put the kettle on.' She raised her hand when she saw Molly exchange glances with Nellie. 'You are having a cup of tea whether yer like it or not. Whenever yer do honour us with yer presence, yer never stay long enough to warm the seat of the chair.

So take a pew, and the tea will be on the table before yer can say Jack Robinson.'

Nellie didn't need telling twice. 'I hope there's biscuits to go with the tea, girl?'

'I can answer that, Mrs Mac,' Archie told her. 'There's always a packet of custard creams in the larder, just on the off chance yer call in.' He thought the world of Nellie, telling everyone she was the best mother-in-law any man could ask for. He loved her crazy sense of humour and down to earth nature. 'Are yer looking forward to Paul's wedding? I bet you and Mrs B. are eager to see what the latest hat styles are.'

Nellie's chins nodded before her head, for they were getting excited about what was going on. 'Me and Molly are going into town tomorrow, lad, but only to window shop. Just to give us an idea of what hats and dresses to go for when we've got the money.'

'Here yer go!' Lily put the tray down in the middle of the table. 'I'll let you be mother, Mrs B., 'cos you're nearest.'

'Where's Archie's mother?' Molly asked as she lifted the teapot. 'I haven't seen her for ages.'

'She's gone to her sister's, Mrs B.' It was Archie who answered. 'Me auntie is in ill health, and me mam goes a few times a week to do a bit of housework for her, and the ironing. I think me auntie plays on me mam's good nature, but talking to me mam is like talking to the wall.'

'Yer mam was always daft even when I sat next to her in school. She's a sucker for a hard luck story.' Nellie's hand moved to the plate with the biscuits on, and picked up two Nice biscuits and one arrowroot, which she dunked in her tea while still talking. 'Your mam often got the cane for talking when it should have been me. The trouble with her is she's no good at telling fibs, she blushes the colour of beetroot. Me, now, I can tell a lie without turning a hair.'

'That's nothing to brag about, sunshine, yer should be ashamed of yerself.' Molly rolled her eyes. 'Yer seem to think it's clever, but it's not.'

'Oh, it is if it stops yer getting the cane, girl! I bet you don't know what it's like getting three strokes of the cane, 'cos ye're too bleeding good to be true.'

'Let's change the subject, Mrs B.,' Lily said, ''cos yer'll never change me mam, not in a million years.' There was a smile on her pretty face when she added, 'Yer should have heard the lies I use to have to tell the clubwoman, or the coalman, when I was a kid. Me mam made me go to the door and tell them she wasn't in. And she'd keep me off school on the days they were due, so I'd have to tell another lie the next day, and say I had a sore throat or a tummy ache.'

'Didn't do yer no harm, did it, girl?' Nellie's hand moved towards the plate again, but she was so busy talking, she didn't see Molly moving the plate out of her reach. And it was only the smiles and giggles that caused her to stop talking and look for the biscuits. 'Where's the bleeding plate gone?'

'Oh, didn't yer see it walk out in disgust?' Molly asked. 'It said yer were so greedy yer'd probably eat the flowers painted on it, so it got out of yer way as quick as it could.'

325

'Ho, ho, very funny, I'm sure. Ye're a thief, Molly Bennett, and a thief is worse than a liar.'

Archie was leaning forward, his elbows on his knees. 'How do yer make that out, Mrs Mac? They're both as bad as one another, I should think.'

'No they're not, lad! Just think on it. If I tell yer a lie, I can always say I'm sorry and didn't mean nothing. But if I stole two of those biscuits off the plate what my mate is hiding on her knee, and I ate them, then I couldn't give them back, could I? So do yer see what I'm getting at, like?'

'I don't know why I bothered actually,' Archie said. 'But in her own roundabout way, I suppose Mrs Mac knows what she's talking about.'

'Does she heck!' Lily laughed. 'My mam never knows what she's talking about, because she never stops talking long enough to listen to herself.'

Nellie's eyes narrowed to slits as she tried to get her head round what her daughter had said. And while Molly, Lily and Archie looked on, they saw her face contort into every shape conceivable. Then, when her features returned to normal, she opened her eyes and fixed them on her daughter. 'That was a daft thing to say. I know very well I can't listen to meself when I'm talking. And d'yer know how I know? Because I've tried it many a time and it doesn't work. So put that in yer pipe and smoke it, 'cos ye're not as clever as yer thought yer were.'

'Let's change the subject, eh?' Lily said. 'Are yer stopping for a game of cards?'

'Oh, we're going to see me ma and da, Lily, 'cos I haven't seen them for a few days, or Tommy and

326

Rosie. They'll think I've forgotten them.'

'I haven't seen Tommy for a few weeks, Mrs B.,' Archie said. 'Is he all right? And the rest of the family, are they keeping well?'

'They're fine, Archie.' Molly had an idea. 'Why don't you and Lily walk round with us? They'd all love to see yer.'

'They wouldn't want a houseful, Auntie Molly,' Lily said. 'It would be too much for Bridie and Bob. Not that I wouldn't like to see them, because I'd love to. But I do think four of us turning up uninvited would be a bit much.'

'Don't be so daft,' Nellie huffed. 'Bridie and Bob love to have visitors, it puts some sparkle into their lives.'

'My goodness, sunshine, ye're coming up in the world, aren't yer?' Molly chuckled. 'That was really poetic, that was. Putting sparkle into their lives is better than anything I could come up with. And ye're right to say they love to have visitors, so yeah, the four of us will go round and surprise them. We'll have a laugh even though it might end up with Rosie sitting on Tommy's knee, and Lily on Archie's. The more the merrier as the saying goes.'

'I'll get me coat.' Lily pushed her chair back. 'The dishes can wait until I get back. They won't mind us going in our working clothes, will they?'

'I could do with having a shave.' Archie fingered his chin. 'I look like a tramp. That's the worst of having black hair, yer really need to shave twice a day.'

'Yer'll do as yer are, lad,' Nellie told him. 'Ye're that tall, most people won't see yer chin unless yer bend down. Besides, who is going to worry about how yer look? Beauty is in the eye of the beholder, lad, and our Lily loves yer, so that's all yer need.' She craned her neck to look at him. 'If she ever gets fed up with yer, she can pass yer on to me.'

Archie managed a look of horror as he held his hands up. 'Oh, not that, Mrs Mac. I love yer to bits, but I don't think I could stand the pace.'

'Ye're safe, lad,' Nellie told him. 'My George knows me inside out, and we're too old to learn new tricks.'

'Can we get going?' Molly said. 'It'll be bedtime before we get there, and I told Jack I wouldn't be late.'

Nellie shuffled towards the front door, her head bent as she muttered, 'Sod Jack, that's what I say.'

'What was that, sunshine?' Molly asked, winking at Lily. 'Did yer say something?'

'No, girl, just that I'll lead the way.'

Chapter Fifteen

When Tommy opened the front door he pretended to stagger back in amazement when he saw the group of four. 'Good heavens, we're being invaded!'

His words were heard in the living room, and Rosie jumped up quickly and ran into the hall. 'What is it, me darling beloved?' Her voice trailed off when she saw the reason for his words. 'Oh, now isn't this a lovely surprise, so it is! Will yer not be standing aside, me darlin', and let the visitors in?'

'I should think so too!' mumbled Nellie as she used the door frame to help her climb the step. 'Your darling beloved has been standing there with his mouth open, like a fish what has just been caught in a net.'

Rosie pressed herself against the wall to let Nellie pass. 'Now Mrs Mac, sure I've never seen a fish as handsome as my beloved, and that's the truth of it. When I caught him in me net, sure wasn't I the luckiest and happiest girl alive?'

Bridie and Bob smiled when Nellie waddled in, for their affection for the little woman was genuine. Then when Molly came in their eyes lit up with love for their daughter, and when she bent to kiss them they gave her a hug. It was when Lily appeared, followed closely by Archie, that the elderly couple showed their surprise and pleasure. 'Well now, will yer look who it is,' Bridie said, in her lilting Irish voice. 'Sure ye're as welcome as the flowers in May, so yer are.' She turned to Bob, whose hand she was holding. 'Sure it's a full house we have tonight, right enough, me darlin', and it's happy we are to see them.'

Tommy was standing on the threshold of the living room, talking to his idol, Archie. They were talking about their jobs when Rosie said, 'Tommy Bennett, have yer no manners? There's not enough chairs, so will yer fetch the one down from our bedroom and we'll try and squash round the table so we can talk to each other.'

'I'm sorry, sweetheart, and I apologize for my

lack of manners. But it's a while since I last saw Archie, and we've got a lot to catch up on. I'll nip up and fetch the chair down.'

They managed to fit six chairs round the table, and Molly thought her ma and da should sit on two of them, so they weren't left out of the conversation. Which meant that Lily and Rosie had to sit on the knees of their husbands, which they did with great pleasure. Playing cards was out of the question, so they exchanged news, with many conversations going on at the same time. Bridie and Bob tried to keep up with them all, but it soon became impossible until Nellie set out to amuse them. The first bout of hilarity came with her telling the tale of the alarm clock. Her exaggerated version of George trying to get two feet in one leg of his trousers, and his falling about all over the place, brought forth hoots of laughter as imaginations ran riot. Even Molly, who knew the truth, couldn't help chuckling at Nellie's words and actions.

'I'm laughing now, but I was so mad at George for putting the blame on me 'cos the alarm didn't go off, I could have clocked him one.' Nellie pointed a podgy finger at Molly. 'Ask me mate, she'll tell yer how mad I was. But thanks to her, everything turned out very well, and I'm tickled to bits.'

'Why, what did I do?' Molly asked. 'Don't bring me into yer squabble with George, 'cos I'd be on his side.'

'Yeah, yer told me that, girl, and I did what yer said I should do! I got meself all dolled up before he came in from work tonight.' Much to the amusement of her audience, she patted her hair like Mae West. Except her hair was as untidy as it always was. 'I mean, like, yer can see I made meself look good for him. And like Molly told me, I greeted him with open arms and a big kiss. Now I'm not one for kissing, really, but the trouble I'd gone to was worth it just to see the look on George's face. He thought I'd lost the run of me senses. Light of my life, I called him, and heart of my heart. Oh, I didn't half enjoy meself.' The table rose with Nellie's tummy, and Rosie nearly toppled off Tommy's knee.

The family and friends were still laughing when Nellie wheezed, 'Ay, girl, yer didn't half give me some good advice.' She winked at Molly. 'I'll treat yer to a pot of tea and a cake in the Kardomah tomorrow, out of the money I cadged off George for being so nice to him.'

'Yer cadged money off him again!' Molly tutted. 'I told yer to be nice to him because you hadn't set the alarm and him and Paul were late for work. I didn't say anything about cadging money off him.' Once again she tutted. 'What am I going to do with yer, Nellie McDonough? Ye're the blight of me life.'

'Well, yer can have a little treat tomorrow out of the money I cadged off George and Paul.'

'Yer mean yer took money off Paul as well, even though the lad is saving up to get married?'

'Oh, I never asked Paul for money, girl, I didn't have to. He gave it to me of his own free will.' The chubby face beamed as Nellie looked round the table. 'And it was you what told me to be nice to George, so it was you what cadged the money, in a roundabout way.'

Molly sat back in her chair, a look of disbelief on her face. 'Nellie, for twenty odd years I've listened to yer cockeyed ways of seeing things, and mostly I've found them funny and had a laugh at them. Not that I could always see the logic in them, mind, because I'd have to be the brain of Britain to be that clever. But this latest trick is something else. How do yer make out that because I happened to say yer should be nice to yer husband, I'm the one what cadged money off him? That's too far-fetched even by your standards.'

All eyes turned to Nellie now, awaiting her response. 'Well, it's like this, yer see, girl, if yer know what I mean, like. I would never have thought about being nice to George. In fact I was more inclined to want to hit him over the head with the frying pan after he'd played merry hell with me for not setting the alarm. But when I got home from your house I thought it would be in me own interest, like, if I was nice to him. Which I was, and it worked a treat! So now can yer understand why we'll be having tea and cakes in town tomorrow?'

'Nellie, sunshine, I may have tea and a cake tomorrow when we go to town, but they'll be paid for out of me own money. And in future I'll keep me mouth shut instead of trying to turn you into a kind, thoughtful, sensible mother, wife and mate. It's just a waste of me time and breath.'

The onlookers thought how unusual it was for Molly to be so serious with her friend, and were a little concerned. But they needn't have been,

332

for no amount of words could dampen Nellie's spirit. Insults had no effect, it was like water off a duck's back. Only with her best mate, though! If anyone else criticized her, she'd clock them one and not think twice about it.

'Ay, girl, tell them about the trouble I caused yer the other week, when Doreen had to help me out of George's chair. Go on, girl, give them a laugh.'

'Yer have one redeeming feature, sunshine, and that is nothing worries yer. Yer don't mind anyone knowing yer made a ruddy fool of yerself, and caused me a lot of worry, and our Doreen into the bargain.'

'Ah, ay, girl, it was really funny and this lot would love to hear it. My ma, God rest her soul, used to say a good belly laugh was better than a feast. Mind you, she was skint at the time, and couldn't afford a loaf of bread, never mind a feast. And our bellies weren't laughing, they were rumbling with hunger.'

'Mam, yer've just told Mrs B. to make us laugh, and then yer tell us a tale which has the tears rolling down our cheeks,' Lily said. 'We don't want to hear hard luck stories, we want to laugh and be happy. So come on, what did yer do with me dad's chair that was so funny?'

Molly leaned forward. 'I'll tell yer, 'cos Nellie will get everything back to front.'

Nellie put a hand on her mate's arm. 'Don't yer mean backside to front, girl?'

'Nellie, who's telling this tale, you or me? If you want to do it, then by all means be my guest.'

'No, girl, I was only saying, like, didn't yer see the connection with backside?' Nellie saw the straight face on Molly and shrugged her shoulders. 'Okay, I'll keep me trap shut.'

'As yer know, me and Nellie have a set routine every day,' Molly started off. 'At half ten every morning, except Sunday, Nellie knocks on my door. We have a cup of tea, biscuits if I've got any, and a natter. Eleven o'clock we leave the house and do whatever shopping we need, then do a bit of visiting to family and friends. Anyway a week or two back, Nellie didn't put in an appearance and I started to worry. Our Doreen came over with a message, and when I told her about Nellie, she said there must be something wrong. Now I've always had a key to the McDonoughs' house, so me and Doreen let ourselves in. And a voice called out, "You took yer bleeding time, didn't yer?"' The memories came flooding back, and Molly was crying with laughter when she described the scene that she and Doreen were met with. And for the next fifteen minutes the house rocked with laughter, the loudest coming from Nellie herself, as her tummy lifted the table and her bosom pushed it down again. Bridie and Bob were clinging to each other as tears rolled down their cheeks, and their pleasure made Molly happy. Archie's laughter was the loudest, Tommy was a close second, while Lily and Rosie wiped their tears away with the backs of their hands.

'Ooh, I've got a stitch in me side, so I have.' Rosie gave her mother-in-law a hug, then Nellie. 'Sure it's lucky yer are to have such a strong friendship, and that's the truth of it.'

Nellie was as pleased as Punch. It didn't worry her that it was due to her clumsiness that they were all laughing. Like her ma had once said, a good belly laugh was better than a feast. And she had a few more belly laughs in her head. But she'd wait until they'd calmed down.

'We'll have an interval now,' Rosie said, 'while me and my dearly beloved make some tea. Sure, I know it's a bit crowded, but that can't be helped. And if ye're enjoying yerself, why let a little thing like that bother yer?'

'Hurry up and make the tea, girl,' Nellie said, 'me throat is as dry as a bone.'

Molly's eyes widened. 'Hey, Nellie Mac, what about me? I've done all the talking, but you're the one complaining about having a dry throat! You can do the talking from now on.'

'Ah, ay, girl, you're better at talking than me, yer have a way with yer. I don't know what ye're talking about half the time, like, but it always sounds good.'

When Tommy carried the tray in and set it down in the middle of the table, Nellie's face lit up, for there were two plates of biscuits, and she could see a wide selection including fig. She patted her tummy, and to the amusement of Bridie and Bob she said, 'Prepare yerself for a treat. But don't yer dare rumble 'cos it's only common people what do that.'

'Nellie, me darlin',' Bridie said, 'if your tummy wants to rumble, then you let it rumble.'

Bob nodded. 'I must be very common, Nellie, because my tummy has always been a rumbler.'

At that moment Tommy came through carrying another tray filled with cups of tea. 'Mam, will you do the honours, please?'

'With pleasure, sunshine, but I'll let everyone put their own sugar in.'

When they were all settled, sipping tea and eating biscuits, Nellie chose her time. 'Ay, girl, do these know I'm a heroine, like what Florence Nightingale was?'

'Oh, we do that, Nellie, and it's proud of yer we are,' Bridie said. 'The whole neighbourhood know what happened; yer were the topic of conversation for days.'

Molly was eating a fig biscuit, and she nearly choked when her thoughts brought on a bout of laughter. 'Oh, I'm sorry, but I couldn't keep that back. I was thinking about how sorry Nellie was because she couldn't meet the other heroine, Florence Nightingale.'

Nellie put a hand flat on her chest, closed her eyes and slowly nodded her head. 'Yeah, it was sad that, 'cos both being heroines, we could have been friends. When did yer say she died, Molly?'

'I don't know exactly, sunshine, but I'll make a guess that it was about nineteen hundred.'

'Ah, I only just missed her then? That's just my luck.' Nellie's eyes slid sideways. 'Did she live round here, girl?'

Archie and Tommy thought it was hilarious. 'Mrs Mac can always be relied on to bring laughter with her,' Tommy said. 'And the funniest part of it is, she doesn't realize how funny she is.'

Nellie was enjoying herself, even though Tommy was right when he said she didn't realize how funny she was. All she knew was, hearing people laugh made her feel good. And she wanted them to keep on making her feel good. Important like, as though she was someone special. So she searched her brain, and came up with an idea.

'Ay, girl, why don't yer tell them about me and Hilda getting stuck in the doorway. You know, how we became bosom pals.'

'Oh, I think we've had enough for one night, sunshine. We'll tell them another time.' Molly raised her brow at Lily, as if to say she didn't want Nellie's daughter to encourage her mother to pass on this particular piece of information, as it wouldn't be to everyone's taste. Certainly Bridie and Bob wouldn't think a joke about bosoms was funny.

'Yes, we've had enough for tonight, Mam,' Lily said. 'If I laugh any more I'll be sick. And anyway, we should be making tracks for home now. Archie's mam will wonder where we've got to. But it's been a really good evening, and I've really enjoyed meself. And I don't need to tell yer Archie has, because he's never stopped laughing since we came in.'

'We'll come out with yer, Lily,' Molly said. 'Jack will be thinking I've run off with the coalman.'

'No he won't, girl,' Nellie said, wanting to stay a bit longer as there were two biscuits still on the plate. 'Not the coalman, he's as ugly as sin. Now if yer'd said the milkman, that would be a different thing altogether, 'cos I think he's the spitting image of Alan Ladd. Tall, with blond hair and blue eyes. I'd run off with him meself if I got the chance. I've given him the glad eye a few times, but the silly bugger just winks back and goes on his way.'

'I hate to disillusion yer, Mrs Mac,' Archie said,

his white teeth gleaming, 'but Alan Ladd is only the same height as you. He has to wear shoes that have been built up to make him seem taller.'

'Oh, sod that for a lark,' Nellie said, looking disgusted. 'I'll stick to Cary Grant or Gary Cooper, I bet they don't have to wear high-heeled shoes.' She pushed her chair back and pulled herself up. 'In fact I'll stick to my George, 'cos I know what I'm getting with him.'

'Now that's settled, and we've got Nellie on her feet, let's get going.' Molly hugged and kissed the parents she adored, and in turn was nearly suffocated by Rosie and Tommy as they kissed her goodnight. And of course Nellie wasn't left out, because she was regarded as one of the family.

On the walk home, Nellie wouldn't leave well alone. If Molly wouldn't tell the others about her and Hilda being bosom pals, then she'd tell them herself. So, despite receiving a few digs from her mate, she told the tale, and Lily and Archie were still laughing when they reached home. Archie put his arm around his mother-in-law and said, 'Mrs Mac, ye're a treasure. And I am lucky to have married yer daughter, who takes after you in many ways.' He touched Molly's shoulder. 'You are in the treasure chest with Mrs Mac, because one without the other wouldn't be the same. Yer need each other.'

Molly and Nellie lived at the bottom end of the street, and when they left Lily and Archie they linked arms and made for home. 'Ay, I enjoyed meself, girl.' Nellie was still as bright as a button. 'It was good, wasn't it? We all had a good laugh, and that's how it should be. Because it doesn't cost anything to laugh, and it beats being miserable.'

They stopped outside Nellie's house, and while she was rooting in her pocket for the door key, Molly said, 'Yes, it was a good night, and I'm glad Lily and Archie were there, we really don't see enough of them. The trouble is, both our families are getting bigger and it's hard trying to keep in touch with them all. But we shouldn't moan, sunshine, because we are very lucky. We should count our blessings that we are all in good health and have so much love all around us.'

Having found the door key, Nellie was standing on the step, her hand poised to insert it into the lock, when she turned her head. 'Yer don't half come out with some nice words, girl, and I often curse meself for not taking in what the teachers tried to drum into us. I was too bleeding clever by far, telling meself they were old-fashioned, talking as though they had a plum in their mouth, and I was much smarter than they were. But look how I've ended up, girl, as thick as two short planks.'

'You are far from thick, sunshine, so don't be running yerself down. Yer've got a husband who adores you, and yer've brought up three wonderful children. I wonder if that teacher ye're talking about has done as well for herself? And I bet she can't tell jokes like you can, or make so many people happy.' Molly planted a kiss on Nellie's cheek. 'Ye're my best mate, sunshine, and I know yer better than anyone. So I can say, in all honesty that you are definitely not as thick as two short planks. Now go in to yer husband, give him a kiss and go straight through to the kitchen and make him a cup of tea. And while ye're standing waiting for the kettle to boil, keep telling yerself ye're as good as anyone. Will yer do that, Nellie?'

'Yeah, I will, girl! Yer've got me going now, and it's God help anyone who dares to call me stupid. I'll knock their block off.'

Molly gave a slight shake of her head before smiling. 'Well, that's a start, sunshine, 'cos yer could have said yer'd knock their bleeding head off.'

'Yeah, I'd do that as well, girl!'

'Okay, Nellie, I'll love yer and leave yer now. Goodnight and God bless.'

'Goodnight, girl. Don't forget we're going into town tomorrow.'

Molly walked the few yards to her own house, calling back over her shoulder, 'I've put it in me diary, sunshine, so I won't forget.'

She was opening the door when she heard Nellie saying, 'What's the matter with this bleeding key? It won't go in the stupid so and so.'

'It'll go in quicker if yer calm down, Nellie. Just take it easy.'

'I am calm, girl, but I can't get the door open and I'm dying to go to the lavvy.'

Then George's voice reached Molly. 'What's all the commotion, Nellie? Ye're making enough noise to waken the dead!'

'Get out of me way, soft lad. Can't yer see it's an emergency?'

Molly was chuckling as she closed her front door. Trying to make a lady out of her mate was going to take a lifetime. Still, the journey had its rewards and they came wrapped in laughter.

'Are we going to call in the market before we go into town, girl?' Nellie asked the next morning when they were having their usual cuppa. 'To see Sadie and Mary Ann, like, and tell them about the wedding?'

'Not on our way into town, sunshine,' Molly told her. 'We'll see how we get on for time first, eh? We don't want to rush around the big stores, there's no pleasure in that. I'd like to take our time and see which are the best shops to go back to when we're ready to buy our hats and dresses.'

'Don't forget we're having tea and cakes, girl, that's what I'm looking forward to. We don't often do that, it's only now and again we get the chance to be ladies of leisure and mix with the toffs.'

'They're not toffs, sunshine, they're flesh and blood, just as we are. Some have a bit more than others, but those who go for tea and cakes at the Kardomah, or Reece's, they aren't out of the top drawer, just ordinary folk who have to work for a living.'

'I don't know about that, girl, 'cos when we've been before, them what sat at the tables near us were talking so far back yer could hardly hear them.'

Molly grinned. 'Yer shouldn't be listening to them, sunshine. It's bad manners to eavesdrop.'

'If they didn't want anyone to hear, girl, they should keep their mouths shut. And why the heck they have to stick their little finger out when they drink their tea, well, I think it's daft.'

Again Molly grinned. 'If yer think it's daft, sunshine, then why do you do it?'

341

'Because if I didn't, they'd think I'm as common as muck.' Nellie had a picture flash across her mind, which caused her whole body to shake with laughter. 'Ay, girl, can yer imagine the looks on their faces if I poured me tea into the saucer and drank it from there, making those sucking noises? Ooh, wouldn't that be funny? Wouldn't yer just like to see their faces, eh?'

'I doubt if anyone would see their faces, sunshine, because I think they'd all walk out in disgust. And I'd be right behind them. Yer'd have the place to yerself until the manager came to turf you out, with a warning never to set foot in there again.'

'Yeah, and I'd tell him where to stick his café, and that's where Paddy stuck his nuts. Anyway, it would be ages before we went back there. They'd have forgotten us by then.'

'Oh, I doubt very much if they'd forget you, sunshine, 'cos it's a case of once seen never forgotten. Anyway, you being barred wouldn't affect me. I could go in any time I liked.'

'Yer wouldn't go in without me, girl, 'cos yer'd be lonely sitting at a table on yer own, with no one to talk to. And if yer saw something funny yer wouldn't be able to laugh, 'cos they'd all think yer were doolally.'

'Nellie, sunshine, if I was sitting at a table on me own in a café, and I was laughing, then I would be doolally. And I'd expect the men in white coats to come and take me away.'

'Oh, I wouldn't let them do that, girl!' Nellie put on her most fierce expression. 'I wouldn't let them get near yer.' She shook her fists. 'I'd knock them out in no time.'

'How could yer do that, Nellie, when yer've been barred from the place? They wouldn't let you in, so yer wouldn't be in a position to help me.'

'Ooh, er, I never thought of that.' Nellie's eyes went round the room as she sought a solution. 'I'm going to have to stop doing it, girl, there's nothing else for it.'

'Stop doing what, sunshine?'

'Drinking tea out of a saucer, that's what!'

'But yer don't drink out of a saucer, do yer?'

'That's what I'm trying to tell yer, girl! I won't do it no more.'

Molly decided it was time to bring the conversation to an end, otherwise there wouldn't be enough time to go into town, and have tea and cakes. And definitely no time for drinking tea out of a saucer. Not when all about them people were drinking out of china cups with their little fingers sticking out.

'It's ten to eleven, Nellie, and we'd promised ourselves we'd get out early today. I think yer can definitely forget going to the market, we'll have to leave it for another day. As it is we'll need a pair of skates to do all we'd set our mind on. Before we go into town we have to shop for whatever we're having for dinner, pick up our bread from Hanley's and bring the shopping back here. I don't want to be lugging it around town with us.'

'What are we having for dinner, girl?'

'I don't know about you, sunshine, but I'm doing mashed potatoes with milk and butter in, and two lightly fried eggs on top. Easy, cheap and tasty.'

'And I'll have the same, girl, 'cos as yer say, it's easy, cheap and tasty.' Nellie chuckled. 'If it wasn't for you, girl, George and Paul would be having fish and chips from the chippy every night. It's you what sets our menu.'

'It would cost you a fortune going to the chippy every night, and George and Paul wouldn't be happy about that.'

'Oh, I wouldn't go to the chippy for them, blow that for a lark. George could pick them up on his way home from work. He has to pass the shop.'

Molly's jaw dropped. 'Nellie, there are times when I think yer mouth is engaged before yer brain.' When she saw the look of bewilderment on her mate's face, she said, 'That means, sunshine, that yer don't know what ye're talking about. If yer gave some thought before yer spoke, yer might realize what you are saying is a load of rubbish. I know George lets yer get away with most of yer stupid ideas, but I doubt even he would give in to yer wanting him to call into the chip shop on his way home from work, and stand in a queue to pick up fish and chips for his dinner. Oh, and Paul's as well!'

Molly pushed her chair back with such force that it almost toppled over. 'I'll wash these cups through and then we'll be on our way. And if I'm quiet for the next half-hour, just leave me be. Don't ask why, or yer might get more than yer bargained for. I'll cool down eventually, but right now my blood pressure must be at boiling point. So while I wash these, you put yer coat on ready to go out.'

As she was carrying the cups into the kitchen,

Molly heard her mate mumble, 'All that over bleeding fish and chips! And I bet she'll have a face on her like a wet week for the rest of the day.'

Molly stepped back into the living room. 'Not all day I won't, sunshine. When we get on the bus to go into town, I'll be my happy self again, looking forward to going round the big shops.'

'Thank God for that!' Nellie said. 'All I've got to worry about now is to think before I open me mouth, and that won't be easy.' She let out a sigh. 'As I've said before, life can be a bugger at times.'

Chapter Sixteen

'I like this material, sunshine, and I love the colour.' Molly fingered the fine crêpe that had caught her eye out of all the bolts of different coloured materials. 'That's the sort of colour and material I'd like a dress in for the wedding.'

'What colour would yer say it is, girl?' Nellie asked, peering over Molly's arm. 'Is it blue?'

'It's between a lilac and a mauve, sunshine, I don't know the exact colour. It would go well with a pale lilac hat.'

'Ay, I'm beginning to get excited now, girl. How far off did yer say the wedding was?'

'Well, we're into July now, and the wedding is on the eighteenth of September, so let me think.' Molly used her fingers to count the number of weeks. 'It's just over eight weeks, sunshine, and that'll fly over. I'll have to start saving up in earnest

345

if I don't want to look like a tramp at the wedding.'

'I can't ask my George for money for my outfit,' Nellie said, "cos he's told me he's saving up to buy a new suit. He wants to look his best for his son's wedding.'

'If our Doreen didn't have so much on her plate with looking after the baby, and Victoria, I'd ask her to make me a dress in this material. I've really taken a fancy to it. But I wouldn't ask Doreen, it wouldn't be fair. So don't you mention it, Nellie, d'yer hear?'

'I won't say nothing, girl, 'cos I'm fed up getting lectures off yer. It's getting that way I'm frightened to open me mouth in case I put me foot in it.'

'You, frightened to open yer mouth!' Molly turned away from the counter and bolts of material. 'That'll be the day when you can't open yer mouth, Nellie, unless yer get lockjaw.'

Nellie squinted up at her. 'What's lockjaw when it's out? I've never heard of it. Is it one of these words what yer come out with to confuse me?'

'No, there is such a word, but I can't for the life of me think what it really means. Except, perhaps, that the jaw locks and yer can't speak. But don't take that as being right 'cos I really don't know.'

'Why don't yer look it up in that dictionary of yours and find out? And let me know, 'cos I don't want me jaw locked so I can't speak.'

'I can think of an answer to that, sunshine, but I won't spoil our shopping trip by telling yer. Let's move away from here because there's a shop assistant watching us. She's probably hoping for a sale, bless her, but seeing as neither of us has enough cash for spending today, we can't help her. Except to give her a big smile as we pass her.'

'It is quiet in here today,' Nellie said. 'There's hardly any customers. Everyone must be skint.'

'It's the weekends they're busy, when people have been paid.' They were passing a counter where gloves were on display, when Molly put a hand on Nellie's arm. 'Ay, sunshine, see those beige gloves on the model, well they're just like the ones I bought last year for your Lily's wedding. I've never worn them since, never had any cause to wear them. They're in one of the drawers in the tallboy, wrapped in tissue paper, and they're just like new, not a mark on them. It would be stupid, and a waste of money, to buy another pair, so I'll wear them for the wedding and that'll save me a few bob.' She grinned down at Nellie. 'That's one thing less to worry about. And I've never worn the shoes I bought to go with them, either! I'm used to wearing flat heels, and a two-inch heel cripples me. I don't know why I bought them. It was vanity, I suppose.'

'I saw yer pulling a face when yer had them on, girl, and I knew yer were in agony.' Nellie linked her mate's arm and they made for the exit door of T. J. Hughes' large store. 'I remember at the reception yer were dancing in yer stocking feet.'

'I can't resist dancing when I hear music playing. Especially the slow, dreamy music, which makes me feel romantic. It takes me back to the day when I first met Jack at a tuppenny hop at the church hall, and I can remember the first time he came over and asked me to dance. He was really shy and red in the face, while I was terrified

347

because I wasn't much of a dancer. I was a raw beginner.'

'Ah, ye're getting all soppy now,' Nellie said. 'All these years we've been mates, and that's the first time yer've mentioned that. Tell me, did yer stand all over his feet that night?'

Molly chuckled. 'We both trod on each other's feet, 'cos he was so nervous he couldn't concentrate, and kept bumping into other couples. If he said "Sorry" once, he said it a hundred times. But it didn't stop him coming over for the next dance, and the one after. And we both did well in that, because it was a slow waltz.'

'Did he ask yer if he could take yer home, girl, like my George did on the first night we met at a dance?'

'He got two for the price of one, sunshine, because I was with a girl out of our street. When I told Jack he couldn't take me home because I was with a mate, he offered to see us both home. That happened a couple of times, until Jack asked me if I'd go to the pictures with him. So me friend, whose name was Nancy, had to go to the dance on her own that night. And good for her, she met a bloke she liked and we both ended up happy ever after.'

'Just like in the fairy tales, eh, girl?'

'Yes, sunshine, just like in the fairy tales,' Molly said. 'Except in the fairy tales the prince doesn't have to go through an interrogation by an Irish woman who asked him so many personal questions he didn't know where to put his face. But, thank God, me ma didn't put him off, and he kept coming back for more.'

348

They stood on the pavement outside the shop, taking in the fresh air and sunshine. 'It's a nice day, Nellie, so we may as well walk down to Church Street. It's a bit of exercise, which we get very little of. We only walk as far as the shops every day, and after that we sit on our backsides.'

'I don't mind sitting on me backside,' Nellie told her. 'It's nice and soft to sit on. That's one good thing about being well padded.'

'Ay, Nellie Mac, I'm not all skin and bone, yer know.' Molly said. 'I might not be as well endowed as you are, but I'm not skinny, either!'

'Let's start walking, and we can argue on the way. Which shop are we heading for, girl?'

'We'll let our feet lead us, shall we, sunshine? The first shop we come to that we like the look of, we'll go in.'

'And what time are we going for our tea and cake?' As usual Nellie's thoughts were on her tummy, and the treat in store for it. 'It's getting near lunchtime, yer know. I bet it's turned one o'clock now. I haven't got a watch, but my tummy is as good as a watch any day. It always lets me know when it's time to eat.'

'Yes, I have noticed that, sunshine. I know yer are very fond of yer tummy. And seeing as yer insist on treating me, we'll go when and where yer want to have our tea and cake. You're the boss now.'

'Don't be too nice to me, girl, or I'll think ye're sickening for something. I can deal with yer when ye're telling me off, or moaning, because I'm so used to it. But when yer go all sickly sweet, I don't trust yer!'

'Thanks for telling me, sunshine. I'll watch what I say in future. Anyway, I don't tell yer off! If I think ye're wrong, then I'll tell yer so. But that doesn't come under the heading of telling yer off. In my book it means putting the record straight.'

'Oh, is that what it is? Keeping records, are yer?' Nellie nodded her head as her mouth did contortions. 'Well, I'll have to get meself a note-book, and write down every time yer have a face on yer what would stop a clock. I'll give yer one bad mark if the clock goes slow, and two bad marks if it stops altogether.'

'When yer go in the shop to buy the book, yer can get me one while ye're at it. Get me one with lines on, 'cos I'm not very good at writing in a straight line.'

'Ah, me heart bleeds for yer, girl, it's a hard life yer've got.' Nellie wasn't as good at sarcasm as Molly, but she did her best. 'Would yer like the line to go across the paper or down?'

'It doesn't matter much, sunshine, because I'm going to draw lines in it meself. Six lines down I'm going to do, so there'll be a line for every day of the week except Sunday, because I don't see yer on a Sunday. And in the six spaces, I'm going to put words like "Nellie swore today", or "Nellie told three lies today"!'

'Ooh, that's going to be some job for yer, girl. It'll take a lot of yer time up. But I'll help yer out, I won't make things hard for yer. I'll make a note of the number of times I say "sod", and you make a note of me "bleedings"'s.' Nellie screwed her eyes up for a few seconds, then said, 'We'll share "bugger", 'cos I don't say that very often. Only when I bang me head or me elbow. Oh, and when I'm chasing after Elsie Flanaghan. That doesn't happen often now though, because she takes to her heels as soon as she sees me. Talk about "now you see it, and now yer don't" isn't in it. And I miss me little spats with Elsie, 'cos they used to liven the day up. I used to enjoy them.'

'You might have done, sunshine, but Elsie certainly didn't and neither did I! There's nothing I dislike more than seeing two grown women fighting in the street.'

'Ay, girl, yer could draw another line in yer book, and put that in it. Put it in under the heading "Common as Muck".'

'Nellie, we've been standing in this one spot for so long, it's a wonder the police haven't moved us on for obstruction. So will yer make up yer mind what yer want to do? Go in Owen Owen or Reece's?'

'I'll let you choose, girl. I don't mind where we go, as long as it's Reece's.'

'Well, one thing ye're not slow on, sunshine, and that's anywhere where food is concerned. And as we're standing right outside, we don't have far to go. So stick yer leg in, and we'll walk up to the café on the first floor.'

Linking her mate's arm, and leaning on it to climb the steps, Nellie said, 'Ay, girl, if I keep forgetting to stick me little finger out, yer will give me a nudge, won't yer? I don't want no one thinking I haven't been brought up proper.'

'Nellie, not everyone drinks with their little finger sticking out. Have yer ever seen me doing it?'

'I haven't noticed, girl, 'cos I'm always too busy looking round at the tables what are near me. I can see you any time, I only see the toffs every blue moon, and I don't want them to think I'm not as good as they are.'

They were at the entrance to the café on the first floor of Reece's and could see the tables were nearly all occupied, and the atmosphere was alive with the various conversations. 'Ooh, we'll never get in there, girl, all the tables are taken.' Nellie looked disappointed. 'That's what we get for standing gabbing for so long.'

'Have some patience, Nellie, for heaven's sake. We've only just got here.' Molly's eyes travelled the room, and it was on her second sweep that she noticed a table for two in the far corner. 'Come on, sunshine, there's a table over in that corner. Let's get over there before someone else spots it.'

'Ooh, you've got good eyesight, girl,' Nellie said, waddling behind and knocking a few elbows on the way. She ignored the dirty looks, telling herself they should keep their elbows to themselves, instead of sticking them out and taking all the room up. It was the little fingers what were to blame, and she wasn't going to bother sticking hers out any more. It was daft pretending to be something yer weren't. When they reached the table, there was a look of despair on Nellie's face. 'I'll never get in there, girl, me tummy wouldn't fit in. Can't we find another table, where we can sit in comfort?'

'I can't see another one, sunshine, but I can see two ladies on the far side who are just about to put their coats on. I'll nip over sharpish, before someone else bags the table. You follow on behind me.'

Molly was just in time to secure the table before another couple reached it, and she was all smiles when Nellie reached her. 'This is better, isn't it, sunshine? The waitress hasn't been to clear the table, but she'll be along soon. And anyway, I don't care as long as we're sitting down. We're not in any hurry.'

'Some of the tables have got cake stands on, girl, and they have a variety of cakes on. Are they only for rich people, 'cos they've never given us a cake stand.'

'That's because we've never asked for one, Nellie.' Molly sucked in her breath, as her brain ticked over. The cake stands came with a selection of cakes, six in total, and you just paid for the ones eaten. It would be nice to have a selection to choose from, but to put a stand in front of Nellie would be asking for trouble, 'cos she would eat the lot. 'I'm quite happy to have a toasted teacake and a cup of tea, sunshine. More filling than a cake which you can eat in two bites and leaves yer just as hungry. How about it, Nellie, shall we settle for tea and toasted teacakes?' Molly could see her mate wavering towards the cream cakes, so she coaxed, 'They make lovely ones here, with lots of butter oozing out of them. My mouth is watering just talking about them, and I can practically feel the hot butter running down me chin.'

Nellie was hooked now, and she licked her lips in anticipation. 'Okay, girl, yer've talked me into it. In fact I'll have two of them, 'cos they sound just the job.'

'Yer can't resist, can yer, sunshine? Why do yer have to have two? If one is plenty for me, it should be enough for you. But, seeing as ye're the one with money to throw around, then you order two for yerself, and I'll order me own.'

'Keep yer hair on, girl, there's no need to be sarky over a ruddy teacake, even if they are oozing with butter. And another thing, Molly Bennett, my George and Paul gave me the money to buy us both tea and a cake. They said it was a treat for us, and they'll be upset if I tell them yer wouldn't let me. They'll be insulted, and yer wouldn't want that, would yer? So when the waitress comes, you order tea and a teacake each, because yer do it better than me.'

Molly could see her mate was getting upset, and it was the last thing she wanted. So she tried to put things right, and a smile back on the chubby face. 'Nellie, I know yer think I'm a miserable so-and-so, but it's only because I worry about you. If I didn't, then I'd let yer go ahead and eat whatever yer wanted. The more cakes and biscuits yer eat, the more weight yer pile on, and it's a strain on yer heart. I mean, in moderation, the odd cake and custard cream wouldn't do any harm, but you don't know the meaning of moderation, and yer stuff yerself as though there's no tomorrow! And it does worry me, sunshine, I can't help it. Ye're me best mate, and I wouldn't be much of a friend if I didn't try and stop yer making yerself ill. If our roles were reversed, you'd do the same. In fact yer'd be more forceful than me, 'cos I know yer've got as much affection for me as I have for you.'

354

'Here's the waitress coming with her pad, girl, so you give the order in, and when she's gone I'll tell yer how much I love yer.'

Molly smiled with relief. 'I'll ask her to clear the table first, sunshine, 'cos I won't enjoy me treat with dirty crockery on the table.'

The waitress was a little hot and bothered because she'd been run off her feet in the last couple of hours, but she quickly gathered the crockery on to the tray and smiled at Molly who was seated nearest. 'I'll clear the table, madam, then come back and take your order.' As she picked the tray up, she again smiled at Molly, and said, 'I couldn't help hearing your daughter saying she loved you, and I thought it was really sweet.' She hurried away, leaving Molly with a choice of laughing or crying. She looked across the table at Nellie, and realized it was easy to see why the waitress thought she was her daughter, for Nellie, sitting on the chair, looked very small, and as she had her head turned towards the table next to them, the waitress hadn't really seen her face. So now Molly didn't see it as the insult that at first left her flabbergasted. She'd tell Nellie, and give her a laugh, even though Molly knew she was asking for trouble, because Nellie would tell everyone she met that she'd been taken for Molly's daughter.

Little knowing what she'd missed, Nellie swivelled back in her chair and told her mate, 'Ay, yer should listen to those two women on the next table, girl, it isn't half interesting. One of the woman's daughters has been courting a bloke for three years, and they were supposed to be getting married next month. And doesn't the sod tell her last night that he'd met someone else, and she'd better cancel plans for the wedding.' Nellie went into her boxing mood, eyes like slits, nostrils flared and hands curled into fists. 'If I could get me hands on him I'd make him sorry he jilted a poor girl just weeks before her wedding. He deserves a good thrashing, the blighter.'

Molly was horrified. 'Nellie, have you sat there listening in to the intimate conversation of strangers? I don't know how you have the nerve! It's a wonder they weren't angry, and told you to mind yer own business. It's a good job they were deep in conversation and probably didn't notice you.'

'Oh, I think they knew I was listening, girl, because they kept looking at me. They knew I was on their side and felt sorry for them 'cos I was nodding and shaking me head at the right times. One of them kept tutting when she was listening to the mother of the girl what got let down, and I tutted with her.'

Molly leaned forward so the two women at the next table couldn't hear her words. 'I think I should have stayed in bed this morning, sunshine, because I think I got out on the wrong side. The first sign it wasn't going to be one of me best days was when you and me had a difference of opinion over yer wanting George to call into the chip shop on his way home from work. I don't like it when we have an argument.'

Her face as innocent as a baby's, Nellie said, 'Yer don't have to worry about being a bit of a misery, girl, 'cos I don't mind. It's like water off a duck's back to me. So don't get yer knickers in a twist. And as for me listening in to what those two women were talking about, well yer missed out on that because it was really interesting, and I'm sorry yer missed a treat. But I know you wouldn't do such a thing because ye're too good-living. So forget what's gone 'cos yer can't do nothing about it now, and pretend the day is just beginning. That should cheer yer up.'

'Oh, you haven't heard the best yet, sunshine. On top of everything else that hasn't been to my liking in the last two hours, the waitress thinks I'm your mother! And if I hear yer laugh, or crack a joke, then so help me I will clock yer one.'

Nellie thought she was having her leg pulled. 'Ay, yer must be feeling better, girl, 'cos it's not very often yer think up something as funny as that! I'm supposed to be the comedian, but I wouldn't have thought that up in a million years. Not that it's really funny in itself, like, 'cos anybody else would think it was corny. But because ye're me best mate, I won't say that.'

'It's not a joke, Nellie, I'm telling the truth. The waitress heard yer say how much yer loved me, and she said she thought it was really sweet. She was run off her feet, and she cleared the table saying she'd come back for our order.'

Nellie stared hard into Molly's eyes, to see if she could see a glint of humour, but her mate's expression gave nothing away. 'Give in, girl, and tell me the truth. Yer are pulling me leg, and it's a joke.'

'Yer can ask her yerself, sunshine, because this is her coming towards us now. She's coming to take our order.'

The waitress had the order pad in one hand, and her pen poised in the other. 'I'm sorry you've been kept waiting, but we are always busy at this time of day. I'll take your order now.' She addressed Molly first, before glancing to where Nellie sat with her elbows on the table. After another quick glance, the woman turned back to Molly. 'Oh, has your daughter left? I do hope it wasn't because she had to wait so long?'

Molly sensed Nellie shuffling to the edge of her chair, and knew she wouldn't be able to resist adding her two-pennyworth. She would do it for a laugh, but the waitress didn't have time for a laugh, not when she was so busy. So Molly jumped in before her mate had a chance.

'No, my daughter has gone on a message for me. As you see, one of my friends turned up, so I haven't been left alone. And now we'll give you the order so you can go about your business. It's a pot of tea for two, and two of your delicious toasted teacakes.'

The waitress scribbled quickly, not wanting to keep the customer waiting any longer. 'I'll be back in a few minutes, and I do apologize for the delay.'

'Don't worry, girl, yer've got enough to do, being so busy, and my friend is quite happy now I'm here to keep her company.'

The waitress scurried away, missing the glint in Nellie's eyes and her chuckle. 'Ay, she thought she was seeing things, I could tell. Yer were right, girl, yer weren't pulling me leg after all. But she must either be stupid, or need her eyes testing.

358

How could she possibly mistake me for yer daughter? Nearly every girl resembles her mother in some way, but you've got blonde hair and blue eyes, while I'm mousy-coloured and have eyes what are light brown. At least that's what I had the last time I looked, if yer know what I mean, like. It's a long time since I saw me face 'cos we haven't got a ruddy mirror what I can see meself in. I know I've still got two eyes and a nose, because I can feel them, but that's about it.'

'I don't really care how or what conclusion she reached, sunshine,' Molly told her. 'But I'm very grateful to her in one way; she did me a favour.'

'What d'yer mean, like, girl?' Nellie's brow was raised. 'She didn't do yer no favour by thinking I was yer daughter. Yer'd have to be in yer sixties to be my mother.'

'Yer don't need to tell me that, sunshine, 'cos I can add up. What I mean by saying she'd done me a favour is that she's made me realize that my lot in life is not so bad, and I should be grateful to her for reminding me of the fact. I mean, just imagine what my life would be like if I was your mother!' Molly was chuckling inside. 'My life wouldn't be worth living if I had to cope with you every day and night. I couldn't bear it.'

'Well, that's charming, that is, I must say! That's not a very nice way for a best mate to talk.' Nellie put on her woebegone look and let out a heavy sigh. 'I'm cut to the quick, girl, me heart is bleeding. In fact, by the time that woman comes back with our order, she'll be wading in blood, that's how much me quick has been cut to.'

Molly laughed. 'I bet yer don't know where yer

quick is, sunshine, no more than yer know where yer heart is. Whenever ye're acting dramatic, and yer want to put yer hand on yer heart, yer put it in the wrong place.'

'No, I don't, girl, I know where me heart is. After all, it is my heart, so I should know where it is.' Her hand went to her right breast. 'It's right here, where it should be.'

The appearance of the waitress carrying a tray was the reason Molly didn't tell her mate that most people had a heart on the left side of their body, for she knew the poor woman would be brought into the discussion on the whereabouts of Nellie's. 'Oh, that looks very nice.' Molly smiled at the small, slim woman carrying the heavy tray. 'Here, let me help you put it down. Those teacakes smell delicious, don't you think so, Nellie?'

Putting on her very best accent, and with a hint of sarcasm, Nellie answered, 'Oh, yes, Molly, they look very inviting. Almost good enough to eat, I think.'

Molly glared at her before telling the waitress, 'My friend will have her little joke, even though it's not always appreciated by others.'

The tray now cleared, the waitress held it down at her side. 'I'm sure you'll enjoy them, madam.' With that she hurried back to the kitchen to pick up the next order. It was on busy days like this that she thought it would have been better if she'd taken the job in Vernon's when she had the opportunity. It would have meant working every Saturday night marking the football coupons, but at least she wouldn't be run off her feet every day, and the wages were five shillings a week more. Still, it was no use wondering what would have been, it was too late to do anything about it. Unless she tried again in the hope that they wouldn't remember she'd turned the job down once. She watched her next order being put on the tray, and blamed all her woes on her boyfriend, especially her aching feet. He was the one who put her off the job in Vernon's because he objected to her working every Saturday evening.

'Christine, will yer wake up!' one of the kitchen staff said. 'Yer mind is miles away, and I'm standing here like a lemon. Get cracking before this tea goes cold.'

The waitress gave a quick shake of her head to clear her mind. And as she picked up the laden tray, she made a decision. On Monday morning she'd call in to the Labour Exchange and ask for an application form for Vernon's. To hell with her boyfriend, it wasn't him who had the sore feet.

Back at their table, Molly was pouring the tea out. 'I wouldn't like her job for all the tea in China. At everyone's beck and call and run off her feet.'

'Yeah, she should get married, like what we did. Then she could live the life of a lady, with bags of time on her hands, and she could please herself whether she spent her day doing housework, or just gave a quick flick of the duster when the dust started to show. That's what she should do, girl, find a husband and have a life of leisure, like what we have.'

'Ay, Nellie Mac, you speak for yerself,' Molly told her. 'I don't live the life of a lady, and I don't know anyone in our street what does. All the menfolk go out to work and the wives work just as hard bringing up the children and struggling to make ends meet. That's besides doing the housework, the washing and ironing, the shopping and the cooking. I'm not moaning, I'm quite happy with my life, always have been. But it is far from a life of leisure.'

'I'm always telling yer, girl, that I don't see any point in dusting and polishing every day. Yer should be like me and leave the dust to mount up for a few days. And then only get the duster out when it's gathered enough to be seen.'

'Nellie, I don't think you'd worry if your backside was on fire. The dust could be meeting George at the front door when he came home from work, and you wouldn't give a toss. I don't know how yer've got the nerve. All I can say is that yer've got a husband in a thousand. My Jack is a good husband, but he'd soon have something to say if I let the housework go to pot.' Molly wiped her mouth with the small paper napkin. 'Not that Jack is the reason for me being house-proud, I've always been fussy. I take after me ma, she's very fastidious.' Molly used the napkin again to wipe her mouth, but this time it was to hide a smile while she watched the contortions on Nellie's face. How long would it be before the little woman found a way of finding out what fastidious meant? She wouldn't ask outright; that wasn't the way Nellie's mind worked.

'I'm just as fast as you are, girl, so don't be so bleeding big-headed. It's a wonder yer can get through the front door the size of yer head.'

362

'Nellie, if ye're referring to the word fastidious, then before yer get yer knickers in a twist, it means fussy.'

Nellie was too worked up to listen, and her knickers were already in a twist. 'How would you like to be called a slowcoach, eh? Right in me face as well! I think yer've got a flaming cheek, Molly Bennett.' Nellie stopped for breath, and when she spoke again it was in a more relaxed voice. 'What did yer say the word meant, girl? Did I hear right when yer said yer were fussy?'

'Yes, Nellie, yer did hear right, and to save any more argument I'll hold me hands up and admit I am fussy. So let's forget all about it now, so when our husbands ask us tonight what we did in town we won't have to say we spent best part of the day arguing over who was big-headed and fussy, and who got their knickers in a twist over nothing.' Molly sat back in her chair. 'You're nearer the tea-pot, sunshine. Will yer see if there's any tea left in it?'

Nellie shook her head. 'It's only warm, girl, not fit to drink.' Then a slow smile creased her chubby cheeks. 'I know what we can do, girl. We can pretend we've just come in, and we can order tea and teacakes all over again. Isn't that a good idea, Molly, 'cos those teacakes were really nice.'

Molly was tempted. 'They were more than nice, they were scrumptious.' She quickly lifted a hand. 'That means they were really nice, sunshine, so don't be giving me dirty looks. And yes, let's go mad for a change and order a repeat.'

'You order, girl, while I sit here with me mouth watering.'

'Okay, sunshine, but yer do know it will mean getting the bus as soon as we leave here? No time to look around the shops because we have to be home to make the dinners. It's up to you, Nellie, it's your choice.'

It was Nellie's turn to lean forward. 'I often say that life can be a bugger, girl, as yer know. But this is a time when life is worth living. So call the waitress over, in yer posh voice, mind, and give her the order. Yer could tell her we're in a hurry, so she'll move herself. If she's a slowcoach, then me mouth won't be just watering, I'll be slobbering like a baby.'

'Behave yerself, Nellie. Don't make a show of me.'

'I wouldn't dream of it, girl! I wouldn't make a fool of someone who is fastidious and thinks teacakes are scrumptious.' She turned away chuckling at the expression on Molly's face.

Chapter Seventeen

'You were late getting in last night, sunshine,' Molly told her daughter as she put her tea and toast down in front of her. 'Yer know yer've been told often enough by me, and yer dad, that half past ten is the limit for you to be out, and no later.' She pulled a chair out and sat facing her daughter. 'You were later than that last night, and me and yer dad were worried.'

Ruthie pulled a face. 'We were only outside

talking. Me and Gordon, and Peter. And we weren't really late, only about five minutes.'

Jack drained his cup, then raised his brows at his daughter. 'It was nearly a quarter to eleven, Ruthie, and that's too late for you to be out. We know yer won't come to any harm with Gordon, but we have to be up early and need to get to bed at a reasonable time. Yer have enough time at the dance to do all the talking yer need. Don't let it happen again, d'yer hear me?'

'Bella's mam and dad wouldn't be very happy, sunshine,' Molly said. 'Yer know how they worry about her.'

'It was because of Bella we were late,' Ruthie told her. 'She probably won't tell her mam the truth, she'll blame us. But honest, Mam, she got on my nerves last night, acting like a big baby.'

Molly's brows shot up. 'It's not like you to talk that way about Bella! I hope yer haven't had a quarrel after all these years of being best mates? She is so quiet and timid, I can't imagine her doing anything to cause yer to fall out.'

'Well she did!' Ruthie's stubborn streak showed in the set of her jaw. 'It wasn't me she made a fool of, it was Peter. And herself, 'cos she was acting like a big kid.'

Jack had a look of surprise on his face. 'It must have been something really out of character for Bella to cause yer to talk about her like that. Never in a million years would I expect to be having this conversation. What did Bella do that was so bad?'

'Everything was all right on the way to the dance, we were laughing and joking, all in a good mood. When we got to Blair Hall, Gordon bought my ticket and Peter paid for Bella. We were fine until the first excuse me. I was dancing with Gordon and Bella with Peter. Anyway, some bloke excused Bella, which is nothing out of the ordinary because it happens to everyone. Then we always meet up after the dance. But last night the feller who excused Bella kept her talking after the music had finished. And while Peter was waiting for her, she stood talking to this bloke and she was laughing and giggling like a school-girl. I don't know what he was saying to her, he's one of those cocky lads who think they're another James Cagney. I felt sorry for Peter, standing there waiting for her while she was being all coy. Gordon was in a right temper, 'cos Peter had paid for her bus fare and the dance ticket.'

'That doesn't sound a bit like Bella,' Molly said. 'She's usually so shy. But I agree with yer that she was wrong to treat Peter like that.'

Speaking through the toast in her mouth, Ruthie said, 'I was really annoyed, and in the end I went over to her. When I asked why she hadn't joined us, the smart lad told me to scram and mind me own business.' When she heard her mother gasp, Ruthie told her, 'That was nothing, Mam, to what he said to Peter, who had come up behind me. Yer know how quiet Peter is, well, when smart lad told him to get lost, I thought there was going to be a fight because Gordon came over.'

Molly's eyes told of her surprise. 'What on earth was Bella doing all through this? Why didn't she walk away with you and Peter?'

'Don't ask me, Mam. She looked as though she was enjoying all the attention. And the lad was sneering, as though he'd clock anyone if they tried to interfere. He's a real tough lad, who'd knock yer for six if yer looked sideways at him. When I asked Bella if she was coming to stand with her mates, the queer lad smirked, and told us she was having the next dance with him.'

'What sort of a place is it that yer go to, pet?' Jack asked, his temper rising. 'Perhaps yer should give it a miss in future. It doesn't sound like a place I'd wish a daughter of mine to go to.'

'There's nothing wrong with Blair Hall, Dad. It's a nice place, never any trouble there.'

'It doesn't sound a nice place, sunshine,' Molly said, 'when there's bad lads go there and cause a fight.'

'It didn't come to a fight, Mam.' Ruthie's face was relaxed and smiling now. 'I got hold of Bella's hand, and the lad tried to pull her towards him, but I put me foot behind his leg and sent him sprawling on the floor. I dragged Bella back to where we always stand, then went back to where the clever lad was getting to his feet. There was a crowd around him and they were all making fun of him. It appears he's not very popular there, being a bit of a bully. Anyway, I was going to tell him what I thought of him when Gordon came up behind me and he told the lad in no uncertain terms that if he came near us again he would be going home with two black eyes. And the crowd around said it was what he deserved. He is a very unpopular lad by the sound of things. Probably makes a play for all the girls, and the fellers don't like it.'

Jack pushed his plate away with his eyes on the clock. 'No time left for talking, pet, or we're going to be late for work. Put a move on, there's a love.'

Molly jumped to her feet. 'I'd forgotten about the time, ye're both going to be late. Put yer skates on, Ruthie, and take that piece of toast with yer. Yer can eat it on the way to the bus.' Then Molly had a thought. 'Are yer still going in to work with Bella, sunshine, or have yer fallen out?'

'I'm still going to work with her, Mam. I'm not so childish I'd fall out with her.'

Ruthie struggled into her coat, a piece of toast between her teeth. Her mother had the front door open and Jack was the first out. Kissing Molly's cheek, he said, 'We'll talk about it tonight. Ta-ra, love.'

Ruthie took the toast from her mouth and kissed Molly. 'Ta-ra, Mam. I'll finish the tale later. I might add to it so it'll be more interesting. She turned when she stepped on to the pavement and grinned. 'I'll do an Auntie Nellie on yer.'

Molly watched her daughter crossing the cobbles to where Bella was standing with her mother, Mary. Not wanting to get involved in a conversation with Mary until she'd heard the full story, Molly waved a hand in greeting before stepping back and closing the door. The Watsons were a nice family who had lived in the Street for over sixteen years. In fact Bella was born not long after they moved in. An only child, she had been wrapped in cotton wool, the wind wasn't allowed to blow on her. With Ruthie being the same age, they'd become friends from when they could toddle. But because of Mary's almost suffocating hold on her daughter, the two young girls weren't allowed to move away from the Watsons' front door, so Mary could keep an eye on her daughter. Molly had, over the years, told Mary she was holding her daughter back, and she should allow the girl to grow and blossom like other children, not smother her. To Ruthie's credit, she had stuck by her friend, even though it meant her missing out on the Saturday matinee at the picture house, and going to the park with a bottle of lemonade and some sandwiches to have a picnic. And now both girls were sixteen, it had been thanks to Molly, with the help and support of Bella's father, Harry, that the girl was allowed to go dancing. And that was only achieved because they went with the Corkhill boys, who were well respected in the Street.

Molly cleared the breakfast dishes, shook the tablecloth in the yard, then put the kettle on for hot water to wash the dishes in, and to make herself a cup of tea. And all the time she was wondering what really happened, and why. She didn't for one second disbelieve what Ruthie had told her and Jack, for her daughter never told lies. In fact it was just the opposite: she was apt to be too outspoken and said precisely what she thought.

Molly pulled a chair out from under the table, put her cup of tea down, then plonked herself on the chair. She felt restless, which wasn't usual. And even after drinking her tea and telling herself she was being ridiculous worrying and fretting over something she could do nothing about, she couldn't talk herself out of her depression. There had been few upsets in the Bennett house, few arguments and absolutely no falling out. All her children got on well with each other, and that had made for a happy home.

Running a hand across her forehead, Molly told herself not to be so miserable over such a stupid thing. If Bella had done something out of place, then it was up to her mother to sort her out. Bella was naïve because she hadn't been allowed to grow up, and it was up to her parents now to deal with it.

So, with that thought firmly in her head, Molly started her housework humming. The fireplace thought it was its birthday, it was so shiny it could see itself in the reflection of the highly polished sideboard. And upstairs in the bedrooms, the bedding was given such a good shaking, it gave a sigh of pleasure and went to sleep as soon as Molly left the room.

When half past ten came, Nellie could hear her mate singing as she raised the knocker, and she was invited in with a waving hand and a face smiling and happy. 'What's got into you, girl? Yer haven't had a sly bottle of milk stout, have yer?'

'No, sunshine, I haven't. But look at those white clouds bobbing and drifting in a beautiful clear blue sky. Doesn't it make yer feel happy, and glad to be alive?'

Nellie squeezed past her in the tiny hall. 'If it's not milk stout yer've had, then the water in your tap must be different from ours, 'cos the blue sky doesn't have the same effect on me. I wouldn't

370

have even noticed it if yer hadn't pointed it out! I don't look up much, yer see.' She made straight to the carver chair and placed it at the table. 'D'yer know why I don't look up, girl? Well, it's because yer never find anything that way. If yer look down, on the other hand, yer might just find a tanner, or a threepenny bit what someone has dropped. A lot of people have holes in their pockets, yer know, and things do fall through.'

'I know you've got a hole in yer pocket, sunshine, but I've never known yer to lose anything out of it.' Molly stood by the kitchen door, waiting for the kettle to boil. 'Anyway, walking with yer head down has its drawbacks. Yer could walk into a lamp post and give yerself a black eye. Or yer could bump into someone, stand on their toes, and they'd give yer a black eye.'

Nellie squinted at her mate. 'Did you and Jack have an early night in bed last night?'

'No we didn't, sunshine! We were late getting to bed as it happens, because Ruthie came in later than usual and got a telling off.'

Nellie chuckled. 'So what ye're trying to tell me, girl, is that yer didn't have the time or the energy?' She tutted. 'Me, now, I'd make the time, and find the energy, no matter what time of day or night it was.'

The kettle began to whistle, and Molly said, 'Saved by the bell.' She then hurried out to switch off the gas before pouring the boiling water into the teapot. 'I'm in a happy mood now, and don't want to know about the shenanigans yer get up to in yer bedroom.' There was silence as she prepared the tray, then she said, 'Anyway,

371

a woman of your age should be past talking about a subject that should only be discussed by man and wife. It's private, and should stay that way.'

Nellie's feet began swinging under the chair. 'I thought it wouldn't last, girl, it was too good to be true. Yer were all smiles when yer opened the door to me, full of the joys of spring. I've been here five minutes and yer've got a face on yer what would stop a clock.'

'I'm sorry about that, sunshine, there's little I can do about it because it's the only face I've got. But if yer don't want to look at it, I don't mind. I don't get upset easily, not like some people I know. Anyway, yer tea's in front of yer, yer've got two biscuits in the saucer, so consider yerself lucky.'

Nellie dunked her biscuits in the tea, and within seconds they had disappeared. Then she wiped the back of a hand across her mouth before putting her bosom on the table and leaning across to be as near to Molly as possible. 'Ay, girl, I've got some news for yer. Phoebe's going into town on Wednesday to choose her wedding dress. She's taking the afternoon off work, 'cos Ellen doesn't work all day, with Wednesday being half-day closing, and they're going together.'

'Oh, that's nice,' Molly said. 'Ellen will be over the moon. The first of her children to get married. I bet her and Corker are delighted. I can picture Corker on the day of the wedding, he'll be as proud as a peacock. And I bet Phoebe will look beautiful, walking down the aisle on his arm. A pretty girl and a handsome man.'

Nellie dropped her head and gazed through her

eyelashes at Molly. 'I told George that I should be going with Phoebe on Wednesday, seeing as Ellen is going. He told me not to be so bloody daft.' She grunted. 'I know Ellen is mother of the bride, but I'm mother of the groom and we should be on equal footing.'

'I'm afraid I feel the same as George about that, sunshine. I mean, I can't see your Paul in a white wedding dress and carrying a bouquet, can you? If ye're going to look at it that way, then Ellen should go with Paul to choose his suit!'

'Don't start getting sarky, Molly Bennett, there's no need for it! I only mentioned it, and I still think Phoebe and Ellen wouldn't mind if I asked them nicely.'

'If yer had the nerve to ask, they would probably say yer could go with them because they wouldn't like to refuse. Yer'd put them in an awkward position, Nellie, and I don't think yer should do that. In fact, if I'm to be honest, I think yer'd have a ruddy cheek! Yer own common sense should tell yer it wouldn't be right. Neither Phoebe nor Ellen are in any way related to you, so yer really shouldn't expect to be involved.'

'I'll be Phoebe's mother-in-law when she marries our Paul, so we'll be related then, and what difference does a few ruddy weeks make?'

'The difference is she is not yer daughter-in-law as yet, and not related to you in any way. Besides all this, no bride wants anyone, no matter who they are, to see the bridal dress until the wedding day. Don't yer see now, after all that, how wrong you are, or have I been wasting me breath?'

'Oh, yer haven't been wasting yer breath, girl,

yer've given me a headache with it.'

'I'm sorry yer've got a headache, sunshine, but yer've brought it on yerself. Yer always want to be involved in everything, even though it's got nothing to do with you. Why don't yer leave Paul and Phoebe to get on with what they want for their wedding? They should be looking forward to the happy day, making plans together, being excited and secretive. Especially Phoebe, who won't even let Paul see her dress until she's walking down the aisle on Corker's arm. Don't begrudge her that, sunshine. Remember when you were young and in love, and how excited yer were on yer wedding day? I remember how it was with me, I couldn't sleep for weeks before me and Jack got married. We weren't well off in those days, so there was no expensive dress or flowers, and no reception. All we had as regards a party was having some neighbours in for a glass of sherry and a piece of wedding cake me ma had made. But we enjoyed ourselves. We were in love, and still are.'

Her mate's words had Nellie going back in time, and there was a gentle smile on her face. 'Yeah, it was the same for me and George. We saved up to buy the rings, and I was married in a second-hand dress, and George had his dad's suit on, 'cos his own was frayed. Our two mothers got together and bought enough eats to have a party in our house. Mind you, there were so many neighbours came, we all ended up in the street having a right old knees-up. As me ma said, "Yer don't need to have money to enjoy yerself, queen, just good friends and neighbours."'

'Your mam was right, sunshine, and we're here

to prove she was right. For twenty-five years we've been both neighbours and friends, and that's good going. Not that there hasn't been the odd difference of opinion now and again, but that is only to be expected. It would be a dull world if everyone thought alike.'

'We've never come to blows, girl, that's the main thing. It doesn't matter if we lose our rag now and again. I bet St Peter loses his temper sometimes with all the bad people in the world. And he can't swear to get it off his chest, not like we can. If I get in a temper, like banging me toe on the table leg, well, I can have a good swear and it makes me feel better.'

'Yer don't have to use bad words to make yer feel better,' Molly told her. 'If yer stub yer toe, like I do sometimes, then "blast" is as good a word as any.'

'That's what I say, girl! I often say blast!'

'Oh, come on now, sunshine, be honest. Yer don't always say blast! When yer banged yer knee on the corner of the sideboard last week, I distinctly heard yer saying, "Damn, blast and bugger it."'

'Ay, girl, I didn't half hurt me knee that day, it left a big bruise on me leg. Yer didn't expect me to say "Oh dear, golly heck", did yer, when I was in agony?'

Molly burst out laughing. 'I can see you, in me imagination of course, sitting in the Adelphi, having tea and cucumber sandwiches, with yer little finger sticking out. And you drop a few crumbs on the floor, look down, and say, "Oh, drat."'

'What does that mean, girl? I've never heard

that before.'

'It's what the posh people say, instead of "Oh, bugger it".'

'Ooh, I'll have to remember that.' Nellie's chins were in complete agreement with her. 'I will remember it, 'cos it's an easy word.' She leaned over the table, grimaced when she crushed her breasts, then a cheeky grin appeared. 'Oh, drat, I've hurt me bleeding bust now!'

Molly's laughter filled the room. 'Helen Theresa McDonough, what am I going to do with yer? Only you could be posh and as common as muck in the same sentence.'

'Ay, I'm going to try that on George tonight, and see if he knows what it means.' She gazed at the ceiling for inspiration, then turned a smiling face to Molly. 'I know what I'll do, girl, I'll drop a fork when I'm giving him his dinner, and say, "Oh, drat!"'

'What good would that do yer, sunshine? Except yer'd have to take the fork out and wash it again.'

'Would I heck!' Nellie said, her eyes rolling to the ceiling. 'George could wash it himself, or else he could eat his dinner with his ruddy fingers. No, girl, I'd only do that to see if my feller knew what "drat" meant! To catch him out, like. He thinks I'm as thick as two short planks, so let's find out if he's as clever as he makes out.'

'Well, if you want to play silly beggars, sunshine, that's up to you. I just don't know what yer'll gain from it, except one dirty fork. Still, to each his own, eh? We're all entitled to our opinion.'

'Ye're right to a certain extent, girl, but if we all

stuck to our opinion, and never gave in, then the world would be in a hell of a state, wouldn't it?' Nellie's face wore a serious expression, as though she was weighing up a matter of importance. Then she narrowed her eyes to slits when she looked at Molly. 'It wouldn't work, yer know, girl, no matter what yer say. Yer could talk to me until yer were blue in the face, but yer wouldn't change my opinion on Elsie Flanaghan. See what I mean, girl? She passed a few comments on me being fat, made rude remarks, and I'll never forgive her.'

Molly's mouth opened wide in disbelief. 'Nellie, Elsie Flanaghan passed a comment which I didn't like, regarding our Jill and Steve when they first went to live with Lizzie Corkhill. She said they were cadging off Lizzie, and I pulled her up over it. But you can't pass her without belting her. She's like a red flag to a bull, yer can't resist fighting with her. Yer've knocked her flying a few times, for no reason at all. She's terrified of yer now, and runs a mile when she sees yer!'

Nellie's head nodded vigorously. 'Yeah, 'cos she knows what she'll get if I ever catch up with her. She can't half run fast, she's like a whippet. But one of these days I'll catch her when she's not looking.'

'And what will yer do then, sunshine? Make a holy show of yerself? It's a pity yer've got nothing better to think of than Elsie Flanaghan, that's all I can say. Why don't yer think of something nice, like yer son's wedding? It's a big day in Paul's life and yours. He's getting a wonderful wife in Phoebe, and you're gaining a lovely daughter-in-law. Yer should be full of the joys of spring, having so much to look forward to.'

Nellie sent the cups rattling in the saucers when she banged a fist on the table. 'Ye're right, girl, as usual. I have got a lot to look forward to. I mean, like, I should be looking at wedding hats, and dresses. Why don't we go into town again and have a good look around? We didn't look proper when we went last week, we spent too long in the café.'

'Whose fault was that, sunshine? You were the one who wanted to go in Reece's in the first place, not me. And yer were the one who wanted a second helping. It was very nice, I have to admit,' Molly said. 'But I would have been happy going around a few shops to see what they had to offer in dresses and hats suitable for a wedding. But let's leave it until Saturday, Nellie, when I've had me housekeeping money off Jack. I put a couple of bob away last week, and I'll do the same this week. It's not enough to buy a dress, or a hat, but some shops will put things aside for yer as long as yer leave a deposit.'

'Ooh, ay, that's a good idea, girl, I would never have thought of that. So shall we definitely go on Saturday?'

Molly nodded. 'Yeah, as soon as we've got the dinner over. I'll leave the dishes to Jack, it'll give us a bit more time, and he won't mind. And now we've settled that, can we get a move on now? I want to call to Doreen's and Jill's before we go to the shops. We won't stay long in each house, just see the babies and have a little chat. Then this afternoon I'll walk round to see me ma and da. I

378

should go round more than I do. With Tommy and Rosie out at work every day, they're on their own and would welcome some company.'

'I'll come with yer, girl, to keep yer company on the way there and back.'

Molly chuckled. 'Nellie, it's only a few minutes' walk! Still, I'd feel there was something missing if yer didn't come. You and me remind me of that song "Me And My Shadow". I'm me, and you're my shadow.'

'Nah, I'm too fat to be your shadow, girl. If I was asked to describe you and me, I'd say we were the long and short of it.'

Molly patted Nellie's back as she followed her to the front door. 'Very good, Nellie! Yer can go to the top of the class for that.'

'Wait until I tell Victoria, I bet she'll have a laugh.'

'I'm sure she will, sunshine. But don't mention Phoebe and Ellen going to town on Wednesday to look at wedding dresses, because they'll think ye're just jealous.'

'Well, I am jealous, girl, and I'd be telling a lie if I said I wasn't. But after George having a go at me, and then you, I've decided two heads are better than one, so I'm going to keep me mouth shut.'

When Nellie stepped on to the pavement, she turned to say, 'Ay, girl, your Jill's pram is outside Doreen's, which means they'll be going for their own shopping.'

'I'll give a knock anyway, sunshine, just to see the babies. And me daughters and Victoria, of course. I wouldn't leave them out, even though it sounded like it.'

Doreen opened the door before Molly had time to knock. 'We saw yer coming, Mam.' She stood aside to let them pass, giving them each a kiss. 'Jill's here, but yer already know that with the pram outside.'

Molly's whole face lit up at the reception she received as she walked through the door. Jill ran to hug her, and the two babies screamed and struggled to reach out to her. 'Anyone would think they were glad to see you, Molly,' Victoria said. 'You're very popular.'

Nellie pushed her mate aside. 'Only because she got in first and is bigger than me. But look at little Moll, she's holding her arms out to me. She knows who her best grandma is.'

Jill passed little Moll to Nellie, and Doreen put Bobby down on the floor so she could talk to her mother and Jill, so her eyes weren't on him as he crawled towards Nellie. He covered the space quickly, then sat back on his bottom with his arms in the air. The only person who saw what happened next was Victoria. Her laughter caught in her throat and brought about a wheezing cough. It was this sound that caused Molly and her daughters to turn. And what a sight it was that met their eyes. Bobby had put his arms up to pull himself to his feet by clutching at Nellie's clothes. But his hands had gone under her dress, and it was her fleecy knickers he'd grabbed and pulled on, and they were now hanging around her ankles.

'He's pulled me bleeding knickers down!' Nellie's face was a picture as she told little Moll, 'Ay, he's starting young, isn't he?'

After a hearty laugh, Molly said, 'Oh, if we only had a camera! It's not often yer see a sight like that, thank goodness.' As she moved to relieve Nellie of little Moll, Doreen swept Bobby up in her arms. 'I'm not going to say you're naughty, darling, because ye're too young to understand. But although I think Auntie Nellie looks hilarious, don't ever do it again.'

Nellie hadn't been able to touch her feet for years because her mountainous bosom and huge tummy got in the way. So she shuffled to the kitchen with the knickers holding her back, muttering under her breath. Then, with her two hands on the sink, she looked down at the bloomers covering her feet. 'I can't reach down to pull yer up, yer silly bugger, so I'm going to have to step out of yer. And if this floor is dirty, don't blame me.'

Three heads popped round the door, and amid the laughter it was Molly who said, 'Ye're not coming to the shops with me with no knickers on, Nellie McDonough. What are yer thinking about? Pull them up and make yerself respectable.'

Nellie turned her head slowly and if looks could kill, then Molly would be dead. 'I can't reach down to take them off, but I can catch them if I kick them in the air. And if ye're too much of a snob to go out with me 'cos I've got no knickers on, then it's just too bad. I'll walk behind yer if it makes yer feel better.'

'Oh, dear, oh, dear,' Molly said. 'What a flipping performance! Just stay as yer are, Nellie, and I'll pull yer knickers up halfway. Yer can manage the rest yerself.' She pushed her two daughters back

381

into the living room. 'Let's have a bit of privacy, shall we? Nellie's not worried who sees her, but I am. So just close the door till I sort her out.'

Molly could hear the giggling as she closed the door, and she had trouble keeping her own face straight. 'Come on, Nellie, let's get it over with.' It was then she noticed the glint in her mate's eyes, and as she pulled the knickers up to the chubby knees she heard a chuckle, then, 'As I've told yer many times, girl, life can be a bugger.'

'My life would be a bed of roses if it wasn't for you, Nellie McDonough. Yer cause me more trouble than my four kids ever did. In fact they were angels compared to you.'

Doreen and Jill had their ears to the kitchen door, and Doreen repeated to Victoria everything that was said, making the old lady shake with quiet laughter.

'It wasn't my fault the baby pulled me knickers down, girl, so if yer want to tell anyone off, well, tell the baby. Your trouble is that yer haven't got no sense of humour. I bet when I tell yer ma and da, when we go round there this afternoon, they'll have a ruddy good laugh. And Tony and Ellen when we go to the butcher's, they'll see the funny side, as well.'

Those listening behind the door missed a treat, for Molly's mouth and eyes were wide with horror. Then came her reply. 'If that is your intention, Nellie Mac, to make a fool of yerself, then yer do it on yer own. I won't be with yer when yer go to the butcher's, and you won't be with me when I visit me ma and da. So see if yer find that funny.'

'I am a burden to yer, girl.' Nellie's face was sad,

but her tummy was shaking with mirth. A fact which didn't go unnoticed by Molly. 'Perhaps yer'd be better off without me. You go and do the shopping on yer own, I don't want to be a hanger-on. I know when I'm not wanted, I can take a hint.'

'Oh, yer poor thing,' Molly said. 'Me heart is bleeding for yer. As yer often say, life can be a bugger. But I'll forgive yer this time, sunshine, 'cos as I say my heart feels sad for yer. So make yerself respectable and we'll be on our way with no harm done.'

Molly was turning away when Nellie said, 'I hate to tell yer, girl, but the elastic in me knickers snapped when I pulled them up. Will yer ask your Doreen if she's got a safety pin I can borrow?'

The laughter from the living room drowned out Molly's reply.

Chapter Eighteen

Ellen and her daughter Phoebe got off the bus outside Lime Street Station, both laughing and excited. It was a very special day in Phoebe's life, and she was glad her mother was with her for support. She wouldn't have the nerve or confidence to look at wedding dresses on her own.

'What do yer want to do first, sweetheart?' Ellen asked. 'Shopping, or a snack in Sampson and Barlow's? I think we'd be better having something to eat and drink first, for we've both come straight from work and we'd feel much better with some food down us, even if it's only a sandwich. The café is right behind us, and the bridal gown shop yer were told about is just a bit further along Lime Street on the opposite side. Yer can see it from here, but yer can't see what they've got on display in the window.'

'I'm so excited, Mam, I've got butterflies in me tummy and feel as weak as a kitten.'

'It's Sampson and Barlow's then, sweetheart. Yer'll feel a lot better with some food inside yer.' Ellen linked her daughter's arm and led her to the stairs up to the café which was over a shop. It was a popular eating-house, serving good food at reasonable prices during the day, but was more expensive in the evening, when it catered for people going to the theatre or cinema.

The café was quite full, but Ellen was fortunate to see two women paying their bill, and she quickly led Phoebe over to the table. 'That was lucky, sweetheart, all the tables are taken.' She picked up the menu, ran her eyes over it, then passed it to Phoebe. 'I'll have the toasted crumpets with a pot of tea. What do you fancy?'

'I don't really feel hungry, Mam. I'm a bag of nerves.'

'Yer'll feel better when yer've had a cup of tea, and you really must have something to eat or yer'll feel worse. Have crumpets with me, they'll set us up for the afternoon.'

The service was quick and efficient, the crumpets were delicious, and the tea was enough to settle Phoebe's nerves. 'I'm glad yer talked me into coming here, Mam. I feel much better now.'

Ellen was delighted. 'Ready to face the world, are yer, sweetheart? Well, I'll settle the bill and we'll go in search of a wedding dress that'll give the neighbours something to talk about. A lovely dress for a lovely bride.'

'I'm not worried about the neighbours, Mam, it's Paul I want to look good for. And you and me dad. I want you to be proud of me.'

'Yer don't have to dress up for me and yer dad to be proud of yer, sweetheart, we've always been proud of yer. You and Dorothy, Gordon and Peter. Yer dad loves all of yer, yer know that. He dotes on yer.'

'He can't love us any more than we love him, Mam. I still remember what our life was like when we were kids, when our real dad was alive. We couldn't play out because no one would play with us. No clothes, no food, dressed like tramps and always starving. And never without bruises. It's terrible to say this about someone who is dead, but we hated our dad. So you can imagine how we felt when you married a man who was the opposite. We all adore the man we used to call Sinbad, who is kind, loving, gentle, and full of fun. And I want him to be proud of me on the day I get married.'

'I made a mistake in marrying Nobby Clarke, Phoebe, and we all suffered because I was stupid. He was a rotter, but like yer say we shouldn't speak ill of the dead. I was weak in those days, and should have left him when I found out he was a drunkard and a violent bully. But I put the past behind me when I married Corker, and my life now, and my family's, is a far cry from those bad days. Let's put all bad thoughts out of our mind, because they serve no purpose.' Ellen beckoned the waitress and asked for the bill. 'There are people waiting for tables, Phoebe, so make a move. I'll pay at the till.'

When they reached the bottom step, Phoebe put a hand on Ellen's arm. 'I'm sorry, Mam, I should never have mentioned Nobby Clarke. I didn't mean to upset yer. It was talking about me dad, and how much he loves us, that raked up the past. And the difference in the two fathers we've had. I'm sorry, don't let it spoil our day.'

'Don't fret about it, sweetheart. I'm strong enough now to talk about the past without getting upset. Thanks to Corker, who I love dearly, Nobby Clarke is a faint memory, and talking about him doesn't upset me. I will only say I hope his soul is at peace now.'

Phoebe leaned over and kissed her mother's cheek. 'I know what you went through, Mam, and I admire and love you very much. So now we've got that over, shall we sail forth to find the most beautiful bride's dress in Liverpool?' She bent her arm. 'Put yer leg in, Mam, and we'll cross over.'

There were two white bridal dresses on models in the window, and Phoebe's eyes were shining with excitement. 'Ooh, they're both lovely, Mam. I wouldn't know which to choose.'

'All brides' dresses look lovely, sweetheart, but yer don't choose the first one yer see. You have to try a few on, to see which one suits yer best. There's so many different styles and material, yer'll be spoilt for choice. And colour, too, for ivory is a lovely colour. Yer might prefer it to white if yer see a dress yer like.'

'Ooh, I think white for a wedding dress, Mam, that's traditional, isn't it? And a white veil.'

'Don't make yer mind up until yer've seen what's on offer. If there's nothing in here that sets yer heart beating faster, then we'll try another shop. So come on, let's take the bull by the horns.'

The bell on the door rang when they entered the shop, and an assistant came through heavy velvet curtains which covered the entrance to the changing rooms. 'Hello, can I help you?' She asked, her smile and tone friendly.

Phoebe's mouth was dry with nerves, so it was Ellen who explained. 'My daughter is very shy, but she'll be fine when her nerves settle. She's getting married soon, and I'm helping her choose a wedding dress and accessories.'

The assistant smiled at Phoebe. 'Most girls who come in are nervous, my dear, but not for long. When they see the selection of wedding dresses we have, their nervousness turns to pleasure and excitement.'

'The dresses in the window are lovely,' Phoebe said. 'Except they would probably be too long for me. I'm only five feet three or four inches.'

'If you were two feet or six foot, makes no difference, we cater for all sizes. If you'll come through to the showroom I can show you the range of dresses we have in. Any of them can be made to fit, in any style, colour or material.' She smiled again at Phoebe, putting her at ease. 'You don't just go into a shop, see a wedding dress you like the look of, and say, "Oh, that's nice, I'll take it".'

'I don't think my mam would let me do that.

She's here to make sure I don't do anything stupid.'

Mother and daughter were waved to two chairs which were upholstered in a deep red velvet, and they were very impressed. And they were more impressed by the four dresses that were brought through, one at a time, from another room, all covered with layers of tissue paper to keep the dust from touching them. Phoebe's eyes were shining and as each dress was held out for her inspection she clutched her mother's arm. 'Oh, Mam, they are all beautiful.'

'Yes, they are, sweetheart, fit for a fairy princess. But yer can't tell just by looking at them that they are right for you. Dresses look different on different people. Yer can't tell until you try them on. And you can't try any on now because yer've come straight from work and I'm sure the assistant wouldn't like you touching them.'

'No, I couldn't allow you to try on today, madam, for the least mark would mean we couldn't sell the dress. Besides, you need to make an appointment if there is a particular dress that you are attracted to. If you could come back one day when you have time to try them on, it would be far better than making any rash decision now. If you do decide to purchase one of our gowns, you would need a fitting, and be measured for any alterations. Your wedding day is probably the biggest occasion in your life, so you want it to be perfect.'

Ellen nodded. 'The lady is right, Phoebe, buying your outfit can't be rushed. You do need everything to be perfect.'

'Is there a particular dress that caught your eye, madam?' The assistant didn't want to put the girl off, because if she bought her wedding dress and accessories from the shop, then she herself would get a bonus. 'Usually one dress catches the attention, I've found.'

Phoebe looked into her mother's eyes. 'Don't tell me, Mam, just nod your head if there is one you favoured, and we'll see if we both liked the same one.'

Now Ellen had fallen in love with one of the dresses as soon as she'd set eyes on it. It was just what she imagined for her daughter, but she didn't want to influence her in any way, so she didn't answer, just smiled and nodded.

The assistant was listening as she covered the end model with tissue paper, and she was intrigued. 'Can I join in? It's a long time since I played a guessing game. I think the last time was when I was still at school. I don't want to butt in, and my boss would have a duck egg if she knew, but I know which dress I'd say was just right for your daughter. So may I join in?'

Ellen and Phoebe laughed. 'Mam, have yer got a piece of paper on yer, and we can tear it into three pieces, so we can't cheat?'

'I've got paper,' the assistant said, 'and pencils. Just hang on, I won't be two ticks.'

'Mam, my tummy is churning over. I'll never sleep tonight, I know I won't.' Phoebe, always the shy one of the family even though she was the oldest, was beginning to realize that her dreams of being Paul McDonough's wife were really going to come true. 'If I'm like this now, what will

I be like on me wedding day?'

'Yer'll be taking many deep breaths in the weeks ahead, sweetheart, because once you've settled on your bridal outfit, yer've got to start thinking about the bridesmaids. The material for their dresses, colour and style. And headdresses. I'm not telling yer this to frighten yer, but there's stacks to be done. Not that yer'll be left to do it on yer own, because I'll be with you all along the way. And if we get stuck we can ask Molly next door, she's been through it a few times and knows the procedures. And Molly would love to help.'

The assistant came back from the front room and handed them a pencil each, and a small square piece of white paper. 'I feel like a child again, and it's a wonderful feeling. You have certainly brightened up my day! Now, how are we going to distinguish the dresses? All of them are white, so colour is out. How about neckline, that's the best. There's a round neck, a square neck, and a sweetheart neck. So if we write the one we liked best on the paper and fold it over, we can mix them up, and each pick one out?

There was plenty of giggling as the pieces of paper were put in a small hatbox and were given a good shaking before the box was offered to Phoebe to be first to pick one. She kept it in the palm of her hand until her mam and the assistant had theirs. Then she opened it up and said, 'Round.' She looked at Ellen. 'What does yours say, Mam?'

Ellen held the paper up. 'Round again.' And when the assistant said 'Third time lucky',

Phoebe and Ellen were delighted.

'Can I come on Saturday and try it on?' Phoebe asked. 'I'll bring someone with me.'

Ellen wanted to ask a few questions seeing as she couldn't be with her daughter on Saturday. 'What material do you have that dress in?'

'The one you saw was in silk, and we can also have a soft cotton which is nice.'

'What about lace?' Ellen asked. 'In an ivory or cream colour?'

'We can make it in lace, in the colours you mentioned, but we don't keep any in stock as they are very expensive and the cost is out of the reach of most people.'

'What sort of price are you talking about?' Ellen pushed aside her daughter's hand. 'It's all right, sweetheart, I'm only making enquiries.'

'It would depend upon the style of dress, madam. A straight skirt would be in the region of thirty pounds. Then you have the headdress and veil to buy, which would take the amount to pay much higher.'

Ellen was shaking her head. 'I was thinking of a very full skirt, but it is up to my daughter. I'm being selfish, saying what I would like; I shouldn't be trying to influence her. But I only want what is best for her. She'll be the first of my four children to marry, and me and me husband want it to be very special.'

'Mam, I don't want you and me dad spending a fortune on me,' Phoebe said, 'and a lace dress would cost a lot of money.'

'Listen, sweetheart, I had strict instructions from your dad that you were to have the very best,

391

money no object. We aren't rich, but we aren't poor, either.' Ellen turned to the assistant. 'I know you can't give an exact figure, but roughly what would be the cost of a full skirted dress, in ivory lace, with a round neck, and long sleeves which taper to a point on the back of her hand?'

Phoebe smiled at the assistant. 'Yer've been very kind, and very patient. Me and me mam will have a good talk, and when I come on Saturday I'll have it all written down.'

Ellen was determined her daughter was going to have the best, and knew if she wasn't with Phoebe on Saturday, her daughter could be talked into anything. 'Can you give me a rough idea of the cost of a dress I have described to you? Plus veil and headdress? I'm not expecting you to give a spot on price because you won't know the number of yards of material until Phoebe has been measured, but just an idea. Yer see, there are three matrons of honour, and two bridesmaids, so a lot to think about.'

'I'll try,' the assistant said, 'but it will be a rough guess on my part and don't hold me to it. Give me ten minutes.'

When they were alone, Ellen held her daughter's hand. 'When I got married to Nobby Clarke, I was wearing a dress that I'd had for ages, me everyday shoes, and a small bunch of flowers. And it was in a register office with just two of me mates as witnesses. A bare room, and we were in and out in fifteen minutes. So I can't look back on my wedding day with fond memories. And I don't want that for you. I want you to have what I never had: a wedding that you'll always remember as the happiest day of your life. So put up with me if I seem to be taking over, for me and yer dad want the best for yer. If yer don't want ivory satin and leg-of-mutton sleeves, then tell me. It's your wedding, you have what you want.'

'Mam, I've come round to thinking ivory lace would be lovely. But it's the money I'm concerned about. There's the bridesmaids' dresses, flowers and everything. It's all going to be too much.'

As the assistant came back in, Ellen told Phoebe, 'We'll talk about it on the way home. And have another look at the two dresses in the window, yer only had a glimpse of them before. Just to make sure you have chosen the right one.'

'I've chosen the right one, Mam, I don't need to look at any others. As soon as I saw it, I knew. And when you and the lady chose it as well, that sealed it for me.'

'This is the best I can do without having measurements.' The assistant held up a piece of paper, but didn't pass it to Ellen whose hand was outstretched. 'I'm sorry, I can't let you have this, it's more than my job is worth. If I was out in the figures, and the customer complained, wanting to keep me to the price I'd given, then I would be in deep trouble. So this is just my estimate. With a very full skirt, and the long sleeves you suggested, in ivory lace, the dress could be anything between seventy and eighty pound. Another ten pound for a headdress, presuming you want a really nice one.'

Phoebe gasped. 'Mam, that's ninety pound! I'd intended to buy me own wedding outfit, I've saved up for it! I can't let me dad fork out that much.'

'Sweetheart, the last thing yer dad said to me this morning when he was going out of the door was, "The best and nothing but the best for Phoebe, no matter what she says."'

'I wouldn't refuse that, madam,' the assistant said. 'If you do, you may hurt him. It sounds as though he's very proud of you.'

Ellen got to her feet. 'We'll talk about it when we get home. And when Phoebe comes on Saturday she'll have all the details we've agreed on. Material, colour, design and accessories. And as I won't be with her, I'd like to thank you now for your kindness and patience. I will see you again, when Phoebe and I can arrange a time when we're both free.' She held out her hand. 'Thank you once again, and I know you will look after my daughter on Saturday. She'll have a companion in the shape of her future sister-in-law, who is chief maid of honour.'

The assistant showed them to the door, then watched as they linked arms and walked towards a post, which was a stop for both trams and buses. What nice people they were. She hoped Phoebe would buy her wedding outfit from the shop, for she'd love to see her in all her finery.

Ellen opened the door to Paul that night, and she felt a warm glow as she smiled into his handsome face. His deep brown eyes were full of laughter, as usual, and Ellen told herself he was just the right person for Phoebe. He would make a loving husband. 'Is my girl in, Mrs Corkhill? Yer know the one I mean, the gorgeous one.'

'Come in, son, she's helping Dorothy with the dishes.' Ellen stood aside to let him pass. 'They should be finished soon, and Phoebe said you were going to the pictures?'

Rubbing his hands together, Paul nodded his head as a greeting to Corker, who was puffing away on a full strength Capstan cigarette. 'Yes, I've booked the whole back row at the Astoria, for me and my girl. Or should I say my future wife? It has a better ring to it, don't yer think?'

Phoebe came in from the kitchen drying her hands on a small towel, and no words were needed to confirm her love for the handsome lad with the dimples, for it was written in her face. 'Who said we're sitting on the back row? You should ask me if that is what I want.'

Paul winked at Corker before saying, 'Oh, I have every intention of asking you, love. But I thought it would be nice to ask yer when we're seated comfortably, with me arm round your shoulder, on the back row of the stalls.'

Phoebe threw the towel at him, but he caught it in mid-air. 'Did yer see that, Uncle Corker? I'm getting a bit worried about her behaviour, she can be a little wildcat when she doesn't get her own way. I'm seeing meself as a henpecked husband, coming home from work every night and having to make me own dinner or starve to death!'

Corker nodded. 'I can understand yer dilemma, lad, but I don't know what advice to give yer. One thing yer don't have to worry about, though, is that yer'll be living with yer parents, and yer mam won't let yer starve. And if Phoebe ever does throw plates at yer, yer mam would throw them back as quick as they came.'

'Well, the plate fight at the McDonough ranch wouldn't last very long, because we've only got three cracked plates, three cracked saucers, and three cups with no handles. I was only telling me mam last night that she'd have to buy another cup, saucer and plate the day before the wedding.' His dimples appeared when he added, 'She promised to go down to T.J.'s and get them. They have seconds there, so she told me, and some of them don't even have a crack or a chip in them.'

Phoebe laughed. 'It sounds as though I'm going to live a life of luxury when I get married. A cup with a handle, I won't know I'm born!'

'Oh, me mam intends going the whole hog for our wedding, pet. I've never known her be so excited before. Well, yer can tell she's putting her heart and soul into it, when I tell yer she's going to scrub the front steps the day before the wedding, and if I lift her up, she's going to clean the windows! How about that, eh?'

Corker had been chuckling softly, but now he let out a loud guffaw. 'Phoebe, me darlin', yer'll not be having a dull life, that's for sure. Yer Auntie Nellie will see to that.'

'But she won't be me Auntie Nellie then, will she?' Phoebe pretended to shiver with fright. 'She'll be me mother-in-law. I don't even know what I can call her then.'

'If I were you, pet, I wouldn't put a name to me mam until yer've lived with us for a week. Yer see, she gets called many different names from people, so wait and see how yer get on with her

396

before yer give her a name. But I will suggest that yer don't bring the name of Elsie Flanaghan into a conversation, because that would be like a red flag to a bull. I can safely say that I don't know any human being who has such a colourful vocabulary as my mam. Sometimes I think she's talking in a foreign language, like French or Polish. I did ask her once if it was Chinese, but I got a clip round the ear, so I've never asked her since.'

Tongue in cheek, Phoebe asked, 'Did it hurt?'

'Did what hurt, pet?'

Phoebe tutted. 'The clip round the ear, soft lad.'

'Well, it's like this, yer see. Me mam isn't big enough to reach me ears, even on tiptoe. And I'm not daft enough to help her by bending down. So I stood there waiting for her to jump high enough. I thought she'd never make it, and she wouldn't have done if she hadn't pulled a fast one on me. She got hold of me tie when I wasn't expecting it, and tugged hard on it until me face was on a level with hers. And then she boxed me ears. It didn't half hurt as well. So I'm nice as pie with her since then, 'cos I've learned it's not pleasant to be strangled.'

'If yer want to call the wedding off, I don't mind,' Phoebe told him. 'Marrying you seems a big risk.'

'Nah, yer'll be all right. I'll stand in front of yer when the plates and pans start flying. Anyway, I've got good news for yer. Me mam likes yer. She was asking after yer just before I came out. She said not to forget to ask yer how yer got on this afternoon, and what's yer wedding dress like?'

Corker chortled. 'I've been trying to get that information since I came in from work. But I have been informed politely that nobody is being told any details about the bride's outfit, or the bridesmaids'. There's nothing to tell yer, anyway, so I understand; nothing has been ordered or bought. And even when things are happening, only Phoebe and Ellen will know. And Lily is one of the helpers, so she'll know. But that's as far as it goes, I've been warned. Not a soul, except the three mentioned, will be given any details until the day of the wedding.'

'But I'm the bridegroom, surely I'm to be let into the secret, because it's my wedding too! I mean, if I don't know what me bride is wearing, I could easy make a mistake and marry some stranger whose face is hidden behind a veil. And Phoebe could end up being married to a bloke she's never set eyes on before.'

Phoebe was putting her coat on, a smile on her face. 'Yer never know yer luck, Paul, yer could end up with someone who looks like Betty Grable.'

'Yeah, if pigs could fly! No, I'm not taking no chances, not with my luck. I'd probably end up with a Flora Robson lookalike.'

'Oh, come on, Paul, the big picture will have started by the time we get there.' Phoebe pulled him towards the door. 'They say women are janglers, but you take some beating.'

'I'll be as quiet as a mouse when I'm sitting on the back row with me arm round yer.' Paul managed to wave a farewell to Ellen and Corker

398

before Phoebe opened the front door. And they both laughed when they heard him say, 'I'll let yer whisper in me ear what yer did today, what shops yer went in, and yer can describe yer wedding dress to me. I'll cross me heart and promise not to tell a living soul.' His voice became fainter when Phoebe closed the door behind them, but they could still hear him talking.

'He takes after Nellie,' Corker said. 'An answer and a joke for every occasion. Our daughter will never have a dull moment.'

In the Bennett house, Jack was in his fireside chair, smoking a ciggy and reading the *Echo*, while Molly sat facing her daughter across the table. The dishes had been washed, the tablecloth had been shaken and folded, and the chenille best cloth had taken its place.

'Is Bella going with yer to the dance, sunshine?' Molly asked. 'Yer haven't mentioned her for a few days. Oh, I know yer still go to work with her, and yer go over to the Watsons' every night as usual. But yer've never really told me whether she's still Peter's girlfriend, or whether he doesn't bother with her after the way she behaved the last time you went dancing?'

'I don't want to fall out with her altogether, Mam, after being friends all our lives, but she gets on my nerves lately, acting so childish. She is coming to the dance because I didn't have the heart to refuse her, but I doubt if Peter will pay for her. Yer couldn't expect him to after the way she behaved. If she doesn't start acting her age, I doubt he'll bother with her again.' Ruthie sighed.

'We'll have to wait and see what happens. I'm going with Gordon, and Bella's coming, but I don't know what Peter's doing. I've told her she should grow up and apologize, but she doesn't seem to think she's in the wrong.'

Jack looked over the top of his paper. 'I always got the impression she really liked Peter. She fell for him when you and her were only fourteen, she never took her eyes off him, and he was the same with her. If she falls out with him, she'll go a long way to find another lad as nice as him.' With those words of wisdom, Jack went back to his paper.

'I'm a little bit confused about this, sunshine. I can't make head or tail of it,' Molly said. 'Has Bella seen Peter since the night of the dance?'

Ruthie shook her head while keeping her eye on the clock. Gordon would be calling for her soon and she didn't want to keep him waiting. 'No, she hasn't seen him. To tell yer the truth, Mam, she said if that other bloke is there and asks her for a dance, she'll dance with him whether Peter likes it or not. The silly nit fell for the flattery he dished out. She said he told her she had a good figure, was very pretty, and he liked her hair and the dress she had on. And she was stupid enough to lap it up. I bit her head off when she said Peter never says nice things to her. Now I know he always tells her she looks nice, but he doesn't harp on it every time he sees her. Gordon always tells me I look nice, but he doesn't keep on about it, and I wouldn't want him to.'

'Oh, dear,' Molly said. 'I would never have thought that of Bella. I'm surprised, and disappointed in her. It would serve her right if Peter washes his hands of her, for he's too nice to be messed about. And if Mary and Harry knew, they'd go mad. They'd put a stop to Bella going out.'

'Don't say anything to her mother.' Ruthie was torn between the girl she'd been close to all her life, and Peter, whom she'd also known all her life. But no matter what the others did, no one would spoil her relationship with Gordon. He was a year older than her, more of a man than a boy, and they got on well together. 'Wait and see what happens tonight. Bella might have given it some thought and come to her senses, I hope. The whole trouble is she's been spoilt all her life, and never allowed any space to grow up. If it wasn't for you having a go at Auntie Mary for not letting Bella have some freedom, Mam, she would be sitting at home every night playing Ludo.'

'I agree with yer, sunshine, that Mary didn't give Bella any freedom, but that was because she was an only child. She still is a child as far as Mary is concerned. So it isn't Bella's fault that she's a bit childish, she's been wrapped in cotton wool since the day she was born.'

There came a loud tat-tat on the knocker, and Ruthie jumped to her feet. 'Here's Gordon, Mam, so I'll let yer know later what happens. If yer go to bed before I'm in, I'll tell yer over breakfast.' With her coat on, a handbag over her wrist and silver dancing shoes tucked under her arm, she gave Molly and Jack a quick kiss. 'I'll see yer later. Ta-ra.'

'Enjoy yerself, sunshine,' Molly called after her,

and waited to hear the door bang before saying to Jack, 'I hope there's no unpleasantness or arguments.'

'If there is, it's not down to you, love,' Jack said. 'Ye're not responsible for Bella. Besides, it's probably a storm in a teacup, and the kids will be laughing and joking while you're worrying yerself sick. Switch the wireless on; Roy Fox and his band are on at eight o'clock, that should cheer yer up.'

'I know that, sunshine. And I know there's a play on at half eight. That's why I bought meself a quarter of Mint Imperials to suck. I'll trade yer two for a kiss.'

Jack folded his paper and put it under the cushion. 'I've got a better idea. Why don't we sit on the couch, and I'll give yer two kisses for one Mint Imperial.'

Molly chuckled. 'That's a bargain at half the price. Ye're on!'

Chapter Nineteen

'Isn't Peter coming?' Ruthie asked, looking up into Gordon's face. 'I've told Bella she can come with us, and I can't knock and tell her she can't come, I'd feel terrible.'

'I don't mind her coming as long as she doesn't expect me to dance with her. I'll pay for her ticket, even though I've got to say it goes against the grain. And as for our Peter, well, Bella will

402

have to do some crawling if she wants him to look at her again. He's gone to the pictures with a mate from work.'

'Ooh, it's a mess, isn't it? I'm sorry about Peter, and I agree with yer that Bella should tell him she's sorry. But I can't make her, she'll have to do it off her own bat. Yer know she's been me friend since we were born, and I don't want to fall out with her, 'cos she's got nobody else.'

'Listen, Ruthie, don't let her spoil our night. She can come with us, but don't expect me to be matey with her, because she's upset you and our Peter. Anyway, knock for her and let's be on our way or we'll miss a few dances.'

Bella opened the door, and after shouting 'Tara' to her mam, closed it behind her. She showed surprise when she saw just Ruthie and Gordon. 'Where's Peter?'

'He's not coming, Bella. He's gone out with a mate.' Ruthie jerked her head, sending her long blonde hair swirling across her face. 'Come on, or they'll be playing the last waltz when we get there.'

But Bella stood her ground, her lips protruding in a pout. 'But why isn't he with you? He always comes. Who am I going to dance with now? He's mean, that's what he is!'

Gordon was blazing, for he had seen how hurt and humiliated his brother had been. And he had strong words on his lips, but they had to remain unsaid when Ruthie spoke. 'I don't blame Peter for not wanting to see you after the way yer treated him. But ye're not going to spoil our night, Bella. Yer can either come with me and

403

Gordon, or go somewhere on yer own.'

'Where can I go on me own? I'll come with you and Gordon, but I haven't got any money on me.'

Ruthie sighed, partly with frustration, but mostly sadness. She couldn't bring herself to speak harshly to a friend who was not used to being considered worldly enough to look after herself. She'd been cosseted all her life and didn't know how to change. 'I'll pay for yer fare and ticket to the dance, and yer can pay me back tomorrow. Now link my arm and let's go.'

Gordon wasn't very happy, but he did understand that Ruthie was piggy in the middle, trying to please everyone. And when the bus came, he told her, 'You sit with Bella, I'll get the tickets.'

The atmosphere was strained between Ruthie and her friend on the journey, because Bella insisted in asking why Peter hadn't come, for she hadn't done anything wrong, had she? Then, not satisfied with Ruthie's reply, she huffed that it wasn't her fault that the bloke had asked her to dance. And she was still bemoaning what she considered to be childish behaviour on the part of Peter in falling out with her when they stepped off the bus outside Blair Hall. 'Will you get the tickets, Gordon, please,' Ruthie asked, 'while we go to the cloakroom?'

Gordon nodded. 'Don't be long, though, because we've already missed a few dances.'

After hanging their coats up, Bella started all over again to moan about having no dancing partner. In the end Ruthie could stand it no longer. 'For crying out loud, Bella, will yer shut up! Yer made a fool of Peter, that's why he's not here, and I don't blame him one little bit. Yer've been his girlfriend for a couple of years, he's been good to yer, and as soon as some lad – a lad yer've never seen in yer life – pays yer a compliment, yer go all childish and fall for it. And before we go in the dance hall, I'm warning yer to behave yerself. Ye're not very popular with Gordon for the way yer treated his brother, so behave yerself.'

As soon as they entered the hall, Gordon claimed Ruthie for his favourite dance, the slow foxtrot. They danced well together, and the music calmed Ruthie down a little. But she knew she'd be happier when the night was over. She couldn't help feeling responsible for her mate, who was standing on her own at the edge of the dance floor. She'll be asked to dance, Ruthie told herself. She's very pretty, some lad is bound to ask her up.

When the music faded, Ruthie plucked up the courage to ask, 'Gordon, let's stand with Bella? I'd feel terrible leaving her on her own. Go on, please?'

Gordon sighed. But looking down into eyes as blue as a summer sky, he couldn't refuse. 'Okay, but I will not dance with her.'

The conversation was stilted until the music started for a tango, and Gordon led Ruthie on to the floor. They talked and laughed together as they always did, but Gordon couldn't help noticing the way Ruthie's eyes kept going towards Bella. 'She'll be all right,' he told her. 'She's got to grow up sometime, and learn she can't have everything her own way.'

'I know, and she's been doing fine until last week. Your Peter was good for her, and I hope she's got the sense to realize that, and apologize to him.' Ruthie just happened to turn her head to where Bella was standing, and her heart sank. 'Oh, no, look, that same bloke is standing talking to her!'

'Just leave it, pet,' Gordon said. 'If she's soft enough to fall for a scamp like him, then she's not worth worrying about.'

Ruthie nodded, but she didn't agree in her heart, and she kept sneaking looks while they were dancing. It was when the tango came to an end, and she was leaving the floor with Gordon's arm round her waist, that she saw the lad who was the cause of all the trouble pulling a reluctant Bella through the double doors of the hall. 'Gordon, that bloke's just gone out with Bella!'

'Leave her to it, if that's what she wants, pet. Ye're not her minder.'

'But he was dragging her out, Gordon! I could see she didn't want to go, she was trying to free her hand! I'm going after them, I've got to. You can stay here if yer want, but I'm going to make sure Bella knows what she's doing, and whether that lad is frightening her. Me mam would go mad if anything bad happened and I didn't help.'

'Ye're not going on yer own, pet, I'm coming with yer. But I think yer'll find Bella's being daft again.'

They left the dance hall in a hurry, expecting to find Bella and the lad in the foyer, but there was no sign. In fact it was quiet and empty, apart from the doorman.

'Have yer seen my friend?' Ruthie asked. 'You know her, she comes with us every time we come.'

'I know who yer mean,' the man told her. 'She's just gone out with some bloke. I was a bit suspicious actually because I know four of yer always come together, and the lad she's gone out with is noted for being a troublemaker. I almost stopped them because yer friend didn't seem to want to go with him, but the lad said they'd be back in ten minutes, they were only going out to get some sweets.'

'Did yer see which way they went?' Gordon asked. 'It's not like our friend to go out without telling us.'

'They turned right, and yer'll catch them up because they'd only gone out of the door when you appeared.'

Gordon was concerned now, and he propelled Ruthie through the door and into the road. 'They can't have gone far. I don't think they'll have crossed over, but you keep yer eyes peeled on this side, and I'll look the other side. Watch out for the alleyways, and listen for Bella's voice. I don't like the sound of this lad.'

They had passed two side streets and were crossing the third when Ruthie pulled Gordon to a halt. 'I'm sure I heard Bella's voice. Listen.'

A few seconds later, Gordon dropped Ruthie's hand. 'That's Bella all right and she's not happy. They're in the first entry, come on.'

As they turned into the entry, Bella sounded distressed as she cried, 'Leave go of me, I want to go back to my friends. Get away from me, I don't like you.'

'Don't be such a baby, give us a kiss.' That's as far as the lad got before Gordon had him by the scruff of the neck and pulled him into the street. Bella was crying and clinging to Ruthie when they heard a blow being struck, then Gordon saying, 'Count yerself lucky I'm letting yer off lightly because I wouldn't waste me breath on yer. And when I get back to Blair Hall I'm going to report you, and I'll make sure ye're banned from ever getting in there again.'

'I haven't done nothing wrong.' The lad tried to bluff it out, 'We were only having a lark, what's wrong with that? A kiss on the cheek doesn't do no one any harm. Can't yer take a joke?'

'Oh, I can take a joke,' Gordon said. 'But I don't happen to think you are funny. In fact I think ye're pathetic and I'm not wasting any more time on yer. So scarper before I black yer other eye for yer.'

Gordon watched the lad run hell for leather to the main road, and waited until he disappeared round the corner. Then he returned to the girls. 'Are yer all right, Bella? He didn't hurt yer, did he?'

Still shaking, Bella shook her head. Neither she nor her friends were to know that in the last fifteen minutes she had finally grown up. Used to being pampered, she was ill prepared for someone like the lad who was cheerful and charming as long as he was getting what he wanted from someone like Bella, who was gullible enough to believe his flattery. 'He was horrible. I didn't want to leave the dance hall with him, but he made me. He said he wanted to buy me some chocolates, and when I said I didn't want any, he pinched my arm.' She showed Ruthie the inside of her arm, which was bright red now, but would turn into a bruise quite soon. 'I hate him, he's horrible.'

'You should have had more sense, Bella.' Gordon spoke softly because the poor girl looked so frightened. 'You must never talk to a strange lad, never mind go off with him. You should have told the doorman what was happening, he would have chased the bloke. He certainly won't get in Blair Hall again, I'll see to that.'

'She's shaking like a leaf,' Ruthie said, her arm round Bella's shoulders. 'And she's not the only one. I'm shaking meself with fright. I hope yer've learned yer lesson, Bella, and yer won't be so daft in future.'

'Yer won't tell me mam, Ruthie, will yer?' Bella begged tearfully 'She'll never let me out again if yer do. Promise yer won't tell her?'

'I'm not going to tell lies for yer, Bella, 'cos fibbers always get found out. But yer mam won't find out from me. We just won't mention it.'

'And don't tell your mam,' Bella sobbed, '''cos she'll only tell mine.'

'I won't mention what happened tonight, I promise yer that. I've never lied to my mam or dad,' Ruthie told her, 'and I'm not starting now. I'll just say we went to the dance as normal, except Peter didn't come. If me mam asks why Peter didn't come, I'll say you upset him at the dance the other night, that's why he's got a cob on. But you're going to call at the Corkhills' tomorrow night and tell him you're sorry, so everything will be back to normal then.'

Gordon huffed. 'Yer'll really have to make it a good apology, 'cos our kid is mad at yer. And so he should be, 'cos yer made a right fool out of him.'

'I will tell him I'm really and truly sorry. And it won't be a lie, Ruthie, 'cos you know I've wanted to be Peter's girlfriend since we left school.' Bella looked at Gordon. 'D'yer think he'll forgive me, Gordon?'

'That's up to him, I can't speak for me brother. But I'll tell him you want to see him tomorrow night. If he's willing to listen to yer, the four of us could go to the park for a walk, away from the street. I won't mention tonight's trouble, and you shouldn't mention it either, if yer want him back again.'

'Oh, I do. I love Peter, and I'll do anything to get him back.'

'Then can we put an end to this now, and go back for the last few dances?'

And it ended up with Gordon in the middle with a girl on each arm, as they walked back to Blair Hall. Of the three dances played by the band before the last waltz, he danced the slow foxtrot and the rumba with Ruthie, and the quickstep with Bella. But wild horses wouldn't have kept him from having the romantic last waltz with his girl, Ruthie.

On the back row of the stalls, Paul was sitting with an arm round Phoebe's shoulder, and holding her hand. He wasn't watching the film, he was only interested in the girl who was soon to be his wife. 'Go on, tell me what the dress is like that yer've chosen. Yer can tell me, I won't say a word to a soul.'

'Will yer stop whispering in me ear, Paul, ye're putting me off the picture. I can't listen to you and watch the screen at the same time.'

'I'm the one you should be looking at all soppy-eyed, not Dick Powell.' Paul blew in her ear. 'I'm the feller ye're going to marry in a few weeks. Besides which, I think I'm better-looking than him, and just as funny.'

Phoebe turned her head, and found herself gazing into eyes that set her heart pounding and her tummy turning over. Her shyness forgotten, she said softly, 'I love you, Paul McDonough.'

'And I love you, Phoebe Corkhill.' Once again he blew in her ear. 'I'm counting the days, and they're not passing quickly enough for me.'

'I'm the same, Paul, but we do have lots to do before the wedding. And the back row of the stalls is not the place to discuss it. We're getting dirty looks off people who want to enjoy the picture they paid to see. So can we watch the film and talk on the way home?'

'Are yer going to tell me if yer've chosen yer wedding dress yet, and what it's like?'

'No, yer can forget that. Yer'll only know what my dress is like when I'm walking down the aisle. And the same goes for the bridesmaids. So can we keep quiet and watch the rest of the film, please? And I mean it. Paul, because it's embarrassing being given dirty looks.'

And Paul had to be content with holding her

411

close until the end of the film when the lights went up and the audience stood for 'God Save the Queen'.

'You go to bed, love,' Molly told her husband. 'I'll wait up for Ruthie.'

'No, I'll wait up with yer. It's a quarter past ten now, not long to wait. Anyway, I don't like going to bed without you. I always feel there's something missing.'

'Well there is, soft lad, I'm missing! And I have to say it's nice that yer miss me. I only suggested yer going to bed because yer were yawning yer head off.'

'It's always the same with me,' Jack said. 'If I yawn once, I can't stop meself, I just carry on.'

'Yer've no need to tell me that because it's contagious. I've only got to see someone yawn in a shop, or on a bus, and it sets me off. The only one I know who isn't affected is Nellie. I don't think I've ever seen her yawn.'

Jack chuckled. 'That's because she hasn't got time, she's too busy talking. But don't tell her I said that.'

'She wouldn't hear me if I did tell her, unless she'd stopped talking to take a breath.'

They heard voices outside the window, and Jack said, 'Here's Ruthie now, I can hear Gordon's voice. I may as well wait and see what's happening with Bella and Peter.'

'Ay, men are not supposed to be interested in things like that. It's us women that are nosy.' Molly pushed herself to her feet. 'I'll open the door for her.'

Ruthie jumped with fright when the door opened, for she was standing on the step with her hand reaching for the knocker. 'Oh, Mam, yer gave me a fright. I nearly jumped out of me skin!'

'Sorry, sunshine, but I heard yer saying goodnight to Gordon, and I thought I'd save yer knocking.'

Ruthie gave her mother a peck on the cheek as she passed. 'I'm going to take a key with me in future, Mam. I'm old enough now to let meself in. Yer know I won't come to any harm when I'm with Gordon.'

Jack smiled at his youngest daughter. 'You look exactly like yer mam did at your age. And that's the biggest compliment I can pay yer.'

Ruthie threw her arms round him. 'Then ye're a very lucky man, aren't yer, Dad, having a lovely wife and three beautiful daughters. Not to forget a very handsome son into the bargain.'

'Yer dad was yawning his head off ten minutes ago, but he wouldn't go to bed in case he missed something. Like meself, he's waiting to find out what the latest is on Bella and Peter.'

Ruthie slipped out of her coat and draped it over a chair. 'Yer didn't wait up for that, did yer, Dad? If so ye're going to be disappointed because there's very little to tell.' She sat down facing her mother. 'Peter didn't come, but that doesn't surprise me. But Bella is going to see him tomorrow night to apologize and ask him not to fall out with her because she really wants to be his girlfriend.'

'D'yer think Peter will make it up with her?' Molly asked. 'I mean, she can't behave so badly, then expect him to take her back. She's really got to learn you can't treat people like that. And Peter's such a nice lad.'

'Gordon has told Bella she'd better pull her socks up if she wants to keep a boyfriend. And he's going to ask Peter to meet her tomorrow night for a talk. Me and Gordon will be there to make a foursome, and we'll go for a walk in the park. We'll let them walk behind us so they can say what they want to without anyone sticking their nose in.'

'It'll blow over,' Molly said. 'A lovers' tiff, we've all had them. It happens to all young people, girls and boys. It only takes a couple of wrong words, there's a falling out, then when they've had time to simmer down they come to the nice part. And that's the making up. A loving kiss, and the couple are all lovey-dovey again. That's life, and that's love.'

'Ay, love,' Jack said. 'The way ye're talking, our daughter will be thinking we were always falling out when we were courting, and that's not setting a good example.'

Molly looked at her daughter and winked. 'No, sunshine, me and yer dad skipped the falling out part, and we stuck to the loving kisses, and the lovey-dovey. We liked that better.'

There was a sly look on Ruthie's face when she asked. 'Is that when yer were sixteen, Mam?'

Molly fell into the trap. 'About that, sunshine.' Then the penny dropped. 'You little tinker!'

Ruthie's laughter filled the room, so youthful it lifted Jack's tiredness. 'Oh, Mam, yer haven't called me a little tinker since I was at school in the juniors! Yer can't call a sixteen–year-old a little tinker, even if I haven't ever had a lover's tiff and made up with a loving kiss. I will try it one of these days though, if I can manage to get Gordon to say a couple of wrong words so I can fall out with him.'

'We'll have less cheek from you, young lady,' Molly told her, hoping she sounded stern. 'The youth of today are much more advanced than they were when me and yer dad were your age.'

Jack left his chair and stretched his arms above his head. 'I'm off to bed, I don't know about you two. But I'd like to add that my mam said the same thing about the generation before ours. So yer see, patents have had to put up with the same problem right through the ages. And Ruthie will be saying it to her children when the time comes.'

'Ah, ay, don't be putting years on me!' Ruthie linked Jack's arm. 'Come on, Dad, I'll help yer up the stairs. It's up to us young ones to help the older generation.'

'Away, both of yer,' Molly said, lumbering to her feet. 'Yer need yer sleep to be bright and breezy in the morning. I'll be up in a few minutes, Jack, I just want to get the dishes ready for the breakfast.' She smiled at Ruthie. 'Sleep tight, sunshine. Goodnight and God bless.'

'Goodnight and God bless, Mam. I'll see me dad to his bed, then when I've undressed and got me nightie on, I'm going to lie on me back, looking up at the ceiling and thinking of a way I can have a lover's tiff with Gordon. Can yer give me a hint?'

'I'll give yer more than yer bargained for if yer don't get up those stairs right now. It's a quarter past eleven, way past our bedtime. Now scoot!'

'It wasn't a bad picture,' Paul said as they came out of the cinema. 'Not bad, but not really my taste.'

Phoebe gave him a sharp dig in the ribs with her elbow. 'How would you know whether it was a good picture or not? Or whether it was to your taste? Yer talked all the way through the big picture, and yer made sure everyone sitting near us didn't hear anything, only the sound of your voice going on and on. It's a wonder some of them didn't ask for a refund on their ticket, because they certainly didn't get their money's worth.'

'Ah, now, fair is fair, I was only whispering in your ear, I wasn't bawling through a megaphone. Anyway, people shouldn't listen in to a private conversation, it's bad manners,' Paul said. 'And what about me? I should get me money back because I didn't even get one kiss! I mean, don't yer know that they invented back rows for that very purpose, so people in love could kiss and cuddle?'

'Paul McDonough, yer've got an answer for everything. I can't get a word in with yer. But I'm telling yer now that after we're married and living in your house, I'm going to get yer mam on my side. She'll soon toughen me up, and between the pair of us yer won't stand a chance. We'll have yer washing the dishes and making the beds in no time. A couple of weeks, and me and yer mam will have yer housetrained.'

Paul's hearty laugh filled the night air, so contagious it brought smiles to the faces of people

416

passing. 'Ooh, that's a good one, Phoebe! Me at the sink with me mam's wraparound pinny on, washing dishes! Ooh, I can just see it. Me mam would be taking the tram down to London Road every day, to buy seconds in T.J.'s half price basket. And as quick as she was buying them, I'd be breaking them! Ooh, that hasn't half tickled me fancy, that has.'

Phoebe was shaking with laughter. How could you fall out with someone who wouldn't let you? Someone who was as handsome, in your eyes, as any film star. And someone you had loved from afar since you first knew the meaning of the word. The handsome prince you never thought, in your wildest dreams, would look twice at you, never mind ask you to be his wife. A shiver ran down her spine at the prospect.

Paul pulled her close. 'You wouldn't really stand by and see yer husband washing dishes, would yer? I mean, if yer would, say so now or for ever hold yer peace.'

'I'm not committing meself at this stage, Paul McDonough, I'm going to wait and see how the land lies. Whether it's in my best interest to take sides with yer mam, rather than you.'

'Oh, I get it now,' Paul said. 'Ye're waiting to see what side yer bread is buttered on?' He let out a heavy sigh. 'Not even married yet, and ye're taking sides against me. If we were married I could divorce you for that. In fact I'll give marriage a three-month trial, and see if I like it. If I don't I'll go back to the register office where yer get the licence, and ask for me seven shillings and sixpence back!'

'They'll not give yer the money back, Paul, because I'll be secondhand goods by then. So if yer marry me, ye're stuck with me for life, whether yer like it or not.'

'Oh, I'll like it, sweetheart, of that I am sure. In fact I'll love it because I love you. I've loved yer for a few years. I didn't know it for quite a while, because yer were so quiet, and shy, while I was fond of a good time, out dancing every night. But I can remember exactly when Cupid's arrow was aimed at me. I was talking to yer one night when I was going to Blair Hall, and you were walking up the street while I was going down. I was acting daft, as usual, and you looked at me and said you were going to meet a girl from work. You had your head held high as you passed me, and our eyes made contact for just a brief second. And with that one look, you stole my heart away. I didn't know what hit me, and I haven't been able to get you out of my mind since.' He pulled her to a halt, put a hand on each shoulder and bent and kissed her. It wasn't a long kiss, because there were people passing, but it brought a sigh of pleasure from the young lovers. 'There now, darling Phoebe, don't you agree we were meant for each other? Or when I kissed you just now, didn't hundreds of stars explode in yer head, and your heart feel a thrill? Mine did.'

Phoebe was so happy she was close to tears. 'All those things happen every time you touch me, Paul. There has never been anyone else but you. I've never even looked at another boy, and although that sounds soppy, it's true. I don't expect you to say yer've never had any other girlfriends, because going to a dance every night for a few years yer must have been out with plenty. But I don't mind that, as long as I'm the one ye're going to marry.'

Paul took her arm and they started walking. 'I have never had a girlfriend, Phoebe, and that's the truth. I had lots of friends that were girls, but they were dancing partners. Dancing was the love of my life until you came along. It's in my blood. I feel free when I'm on the dance floor. I love the freedom and the rhythm. And I hope when we're married you'll come dancing with me now and again. Like our Lily and Archie, who still go dancing since they got married.'

'Of course we'll go dancing. I love it meself,' Phoebe told him. 'And I love being in your arms. We're not going to change into an old married couple after the wedding, love, we're young and we're going to stay young, and enjoy life. And we're going to be as much in love in fifty years' time as we are now.'

'I agree with everything yer said, love, and I'll keep reminding yer of those words. But I have one exception. Yer won't expect me to be as good a dancer in fifty years, will yer? I'll do me best, like, and I'll probably manage the waltz, but I doubt if the old legs will manage a quickstep or a rumba.'

A voice behind them said, 'I think yer main problem in fifty years' time, lad, will be getting on the bus!'

The couple turned to find Lily and Archie behind them. 'Have you been following us for long?' Paul asked his sister. 'That's not fair, yer know, our kid, 'cos me and me wife to be were having a private conversation.'

Lily and Archie chuckled. 'We haven't been behind yer for more than a minute or so,' Lily told him. 'Only long enough to hear from the time yer said yer wanted to be still dancing after you were married, or words to that effect. Oh, and I thought it was nice that Phoebe said yer'll still be as much in love in fifty years' time.'

Phoebe was glad it was dark, and her blush wouldn't be noticed. But she told herself she really must stop being so shy, for she was about to marry into a family who were very open, said what they thought, and had never been known to blush. 'I'm sure you and Archie are hoping for the same thing. Wouldn't it be great if the four of us were getting on the bus together in fifty years' time, on our way to Blair Hall?'

Archie began to walk at Paul's side, while Lily took Phoebe's arm. 'It's a nice thought, girl, but me and Archie want to get a lot of living in by that time, I don't want to waste time worrying about the future, when I'm old and grey. Live life to the full while we've got the chance. For when we start a family, we'll have to nip a few things in the bud. There'll be no dancing or nights out at the pictures, unless we can get our mothers to mind the baby. Or babies, as the case may be.'

'We'll have a year of enjoying ourselves,' Archie said, talking man to man with Paul. 'Me and Lily have agreed to a year of freedom, to enjoy our married life, before we think about starting a family. But I'm looking forward to being a father.'

This time, Phoebe's blush was pale pink compared to Paul's deep red. He didn't know

420

what to say to Archie. So he decided not to say anything, but let his brother-in-law carry on. Which Archie did. 'I can't wait to have a son, so I can take him to see Liverpool play. That's one of my ambitions in life.'

Lily, being a bit more sensitive to Phoebe's embarrassment, changed the conversation. 'Let's walk on a bit, I want to talk to yer where no one can stick their nose in.' When they had put a safe distance between them and the men, she said, 'I'm looking forward to going into town on Saturday with yer. I bet ye're getting excited now ye're getting to the wedding dress stage. I know I was, I didn't get a proper night's sleep for weeks.'

'Yeah, my nerves have started to play me up,' Phoebe said. 'I'm glad ye're coming with me on Saturday, Lily, 'cos two heads are better than one. And once I've got my outfit sorted, I'll be able to get started on the bridesmaid dresses. They'll be the next big purchase on my list. Me dad is seeing to the reception and most other things.'

'Seeing as I'm a maid of honour, can I ask what colour ye're thinking of for the bridesmaids?'

'I haven't given it any thought really, Lily, I was waiting until I got my own dress and accessories. Have you got a colour in mind that you'd like? It would have to be a colour that would suit all of you, 'cos I want the dresses all the same. But I'll be grateful for any suggestions.'

Lily looked behind to make sure the men weren't listening, before saying, 'I think with the bride all in white, or maybe ivory, the bridesmaids would look nice in a colour that would be in stark contrast. It would be stunning. Like a

421

purple, or even deep red, the colour of wine.'

Phoebe's heart was beating faster. 'Ooh, that sounds a very good idea, Lily I want everything perfect for Paul, and me mam and dad. I want them to be proud of me, and Paul. I want to give them a day they'll always remember. So will you help me out with ideas?'

'Nearly all the bridesmaids are fair; your Dorothy, the three Bennett girls and meself. The only exception is Rosie, with her black hair. I think the best colour, the one that would suit all, is the deep red wine colour. But we can discuss it again on Saturday, once you've sorted your outfit. Yer mam said I'm to take good care of you, and I'm to be honest about whether I agree with the dress yer've chosen. She's set me some task, eh?'

Chapter Twenty

'Mam, can I leave yer to wash the dishes yerself tonight?' Ruthie asked, halfway through the meal. 'Bella's calling for me at seven and Gordon and Peter will be waiting outside their house for us. We made it early because they lock the park gates when it starts to get dark.' She was eating as she talked, much to Molly's disapproval. 'And I want to get washed and changed as soon as I've finished me dinner. And do something with me hair. It needs washing really, but I won't have time.'

422

'Yer hair looks all right to me, pet,' Jack told her. 'It always looks nice. And yer can thank yer mam for that, because yer inherited it from her, same as Jill and Doreen.'

'I know that, Dad!' She grinned at Molly. 'Thank you, Mam.'

Molly smiled back. 'Yer must get fed up hearing that, sunshine. Every time yer mention yer hair, and the same goes for Jill and Doreen, yer get it thrown up at yer. Yer dad probably thinks that if it wasn't for me, his three daughters would have been bald.'

While Ruthie was giggling, and swinging her legs under the chair, her father was defending himself. 'Yer should be flattered, love, that I'm so proud of yer,' Jack said. 'And anyway, it is true, because if I'd have married a redhead, they'd have had red hair, instead of being beautiful blondes.'

'And what would have happened to Tommy if yer'd married this never-heard-of-before red-head?'

'Well, he'd have taken after me no matter who I'd married! He'd still have been the way he is now, with my colour hair and as handsome as they come.'

Shaking her head and tutting, Molly said, 'There's nothing like blowing yer own trumpet, Jack, and when I see Tommy I won't forget to tell him that he should thank you for the way he looks. I won't mention the red hair, because that would make it more complicated.' She looked across the table to where Ruthie sat, and said, 'If yer ever mention washing yer hair again when we're having our meal, don't be surprised if I tell

423

yer to leave the table. Or wash yer hair without telling us.'

'Okay, Mam, I'll remember that. Now I've finished me dinner, can I go and get washed before yer take the sink over to do the dishes? I'll be as quick as I can be, I promise.'

'Oh, all right, sunshine, I'm not desperate to wash the dishes, me and yer dad are not in any hurry. We may as well have another cup of tea and relax, 'cos we ain't going anywhere.'

Ruthie was off her chair like a shot. 'Thanks, Mam, ye're an angel.'

'Oh, my generosity comes at a price, sunshine!' Molly chuckled. 'You scratch my back and I'll scratch yours. In other words, you can have the sink to yerself for a while, and in return, me and yer dad get to know what happens tonight between Bella and Peter. Does he forgive her and take her back, or does he tell her to get lost? Fair exchange is no robbery.'

'Yer drive a hard bargain, Mam, but yer've got me on a spot, so there's not much I can do only give in. But I can't promise to tell yer word for word what Peter says, that wouldn't be fair. What I will do is tell yer whether they get back together again. No details, just the end result.'

'That's all we want to know, sunshine, we're not interested in what they had for dinner, or how many blankets they've got on their beds.' Molly reached for the teapot. 'It's not very hot, love,' she told Jack. 'D'yer want to chance it, or not?'

He shook his head.' I can't stand lukewarm tea, I'd rather do without. Leave it until Ruthie is finished in the kitchen, then I'll make us a fresh

424

pot. I'll have a ciggy while I'm waiting.'

'You haven't been to see me ma and da for a while, Jack,' Molly told him. 'They'll be forgetting what yer look like. D'yer feel like a walk round there tonight? They'd be happy to see yer. And yer son and his wife.'

'Would yer mind if we left it until tomorrow night, love? I haven't the energy tonight, I'm bushed. I was hoping for an early night. Me boss is a slave-driver, he's got his eyes on the line the whole day and doesn't miss a thing. When his dad was running the place he didn't mind yer going to the toilets for a crafty smoke, he turned a blind eye. But his son is a different kettle of fish. He makes sure he gets his money's worth out of the men. He's not happy unless he can see the sweat pouring off us.'

Molly was surprised, for her husband had never mentioned this before. In fact he seldom mentioned his job at all. 'Well why don't yer go to bed when yer've had a hot cup of tea? If yer got a good ten hours' sleep it would do yer the world of good. I'll wait up for Ruthie, and I'll get undressed down here so I won't have to put the bedroom light on. And I'll crawl into bed without disturbing yer.'

Ruthie had been listening in the kitchen, and after putting the finishing touches to her hair she walked through to the living room. 'Why don't yer do what me mam said, Dad? A good night's sleep would work wonders. I'll be as quiet as a mouse when I come in, I'll not make a sound. I won't even breathe, or stand on the stair that creaks.'

Jack chuckled. 'There's no need for either of yer

to put yerselves out for me, but I'm grateful for your concern. What I will do is have an hour's kip on the couch, then go to bed as soon as you come in, Ruthie. So try not to be late.'

'Yer heard what yer dad said, sunshine,' Molly caught hold of her daughter's arm, 'so it would be nice if yer could try and be in for ten o'clock. Ye're not going anywhere, only for a walk, so it won't hurt yer to be home early for once.'

'Okay, Mam, I'll get home early. Gordon's got a watch, so I'll know the time. Anyway, the park gates get closed early, and the only place we can go to is the herbalist shop for a glass of dandelion and burdock or sarsaparilla.'

'I think the time and events of this evening lie in the hands of Peter,' Molly said. 'If he intends finishing with Bella, then it could all be over in ten minutes.'

'It depends upon Bella, Mam, I think. If she talks to him like a grown-up, and looks and sounds as though she really is sorry, then I think Peter will listen to her. After all, he did have more than a soft spot for her. I just hope she doesn't start acting daft, like she does at times. If she does, and Peter decides she's not worth bothering about, then it's her own fault, and she's no one to blame but herself.'

Ruthie had just finished speaking when there was a tap on the window. 'I'll go straight out, Mam, that'll be Bella.' A quick kiss for her mam and dad, and she was gone.

Closing the door behind her, Ruthie smiled at Bella. 'Are yer feeling all right?' When Bella

426

nodded, Ruthie said, 'Gordon and Peter are just coming out. Try and look pleased to see Peter, but don't start gushing, 'cos that might put him off.'

Gordon cupped Ruthie's elbow. 'Let's move on, or the neighbours are going to start getting curious if we stand here for long.'

Peter was standing looking down at the ground, and Ruthie thought that wasn't a good sign. So as she was being propelled forward by Gordon, she glared at Bella, and mouthed, 'Go and speak to him!' And she felt relieved when she heard her friend say, 'Hello, Peter, I'm glad you came. Are yer going to walk to the park with us, 'cos I've got a lot I want to say to yer. I'll understand if yer don't want to be with me, but I'd like yer to listen to what I've got to say.'

Ruthie was too far away by now to hear all that was said, but when she turned her head, it was to see Peter walking at Bella's side. They weren't speaking, in fact Peter had put a distance between them, but at least he hadn't refused point-blank to make up the foursome. That was something. Now it was up to Bella.

'Aren't yer going to speak to me, Peter?' Bella asked. 'I know ye're angry with me, and yer have every right to be, but I can't bear yer not talking to me. Won't yer even look at me?'

'It's not up to me to talk to you, not after the way yer belittled me. I wouldn't be here if our Gordon hadn't talked me into coming because Ruthie asked him to.'

'I know, Ruthie has told me off because of what happened. She told me to act me age, and grow up. And I'm really sorry, Peter, so won't yer be

427

friends with me? I promise I won't do anything like that again.'

Peter could hear the tears in her voice, but she'd hurt him so much he was angry. 'How would you like it if I stood with a girl, holding her hand, and left you on yer own?'

'I wasn't holding that boy's hand, he was holding mine and wouldn't let go.' Bella remembered what Ruthie had said about telling lies, and felt guilty. 'You have every right to be angry with me, 'cos I could have got away from him if I'd really tried. Ruthie would have done, but I'm not like Ruthie! I wish I was, but I'm too shy and frightened. I shouldn't be trying to make excuses for that night, I should be telling you how sorry I am that I was stupid. Which I am, Peter, I'm really, really, sorry and ashamed of meself. So will yer give me another chance, and be friends with me?'

Peter could tell she was close to tears, and said gruffly, 'Don't start crying, that won't do yer any good. Besides, ye're too old to be crying just because yer can't have everything yer own way. It's about time yer grew up. Yer wouldn't see Ruthie crying, and yer wouldn't see her holding hands with a strange bloke while our Gordon was standing like a lemon. If it had been our Gordon yer'd done it to, he'd have given yer the heave-ho, told yer to get lost and never looked at yer again.'

Bella saw a glimmer of hope. 'But I'm not like Ruthie, and you're not like your Gordon. I wish I was like me friend, but no one can help being what they are.'

Peter glanced down at her. 'People mightn't be

able to help the way they are, but they can change if they really want to. That's if they care enough.'

'Oh, I do care for yer, Peter, I always have done. So say we can be friends again, and I'll do me best to be more like Ruthie.'

'I'm not expecting yer to be like Ruthie, nor do I want yer to be. I was quite happy with yer the way yer were.'

'So ye're going to be me boyfriend again, are yer, Peter?' Bella plucked up the courage to link his arm. 'Go on, tell me, so I can smile again, and swallow this big lump in me throat.'

'I'll give yer a week's trial,' Peter said. He'd known all along he'd give in, because he wanted to. 'If I'm not satisfied I'll trade yer in for another model.'

She was so happy she felt like singing. 'I'm going to be the best girlfriend yer could ever have, Peter Corkhill, so yer won't even want to look at another girl. And I'm going to be more grown up, and more sure of meself. I'll make yer really proud of me, I promise yer.'

'Ay, don't you go changing too much, or I won't recognize yer.' Peter too was feeling light-hearted. He'd been miserable the last few days. He was a quiet lad, not as outgoing as his older brother Gordon, and Bella was his ideal girl. 'And ye're still on a week's trial.'

Smiling up at him, Bella asked, 'When we get to the park, if your Gordon gives Ruthie a kiss, will you kiss me?'

'I told yer you are on a week's trial,' Peter told her, a smile on his face. 'Yer don't get kisses when

429

ye're on trial.'

Bella squeezed his arm and giggled. 'Can we start the trial tomorrow, instead? I mean, one day won't make any difference.'

Peter pretended to give that some thought. 'I'll tell you what I'll do. Whatever out Gordon does, I'll do. And I'm sticking to that, so don't try and coax me.'

'I won't have to coax you! It's Gordon I'll have to coax, to kiss Ruthie. If I'm nice to him he might give her two kisses, and if you stick to your words, I'll get the same.'

Young and happy to be friends again, the pair caught up with Gordon and Ruthie, swinging hands and laughing with pleasure. When Gordon saw them he raised his brow at Ruthie and said, 'I told yer so, didn't I?'

When the two boys had gone out, Ellen asked Corker, very casually, 'Are yer going for a drink tonight, love?'

'I will be, me darlin', but not until later. Why do you ask?'

'Well, while Dorothy and Phoebe are both in, I thought we could discuss the bridesmaids' dresses. Time is marching on, and I don't want to be rushing everything at the last minute, I'd be out of me mind. So I wondered if yer'd be an angel and go for an early pint.'

'Surely my being here won't stop you from talking shop? I won't be in the way. I'll read the paper and have a ciggy, and yer won't know I'm here.'

'Corker, we three females want to talk without

a man being present. And it's not often Dorothy and Phoebe are both in at the same time.'

Dorothy, a year younger than Phoebe, was courting a nice lad, and she saw him nearly every night. But she'd put him off that night at her mother's request. And she was eager to hear what her bridesmaid's dress was going to be like. So she added her voice to her mother's. 'Go on, Dad, leave us girls to ourselves. Yer wouldn't be interested, yer'd be bored stiff.'

'If it's the wedding yer'll be nattering about, then I would be very interested, seeing as it's my daughter who is getting married. But I can see I'm outnumbered, so like a good little boy I'll do as I'm told and leave you in peace.' He dwarfed everything in the room when he stood up. 'I hope yer remember, when I come home drunk, that you were the cause.'

'Don't you dare come home drunk, James Cork-hill,' Ellen said, 'filling the neighbours' mouths.'

'I don't normally go out for me pint until an hour before closing time, just enough time to have two pints and a couple of ciggies. It's only a quarter past seven now, time enough for six or seven pints. So on yer own heads be it, ladies. But I'll try not to sing too loud, or wrap meself around a lamp post.' With a salute, he lowered his head to get through the door, and they heard him whistling as he passed the window.

'He won't get drunk, will he, Mam?' Dorothy asked. 'Perhaps we should have let him stay in.'

'They haven't enough beer in the pub to get yer dad drunk,' Ellen told her. 'After all those years going to sea, and nothing to do when he went ashore except drink, he's immune to it now. It has very little effect on him. He may get merry, and talk a lot, but never really drunk.'

'Well, can we discuss the dresses now, Mam?' Phoebe asked. 'Have yer mentioned to Dorothy what Lily said about the colours?'

'I haven't, sweetheart, I thought I'd leave it to you.' Ellen said. 'I think it's a marvellous suggestion, but I'm not the one who will be wearing the dress.'

Phoebe turned to her sister. 'It was Lily McDonough who put the idea in me head, and the more I think of it the more I like it. But it's up to you all what you want. Anyway, I'll see what you think.' Phoebe told her what Lily said about a dark red material looking very dramatic against a white or ivory bridal gown. 'Can yer imagine yerself, Lily, Rosie, and the three Bennett girls, in deep wine-coloured dresses? I know it sounds unusual, but I think they would stand out against my dress. Yer could have flowers in yer hair and posies to match.' She searched her sister's face for her reaction. 'Well, our Dot, what do yer think?'

'The word wonderful comes to mind, Phoebe. I really like the idea, it would be different and very posh.' Dorothy clasped her hands with excitement. 'I'm definitely in favour, our kid, and I'm sure the others will be.'

'Well, I know for sure that Lily is, for it was her suggestion. So there's the three Bennett girls to ask, and I think Rosie will agree. I'll nip over to Doreen's when we've finished here, and Jill's if it doesn't get too late. If I could get them here, with Lily, we could talk about the pattern for the

432

dresses. And the headdresses. Then apart from the making of the dresses, I'll be straight in me head. One thing less to worry about. When I go to try my dress on, on Saturday, I'll ask if they'd make the bridesmaids' as well.'

'Ay, our Phoebe, it'll cost a fortune to have six dresses made in a posh shop. Why don't yer try and find a dressmaker locally? It would cut the cost in half.'

'I'll see what the assistant in the shop says. Apart from Ruthie, who is not as tall as the others, there's not that much difference in height and figures. If she measures Lily, she could give me a rough idea what the cost would be. I've got money saved up, and I want to buy the dresses, because me dad is forking out enough with paying for my dress, and the reception.'

Ellen was nodding. 'It's once in a lifetime, and it's no good spoiling the ship for a ha'p'orth of tar. Now, while ye're here, why don't one of yer go and bring Doreen over, and the other nip up for Jill? As ye're seeing Lily on Saturday, that only leaves Ruthie and Rosie, and they'll be happy whatever yer choose.'

Dorothy was the first to her feet. 'I'll go to bring Jill down, and I can see me grandma while I'm there. I don't see much of her, and I feel a bit guilty.' Corker's mother, Lizzie, wasn't a true grandma of Ellen's children, but they treated her like one, for they loved her dearly. 'I won't stay long, though, so don't start without me.'

Phoebe stayed in Doreen's house long enough to have a little chat to Victoria and Phil. And she grinned when she heard Doreen giving Phil his orders. 'Don't forget to listen for Bobby, now, so don't have the wireless on too loud. And if he does cry, don't lift him out of his cot because he'll get used to it. Just put his dummy in his mouth and leave him. He'll drop off eventually, because he's had plenty of fresh air today.'

Crossing the cobbles to the Corkhill home, Phoebe said, 'Yer've got Phil well trained by the sound of things. Does he always do as he's told?'

'Does he heck! He'll do his share with the baby because he loves him, and is very proud of him. But I know my limits, and apart from tonight, with you giving me a reason to come out, I don't push me luck. He's a smashing husband, and a hard worker, and I love the bones of him.'

The door had been left ajar, and the couple walked in to find Jill there, with Dorothy. 'We beat yer to it, and yer only had to go over the road. Yer can't half jangle, our Phoebe.'

'I was only being polite. I couldn't just run in and drag Doreen out without having a word with Aunt Vicky.'

'All right, stop wasting time,' Ellen said, pulling two chairs from under the table. 'We haven't got all night, because we've got two mothers of young babies here. So sit yerself down and let Phoebe tell yer about an idea for your bridesmaid's dresses, and see whether yer approve or not. I'll put the kettle on for a cuppa.'

Phoebe told them she'd chosen a dress, but not the style or colour. 'I have to try it on first. They'll measure me, then I go back for a proper fitting. Lily is coming with me on Saturday, 'cos I'm hopeless on me own, and I can try it on and see if it's what I want. If it is then I'll choose me head-dress and that's me sorted. So now we have to start thinking about the dresses for the six brides-maids. I want to hear your views on what you would like, but first listen to Lily McDonough's suggestion. I love it, but let me know what you think.'

Ellen was in the kitchen, setting cups and saucers out as she listened to Phoebe. And she smiled when she heard excited voices all speaking at once, and all delighted with the idea of the bridesmaids wearing dresses in a deep red colour. There was a buzz of happy discussion, and Ellen was pleased for her daughter. And when she took the tray in with cups of tea and biscuits, the con-versation turned to style. Phoebe had a pattern in mind, and asked if they agreed. Full skirts, low round necklines, and puff sleeves to the elbow. This was also greeted with nodding heads and words of agreement. Now the girls were involved in the wedding outfits, they were beginning to feel excited, and looking forward to the occasion.

'I'll let yer know more after Saturday, when I've got meself sorted out. Then things are going to have to move fast. I don't want to leave everything until the last minute. It would be wonderful if the bridal wear shop I'm getting my dress from could do your dresses as well. I'll ask when I go on Saturday, and keep me fingers crossed. It would take a load off me mind if we could get everything from the same shop.' Phoebe remembered something she had to ask. 'Oh, about shoes. They need to be silver, and I wondered if any of you had decent silver dance shoes? It would save a bit of expense if yer have, but otherwise I'll pay for them.'

Jill and Doreen looked at each other and smiled. 'I've still got mine,' Doreen said. 'I kept them in the hope that one day, when Bobby's a bit older, me and Phil will be able to trip the light fantastic occasionally, when we can get someone to babysit. The shoes are silver with straps, and as good as new. So I'm sorted in that department.'

'Me too!' Jill told them, her lovely face lit up in a smile. 'They are years old, but still in the box and hardly worn. Me and Steve were never dance mad, like Doreen and Phil. The plain truth is, we're lousy dancers. So I'm all right for shoes as well, and one less worry for you.'

Doreen had a thought. 'Yer can forget our Ruthie, too, because she's got two pair of silver shoes. And I'm sure Rosie will have a pair.'

'That's everyone accounted for, then, sweetheart,' Ellen said. 'Our Dorothy is sorted, and I know Lily will be, because her and Archie still go dancing a few nights a week.'

Phoebe sat back in the chair. 'I'm glad you could come over tonight. I feel a lot lighter, not so much to worry about. Except for the wedding itself, that is. I'll be a nervous wreck, and instead of a happy, radiant bride, Paul is going to have a quivering, crying baby who wants to run home to her mam.'

'It wouldn't do yer any good to run home, sweetheart, because I won't be here. I'll be too busy enjoying meself. Someone will have to celebrate with yer new husband. And if I'm buying meself an outfit for the wedding, then I'll want to show off. It's not every day I get to be the mother of the bride, and I intend making the most of it.'

'Don't worry, Auntie Ellen,' Doreen said. 'With six bridesmaids, and a handsome man waiting for her at the altar, Phoebe will be in heaven when she's walking down the aisle with Uncle Corker. A good-looking man on her arm, and another one waiting for her, what more could she ask for?'

'If our Phoebe chickens out,' Dorothy said, 'then I'll take her place. I've always had a soft spot for Paul McDonough.'

'You keep yer eyes off him, our kid, if yer know what's good for yer,' Phoebe said. 'Besides, yer've got a boyfriend, yer don't need another.'

Jill pushed herself to her feet. 'I think I'd better go, the baby will be ready for her feed. I'm glad I came, though, because I don't get out very often, and now I've got plenty to think about, and I've enjoyed it.'

'I'll leave with yer,' Doreen said. 'Thanks for inviting us, Phoebe, and I hope all goes well for yer on Saturday. Let us know.'

'Before yer dash off, can I ask yer not to tell anyone about the dresses, style or colour? I want everything to be a surprise on the day.'

'Not a word eh, Jill?' Doreen said. 'Even under torture.'

Chapter Twenty-One

'Good morning, sunshine,' Molly said when she opened the door. 'Dead on time as usual.'

Nellie brushed past without a word, her lips set in a straight line and her eyes like slits.

Molly pulled a face as she closed the door. 'Yer don't believe in the niceties of life, do yer, Nellie Mac? I thought it was a really nice morning, with the sun shining in a clear blue sky. That was before I opened the door and was greeted with a face like thunder. What's happened to ruffle your feathers, or am I a fool for asking?'

Nellie picked her carver chair up, carried it to the table, then plonked herself down. All without a word, and her face set. And with her fingers tapping the table, she stared at the wall, ignoring her best mate. 'Okay, if that's the way yer want it, sunshine, it suits me,' Molly said. 'I'm not in the mood for talking either. So you sit and stare at that wall, and I'll stare at the other. See who gets fed up first. It means the tea going cold, but it won't kill us not to have a drink before we go to the shops.'

Nellie turned her head. 'Some best mate you are, when yer keep things from me. It's my son getting married, and yet nobody tells me nothing, not even you, what hasn't got nothing to do with the wedding.'

'I know I've got nothing to do with the wed-

438

ding, sunshine, I'm very well aware of it. And I don't know any more about it than you do. So why ye're sitting there giving me daggers, I haven't the faintest idea. But I do know that if looks could kill, I'd be a dead duck by now. In me own house as well!'

'I suppose ye're going to tell me that yer didn't know Corker went to the pub just after seven last night, eh? And that less than twenty minutes later, your Doreen and Jill went in Ellen's house, and were in there for an hour or more.'

Molly's face was blank. 'I don't know what ye're talking about, Nellie. I really don't have a clue. How would I know what time Corker went to the pub? He doesn't have to pass this window, and I wouldn't think anything of it if he did! It's a free country!'

'I never said it wasn't, girl, did I?' Nellie knew she'd put her foot in it, 'cos she'd never thought on that Corker wouldn't pass Molly's on his way to the pub. 'But what about yer two daughters? Yer can't say yer didn't see your Doreen come out of her house with Phoebe, because she lives right opposite, yer couldn't miss them.'

'Oh, yes I could! If I wasn't being nosy, looking out of the window, then I could easily miss anything that was going on in the street. And to be quite frank with yer, Nellie, I don't care one way or the other what goes on. If you've got nothing better to do, then I feel sorry for yer.' However, even as she was talking, Molly couldn't help being inquisitive. Corker never went to the pub that early, and it was unusual for Doreen and Jill to leave their babies when it was near their bedtime. 'Are yer making this up, Nellie? Having me on, like?'

Now Nellie was having second thoughts. Not about Corker or the girls, 'cos she'd seen them with her own eyes. But Molly never told lies, so perhaps she didn't know what was going on. Oh, dear, Nellie told herself, me and my big mouth. I'm in for a right lecture now, and it's me own fault. 'I haven't made it up, girl, and I'm not having yer on. What I've told yer is what I saw, and it's true.'

'Is that supposed to be an apology, sunshine?' Molly kept her face straight. 'Yer walk in here without a by your leave, and accuse me of being underhanded. Oh, and a liar into the bargain! Well I think yer've got a ruddy cheek! What Corker does is his own business, he doesn't have to answer to you for his movements. And neither do my two daughters. They'd probably tell you if yer asked them, which would be the proper thing to do, instead of coming moaning to me.'

Nellie was hard-skinned, and she was seldom sorry for anything she said, or her actions. But although she would argue with her mate until the cows came home, she didn't like hurting her. And the thought of falling out with the one person who had been her friend, and kept her on the straight and narrow, for twenty-odd years, didn't bear thinking about. 'Don't be getting all narky, girl, just because I made a mistake. How was I supposed to know yer didn't know what was going on? They're your daughters, and I'm not a flipping mind-reader.'

'No, but yer've got a bad mind, Nellie. Yer

always believe yer friends are not treating yer right because they don't come running to yer with every bit of news they've got. And that is wrong because nobody owes yer anything. Or me for that matter.'

Nellie gazed down at the cloth on the table for a few seconds, then looking all meek and mild asked, 'Aren't we having a cup of tea this morning, girl? I mean, like, yer can't take it out on me tummy because I've got a bad mind. Me tummy hasn't done yer no harm.'

'Nellie, yer've got a cockeyed way of looking at life. If we all had your attitude, we wouldn't have a civilized society, we'd have chaos!'

'Yeah, I know that, girl.'

'Yer know that!' Molly's voice was shrill. 'Yer mean you agree?'

'Listen, girl, I'll agree to anything yer say. If you tell me the rain is pouring down I won't argue with yer. Just put the bleeding kettle on before I die of thirst.'

'Now this is where I put me foot down, Nellie Mac. I've put up with yer shenanigans over the years, but no more. Under no circumstances will I allow yer to die in my house. The least yer can do after us being friends for so long is to show me some consideration. So if yer feel yer time has come to kick the bucket, please go home now And if yer have time, when yer get home, leave a note on the table for George with a loving message on. He deserves that much.'

'Ah, give us a break, girl! Yer know I can't write a bleeding word! I can't even spell me own name.'

'Yer can spell "Nellie", and then George will

441

know it's from you.'

'Ah, yes, I can spell Nellie, but that's not me right name, is it? Me real name is Helen Theresa McDonough, and I can't spell all that. I couldn't even sign me marriage licence, George had to put his hand over mine and move it around. I had a pen in me hand, like, what the woman behind the desk had lent us. He did a good job of it too, did George. I didn't even recognize meself.'

Molly opened her mouth, then closed it quickly when a little voice in her head told her she'd be wasting her time if she asked Nellie what she meant when she said she didn't recognize herself. And time wasn't something they had plenty of, because they were way behind today. 'I'll put the kettle on.'

She was putting a light under the kettle when she heard Nellie muttering, and she cocked an ear. 'I don't know, we've been all round the bleeding houses thanks to her. She might know a lot of words, but she's not half slow. She's had me dead, not in her house, mind, I had to go in me own house and die on me own couch. And she said I had to do the job properly and leave a note for George. She wouldn't half get her eye wiped, because my George would die if he saw a letter from me, he's never had one off me in his whole life. And there isn't enough room on my couch for two dead bodies, so it would be the floor for George.' Nellie was talking to the flowers on the wallpaper. 'I've gone all through that, without any complaint, and still haven't got a bleeding drink. It reminds me of a picture I saw once, where the goodie had been dragged halfway through a desert

442

by the baddie, and left there to die. I forget who the film star was now, but he was crawling through the burning sand, with the sun beating down on him, and he was crying out for water. The silly nit should have known there aren't no taps in the desert. I think he was hoping to come across one of those osis things, so he could have a drink. I thought it was a bit far-fetched meself, but I have to say I know how he must have felt. I'm dying of thirst meself right now, and I'm not even in a bleeding desert!'

Molly was standing just inside the kitchen, listening. She didn't make a sound in case she interrupted her mate, for she found Nellie's tale very interesting. When she was in the mood, there was no one who could come up to Nellie for entertainment. It was a great pity she couldn't write, for she would make a fantastic author.

Molly poured the boiling water into the teapot, then carried it through and stood it on a stand so it could brew while she was seeing to the cups. 'I remember that film, Nellie, and I've racked me brains trying to think who the star was. I can see his face, dark-skinned and black hair, but I can't for the life of me remember his name.' She turned to go back to the kitchen, when she had a thought. 'Oh, by the way, the word yer were looking for was oasis.'

'I wasn't looking for no word, girl, it was Tyrone Power what was looking for it.'

'Ooh, ye're a dark horse, Nellie, when yer want to be. Yer knew it was Tyrone Power all the time!'

'I did, girl, but me mouth was too dry to say it. I could do with an osis meself right now.'

'It's oasis, Nellie, that's what yer want.'

'No, it's not, girl, I know what I want better than you know what I want. I'm beginning to think ye're losing yer marbles. Yer fetch a pot of tea in, no cups, mind, and tell me I need an osis!'

Molly threw her hands up in the air. 'I give in, sunshine, I surrender.' She made for the kitchen and the cups, muttering. 'She'll have me as bad as herself if I don't watch out. I should have known it was going to be one of those days when I opened the door this morning. She had a face like thunder on her. And there was me, full of the joys of spring, thinking it was such a lovely summer's day you couldn't help but be happy. How flipping wrong I was.'

'I can hear what ye're saying, girl, I'm not deaf. And I'm not a slowcoach, either! It doesn't take me half an hour to make a visitor a cup of tea. Ye're taking so long I'm beginning to think the blinking tea is begrudged.'

'Ye're right and wrong there, sunshine,' Molly said as she came in with the tray. 'Ye're wrong in saying I'm taking a long time to make yer a cup of tea, and ye're right in saying it's begrudged. Now if it's not too much trouble, will yer pour the tea while I see if I can rustle up a few biscuits for us.'

Now, they were magic words to Nellie, and she brightened up. 'Aye, girl, yer were right about it being a nice day. Just look at that blue sky. It makes yer feel happy, and interested in life.' She had two biscuits in her hand before Molly had time to put the plate on the table. 'Are we going to Doreen's to see the baby? She might have

444

some news for us.'

'Nellie McDonough, ye're as crafty as a box-load of monkeys. Yer can't bear to be left out of anything. Yer can't ask Doreen questions she might not want to answer.'

'Oh, I won't ask her outright, girl, I'm not that hard-faced. No, I'll do it in a roundabout way, so she won't even know I'm being nosy.'

'If yer tell her yer saw her crossing the road to the Corkhills', she'll know yer were watching through the window.'

'If God didn't want us to be nosy and keep tabs on what was going on, then He wouldn't have invented windows, would he? Now, find an answer to that if yer can!'

'That's easy, sunshine, because God didn't invent windows.'

'Who did, then?'

'How the heck do I know!' Molly was getting frustrated. 'I don't know anything about windows, but I can tell the time, and it's marching on. We should have been out ages ago. So you put yer chair back while I carry these dishes out.'

Nellie lumbered to her feet, picked up the carver chair and put it back in its place at the side of the sideboard. And as she turned round, she caught sight of Jill putting the brake on the baby's pram outside Doreen's house. 'Ay, girl, your Jill is over the road, so I'll have two chances to find out what was going on last night.'

'Look, Nellie, why do yer have to have something to worry about over the wedding? Why don't yer leave Phoebe and the young ones to get on with it? They want to keep everything secret, and I can understand why. So why don't we older ones have our secrets? It's about time I had something to cheer me up, something nice to look forward to.'

The goings-on of the future bride and brides-maids were forgotten as Nellie sensed excitement and intrigue. Rubbing her hands in anticipation, she said, 'Whatever yer've got in mind, I'll go along with 'cos it sounds good to me! So out with it, 'cos I've been starved of excitement for too long, and I'm raring to go.'

'First of all, we're going to do what we always do, and that is to call to see Doreen, Jill and the babies. Talk to Victoria about anything but the wedding. No questions, Nellie, don't ask, please. Then, after spending time with the babies, we'll start our normal routine of shopping. And when we pick up our bread from Hanley's, we'll start the cheering up process by treating ourselves to a cream slice, which we'll have with a cup of tea this afternoon.'

'Ooh, ay, girl, ye're really breaking eggs with a big stick. It's not like you to go mad and buy yerself a cake. And yer never make me a cuppa in the afternoon.' Nellie looked into Molly's face. 'Are yer feeling all right, girl?'

'I've never felt better, sunshine. I've been lost lately, with nothing interesting happening to keep me mind occupied. I don't half miss the noise and laughter there used to be all the time, before the girls and Tommy got married. I know I see them most days, and they were bound to marry and leave home some time, but I can't help the way I'm made.' She let out a sigh. 'When you were sitting muttering to yerself before, I gave meself a good talking to. I need something to spice up me life, something to look forward to. And I suddenly thought about the wedding. I know I won't have a big part in it, not like you'll have being the groom's mother, but the Corkhills are like family, we've known them since we've lived in the street. And I'll be going to the wedding, I've already had me invitation, along with Jack. So if it suits you, Nellie, we could start preparing for it, and that will give us both something to look forward to. We'll have plenty to talk about and do. What do you think, sunshine?'

'Yer mean we'll be going into town to buy our hats and dresses?'

Molly nodded. 'We'll have a chinwag this afternoon, and discuss when we'll have enough cash to look around for something that takes our eye. But we won't let on to anyone, we'll be as secretive as the girls are. Then on the day of the wedding we'll all get a surprise.' She chuckled. 'A nice one, I hope. We can't keep up with the young ones, but we're not too old to look nice. I fancy meself in a dress that's the height of fashion, and a stunning hat to catch the eye.'

'Ay, I'm the one what needs to stand out, girl, so give me a break, will yer? I'd like a hat as big as a – er – as big as a bicycle wheel! How about that, eh? That should give them something to talk about.'

'We'll pool our ideas this afternoon, sunshine, when we've done our shopping and got the dinner on the go. Jack said he fancied a ham shank, so I'll cook that with peas and pearl barley. If

Tony's got any ham shanks, that is. If not I'll get a lean breast of lamb and cook that with the peas and barley. We could put them on a low light, and leave them to boil for a few hours. Are you having the same, sunshine?'

'Don't I always, girl, don't I always?'

'Well, if that's settled, we'd better go across the road and see the family. And not a word out of place, Nellie, d'yer hear?'

'I can't go there and not open me mouth, girl, they'll think there's something wrong with me. But I promise I'll watch every word what comes out, and if I think it's wrong, I'll push it back in and use another one.'

'I think yer'd be better watching Bobby than yer words, sunshine.' Molly smiled as a vision flashed through her mind. 'We don't want a repeat of seeing yer with yer knickers round yer ankles.'

'Ooh, yeah, that wasn't half funny. But I'll keep me eyes on the little tinker from now on. It's to be hoped he grows out of it, 'cos he'll get plenty of black eyes if he keeps it up when he's in his teens. It doesn't bear thinking about, does it, girl?'

'Then why are yer, sunshine?' Molly tutted. 'Mention it in the butcher's, Nellie, and so help me, I'll throttle yer.'

'Have yer put yer ham shank on a low light, sunshine?' Molly asked when she opened the door to Nellie at half two that afternoon. 'It'll boil all over the place if yer haven't.'

'Go and teach yer mother how to milk ducks, girl. I know I'm not very clever, but I'm not daft,

448

either! Of course I've got the pan on a low light, and the peas and barley are in with the shank. In two hours my little kitchen will smell delicious.'

'I'll go one better than delicious, sunshine, just get a load of this.' Molly wiggled her nose. 'The aroma pervading the Bennetts' kitchen will spread through the house, causing the family to become deliciously hungry, and they will be fighting their way into the kitchen, with their noses twitching like the Bisto Kids'.'

'It's no use yer showing off, girl, because yer've picked on the wrong one to say it to. It would be the price of yer if it was your pan what boiled over, and then the Bennett family would have something to make their noses twitch all right. They wouldn't be getting a delicious meal, they'd be getting a burnt offering.'

'It's not likely that I wouldn't smell me pan boiling over, is it?' Molly asked. 'I've got a good sense of smell and good hearing. I'm lucky in that respect.'

Nellie's face was straight when she said, 'Well, what's all the spitting and banging I can hear? It sounds like a pan lid going up and down to me.' When Molly pushed her chair back with such force it toppled over, there was a smirk on the chubby face. And she muttered, 'Even a ruddy dictionary didn't do her no good there.'

'Nellie Mac, ye're hearing things.' Molly picked her chair up and sat down. 'The dinner is simmering away, just as it should, and it smells good already.'

'Oh, yer've come down in the world, girl,' Nellie said. 'Yer dinner just smells good now, does it? A few minutes ago it was delicious and yer nose was twitching with the room.'

'Me nose twitching with the room!' Molly asked, 'How can me nose twitch with the room?'

'How the hell do I know, girl! Yer use so many strange words I don't know what ye're talking about. But I do know yer've done nothing but jabber since I came in, and I'm waiting for me tea and me cream slice. So d'yer mind getting off yer chair again, and seeing to yer visitor? Yer were full of talk about what we were going to discuss regarding our clothes for the wedding, but at this rate the wedding will be over before we start.'

When the tea was finally ready, Molly carried it through. 'The cakes are on a plate near the sink, Nellie. Will you bring them in while I pour out? Oh, and I know now how yer made a mistake about me nose twitching with the room. I didn't say room, I said aroma.'

Nellie's face was comical. 'Oh, dear,' she said in what she hoped was a posh voice, 'I ham sorry, how silly of me. Hi should have known yer said haroma.'

'It's not haroma, Nellie!' Molly was beginning to get exasperated until she noticed the devilment in her mate's eyes. 'I'm a fool, I am, 'cos I fall for it every time. I ought to know by now that when yer have that certain look in yer eye the alarm bells are ready to ring. But can I just ask that we be serious for a while, and talk about the reason for you sitting at my table at this time of the day?'

Nellie shuffled forward on her chair, and to show she was really interested she lifted her bosom on to

450

the table and folded her arms round it. 'I'm all ears, girl, so go on, tell us what the reason is for me being here?'

Molly was so taken aback she outdid Nellie for facial contortions. Her voice cracked when she asked. 'What d'yer think ye're doing here, Nellie? Haven't yer the foggiest idea what yer came to talk about, or are yer pulling me leg again?'

Nellie's face changed to her angelic look. 'I'm not pulling yer leg, girl, I'm sitting here nice and comfortable, just waiting for yer to start telling me when we're going to start this exciting life yer mentioned. So why don't yer begin, because my ears are waiting. In fact they've been waiting so long they'll be dropping off to sleep soon, and then I won't hear a word you say.'

'I'll let yer off this time, sunshine, because as yer say, time is marching on. So I'll just have a look in the kitchen to make sure the shank's not boiling over. I want it to simmer so the peas and barley don't clog up together. It's starting to smell nice, and I'm going to enjoy it. I won't be a second.'

'Will yer have a look at mine while ye're at it?' Nellie joked. 'Give it a stir for us, save me getting off me chair.'

Molly came back with a satisfied smile on her face. 'It's doing just right, simmering gently.'

'I wonder if I should nip home and make sure mine is okay?' Nellie asked. 'Every time I cook any kind of stew, I burn the backside off the pan. I've thrown dozens of pans in the bin over the years.'

'Why did yer have to throw them out?' Molly asked. 'I've burnt the odd pan meself over the

451

years, but I've never had to throw one out. A bit of elbow grease and a piece of wire wool, they come up like new. Money is too hard come by to be throwing it away.'

'Yer'll not catch me standing for an hour trying to get the burnt goo off the bottom of a ruddy pan what is as black as the hobs of hell. Easier to throw it out and buy a new one.'

'Does George know what yer do with his hard-earned money? Yer'd spend a couple of bob on a new pan, just because yer can't be bothered to scrub it? Yer should be ashamed of yerself, Nellie McDonough.'

'Oh, I am, girl, I am! I'm downright ashamed of meself. Just think of all those cream slices I could have bought with the money.'

'Nellie, I don't want any wasted money on my conscience, so go and check on yer dinner.'

'I've got a good idea, girl, to make sure me pan doesn't get burnt.' Nellie sounded eager. 'I could bring me pan in here, and put it on your stove. That way we can keep an eye on it and make sure it doesn't boil over.'

Molly fell back on her chair. 'Well, yer've pulled some stunts over the years, sunshine, like cadging sugar when yer ran out of it, a penny for the gas meter so yer could cook yer dinner, and getting down to the shops only to hear yer say yer'd come without yer purse and would I lend yer some money till we got home. Then I'd have to wait until yer were too ashamed to make any more excuses on why yer couldn't pay me back.' Molly took a deep breath, then let it out slowly. 'But wanting to cook yer dinner on my stove is the cheekiest yet.

I've never known anyone with the nerve you've got. Yer don't give a continental for anyone. Yer wouldn't care if yer backside was on fire.'

Nellie was quick to put her hand up. 'Ah, now yer can't say that, girl, 'cos of course I'd worry if me backside was on fire. I've only got two pair of knickers, and if one pair went on fire I'd be in a right state. It wouldn't be so bad in the summer because I could wash them at night and they'd dry out on the line in time for me to call here for me morning cuppa. But it would be terrible in the winter only having one pair, they wouldn't dry quick enough.'

'There is a way round that, Nellie, yer could buy yerself another pair of knickers. And the next time yer burn a pan, don't put it in the bin. Scour it out yerself, and with the money yer save by not having to buy another yer could buy yerself a few pair of bloomers. Yer'd be well off then, yer'd have a stock for emergencies.'

'Did yer go all through that just to tell me I can't bring me pan in here? Well, don't talk to me about wasted, 'cos yer've just wasted half an hour, and yer breath!'

Molly couldn't help but chuckle. 'Ye're a case, sunshine, no doubt about it. I've never known anyone like yer for cheek. But yer can talk till ye're blue in the face, and ye're still not bringing yer pan in here.'

'Oh, I got that message long ago, yer miserable beggar. So as I need to go to the lavvy, I'll use yours, then slip home and see if the house is on fire. I'll go out of your entry door, and into mine. I'll be back in two shakes of a lamb's tail, and then perhaps we can talk about out wedding hats. As long as yer remember mine has to be bigger and brighter than yours, seeing as I'm the groom's mother, and all eyes will be on the creation I'm wearing.'

'Nellie, if yer don't move now, yer'll miss the ruddy wedding and won't need a hat!'

Nellie waddled to the kitchen door. 'Yer can time me if yer like, girl, and I bet I can do it all between five and ten minutes. Keep yer eye on the clock and yer'll see. I can move when I want to.'

As the back kitchen door opened, Molly shouted after her mate. 'Don't forget to wash yer hands after yer've been to the lavvy.'

Pulling herself back up the kitchen step, Nellie popped her head into the living room. 'Yer wouldn't like to come and wipe me bottom for me, would yer?'

'I'll have to turn that invitation down this time, sunshine, because my tummy is feeling a bit queasy right now.'

Molly cocked her head, knowing Nellie wouldn't it let pass without an answer. And sure enough, she heard her mate saying, 'Yer never know where yer are with that one. She can be as nice as pie one minute, then as miserable as sin the next. If my old ma was here, God rest her soul, she'd say Molly was fickle, moody, and unreliable.'

'Would yer ma say I was all those things in one go, Nellie, or would she mean I would be in a different mood each day?'

'I can't answer that now, girl, 'cos desperation has set in, and if I don't scarper I'll disgrace meself.'

454

Molly hurried to the back window and chuckled when she saw Nellie hotfoot it down the yard, then kick the lavatory door open. 'I hope she hasn't kicked it off its hinges,' she said, 'the door is falling to pieces as it is.' She didn't wait for Nellie to come out of the toilet, instead she began to clear the table. When Nellie came back they'd better get down to business or the afternoon would have been wasted. A good idea would be to have a pencil and paper ready, so they could start writing down what they needed and what they'd like.

So when Nellie came bounding back into the room, a grin on her face and saying, 'Ooh, I don't half feel better now,' Molly pointed to the piece of paper and pencil in front of the carver chair.

'It's down to business now, sunshine. No messing about, so we'll get straight on with making a list of what we want for the wedding. And I thought we'd start with you, because ye're more important than me.'

That flattering remark added two inches to Nellie's bosom. 'That's really nice of yer to say so, girl, and I'll make sure that you're getting some attention as well. It won't be as much as I get, but then yer couldn't expect it if yer hat is only half the size of mine and the colour won't be as outstanding.'

'What makes yer think that, sunshine? I intend to push the boat out to celebrate Phoebe's wedding. And Jack will be wearing top hat and tails, to match the splendiferous outfit I'll be wearing.'

'Yer'll swallow yer tongue one of these days,

coming out with words as long as our yard.' Nellie's eyes narrowed. 'My old ma, God rest her soul, used to say liars always get found out. And she was right, because I've just found you out in a lie. Yer told me your Jack wasn't getting a new suit because he's only worn the one he got for Tommy's wedding twice. So there, Mrs Clever-clogs, yer can't fool me. And let me give yer a little warning, girl. If yer turn up at the church with a hat what has a wider brim than mine, then I'll pull it off yer head and stamp me feet on it until it's too battered for yer to wear.'

Molly grinned. 'Ay, we're going to have some fun at this wedding, sunshine, I can feel it in me bones. It'll keep us going until the wedding after Phoebe's, whoever that will be.'

'There's only your Ruthie left, girl. She'll be the next.'

Molly's jaw dropped. 'She's only sixteen! Don't you go putting years on her! There's Dorothy Corkhill after Phoebe, and she said she's not getting married for a year or two. But it'll definitely be before our Ruthie.'

'We've gone off the track again, girl, so can we get back to us going into town to look for whatever it is we fancy? I'll scrounge some money off George, in case I haven't got enough in me purse. How are you off for money, girl? It's no use going with an empty purse.'

'I've got a couple of pound,' Molly told her. 'I have been saving a few bob every week. I might have enough for one decent item, either the dress or the hat. We'll have to wait and see. My Jack doesn't earn as much as your George, but I think

I handle me money better than you. I make it go further.'

There was a tap on the window, and Molly looked up to see Doreen making signs for her to open the front door. Of course Molly's first thought was Bobby. 'What's wrong, sunshine?'

Doreen clicked her tongue on the roof of her mouth. 'Why do yer always think the worst, Mam? Everything is fine. So can I come in now, just for five minutes 'cos I've got the dinner on.'

Nellie looked up when Doreen came in the room. 'Hello, girl, are yer on the cadge?'

'Don't be so bad-minded, Auntie Nellie. I haven't come on the cadge, I got everything I needed when I went to the shops. On the contrary, I come bearing gifts.' Doreen took out two small white envelopes which she'd hidden under her cardigan. 'Mam, it's yer birthday next week, and me and Jill were wondering what to buy yer. Our Tommy was asking what he could get yer, as well. Anyway, in the end we decided it would be better to give yer the money, so yer could buy what yer wanted. Especially with the wedding coming up.' She handed one of the envelopes over. 'Me and Jill and our Tommy are coming for our tea here that night, so we can all be together for yer birthday tea.'

Molly fingered the envelope. 'I don't like taking money off yer, sunshine, yer know that. A birthday card would do, I'd be more than happy with that.'

'Its too late now, Mam, so buy yerself something that yer like or need.'

'Don't look a gift horse in the mouth, girl,' Nellie said. 'I wouldn't refuse if it was me.'

'Oh, you haven't been left out, Auntie Nellie, 'cos this envelope is for you. Our Tommy happened to mention to Archie that it was me mam's birthday and we were thinking of giving her the money to buy herself a hat or something for the wedding. And as it is with families, one tells another one, and Archie told Lily. So it ended up with you getting the same as me mam.' As she passed the second envelope over, Doreen warned, 'Archie said to tell yer it's an early birthday present, so don't be expecting much when the day comes.'

Nellie's face was a joy to behold. 'Ay, girl, shall we open them to see what's inside?'

'Just hang on the bell, Nellie,' Molly said. 'Aren't yer going to thank Doreen, and the others when we see them?' Molly hugged her daughter. 'Thank you, sunshine. I'll see Jill tomorrow. But I hope yer haven't left yerselves skint?'

'Don't be silly, Mam, it's only a couple of pounds. If yer use the money for a hat, make sure it's as big as Auntie Nellie's.' She gave Nellie a quick peck, then turned to the door. 'I'd better get back to Bobby. I'll see yer tomorrow.'

Molly followed her to the door. 'Thank you, sunshine, I'm very grateful. I'll see Jill and Tommy tomorrow. Ta-ra.'

When Molly came back, it was to see Nellie holding her envelope up to the light coming from the window. 'Ay, girl, I wonder how much is in here.'

'Whether it's ten bob or a pound, yer could have shown some gratitude, Nellie. It's not the present, it's the thought that counts.'

The chubby face spread into a beaming smile. 'I'll do more than thank them, girl, I'll give them a hug and kiss like you do. So will yer sit down now, so we can open the envelopes, please.'

They had reason to be more than grateful to their children, for there were ten one pound notes in each envelope, and they were so astonished they couldn't speak for a few seconds. 'Oh, my God,' Molly said, 'I didn't expect anything like this!'

'Me neither, girl, but isn't it great!' Nellie's bottom was working overtime on the seat of her chair. 'I can buy a smashing hat with this.'

'Don't forget what our Doreen said, sunshine. I've got to buy a hat as big as yours. And I intend to do that. This will buy me a dress and a hat. And I've got the money I've been saving up.' Molly became emotional. 'We've got wonderful children, Nellie, so thoughtful and loving.' The tears were glistening in her eyes. 'We are very lucky, sunshine.'

'Yeah, we're lucky with our families, and out friends, girl. I might not always show it, but I do know how well off I am.' These were serious words from Nellie, but she was soon back to her usual self. 'Ay, girl, we don't have to wait until pay day now, we can go to town tomorrow. What d'yer say?'

'I say life is wonderful, sunshine, and going to town tomorrow is the icing on the cake. We'll leave here at half ten, and we'll have time to look around. And treat ourselves to a snack. Oh, boy, happy days.'

Chapter Twenty-Two

Molly and Nellie were walking down the street, arm in arm, when a voice behind them asked, 'Where are you two off to? Got a heavy date have yer?'

The friends turned to find Phoebe and Lily just a yard behind them. 'We have got a date,' Nellie said, 'but don't tell yer dad 'cos yer know he's got no sense of humour.' Her eyes narrowed. 'Are you and Phoebe going to see about the dresses for the wedding, or is that still a secret?'

'It's no secret that we're going to see about the dresses, Mrs Mac,' Phoebe told her. 'But the dresses themselves are secret, and will remain so until the wedding.'

Molly nodded. 'Quite right too, sunshine. You keep them under cover until the big day.'

'Shall we move on, we're in people's way,' Lily said, smiling as she moved back to let a neighbour with a pram get past. 'If we're all going into town we may as well get the same bus. Or tram if one comes along first.'

Molly's eyes widened as she looked over Nellie's head at Lily. 'Oh, no, you go on ahead, yer walk quicker than us.' She was thinking that if they got off at the same stop in town, it could be near the shop where Phoebe was getting her dress, and if Nellie knew, wild horses wouldn't stop her from sneaking in. So Molly sent a clear

460

message with her eyes and shaking head. 'Go ahead, we'll follow at our own pace.'

And this time Lily got the message. 'Come on, Phoebe, we can run faster than these two, our legs are younger.' She cupped Phoebe's elbow and urged her forward. 'I'll see yer tonight, Mam! Ta-ra, and happy shopping.'

Nellie watched the two girls hurry away, then when they'd turned the corner into the main road she said, 'Well, how d'yer like that! They could have waited and walked with us, we're not two doddering old women what can't keep up with them. Just wait until I see our Lily tonight. She won't half get a piece of my mind.'

'It was me that encouraged them to go on ahead, sunshine, and I did it on purpose. What if they said they'd meet up with us when Phoebe had sorted her dress out? I mean, they're not going to be hours in the shop, are they? And I don't want anyone with me when I buy me hat, or dress. The hat is the main buy for me, it's what people see before anything else. Especially if it's got that film star look.'

Nellie's lips were clamped together and her head was nodding as she listened to Molly's words. 'Good thinking, girl, good thinking. You and me are going to be the stars of the show. We'll knock 'em dead when we walk in the church.'

'Well, I wouldn't like anything as drastic as that to happen, sunshine. And Phoebe and her bridesmaids are going to be the stars of the show, that's only fair. But you and me can be a close second.'

That satisfied the little woman, and her chubby face creased. 'Ye're right as usual, girl. And if we

461

happen to spot Phoebe and our Lily while we're going round the shops, we'll do a bunk so they won't see us. It's tit for tat, isn't it? They won't let us into their secret, so sod them, that's what I say. We won't let them into ours.'

Molly put an arm across Nellie's shoulders. 'That's right, sunshine, we'll keep everything under wraps. And now we'd better get a move on, or the day will be over before we start.'

The two mates walked towards the bus stop, and they reached it just as a bus came along. 'Perfect timing,' Molly said. 'Go on, you get on first and see if there's an empty seat for two. I'll pay the fares going, and you can pay coming home.'

Nellie claimed a window seat, leaving Molly perched on the outside and holding on to the back of the seat in front, so she wouldn't fall off. Every time the bus swayed, Molly expected to slide into the aisle, and she gripped the seat in front so hard her knuckles were white. All the time, Nellie was gazing out of the window and giving a running commentary on the shops they passed, and the Mary Ellens on the corner of each street with their carts, selling fruit and veg, or flowers. They added colour to the streets of Liverpool as they vied with each other for trade.

'Ay, I'd make a good Mary Ellen,' Nellie said. 'I could shout louder than them, and I'd get more custom.' The more she turned, the more Molly had to hang on like grim death. In the end she said, 'For heaven's sake, Nellie, will yer keep still, or yer'll push me off the seat altogether.'

'Ah, are yer not comfortable, girl?' Nellie cast

an eye out of the window and saw they were nearing London Road. 'I'd swap places with yer, but it's not worth it now, we're nearly there. Just hang on until the next stop, that's where we'll be getting off if we want to look in the shops down here.'

Even though Molly was uncomfortable and praying for their stop to come, she couldn't help laughing at the expression on her mate's face. Most people could appear sympathetic without trying, but not Nellie. She had to make a big show by pushing her lips upward to meet her nose, and her eyes screwed up so much they disappeared completely for a few seconds. Then out of a face that was unrecognizable, she said, 'Ah, I'm really sorry, girl, my heart bleeds for yer.'

'Nellie, yer kindness is killing me. But could yer turn sideways so my bottom can feel the seat. It doesn't know where it is because it's numb.'

Now Nellie was never good on thinking of the best way to do things, and this was no exception. Instead of turning her back to the window to give more room to Molly, she turned her back on her mate and in the process knocked her off the seat completely. If it hadn't been for the woman sitting in the seat opposite, who was aware of Molly's difficulties and acted quickly to lend a hand, Molly would have ended up on the floor in the aisle.

'What are yer doing, girl?' Nellie looked surprised. 'Yer gave me a fright then. I thought yer were going to fall on yer backside! It's not like you to be so clumsy.'

Strong words were ready to come from Molly's mouth, but Nellie was saved by the bell being rung by the conductor. And as it was their stop, they were standing on the pavement before Molly was able to give vent to her feelings. 'Ye're a smasher, Nellie, no doubt about that! I could have broken me ruddy back, there, and you didn't turn a ruddy hair!'

Nellie pursed her lips while her brain repeated Molly's words. Then she said, 'Ooh, yer must be in a real bad temper, girl, 'cos yer used the word "ruddy" twice, and that's not like you. I hope yer don't keep it up for long or it's not going to be very nice for me if I'm trying posh hats on, and you've got a face on yer what would stop a clock.'

'Is that all ye're worried about, Nellie? It's a pity yer haven't got better things to do than think about yerself. I could have come a cropper on that bus because of you, but all you're thinking of is a flaming hat!'

'Not a flaming hat, girl, but me wedding hat! And yours if it comes to that. Mind you, no respectable hat would want to be tried on by you, not with the gob on yer.'

Nellie's expressions never failed to bring Molly round. How could you fall out with someone who had the face of a cherub? 'Okay, I should know by now that yer don't know what an apology is, so I shouldn't expect one. It would be nice to have one, though, but who am I to try and change the habits of a lifetime? So let's put our differences aside and set out to enjoy ourselves courtesy of our very generous children. Put yer leg in, sunshine, and let us sally forth.'

Nellie's face was a study. Why the hell couldn't her mate speak English like everyone else? Or were some of the words she used made up out of her head? Perhaps she didn't understand them herself, and was just showing off. Best to say nowt and let her get on with it. It takes all sorts to make a world, as her old ma used to say, God rest her soul, and she was right. But what would the old girl have thought about Molly, with her fancy words? She'd have had a ruddy good laugh, that's what she would have done. There was nothing her ma liked better than a ruddy good belly laugh.

'Ye're very quiet, sunshine,' Molly said. 'What are yer looking so serious for? Come on, tell me what's on yer mind.'

'Well, to tell yer the truth, girl, I was wondering what my old ma would have made of you. I think yer'd have got on very well together, because yer wouldn't have been able to understand each other. She'd think you were hoity-toity and laugh at some of the words yer come out with. And with you never swearing, well, you wouldn't know what to say to each other.'

'Nellie McDonough, it's not me that's the snob, it's you,' Molly told her. 'I was born in a two-up-two-down house, and I still live in one. And what's more, I wouldn't want to live any-where else. Like yerself I've many a time been skint, not knowing where the next penny was coming from, robbing Peter to pay Paul. I've shared a loaf of bread with yer when the kids were little, so don't you dare say I'm a ruddy hoity-toity snob!'

Nellie's whole body was shaking by this time. 'That's more like it, girl, you give me hell and yer'll feel a lot better. And when yer've got it all off yer chest, then perhaps we can start enjoying ourselves.' She gave Molly a dig in the ribs. 'Ay, girl, it's a good job it's not me what's got to get it off me chest, 'cos the size of mine, we'd be here until it was dark.'

'Right, well, where shall we start, sunshine? There's Lewis's, Owen Owen, and that shop in Bold Street. None of them are cheap, but we can always walk out if there's nothing suitable. And there's plenty of smaller shops we can look in. We've got time on our side because I've told Jack I don't know when I'll be home. He can always send Ruthie to the chippy if their tummies start rumbling.'

'George and Paul said they'd do some cheese on toast for themselves to tide them over till I get back. But I hope they don't expect me to make a hot meal for them, because they're in for a disappointment. Me feet will be too tired to stand by the stove by then.'

'Let's walk up Bold Street, then make our way down to Church Street, and Lord Street.' Molly said. 'We can stop for a snack if we get hungry, or our legs get tired.'

The friends passed the flower sellers at the bottom of Bold Street, and they admired the beautiful colours of the roses, carnations and flowers they didn't know the names of. The women with their shawls over their shoulders were calling out to passers-by, and they seemed to be doing a roaring trade.

'They smell lovely, don't they, girl?' Nellie said. 'All the different scents, it must be nice for the women to be sitting by their buckets with all those under their noses.'

'It's a job, sunshine, that's how they make their living. It's all right for us, walking past admiring the flowers, but the women have to sit on those stools for hours on end, until all their flowers are sold. It's a nice day today, good for their business, but it must be a lousy job in the winter.'

The couple were walking up Bold Street, arms linked, and they stopped occasionally to look at the window displays. One shop in particular caught Molly's eye, and she pulled Nellie towards it. 'Those dresses look nice, sunshine.' She nodded to the three models. 'I like that deep lilac one, it's very attractive. I like the colour and the style.'

'It's a bit like the colour of the material we saw the other week, remember? Yer didn't half like that material.'

Molly nodded. 'I did, yes, but I don't know any dressmakers so I'll have to buy a dress. And although this material is a bit darker in colour, I really like it. But it hasn't got a price on, and it's probably more than I can afford. I've got the hat to buy so I'll have to keep count of me money.'

'There's no harm in walking in the shop and asking how much it is,' Nellie said. 'Yer don't have to buy it, yer can just walk out. If yer don't try, girl, then yer'll never know. Shall I go in and ask for yer?'

'No, we'll go in together, sunshine. If the dress is more than I can afford, then as yer say, we can

467

just walk out.'

So, with Nellie bringing up the rear, Molly pushed the shop door open. Her first reaction was one of surprise, for the shop was much bigger inside than she'd imagined. There were a few dresses on models, but there were several long racks filled with garments of every colour and length. There wasn't time to stand and stare, as the assistant appeared before them like the genie from Aladdin's lamp. 'Can I help you, ladies?'

Molly swallowed hard. There was no smile or friendliness on the assistant's face, and that was quite off-putting. Then Molly told herself she was as good as anyone, and stared at the woman. 'I was going to enquire about the lilac dress in the window, but I won't bother if you're busy. My friend and I will try elsewhere.'

The change in the assistant was nothing short of miraculous. 'Oh, I'm not busy, madam, I'm here to help, that's my job.' Her hand fluttering, she pointed to a long, velvet-covered bench. 'Please be seated.' She waited until the friends were comfortable, then clasped her hands. 'Was it the lilac dress you were interested in? It's a very pretty dress, I must say, and the colour would suit you. Shall I get it out of the window, for you to have a closer look? We do have it in other sizes.'

'Before yer go to any trouble, I would first like to know the price, for I may not have enough cash on me right now.'

'I'll have to reach into the window,' the assistant said. 'We do have some in the back room, but the price depends upon the size.' She drew aside the white net curtain and stepped into the win-

468

dow. 'The price is three guineas, madam.' Her head appeared through the join in the curtains. 'Should I take it off the model for you to see?'

Molly gave Nellie a dig, and whispered, 'I thought it would be at least twice that much.' Then she answered, 'If you would, please, I should be grateful.' While the assistant was busy in the window, Molly asked her mate, 'Are yer going to see if they've got a dress you'd fancy? There's plenty on those rails, yer might just find one that catches yer eye. The lilac one isn't nearly as dear as I thought it'd be. I've got a feeling this is going to be a lucky day for us, sunshine.'

Nellie kept her voice low when she asked, 'Ay, girl, have yer got clean undies on?'

'Of course I have, yer cheeky beggar! I always have clean undies on, no matter what day it is, or where I'm going,' Molly said. 'That's because me ma drummed it into me that I should always have clean knickers on in case I get run over.'

'Would Madam like to come through to one of the cubicles to try the dress on?' The assistant had been holding the dress for Molly to finger the material, and smiled for the first time when Molly showed signs of enthusiasm. 'I think this one will fit you, but we do have other sizes, although they are not all the same shade.'

'I'll try it on, and hope it fits, for I do like it.' Molly was about to follow the assistant when she looked at her mate, who was still sitting down. 'Come on, sunshine, you can give me your opinion on whether it suits me or not.'

Nellie waddled after her, muttering, 'With your luck it's bound to suit yer. If yer dropped a

469

sixpence, yer'd find a shilling.'

When Molly came out of the cubicle, it was to see Nellie looking at the dresses on a long rack. 'How do I look, sunshine?'

'Yer look a treat, girl, yer really do. Turn round and let's have a good look.'

Ignoring the watching assistant, Molly put her hands on her hips and swayed down the room. She felt good in the dress, which had a square neckline and was fitted into the waist, with a full flared skirt and three-quarter sleeves. 'Will I do, sunshine?'

'Yer look smashing, girl, it really suits yer. Yer hopped in lucky, seeing that in the window.'

Molly nodded towards the rail. 'Have yer seen anything on there that yer like?'

'Oh, there's a few I like, girl, but they won't have them in my size. Yer know I always have trouble getting anything to fit me.'

The assistant, sensing two sales, approached Nellie. 'Oh, I'm sure we have something to fit you, madam, we stock all sizes. I'll help you when your friend had decided if she intends to buy the dress she has on, which I think looks lovely on her.'

'There you are, sunshine, we could both be lucky. I certainly feel this is the dress for me.' Molly fingered the material. 'It feels good on me. I don't think I could do better.'

'If you would like to change into your own clothes, madam, the assistant by the counter through those curtains will wrap it carefully for you and put it in one of our bags.' The assistant was sweetness itself now she knew she would be getting a bonus. 'She will give you a receipt for your money also.'

Nellie wasn't feeling too sure of herself. She wasn't used to posh shops and assistants, and would be lost without her mate. 'I'd rather look through the dresses with you, girl, 'cos you know what suits me.'

'All right, sunshine, I'll help yer look for something nice.' Molly had noticed how her mate had been looked at by the assistant, and it had irritated her. Nellie was a better person than most stuck-up snobs, and Molly made up her mind that Nellie would get the same attention as she herself had been given. So, opening her purse, she counted out three pound notes, half a crown, and a sixpence, which she held out to the assistant. 'Perhaps you'd be kind enough to have the dress wrapped while I stay with my friend. You can put the receipt in with the dress.'

When the two mates were alone, Nellie said, 'Stuck-up cow! Did yer see the way she was looking at me? I felt like clocking her one!'

'She's not worth getting upset for, sunshine. People like her don't know what life is about. A bloody good laugh would kill her.'

Nellie's eyes flew open. 'Oh, yer used a swear word there, girl, and that's not like you.'

'Forget it, sunshine, and let's get you sorted out. I'm not going home with a dress unless you've got one too, so that means yer have to find something yer like. Have yer seen one that takes yer fancy on this rail?'

'There is one that I really like, I'll show yer.'

'Give me two minutes to put me own dress

471

back on, sunshine, I don't want someone to walk in and see me in me underskirt. You get the dress off the rail and I'll be back before yer can say Jack Robinson.'

And when Molly came out of the changing room, Nellie was waiting for her, holding a hanger from which a dress was nearly touching the floor. 'Be careful, sunshine, give me the hanger.' Molly held it up, and she was smiling. 'I love it, sunshine.' The dress was in a rich tan colour, plain in style, with a round neck and long sleeves. It was ideal for Nellie who didn't suit fussy, fancy clothes, because of her more than ample figure. 'This would look lovely with a large-brimmed beige hat, Nellie, it's such a rich colour. D'yer think it'll fit yer?'

Nellie shrugged her shoulders. 'I couldn't tell yer, girl, I was terrified of taking it off the hanger. It looks outsize, so it might fit. I hope so, 'cos I do like it.'

'Open yer coat up, sunshine, before Tilly Mint comes back.' Molly took the dress off the hanger and held it against her mate. 'I'd say yer've hopped in lucky, Nellie, but go in the changing room and try it on. But if it feels too tight take it straight off in case yer split it. Give me yer coat and look sharp.'

Nellie was never quick with taking clothes off, or putting them on, because of her size. When the assistant came in with Molly's purchase in a posh carrier bag, she asked, 'Is your friend trying on a dress?' When Molly nodded, she was asked, 'Does she require any assistance?'

'She'll call if she needs help.' Molly stared the

472

assistant out. 'If she finds it's not the right size then you can be assured she won't try to struggle into it. After all, there would be no point, would there? If you would put that bag on the bench, I'll pop my head in and see how she's managing.'

A voice floated out to them. 'It fits like a glove, girl, but it would need a hem on, that's all. I'll come out and yer can tell me what yer think. This cubicle is too small for me – I can't turn round proper.'

Molly was pleasantly surprised when Nellie appeared, for the colour suited her, giving some colour to her face. 'Oh, I say, sunshine, that looks a treat. The plain style is better for you than patterned material. As yer say, it needs taking up about two inches, but that isn't a problem because our Doreen could do that for yer, and make a professional job of it. I'd go for it, Nellie, because I don't think yer'd find one to suit yer any better, even if we traipsed the whole of Liverpool.'

'Ye're right, girl, and I'll take it.' Nellie looked at the assistant. 'How much is this dress?'

'It's more expensive than your friend's, being a larger size. It's three pound ten shillings.'

Like Molly when she had been told the price of her dress, Nellie was agreeably surprised. 'Will you pay the lady, girl? Yer'll find me purse in me handbag. I'll go and put me old dress on and hand this out to yer to get wrapped. And I want it in a bag like the one you've got.'

Molly stood with the assistant at the counter in the front of the shop, paying for Nellie's dress and waiting for it to be wrapped. 'I'm glad we came up Bold Street, we've both been very fortunate. All we need now to make the day perfect is to find a milliner's with plenty of wedding hats to choose from. Let's hope we stay lucky.'

'Well, I think you might, madam, because there's a hat shop about four or five shops up the road. They have a good selection, I know, because I bought a wedding hat from there a few months ago.'

When Nellie came through, Molly handed her the posh bag with the shop's name on in large letters. 'This seems to be our lucky day, sunshine, because this lady has just told me there's a good hat shop just a few doors away.' She bent her arm. 'Put yer leg in, sunshine, and let's go on another adventure.' They smiled at the girl behind the counter and left the shop two happy women.

They found the milliner's shop, and stood in awe of the half-dozen hats on show. 'Ay, girl, it looks very posh,' Nellie said, her eye picking out a large-brimmed creation in beige, with a ruche trimming of lace around the brim. She gave Molly a sharp dig. 'How much would yer think that hat would cost, girl? That one there, with the fancy lace on it? D'yer think I'd have enough money for it?'

'I couldn't say, sunshine, and as none of them have got a price ticket on, the only way to find out is to go in and ask.'

Nellie pulled a face. 'You go in, girl, I'm hopeless at doing things like that. I go all tongue-tied and can't get me words out.'

'That'll be the day when you go tongue-tied, sunshine. Yer do more talking than I do. But I

474

agree yer have a problem with words, except swear words. So to save your tongue being tied, and to spare my blushes, I'll go in and ask the price of that hat. D'yer want to come in with me?'

'No, I'll stay here, girl, because if they say the hat is ten pound, I'll probably faint. And yer wouldn't like that, would yer?'

'I wouldn't know, Nellie, because at ten pound, I'd have fainted with yer. I wouldn't pay that much for a hat I'll only wear once, even if I was rolling in money.'

Nellie sighed. 'That means we'll never find out, doesn't it, girl? If you don't go in, then we may as well carry on walking.'

'Nellie, I'd rather go in and make a fool of meself than put up with you moaning about how yer'd seen a hat yer liked, but I put yer off it! Anyway, see that pale beige hat with the turned-up brim? Well, I've fallen in love with that. However, I think the prices in this shop will be beyond our limits.'

Nellie wasn't going to give up, though, because the dress in the bag she was carrying and the hat in the window, well, they were made for each other. 'There's no harm in trying, girl. And if we haven't got enough money on us, we could put a deposit down and come back for the hats next week.'

Molly grinned. 'Okay, yer've talked me into it. But only if we both go in together. At least I won't feel as daft if there's two of us.'

There was a girl behind the counter who greeted them with such a friendly smile, the two mates relaxed a little. 'I'm sorry to bother you,'

Molly told her, 'but could you tell us how much two of the hats in the window are?'

'We've got a large selection of hats in these drawers, if you'd like me to show you some?'

Molly shook her head. 'If yer'd just tell us the price of the two we've taken a liking to, we'd be grateful. One is the beige with the lace trimming, and the other is the pale beige with the turned-up brim.'

'I'll get them out of the window for you. I have identical hats in the drawers, for hats vary in size, so if they are too loose or too small, I'll be able to replace them with ones that fit.'

There were huge mirrors round the walls, and soon Molly and Nellie were preening themselves in front of them. Molly's hat fitted her like a glove, but Nellie's came down to her eyes. She was so eager to own the hat, though, she would have been happy with it as it was.

'How much did you say the hats were?' Molly smiled at the young assistant. 'I think I asked, but was so keen to try this one on I don't remember what you said. My friend and I may not have enough money with us, for we have each just bought a dress, but I understand a deposit would probably secure a purchase for a week.'

'A deposit would have to be half the price of the hats, for we've been let down by people leaving small deposits and not coming back. Both hats are four pounds two shillings and elevenpence. That would mean a deposit of two pound one and six.'

While Molly was smiling, Nellie was doing her little war dance, with the hat now covering her eyes. 'We have enough money on us, dear,' Molly told the girl, 'so you don't have to worry about a deposit. But could you see if you have a smaller size for my friend?' She couldn't help laughing. 'We need them for a wedding, and if she takes that one she's going to miss seeing her son getting married.'

From one of the deep drawers, the girl brought out a hat the replica of the one on Nellie's head. But when the little woman tried it on, it was still a size too large. Better than the first one, but still not a good fit.

'It'll do,' Nellie insisted. 'I can pad it with a cloth.'

'Oh, I can do something about the fit,' the girl said. 'I can put a piece of binding all round the inside. It has an adhesive on one side, and it really is very good. We use it often, as it makes for a good fit. I can do it for you now, if you're sure you really want the hat. I like it on you, but it's your decision.'

'Yeah, you go ahead, girl, 'cos that's the hat for me.' Nellie was over the moon. She wasn't really clothes conscious, only when there was a wedding and she could show off. Be the centre of attention, like. And she intended to be the main attraction at her son's wedding. Except for Phoebe, of course, she mustn't forget that. 'Ay, girl, take the money out of me purse while you're getting yours out, and we'll have it ready for when the girl's finished with me hat.'

Molly counted the correct money out for the two hats, and she winked at her mate. 'Not a bad day, eh, sunshine?' She raised her eyes to the ceiling. 'Someone's been looking down on us today'

'That's my friend St Peter,' Nellie said, looking smug. 'He keeps his eye on me, makes sure I come to no harm.'

'Here you are, madam.' The girl handed the hat over. 'Try it on for size now.'

And the fit was just right. So after the hats were placed carefully in strong bags, and the money was passed over, two very happy women closed the door of the hat shop, and stood facing each other on the pavement. 'It's hard to believe, isn't it, sunshine?' Molly said. 'I never thought we'd get hats and dresses in the one day.'

'And we've got money over, haven't we, girl? Have we got enough for tea and buttered teacakes?'

'More than enough, sunshine. So let's turn about and make for Reece's, and a little celebration.'

As the two mates walked away from the hat shop, a short distance away two other women came out of a shop selling bridal wear. And they too were linking arms and laughing.

'I can't believe we've done so well, Lily.' Phoebe's pretty face was aglow with happiness. 'My dress will be ready for a fitting next Saturday, and I've got the design me mam liked and in ivory satin.'

'Yer've done well, Phoebe. I have to say, I love the pattern yer've chosen. Our Paul will fall for yer all over again when he sees yer walking down the aisle. And I liked your idea for the headdress as well.' Lily grinned at Phoebe's excitement, and could remember feeling the same herself when she married Archie. 'It seems the deep red colour for bridesmaids has been used quite often, otherwise she wouldn't have had a sample to show you. The material is lovely and soft, and will fall into folds.'

'I feel like pinching meself to make sure I'm not dreaming.' Phoebe squeezed Lily's arm as they walked towards Church Street. 'You've been measured, so yer'll be going for a fitting soon. I'll have to ask Jill and Doreen to go in on Wednesday, now I've told the assistant. They should be able to manage it, 'cos your mam and Mrs B. will mind the babies for a couple of hours. That leaves our Dorothy, Rosie, and Ruthie. What time did I say they'd go in next Saturday to be measured?'

'Yer told the assistant three o'clock, so you'll have been in for your fitting before they arrive. They won't see yer, yer'll be on the bus on yer way home.'

'I better had be, Lily, because Paul is complaining that he's beginning to forget what I look like, as he sees so little of me.' Phoebe began to giggle. 'Yer know what your Paul's like, he's as bad as yer mam for acting daft. Well, he told me last night that he put his arm round a girl's waist when he was coming home from work, and gave her a kiss on the cheek. It was only when she slapped his face he realized it wasn't me. And if he does it again, and lands in jail, then I'll be to blame and will have to go to the police station and tell them. Oh, and I'd have to postpone the wedding because he might be old and grey by the time he gets out.'

Lily's laugh was hearty. 'He's dead funny is our Paul, but it runs in the family. And I hope yer realize, Phoebe Corkhill, that when yer marry Paul it will really be a lucky day for yer. Because that's the day Helen Theresa McDonough becomes yer mother-in-law.'

'Ooh, I can't wait.' Phoebe laughed. 'What d'yer think I should look forward to most? New husband, or new mother-in-law?' She lifted a hand. 'Yer needn't answer that, Lily. I'll work it out for meself.'

Chapter Twenty-Three

Paul McDonough was waiting at the corner of the street for Phoebe. She'd told him she'd definitely be home by half past five, but so far there was no sign of her. Each bus and tram that stopped, he expected her to jump down the steps with his sister Lily, but there was neither sight nor light of either of them, and it was ten past six. And he asked himself why it was that women were always late for a date? Then he told himself it was because men were daft enough to wait for them.

'What are yer standing here for, Paul Mc-Donough? Are yer hoping to get a click?'

He spun round to find himself looking into Phoebe's laughing eyes. 'Where the heck have you come from? I've been standing here like a lemon since half past five! I thought a bobby was

480

going to lock me up for loitering!'

'I'm sorry love, but I didn't expect yer to wait for me getting off the bus. Me and Lily got off at the stop before, because she wanted to do a bit of shopping. And we cut through the entries for quickness, which is why yer've missed us.'

'Never mind making excuses, Phoebe Corkhill, I've been stood here for nearly an hour. I don't want an apology, I want a kiss to heal me wounded pride. So pucker yer lips up, woman, and give me a kiss that will make me see stars, turn me legs to jelly, and make me heart beat so fast it'll sound like a steam engine.'

'I'm not kissing yer in the middle of the road, Paul McDonough, so get that out of yer head.'

'We're not in the middle of the road, we're standing on the corner. And I'm sure no one would be upset to see a man and his wife to be indulging in an innocent kiss. In fact it could catch on, love, and everyone will be kissing each other.'

'Everybody can do what they like, my love, but I'm not in favour of kissing in public.'

Paul cupped her elbow. 'The nearest entry is about six yards away, and I'll try and last out until we get there.' He propelled her forward so fast her feet barely touched the ground. And once in the entry, he put his arms round her waist and lifted her in the air. 'Now, wench, I want a long, bobby-dazzler of a kiss. And when I come up for air, I want another!'

A woman's voice asked. 'And what's going on here, may I ask?' Phoebe's face was the colour of beetroot when she turned to see one of their neighbours whose back door faced hers.

'It's only Paul acting daft, Mrs Pendleton. Yer should know what he's like by now, yer've known him long enough.'

'It's you I'm surprised at, not him.' The woman's head was jerking with disapproval. 'What would yer dad say if he knew yer were picking lads up in an entry and kissing them?'

'I think yer've got it the wrong way round, Mrs Pendleton,' Paul said, laughter in his voice. 'It's me down here, and Phoebe up there, so it was me doing the picking up. And I'm entitled to kiss the girl who is soon to be me wife. They can't lock me up for that.'

The neighbour thought she better get her facts right, or she'd have Nellie Mac after her. And that didn't bear thinking about. So, her voice softer now, she asked, 'Are yer really getting married, Phoebe?'

'Yes, I am, Mrs Pendleton. I've just come back from town where I've been getting fitted for my wedding dress. That is why I let Paul kiss me, because I'm so happy.'

'Oh, fancy that now! I didn't know you two were courting serious.' Mrs Pendleton wasn't as much of a nosy parker as Nellie Mac's archenemy Elsie Flanaghan, but she ran a close second. And as no one had mentioned a wedding to her, well, she'd be the first to spread the news. So she was happy to say, 'I'm very pleased for yer, and when I know the date of the wedding I'll be along to the church for the happy event. Just to wish yer luck, like, with us being neighbours. And now I must be on me way before the corner shop closes. I've run

482

out of sugar, and my husband has a sweet tooth. He can't stand tea without two spoonfuls of sugar. So I'll say ta-ra for now.' With those words she made haste to the corner shop, to be first with the news. She was to be disappointed, though, because Maisie and Alec had known for weeks about the wedding, being good friends of the Bennetts, McDonoughs and Corkhills. They even had their invites.

Paul waited until the woman was out of the entry before lowering Phoebe to the ground. 'Some people lead a very sad life, don't they, love? I hope you and me don't end up like that. I don't think that one ever smiles.'

'We've got about thirty years before we get to her age, and besides, she hasn't got the family we've got. So let's forget her and give me the kiss you asked me to give you. One that yer called a bobby-dazzler. I've never had one of those before.' The love shone in Phoebe's eyes, and Paul pulled her to him.

'Then pucker yer lips, sweetheart, and fly with me to the moon. And we'll stay there until the stars come out, then we'll come back to earth on a star. Now yer can't have anything more wonderful than that, so pucker up.'

'But me mam and dad...' That was as far as Phoebe got before she was transported to a wonderful place where her heart sang and her whole being tingled as she was wrapped in Paul's arms, and their lips met in kisses that really were bobby-dazzlers.

'Where have yer been, sweetheart?' Ellen asked

when she opened the door. 'Me and yer dad were worried about yer.'

Paul was standing behind Phoebe, and he answered his future mother-in-law. 'I met her at the bottom of the street, Auntie Ellen, and I'm the one to blame for her being later than expected.' His dimples appeared when he grinned. 'To be quite frank with yer, I'm getting a bit fed up with all this preparation for the wedding, 'cos it's knocking my nose out of joint. I hardly get to spend any time with Phoebe, so I lay in wait for her tonight, dragged her down the entry so I could give her a kiss, and lo and behold, doesn't Mrs Pendleton come out of her yard door and catch us at it. The whole neighbourhood will know by now that your daughter is a loose woman.'

Ellen chuckled. 'Come in, the pair of yer, and yer can pour yer heart out to Corker. Not that yer'll get a lot of sympathy, though, because his life had been disrupted as well. Still, yer can both be miserable together.'

Ellen was leading the way into the living room when Paul said, 'Oh, I won't say I'm miserable right this minute, but I was half an hour ago. Yer see, since then me and Phoebe have been on a lovely trip, haven't we, pet?'

Corker was puffing away on his Capstan Full Strength when he saw the blush creeping across his daughter's face. 'What's me laddo been up to now, me darlin'?'

'Take no notice of him, Dad, he's in one of his funny moods.' Phoebe tried to catch Paul's eye, to stop him saying anything that would embarrass her, but she was too late.

'Women are never satisfied, are they, Uncle Corker? Now just tell me how many men yer know that have taken their girlfriends up to the moon? Not many, I bet! And I offered to stay up there with her until the stars came out, but she was worried that you and Auntie Ellen would worry! There was no need for it, 'cos I'd have brought her down safely on one of the brightest stars.'

Corker's weather-beaten face smiled at his daughter. 'Yer didn't turn an offer like that down, did yer, me darlin'? Now that would have been the trip of a lifetime. I sailed the seven seas for thirty years, but never had the opportunity to make that trip. Now if Paul had invited me, I'd have jumped at the chance.'

'Oh, I don't think that would have worked, Uncle Corker, 'cos even a galaxy of stars couldn't carry your weight. And I couldn't close me eyes and imagine I was kissing Phoebe, not with your beard and moustache.'

Corker chortled. The more he saw of this handsome young man, the more he liked him. He was a chip off the old block all right, except his language wasn't as colourful as Nellie's. Which was just as well, for otherwise Phoebe would spend her life with a face the colour of beetroot. 'It took me a long time to grow this beard and moustache, son, and I'm very fond of it. The wife wasn't that keen at first, 'cos she said it scratched her skin and made her face sore. But she's got used to it over the years and it doesn't hurt now. Mind you, her skin is like emery paper, but we're used to each other.'

Ellen was standing by the table, shaking her head. 'Don't mind me, Jimmy Corkhill, just pretend I'm not here. In fact yer may as well carry on talking to yer future son-in-law, while I ask me daughter how she got on today regarding the wedding arrangements. The moon and stars, and beards and moustaches, are all very well and could interest a certain class of people, but Phoebe and meself are not in that class.'

'Before I tell yer what a wonderful day I've had, Mam, I've got to stick up for my soon to be better half, and say there is a certain magic in a trip to the moon. Definitely recommended.'

Ellen smiled and nodded. 'I know, sweetheart. I'm not so old I've forgotten the number of times yer dad and I went there. Lovers haven't changed much over the ages, it's been the same since time began. Although there are some people who have never known what it's like to love and be loved.'

'Yeah, we know that, Auntie Ellen,' Paul said, ''cos we've just met one in the entry, name of Mrs Pendleton.'

His head thrown back, Corker's guffaw ricocheted around the room, bringing smiles to three faces, 'Oh, dear, ye're way off course there, son, for Aggie Pendleton has seen and received more in the love stakes than anyone else round here.' Another loud guffaw, then he told the wide-eyed Paul, 'She should have, she had seven children. She's only got two at home, for the others are all married with families of their own. But she's had her moments has Aggie. Yer shouldn't judge a book by its cover, son, so let that be a lesson to yer.'

486

Paul gazed at Phoebe, and in a soft voice he begged, 'I want yer to promise me something, Phoebe, before we get married. Will yer do that?'

'I can't promise anything until yer tell me what it is, can I, soft lad?'

'I want yer to make a solemn promise that yer won't look like Mrs Pendleton after we've had our seven children? How d'yer think I'd feel walking into Blair Hall with you looking like her? The doorman would think I'd lost me marbles.'

'I think the man on the door at Blair Hall now will have lost more than his marbles by that time, soft lad, because he's over fifty now!' Phoebe was giving him daggers. Fancy talking about them having children when they weren't even married yet! And in front of her mam and dad! Wait until she got him on his own, she wouldn't half tell him off.

'Aren't yer going to sit down?' Ellen asked. 'We don't charge, yer know. And I'm eager to know how yer got on at the dress shop. So sit down, and we'll all keep quiet while yer tell us.'

Paul chuckled as he sat next to Phoebe. 'I think there was a message to me there, Auntie Ellen, so I promise to sit very quiet and listen.' He took Phoebe's hand. 'The floor is all yours, pet, so go ahead.'

'Oh, I'm afraid ye're going to get yer eye wiped, Paul, because I've got nothing to say that will interest you.' Phoebe looked across at her mother. 'Me and Lily are sorted, Mam. We've both been measured and I'm going for a fitting next Saturday. I'm going to see Jill and Doreen tomorrow, and ask them to go in one day to be

487

measured. I'm sure Auntie Molly and Mrs Mac will mind the babies for a few hours. Then there's our Dorothy, Rosie and Ruthie. If they can manage to get into town after me on Saturday, then it will be a load off me mind. All the bridesmaids sorted, and the assistant said the dresses would be ready two weeks before the wedding. I've got everything I wanted, Mam, and I can't keep the smile off me face. I'm so happy and very lucky.'

'And very beautiful, pet,' Paul said. 'Yer don't think I'd marry a girl who wasn't beautiful, as well as happy and lucky?'

'The material? Did yer get what yer wanted?' Ellen's eyes were asking questions. She didn't want to let the cat out of the bag, because Phoebe was determined that no one should know what to expect on the wedding day, it must be a surprise. But Ellen wanted to know if her daughter had been able to get the colour she wanted for the bridesmaids. 'Was Lily pleased?'

Phoebe nodded. 'Yeah, she's over the moon, Mam. I was glad she was with me, she was a good help. Everything has been sorted now, as regards dresses and accessories for the bride and the bridesmaids. I feel really chuffed with meself. That's really all my jobs done. Me dad's seeing to the reception and drinks, Paul's paying for the flowers and presents for the bridesmaids. That's it!'

Paul winked at Corker. 'Yer know, I'm glad I wasn't born a girl. All I've got to worry about for me wedding is a new suit, shoes, shirt and tie. Oh, and have a haircut and shave.'

'Yer've forgotten something, Paul,' Phoebe told

him. 'Father Kelly won't marry us if yer haven't got a wedding ring to put on me finger. And yer can't fool him with a brass curtain ring, 'cos he's got eyes like a hawk and would spot it in a second.'

Paul slapped an open palm on his forehead. 'D'yer know, I kept telling meself there was something missing, but I'm blowed if I could remember what it was! It's a good job yer mentioned it, love, or on the eighteenth of September I'd have been taking me mam's curtains down and pinching one of the rings. But don't put all the blame on me, 'cos ye're keeping everything about the wedding secret, so yer don't talk to me about it. And we hardly have any time on our own.'

'I'll make up for it,' Phoebe told him. 'On Saturday, after I've been for my fitting, we'll go and choose a ring. Will that suit yer?'

Paul shook his head. 'No, ye're too late now,' he told her, his hand going to his pocket. 'I can't wait for you to have half an hour to spend with me, yer beloved husband to be, so I went ahead and did the job on me own.' Then he put a square, padded black box on the table in front of her. 'If it doesn't fit, the man said yer could exchange it.'

Phoebe gazed down at the box, then into Paul's face, and her heart swelled with emotion. 'I hadn't forgotten the ring, Paul, I was going to mention it tonight. I know that these days it's usual for bride and groom to exchange rings at the ceremony, so I was intending to ask yer to meet me on Saturday so we could try the rings

489

together. But yer've beat me to it.'

Corker was getting impatient. 'Well, aren't yer going to open the box, sweetheart?'

'Yer better had,' Ellen said, 'because it may not be the right size for yer.'

Paul reached across and picked up the box. 'Don't open it now, love. Let's do as yer wanted to do, and go together on Saturday to choose both rings. I think that sounds more romantic. The man in the jeweller's shop said I could take it back and exchange it, so we'll do that, eh? Then yer can choose one that you like for yerself, and yer can choose one for me. And when we come out of the shop, I want to spend the rest of the day together. I've never been in the Adelphi hotel, and I don't think you have. So we'll go there for afternoon tea, then go on to the Odeon. Let's live it up for the day, eh?'

Corker and Ellen exchanged glances, both surprised, but delighted that dance-mad Paul McDonough had changed into a serious, likeable, and loving young man. Phoebe had certainly captured his heart. 'That sounds like an offer yer can't refuse, me darlin',' Corker said. 'Hobnobbing with the elite, no less.'

'I won't be dressed for going into the Adelphi,' Phoebe protested. 'I'd feel uncomfortable, like a poor relation.'

'Don't put yerself down, sweetheart,' Ellen told her. 'It's not what yer wear, but how yer wear it. Just imagine two women standing side by side, both wearing dresses the same style and colour, except one woman has paid ten pound for her dress, which has been bought from a posh shop, and the other woman only paid twelve and eleven for hers from T.J.'s. But when they walk into a room no one notices the difference in quality, because the poorer woman walks in with her head held high and her back straight. And she was the centre of attention. Just bear that in mind, sweetheart. It's not what you wear, but how you wear it.'

'Ay, that was good advice, Auntie Ellen,' Paul said. 'And I bet it's true, as well! So I'll buy yer an early wedding present, Phoebe, if yer'll let me? I'll buy yer a new outfit, coat and dress. Then, like yer mam said, yer can walk into the Adelphi feeling good.'

'You can't afford to do that,' Phoebe said. 'Yer've got yer suit and lots of other things to buy that are more important than buying me clothes just so I feel I'm as good as anyone else in the Adelphi. I'm not letting yer waste money on me.'

'If I didn't have the money, and couldn't afford it, then I wouldn't be offering! I haven't been spending any money for the last few weeks, because we seldom go out. I've got a hundred and thirty pound, and I want to spend some of it on you. Is that so bad?'

It was Corker who answered. 'Not bad at all, son. I think yer've done very well. And I think Phoebe should throw caution to the wind and get out and do something different while she has the opportunity.' He looked with affection at his daughter. 'Live dangerously for once, me darlin', and see how the other half live. Don't worry about what yer look like, and remember what I've always told yer. That ye're as good as anyone and better than most.'

Phoebe gripped Paul's hand and smiled into his face. 'Yes, let's go mad, eh, and mingle with the rich? If we never do it again, we can always look back and remember. And brag about it to our mates. And as long as you're with me, I won't care about anyone else.'

Paul lifted her hand and kissed it. 'It's a date, then, next Saturday But don't get too dressed up, I don't want men taking a fancy to yer.'

Puffing away on his cigarette, Corker threw a spent match into the hearth. 'Now yer've reached agreement on that, can I change the subject and ask how yer mam is, Paul? Is she going to cause a stir at the wedding, with a hat the size of a cartwheel? She gets noticed, does Nellie, with her hats. In fact most people keep their eyes on the door for her entrance. And she loves the attention, God bless her, walking down the aisle as though she's a member of the nobility.'

'Me mam came in just before I left the house, and if yer'd been there, Uncle Corker, yer'd have laughed yer socks off. She is so funny, and doesn't really know she's being funny! Her and Mrs B. had been in town shopping for wedding outfits, and all me mam would let me and me dad see was the flipping bag they were in! It was a posh bag, with handles and the name of the shop on, and yer know how me mam can pull the funniest faces imaginable, well she surpassed herself with that bag.' Paul began to laugh as he relived the scene in his mind. 'She held it right up to me dad's face, and said, "See that, George McDonough, well that's class that is. We're going up in the world."' He began to shake with laughter, so contagious it set off Corker, who had a lot of affection for Nellie. And when the giant of a man shook, the whole house shook with him. And he was wiping his eyes when Paul, having brought his breathing under control, spoke again. 'Yer know how quiet me dad is, he never raises his voice. Well, he looked at this bag being held up to his face, and he looked up at me mam, nodded to the bag, and asked. "So that's what ye're wearing for the wedding, is it?"'

'Let me guess,' Corker said. 'Yer mam hit him over the head with it?'

'Did she heck! What she said was, "I'd give yer a clout, but I don't want to put a dent in the bag!"'

'They're a good match, your mam and dad,' Ellen said. 'They're just right for each other.'

'Did yer mam and Mrs B. get their wedding outfits?' Phoebe asked. Then, without waiting for an answer, she wanted to know, 'Has she got a big hat?'

'I couldn't tell yer, pet, because she said not a single soul is going to see her outfit until the wedding. All she'd tell me and me dad was that her and Auntie Molly would be the best-dressed guests on the day. They'd found a shop in Bold Street that sold dresses to suit any occasion, and this is what she said, "Yer've never seen nothing like it, all the bleeding toffs shop there. Can't yer tell by the bag? That's what yer call quality." And off she went up the stairs, carrying that ruddy bag as if it contained the crown jewels.'

'I hope yer won't think I'm making fun of yer

mam, or that I think she's stupid,' Corker said.
'But Nellie would be the first one to laugh if I
said that she wouldn't swap that bag for the
crown jewels, because she wouldn't believe yer if
yer told her what they were. She'd laugh in yer
face and tell yer not to be so bleeding stupid, 'cos
she wasn't born yesterday, and she'd recognize
Woolworth's beads anywhere.'

'She'd have had fun with a crown, though,' Paul
chuckled. 'She'd parade up and down the street
acting daft, not knowing she had a fortune on her
head. Enough money to keep her in cream slices
for life. And her mate, of course, 'cos me mam
would be lost without Auntie Molly to keep her
on the straight and narrow.'

'They are the best mates I've ever known,' Ellen
said. 'Tony loves them coming in the shop
because he thinks they're hilarious. They never
fail to make us laugh, not like some of the miserable customers we get in. Mind you, when
Nellie's in full flow we don't have any miserable
customers because she wouldn't allow them to be
miserable.'

Paul became serious. 'I can honestly say, hand
on heart, that I have never known a miserable
moment in our house. When we were kids, and
money was very tight, we lived on laughter, provided by me mam. That's why our Steve, Lily and
meself love the bones of her. And we feel the
same about Auntie Molly, who is like a second
mother to us.'

Corker nodded knowingly. 'Yes, Mrs B. has
been a restraining influence on yer mam, without
a doubt. When Nellie was ready to fight with the

neighbours in the street, it was Molly who pulled her away and calmed her down. But it cuts both ways, for they're good for each other. Molly would be the first one to admit that her life would have been very dull without her best mate.'

Phoebe tugged on Paul's arm. 'Ye're moaning that yer don't see anything of me, and yet when yer have the chance yer don't take it, yer just sit gabbing! Let's go for a walk for a bit of fresh air. It's too late now to go to a dance or the pictures.'

'Okay, boss.' Paul chucked her under the chin. 'But don't get the idea yer can order me around when we're married, because I intend being master in me own house.'

'But it won't be yer own house, soft lad, it's yer mam's house.'

'I'll soon sort that out. I'll bribe me mam into letting me be the boss. The promise of a cream slice every day, and she'll hand the keys over.'

Paul was opening the front door when Corker and Ellen heard Phoebe asking, 'What kind of cigarettes does yer dad smoke, Paul? I think a packet of twenty twice a week, should get me a set of keys, so we'd be level pegging.'

The door was pulled shut after the couple, and Corker said, 'That's one daughter we'll never have to worry over, Ellen, for she'll have a life of love and laughter when she becomes Mrs Phoebe McDonough.'

'Shall we walk round to me ma's, Jack, and have a game of cards with them?' Molly stood by the kitchen door, a tea towel in her hands. 'I don't feel like staying in. It's been a smashing day for

495

me, getting a hat and dress for the wedding. I'm all fixed up now.'

'Don't I get to see yer new gear? I thought yer'd be trying it on, and showing off.'

'I've put it in the wardrobe because I don't want Ruthie to see it. Yer know she can't keep anything to herself. Yer'll see it soon enough, it's not that far off the wedding. Anyway I want to see Rosie to tell her about getting measured for her dress next Saturday, with Ruthie and Dorothy. So make an effort and comb yer hair, then we'll walk round.'

'What about Nellie,' Jack asked. 'Are yer going to give her a knock?'

'I've been with her all day, yer'd think we'd be sick of the sight of each other, wouldn't yer? But if George goes for a pint with Corker, she'll be left on her own, and my conscience would play up, and I'd feel guilty.' Molly was thoughtful as she cupped her chin. 'I know, you'd prefer to go to the pub with the men, wouldn't yer?'

Jack smiled up at her. 'Well, I haven't had a pint all week, love, so I'd like a drink and a natter with Corker and George. I could go and see yer ma one night in the week.'

Molly nodded. 'I should have thought about that meself, love, yer deserve a pint after working all week. In fact yer deserve more than one. I've been out all day with Nellie, buying clothes for meself, then I'm selfish and thoughtless in expecting you to come round to me ma's for a game of cards! I should have had more sense. So I'll put me coat on and give Nellie a knock, and I'll tell George yer'll be going for a couple of pints with him and Corker. And yer needn't worry about getting home in time for Ruthie coming in, love, 'cos I'll make sure I'm back in time.'

Molly slipped her coat on, then bent to kiss her husband. 'No coming home drunk, though, sunshine. I want you to be sober when we go to bed.'

Jack chuckled. 'Am I on a promise, love?'

'Well, I've got a nice new hat and dress, so I think you deserve a little present.' She moved away quickly when he made a grab for her. 'Don't be so impetuous, sunshine! You appreciate a thing much more when yer have to wait for it.' After another kiss, she made for the door. 'My mate will be delighted when she knows where we're going. But I pity me ma and da, and Tommy and Rosie, because she'll talk the ears off them. Still, there'll be lots of laughter along the way.'

Nellie was over the moon when she heard what Molly had knocked for. 'Ooh, come in, girl, while I put me coat on and comb me hair. Say hello to my feller while ye're waiting.'

'What are yer going upstairs for, Nellie?' Molly asked as she watched her mate bouncing effortlessly up the stairs. For someone of her size, she was as light as a feather on her feet. 'Yer coat's here, on the hook.'

'I know that, girl, and it won't run away. It'll still be there when I come down.'

Molly was shaking her head when she walked into the living room, wondering what her mate was up to. 'Hello, George. I'm going round to me ma's and I thought Nellie might like to come for an hour. And before I forget, Jack will be going for a pint with you and Corker. He'll be knocking for yer in a few minutes.'

'I'll be ready for him.' George McDonough was a quiet man with a gentle sense of humour. 'It'll be good to get out 'cos Nellie's given me a headache. She's never stopped talking since she came back from town. I feel sorry for Bridie and Bob. Tell them I said to put cotton wool in their ears.'

'George, they both love Nellie, like all my family, for she never fails to cheer them up. So do Tommy and Rosie, they love the bones of her because she's like a ray of sunshine.'

'Is her dress and hat as good as she says they are?'

Molly chuckled. 'Now George, don't be asking me to tell tales out of school, or she'll have me life. Besides, Jack hasn't seen my purchases, so I'm not giving the game away on me mate.'

They heard Nellie humming as she came down the stairs, and when she entered the room she left them lost for words, stunned into silence. For in her hand she was holding the bag from the dress shop. Swinging it high by the plaited string handles she swayed her way round the table to stand in front of her husband. It was a big, strong, colourful bag, with the name of the shop in large letters. And such luxury was seldom seen in their neighbourhood. 'See, lad, we've gone up in the world, us McDonoughs, and yer'll not see another like this around these parts.'

'Nellie, go and put it back upstairs, sunshine, and we'll go on our way before it gets too late.'

'I'm taking it with me, girl, to show yer ma and

da. They'll get their eyes opened.'

'What have yer got in it?' Molly asked. 'I thought yer were keeping yer dress and hat a secret. Mine are hanging in the wardrobe, covered with an old sheet, and the bag is on the bottom so our Ruthie doesn't see it.'

'I haven't got nothing in it, girl, the bag's empty. But I bet Bridie would love to see it.'

'Yer taking an empty bag to me ma's house? She'll think ye're crazy, sunshine, and I'd agree with her!' Molly tried to sound angry, but she could see the funny side, and knew her parents would. 'Okay, if yer want to look daft, then that's your lookout. But hurry and put yer coat on or I'll go without yer.'

While Nellie was getting her coat, George told Molly, 'Yer've a lot of patience, lass, and yer know I'm grateful that yer've stuck by Nellie all these years. She'd be lost without you.'

'George, Nellie is as good a mate to me as I am to her. We'd be lost without each other.'

'I'm ready, girl.' The look of pleasure on the chubby face was like the sun appearing from behind a cloud, and Molly held out her arm. 'Put yer leg in, sunshine.'

'Well don't squash me bag, girl, or yer'll spoil the look of it.'

'Now wouldn't that be terrible if the bag got squashed?' Molly said.

The door was closing on the couple when George heard his wife say, 'It would be terrible for the one what squashed it, girl, 'cos I'd clock them one.'

'They're taking long enough,' Nellie said. 'Knock again, girl.'

'No need to, I'm here now,' Tommy said when he opened the door. 'There was only five seconds between you knocking and me answering.'

'Never mind that,' Nellie said, the bag held away from the wall. 'Stand aside and let me pass.'

Seeing the carrier bag, Tommy asked, 'Have yer brought yer carry-out with yer, Auntie Nellie?'

Nellie eyed him up and down. 'Listen, lad, if yer touch this bag, lay a finger on it, then I'll give yer such a clout, yer'll wonder what hit yer.'

Tommy flattened himself against the wall as Nellie passed him, and he raised his brow to Molly 'She means business, Mam. What's she got in the carrier?'

Molly cupped his beloved face, then grinned. 'That carrier bag is going to be the centre of attention all night, sunshine, but it will be worth it, I promise yer.'

And Molly's promise came true, for, as Bob was to say to Bridie as they were getting ready for bed, 'Nellie McDonough is Laurel and Hardy, Charlie Chase and Charlie Chaplin, all rolled into one.' And when Bridie reminded him he'd left out Buster Keaton, Bob replied, 'Aye, him as well!'

When Molly and Nellie first arrived they all thought there was something special in the bag, and they tried to peep when she held it out to them. But Nellie soon put them wise in no uncertain terms. They could look, but not touch. She did her Shirley Temple's 'On The Good Ship Lollipop' with the bag hanging from her arm, and Mae West's 'It's not the men in my life, but the life in my men' with her face copying the famous actresses' expressions. And the more her audience laughed, the more outrageous she became.

It was when Bridie called a halt while they had a cup of tea that the loudest laugh of the night came. Molly was sitting at the table with her ma and da and Nellie, while Rosie and Tommy made the tea. Nellie had stood the bag in the middle of the table for safety, but Tommy wasn't to know this, and he put out a hand to move it. 'You touch that bag, lad, and I'll knock yer into the middle of next week.'

'It's only a bag, Auntie Nellie,' Tommy told her.

'Only a bag!' Nellie's expression was indescribable. 'That's not one of the cheap paper bags yer get in shops round here. That's strong, and it's got handles. And it's made of linoleum, like what my tablecloth is.'

'It is strong, Auntie Nellie.' Tommy thought it was really hilarious. 'But it's still only a bag. An empty bag, at that. My Rosie's bag is made of hessian, and that's just as strong.'

'Oh, now, me darling beloved, my bag isn't as good as Mrs Mac's. Look at the lovely shine on hers,' Rosie said. 'Sure mine isn't a patch on it.'

Tommy loved seeing his Auntie Nellie in action, so he egged her on. 'It's still only a bag, sweetheart. It can't talk or do anything useful, like going for a walk. I can't see what all the fuss is about.'

Nellie's head was jerking from side to side. 'If yer don't stop insulting my posh bag, the one what I carried me wedding outfit in, lad, then yer'll have a lot of explaining to do to yer boss and mates when yer go into work on Monday, because yer'll be gummy after I've knocked all yer teeth out.' She turned to Molly 'He won't be yer handsome son any more, or Rosie's dearly beloved.'

The loudest laugh came from Tommy. 'Oh, Auntie Nellie, yer never change, do yer? That's why I love you so much I'd be willing to let yer knock me teeth out, if it wasn't for Rosie. Yer see I don't think I'd get many kisses if I was gummy.'

Molly received a sharp dig in the ribs before Nellie told her, 'I would have thumped him, yer know, even though he is yer son. The only thing stopping me was that I'd have to jump up and down to reach him, and everyone would see me knickers.'

Molly tried to look sympathetic. 'I understand, sunshine, and I think we should be making tracks home because it's getting late.'

'I'll walk with yer, Mam,' Tommy said, ''cos it's getting dark out.'

Nellie looked suspicious. 'Yer needn't bother, lad, because me and yer mam can look after ourselves.'

'I know yer can, Auntie Nellie, but the question is, is the bag going to be safe? What if someone saw what a posh bag it is, and wanted it for themselves? They could whip it out of yer hand and run hell for leather, before yer had time to stop them. So I'll walk yer home to make sure your proud possession arrives safely.'

Nellie was now all milk and honey. 'Ah, God bless yer, lad, that's really thoughtful of yer.' She smiled at Molly. 'I've always said what a good lad your Tommy is, girl, and yer can't say I haven't.'

Bridie, Bob and Rosie went to the door to see

them off. And they watched the trio walking down the street with smiles on their faces, for it really was a sight to behold. Nellie at four foot ten, Molly at five foot five, and Tommy towering over them at six foot one. But the laughter coming from the three of them, which rang out in the empty, quiet street, was of equal volume.

Chapter Twenty-Four

'This is where we get off, pet.' Paul stood aside to let Phoebe out of the seat by the window. 'The shop is only a few minutes' walk from here.'

'I'm so excited now, what am I going to be like when the big day arrives?' Phoebe linked Paul's arm. 'I'll probably make a fool of meself and cry me eyes out or faint in front of Father Kelly.'

'If ye're going to faint, sweetheart, yer do it in front of me, so I can catch you in my arms, like a knight in shining armour.'

'To be a really true knight, Paul, yer need a horse, and I can't see yer getting one before the wedding. And then yer'd need permission from Father Kelly, so I think I'll just have to make sure I don't faint.'

Paul pulled her to a halt outside a jeweller's shop. 'This is where I bought the ring from, pet.' They looked in the window at the many displays, and Phoebe sighed. 'There's so many, I won't know where to start. It will be difficult to choose because they are all beautiful.'

Paul cupped her elbow and steered her towards the entrance. 'It's easier to look at them inside. The assistant will bring a few trays over for you to see. And Phoebe, love, don't look at the price, look at the ring. I want yer to have one yer really like, because it has to last a lifetime.'

'The same goes for you, Paul, since I'm buying one for you. I'm all right for money, and I want you to have the best.' Phoebe giggled nervously. 'Not a hundred pound one, like those in the window, but a nice one.'

The assistant recognized Paul, and he approached them with a smile.

'Did the ring not fit, sir?'

'We didn't even take it out of the box,' Paul told him, holding on to Phoebe's arm, for he could feel her trembling. 'My fiancée decided that we should both have a ring, and we'd buy them together.' He took the box from his pocket, with the receipt, and put them on the counter. 'So would you let my girlfriend and meself see what yer have in ladies' and gents' wedding rings?' He nodded towards the box which the assistant was picking up, with the receipt. 'I'll settle the money difference when we've made our choice.'

Four trays of rings were brought to the counter, and the couple were so thrilled they found it hard to keep smiles from their faces. 'Is Madam wanting a plain gold ring, or one with a pattern?' The assistant hovered over them, wanting to help the attractive couple. 'Don't be afraid to try them on, for a wedding ring is for ever.'

Phoebe looked at Paul. 'I prefer a plain gold band, Paul. What do you think?'

'It's up to you, pet, I don't want to influence you in any way. Try a few on and take yer time, there's no hurry. I don't want yer to get home, then wish yer'd chosen a different one.'

Phoebe whispered, 'What about the ring you bought for me? Could I see it, please? If I don't, I'll always wonder whether I should have at least tried it on.'

The assistant bent to bring the box from under the counter, where he'd left it, in the belief that the young lady would want to see it, if only out of curiosity. 'Here you are, madam, and may I say your fiancé has good taste.'

Phoebe smiled and took hold of the box. 'Yer must think me and Paul are nuisances, and don't know what we want. But it's only me that's a nuisance, Paul is very easy-going.'

'Open the box, Phoebe,' Paul told her. 'We can't stay here all day, we've got shopping to do. And don't forget yer've got my ring to buy. I've looked at all the gents' rings on the tray, and I want you to buy me the one you like the best.'

Phoebe pressed the little stud and opened the box. She gazed down at the plain gold band and became emotional. Although there were dozens of rings in the trays, all the same except for the thickness of the band, she knew this was the one she wanted. It was Paul's choice, and that made it different from all the others. 'Please don't think I'm contrary, Paul, or stupid, but this is the one I want. Really and truly, I've fallen in love with it.'

He put an arm across her shoulders, and to her embarrassment, and the assistant's pleasure, he kissed her cheek. 'I'm glad you like it, pet, and it shows yer what good taste I've got in rings, and girlfriend, soon to be wife. And now I'm going to let you choose a ring for me. But I know yer've got excellent taste as well, because yer've chosen me to be yer husband.'

It didn't take very long for Phoebe to choose a ring she liked for Paul. The ring Paul had bought for her, and the receipt, were returned, and Phoebe was handing over the money she owed when she suddenly asked, 'Can you have the rings inscribed with our names?' She turned to Paul, her face showing her excitement. 'Wouldn't it be lovely to have our names on, love, and maybe the date of the wedding?'

'Yeah, that would be great! But would they be ready in time for the wedding?'

'I could have them back by next Friday, if that's not too late? And of course there'll be a charge of five pounds for the two rings.'

'I'll collect them next Saturday, I have to come into town.' Phoebe was floating on air, as everything was going so smoothly. 'Do you need the money now?'

The assistant shook his head. 'You pay when you are satisfied, madam, but I have to know what inscription you would like.'

'Just our names, I think,' Paul said. 'I've never had a wedding ring before, so I haven't a clue. What do most people write?'

The assistant, who at a guess would be in his forties, hesitated for a few seconds, then told the couple. 'When my wife and I married, we had both names inscribed, and in between the names we had two hands joined together.' The man looked bashful as he added, 'It's not to every-one's taste, but it was what my wife and I wanted.'

'Oh, I think that's a wonderful idea, so romantic! Don't yer think so, Paul?'

Paul was all for it. 'Let's have the same, eh, Phoebe?' He faced the assistant. 'That's if it's possible? Perhaps your rings were wider than ours?'

'No, about the same. There would be no prob-lem if you decided that is what you want. Perhaps you would like to discuss it before committing yourselves. Once the order goes in, it will be too late to change your minds.'

Phoebe and Paul put their heads together. 'Well, what do you think, pet?' Paul asked. 'Whatever you want, I'll go along with.'

'But you like the idea?' Phoebe was beginning to believe all was going so well, she must be the luckiest girl alive. 'It would be the icing on the cake. The finishing touch.'

'When yer smile like that, love, I couldn't refuse you anything. I told yer that you stole my heart away a few years ago, and you still have it.'

'I can beat that, Paul McDonough,' Phoebe told him, her eyes shining with tears of emotion. 'I lost my heart to you when I was about twelve, before yer even noticed I lived two doors away from yer. My mam didn't have any money to give us kids to go to the pictures, but you were my film star, my hero. And you still are.'

'You won't be telling Father Kelly all this when yer go to confession before the wedding, will yer?'

'Why d'yer think I'll be going to confession, Paul? I haven't committed any sins. If your conscience was as clear as mine, you wouldn't have brought Father Kelly into this.'

Paul tapped his forehead. 'As pure as the driven snow, pet, I promise. And will yer put the kind assistant out of his misery and tell him what we want. Don't forget, we're got some more shopping to do before we go for afternoon tea at the Adelphi.'

When they got outside the shop, Phoebe squeezed Paul's arm. 'This has been a wonderful day so far, Paul, everything is slotting into place. This time next week I'm hoping to have me bridal outfit, and the girls' dresses may be ready, please God. I feel very happy and very lucky.'

'I thought the girls were only being measured this week. I didn't expect them to be ready next week.'

'They had a couple in stock which were the right size, so they don't have to make them all up. They're going to try and have them ready for next Saturday, but if not they'll definitely be ready on the Tuesday. And I can pick the rings up before I go for my dress.'

They were walking arm in arm up Church Street when Paul said, 'I'll come with yer to help carry yer dress. Yer might get it ripped or dirty, getting on the bus with it.'

Phoebe chuckled. 'Nice try, Paul, but no way am I letting yer come with me. Our Dorothy is coming to give me a hand, and your Lily. The first time you'll set eyes on me outfit will be when I'm walking down the aisle towards yer. And I hope I knock yer for six.' She chuckled again. 'If yer don't like what yer see, yer can marry our Dorothy instead. She's got a soft spot for yer, and yer'd still be in the family'

'I like your Dorothy, but not to the extent I'd want her for me wife. I'll stick with you, pet, 'cos as me mam says, it's better the devil yer know than the devil yer don't. Besides, you just fit in me arms nicely, and I'm used to you. Yer know what I mean, pet, like yer get used to a comfortable pair of slippers and yer hate parting with them.'

'If yer keep that up, Paul, yer'll have us like Darby and Joan before we even get to the altar. Don't make us old before our time.'

'We're never going to grow old, pet, we're going to stay young, like me mam and Auntie Molly. They enjoy life, always on the go, helping where they can, and always ready for fun and laughter.' Paul put his arm round her waist and pulled her close. 'Next thing on the menu is shopping for some new clothes for you, then the Adelphi. So let's look sharp and put a move on.'

'You don't need to buy me any clothes, Paul, I've enough.'

'What about for after the wedding?' Paul asked. 'I thought women had going away outfits?'

'But we're not going away! I can change into one of my dresses after the reception, when the party starts.'

Paul kept his secret. 'If other brides have going away outfits, then so is my girl, and no arguments. Do as ye're told.'

Phoebe was nervous walking into the dress

shop, but she soon relaxed with an assistant who had a permanent smile on her face, and an infectious giggle. And, of course, Paul's easy-going nature helped enormously He was always relaxed, which had an effect on others, and soon Phoebe was looking at dresses in her size as though buying clothes was something she did quite often. She consulted with Paul over the colour and style, and soon the assistant was carefully folding a dress of pale blue in tissue paper to stop it from creasing. And as the woman behind the counter was putting it in a bag, Paul whispered in Phoebe's ear, 'Don't let me mam see that bag, or she'll want it off yer.'

'She won't get it, though.' Phoebe's face was animated. 'I'll be putting it in me drawer when I get home, and keeping it as a memento.'

'Well, yer'll be getting another one before we leave the shop. Yer've got a coat to choose now.'

'Yer've no need to buy me a coat as well, Paul. I don't want yer spending more money on me! Besides, the coat I've got will last me a while yet.'

'Don't argue with me, wench.' Paul smiled and his dimples deepened, sending the heart of the assistant fluttering. 'I'm buying yer the going away outfit we talked about.'

'But we're not going away!'

'Don't start that again, Phoebe. Just let's pretend we are, and let me buy yer a coat.'

Phoebe couldn't refuse him anything, and half an hour later they left the shop carrying two bags. Phoebe's held the dress, while Paul carried the heavier, containing a coat in a darker shade of blue than the dress.

And the young couple looked the picture of happiness, until Paul said, 'Now to the Adelphi, to see how the other half live.'

'Oh, Paul, do we have to go there? I'd much rather go to a small café somewhere. I wouldn't mind if I was wearing me new clothes, but I look too dowdy to go in there today.'

'Okay, have it yer own way, pet, but I'm going to take yer to the Adelphi one day, even if I have to carry yer in!'

The Wednesday before the wedding, the Corkhill house was taken over for the trying on of dresses, and a rehearsal. Gordon and Peter couldn't go with their dad to the corner pub, because they were under age, so they reluctantly went to the pictures, while Corker sat in the pub with Jack Bennett and George McDonough, downing pre-wedding pints.

'Right,' Ellen said, pushing the table up to the sideboard to make more room for Phoebe and her six bridesmaids. 'That's given us a bit more space.'

'I'm not putting my dress on,' Phoebe told them, 'in case it gets any marks on it. Besides, I know it fits me fine, and me headdress. You can use the two bedrooms to put your dresses on, and will one of yer help Ruthie with hers, please?'

'Me and Doreen will help our Ruthie,' Jill said.

'You Bennetts take one room, then,' Lily said, 'and Dorothy and Rosie can come with me in the other. We can help each other.'

'When ye're ready, come down and we can have a mannequin parade, so me and me mam can see how lovely yer look.' Phoebe's tummy was doing somersaults, she was so excited. 'Then when yer take them off, we'll have a pow-wow round the table to go over all the details, and yer can tell me if I leave anything out.' As there was a scramble towards the stairs, she shouted after them, 'Oh, there'll be tea and cakes, provided by me mam.'

Everyone agreed the dresses were beautiful, fitted to perfection in the beautiful wine colour that suited everyone. After whirling and twirling, the girls again made for the bedrooms to change back into their day clothes, and cover their bridesmaids' dresses. And while they were busy upstairs, Ellen was busy in the kitchen while Phoebe moved the table back to the middle of the room, and sorted out the chairs. They were two short, but no one would mind sharing.

There was much laughter and animated chatter when Phoebe read from a prepared list of details. As four of the girls were married, they knew the routine, but Ruthie and Dorothy were wide-eyed and listened very carefully.

The first car would take Paul and his best man, Steve, to the church along with Gordon and Peter. Half an hour later two cars would come to take Ellen, Molly and Nellie, and other guests to the church. The two cars would then come back for the bridesmaids, leaving Phoebe with her father to wait for the wedding car, which would be decorated with ribbons.

It sounded easy, talking about it with her mam and her friends, sitting round the table, laughing and joking. But Phoebe knew she'd be a bag of nerves when the day came. But she also knew she'd go through fire and water to marry the man she'd loved nearly all her life. The handsome man whose very touch made her tingle, and whose kiss sent her heart soaring as though it had taken wings. Oh, yes, even if her knees turned to jelly, she'd make it down the aisle with a smile on her face and love in her heart.

Thursday, the seventeenth of September, the day before the wedding, was a lovely sunny day with clear blue skies. And before he went to work, Corker wrapped his arms round his daughter. 'Nearly there, sweetheart. And if the weather is like this tomorrow, it'll be a wonderful day for you and Paul. But don't forget to tell yer future husband that under no circumstances is he to call here tomorrow, because it's bad luck, so they say, for a groom to see the bride before she's walking down the aisle in all her finery.'

'Oh, I've already told him, Dad! He's been well warned. I'm seeing him tonight for an hour, and we're going for a walk in the park, plenty of fresh air to make us sleep.'

Corker's huge hand cupped her chin. 'Yer'll make a lovely couple, me darlin', and I'm going to be a very proud man tomorrow.' A quick kiss on the cheek and the big man was gone, leaving Phoebe to finish her breakfast. Gordon and Peter and Dorothy had already left for work, and Ellen was washing the breakfast dishes.

'Leave those, Mam,' Phoebe said, 'I can do them when yer've gone to work.' Standing by the kitchen door, she told her mother, 'I'm sorry I asked for the day off now, because it's going to be

513

a long day, on me own with nothing to do except worry about tomorrow. I'd have been better at work, with something to occupy me mind.'

'Are yer going to the hairdresser's to have yer hair set? That will pass some time away.'

'No, Lily is going to do my hair for me. I'll put it in rollers first thing in the morning, and Lily will comb it out for me.'

Ellen looked at the clock. 'I'm going to have to leave yer, sweetheart, I don't want to be late. Tony's been good about me taking tomorrow off, and I don't want to take advantage of his kindness.' She reached to take her coat down from a hanger in the hall. 'Why don't yer call at Nellie's about half ten, and go to Molly's with her? Yer could have a cup of tea there, and perhaps walk to the shops with them. It would give yer something to do, and yer could get to know the woman who'll be yer mother-in-law tomorrow. Plus ye're guaranteed a good laugh.'

'That's an idea, Mam, I'll do that. I believe they go to the butcher's every day, so I'll see yer in there. And don't worry about here, I'll make the beds and tidy up. It'll give me something to do before I call to Mrs Mac's.'

Ellen was going out of the front door when she said, 'If yer come to the shop, I'll give yer the makings of a pan of stew, and yer can put it on for me. Yer may as well get yer hand in, ready for when ye're married with a husband to feed.'

Phoebe ran to the door to call after her, 'I can cook, yer know, Mam! Not as good as you, but I wouldn't poison Paul.'

Ellen turned, a huge grin on her face. 'If Paul

was content to have stew every day, then yer'd be laughing sacks, sweetheart, but the day he decided he'd like roast beef and Yorkshire pudding, then that's the day yer'd be up the creek without a paddle.'

'I'm a quick learner, Mam, you'll see!'

Ellen waved a hand and quickened her pace. She had a smile on her face when a vision entered her mind, of Nellie in the kitchen with Phoebe, and her daughter asking her new mother-in-law how to make a Yorkshire pudding. Ellen could see Nellie's face, and imagined what her answer would be. 'How the hell do I know how to make a bleeding Yorkshire pudding? Yer better ask Molly, she's the clever bugger.'

'What have yer been doing with yerself all day, pet?' Paul asked when he put an arm round Phoebe's shoulders as they walked towards the park. 'A lady of leisure for a day. But I bet yer were bored stiff after a while.'

Phoebe looked up at him. 'I went out with yer mam and Auntie Molly, didn't yer mam tell yer?'

'Yeah, she said yer'd been to the butcher's with them, that's all. But that wouldn't have filled yer day, surely?'

Phoebe giggled. 'Going shopping with your mam is a real experience. She had the shop up, with Tony and the customers in stitches. Mrs B. had asked for three lean pork chops, and yer mam said she'd have the same. Now, yer'd think that would be easy, wouldn't yer? In an out of the shop in no time. But we were in there twenty minutes because yer mam would have it that

Auntie Molly's chops had more meat on than hers, and they were a better colour. As yer mam put it, they looked younger and must have come from a healthier pig.'

Paul was chortling. 'That's my mam for yer. What happened then, did she throw the chops at Tony?'

'Well, Auntie Molly told Tony that yer mam could have the ones he'd weighed for her, and she'd have the other three. But yer mam wasn't having that! "You keep yer hands off them chops if yer know what's good for yer, Molly Bennett, until I make up me mind. Yer don't expect me to buy three pork chops without making sure they're what I want. The price they charge, I'm entitled to take me time."' Phoebe was doubling up with laughter. 'I've never known anyone like her in me life. And d'yer know how it ended up? Well, Auntie Molly is as funny as yer mam, I found out today. She winked at Tony, and said, "Let me mate have whichever of those chops she wants, save any bother, and I'll have three lamb chops out of that tray in the window." And the change in yer mam was nothing short of miraculous. Her face beamed, and she said in a very quiet voice, "I'll have the same as me mate, please, Tony, 'cos I always have what she has, and I don't want to upset her." No wonder my mam likes going to work. She enjoys the laughter, and the goings-on of the customers.'

'Laughter keeps yer young, pet,' Paul said. 'It's better than going through life with a long, miserable face. Take your dad for instance. Uncle Corker is a fine figure of a man, and he has the heartiest laugh I've ever heard.'

'If yer'd been shopping today with yer mam, Auntie Molly and me, you would have had a pain in yer side with laughing. We went from the butcher's to the greengrocer's, and my future mother-in-law told Billy his carrots looked anaemic and his cabbages looked as though they were on their last legs. What's more she wasn't paying tuppence a pound for potatoes what were sprouting, and had so many eyes in that by the time they were cut out there'd be no potato left. And anyway, her feller didn't like spuds what had eyes in.'

The couple had reached the park gates by this time, and Paul said, 'Can we forget me mam and Auntie Molly for a while, so I can hold yer close and kiss yer?'

'I've nearly finished, anyway,' Phoebe told him. 'All there is to tell is when we went into Hanley's cake shop, and yer mam made Mrs Hanley take the tray of cream slices out of the case so she could see them proper, like. And she insisted on having the cake with the most cream in, while all the customers in the shop looked on. Then she...'

Paul's lips cut off her words, and his kiss took Phoebe away from the antics of Nellie and Molly to a place where she found perfect happiness in the arms of the man who, in twenty hours, would be her husband.

Chapter Twenty-Five

Ruthie shook her mother's shoulder gently, and spoke in a whisper so as not to wake her sleeping father. 'Mam, it's time to get up.'

Molly stirred, grunted, and pulled the bed-clothes over her shoulder. But her senses had been alerted, and she turned her head to where her daughter was standing at the side of the bed. She blinked rapidly for a few seconds, then brought a hand out from under the cover to rub her eyes and clear her vision. Then, seeing her daughter, her voice croaky, she asked, 'What's wrong, Ruthie, have we overslept?'

'No, Mam, but have yer forgotten it's the wedding day?'

Molly struggled to sit up without disturbing her husband. 'What time is it, sunshine?'

'Eight o'clock, Mam, time to get up.'

'Go down and put the kettle on, sunshine, I'll be down in a minute. I don't want to wake yer dad yet, we'll give him an extra hour. He's taken the day off work for the wedding, and he may as well make the most of it. So don't make a noise going down the stairs. I'll be right behind you.'

Ten minutes later mother and daughter faced each other across the table, a cup of tea in front of them. 'Couldn't yer sleep, sunshine?' Molly asked. 'Nerves get to yer, did they?'

Ruthie nodded. 'I tossed and turned all night. I

518

tried counting sheep but it wasn't a ha'p'orth of good, me mind was too active. I know I've been a bridesmaid four times, but I can't help being nervous.'

Molly grinned. 'That's because yer've got a steady boyfriend now, and it's Gordon's sister who is marrying yer Auntie Nellie's son. And yer want to look nice for Gordon, it's only natural.' Molly put her cup down and pushed her chair back. 'I'll make us a round of toast, to keep the hunger at bay for a few hours, then you can have the sink to wash yer hair.'

'This will be the first wedding that me and Bella won't be doing each other's hair. When Bella won't be a bridesmaid with me.'

'Ruthie, the time has to come when you and Bella don't do everything together. Yer couldn't expect Phoebe to ask her to be a bridesmaid, she hardly knows the girl. And she's got six bridesmaids as it is! Besides, Peter will be there for her, so she's not being left out.'

Ruthie had a thought which brought a bout of giggling. 'If we're still going out with Gordon and Peter when we're old enough to get married, what's the betting Bella will want a double wedding?'

'That's a long way off, sunshine,' Molly told her. 'Yer've got five years before ye're twenty-one, which is the time to start thinking of settling down with the man you love, and who loves you in return. So make the most of those years, and enjoy them while ye're waiting for Mr Right to come along.'

'Okay, Mam, I'll do as yer say and enjoy meself.

I didn't need telling that, really, because I've been enjoying meself since I left school. And I'm going to enjoy meself today, if I can stop me tummy turning over and me hands shaking.'

'Yer'll be with Doreen and Jill, so yer won't be nervous. The three Bennett sisters.' Molly stood by the kitchen door feeling quite sentimental. 'I'll be really proud to see my three pretty daughters together.'

'What time are they coming here, Mam? I hope they don't leave it late, 'cos it'll take us ages to put our dresses on, do our hair and put some make-up on.'

'They'll be here in plenty of time, don't worry. And remember, Rosie is coming here to get dressed too, to give Lily and Dorothy more space to help Phoebe into her wedding dress. It'll be a tight squeeze, but we'll manage. We'll be the late ones if we don't put a move on. You run up and wake yer dad, while I make him some toast. While he's having his breakfast, you can have the kitchen to yerself, but don't hog it for too long because we've got loads to do.'

When Jack came down his eyes were blurred with sleep, and his hair was standing on end. 'Yer could have left me another half-hour, love, 'cos it won't take me very long to get ready.'

'You're the least of me worries, Jack, because men don't have to do much to be ready. Not like us women.' Molly poured out two cups of tea and sat next to her husband. 'It'll be crowded in here after twelve o'clock, yer won't be able to move. So if I were you, I'd make sure I was ready before then because yer won't be allowed in the bedrooms. It will all turn out fine, it always does, but it's the getting there that's the worst part.'

'We know the drill by now, love, or we should do. After all, three of our children are married. I won't get in the way, I'll make meself scarce. When Doreen comes over here, I'll go across and help Victoria with the baby. That'll be one less for yer to worry about.'

'Doreen will be giving Bobby a bottle at half eleven, and he should then sleep for at least two hours. Jill is doing the same with little Moll, so that takes care of the babies until it's time for everyone to leave for the church, and then Mary Watson promised to sit with Victoria and keep an eye on them.'

Jack coughed when a piece of toast went down the wrong way, and Molly slapped him on the back to clear his throat. He took a few sips of tea, then grinned at his wife. 'I picked a fine day to choke meself, didn't I? I shouldn't try to talk with me mouth full. What I was going to say was, our families, the Bennetts, McDonoughs and Corkhills, are growing so big we'll soon have to move to six-roomed houses.'

'We only notice how small these houses are when there's a wedding or a birthday party. Otherwise we manage fine, and I wouldn't want to move from this house anyway, because it holds so many memories. All the children were born here and we've had a good life, thank God. Apart from having a cold or a toothache, there's never been any serious illness, and there's always a feeling of warmth and love. I feel it every time I open the front door. We'd lose all that if we moved to an-

521

other house. No, I wouldn't swap this for a palace, never mind a six-roomed house. And I bet the McDonoughs and Corkhills would feel the same. We'd never get neighbours and friends like them, we are very lucky.'

The kitchen door opened and Ruthie came through with a towel wrapped round her head. 'Well, that's me done, Mam, so you and Dad can fight over who bags the kitchen next. I'll go up and put an old dress on until it's time for our Jill and Doreen to come. One of them can do me hair for me.'

'I'll get ready when I've cleared the table.' Molly said, pushing herself to her feet. 'I'll take the kitchen over, Jack, so don't be coming out for anything because I'm getting stripped to have a good wash, and do my hair. I'm not the bride, but I'm going to make the best of meself. I can't let the side down. Me and Nellie only get the chance to doll ourselves up when there's a wedding, so we're going to make the most of it.'

'When ye're finished, yer can put the kettle on for me, love,' Jack said. 'I'll take your advice and get ready before the girls arrive, while there's still room to breathe.'

Molly hesitated at the kitchen door. 'I think we should have something to eat about twelve, because it's going to be a few hours before the reception. More than a few, probably more like four or five. We couldn't last out all that time, so I'll make enough sandwiches for us three and the girls. I'd hate to hear tummies rumbling in the church, because they'd echo.' She came back into the room. 'Would yer do us a big favour, love,

522

and go to the corner shop for a loaf, a quarter pound of boiled ham and a piece of red cheese? I know yer hate going into a shop, but Maisie and Alec are our mates, so yer won't feel awkward. It would be a worry off me mind.'

Jack's eyes rolled to the ceiling. 'Yer know how I hate shopping, love, but I'll do it this once because it's a special day.' A grin crossed his face. 'And because I don't want my tummy to be one of the rumblers. What was it again? Bread, boiled ham and cheese, is that right?'

'Ye're learning, sunshine. Take six bob out of me purse, that should cover it. Shut the front door after yerself so no one can walk in, 'cos I'd die of shame if someone caught me in me birthday suit.'

Jack nodded. 'I'll take the key and make sure the door is securely shut. Now you get cracking, so I can have the kitchen when I get back.'

It was twelve thirty, and the Bennett house was bursting at the seams, and as noisy as Paddy's Market. The four bridesmaids were having a cup of tea and a sandwich standing up, and they were all talking at once, leaving Jack to say he'd go for a walk out of the way 'cos his head was splitting. 'Don't stay out too long,' Molly warned, 'I don't want to be walking the streets looking for yer.'

'Half an hour, love, and I'll be back. I'll only go as far as yer ma's. The girls will be sorted by then.'

Molly, wearing her new dress under a wrap-around pinny, went to the door with him. 'I'll have to chase the girls upstairs 'cos they've got just under an hour to be ready. Me nerves are on edge, but I'll calm down when everything is under control.' She gave him a kiss before pushing him down the steps. 'Next time yer see me, I hope to look like a glamour model.'

From the pavement, Jack told her, 'Yer always do to me.' He waited until the door was closed before moving away. And as he passed the Corkhills' house next door, he grinned, for the noise he could hear coming from inside was even worse than the noise he'd left.

However, Jack didn't know how wrong he was, for it was quite orderly in his neighbours' house. The noise he heard was Corker singing along to Harry Roy's band on the wireless. And the big man didn't sing softly, either. His rendition of 'Somebody Stole My Girl' had the rafters ringing.

'It's all right for some,' Ellen told her giant of a husband. 'You are the only person in the house who isn't nervous. Yer daughter is being helped on with her wedding dress by Lily and Dorothy who are talking fifteen to the dozen to try and keep her nerves from going haywire. I'm nervous, the two boys are combing their hair every five minutes because of nerves, and here's you, as happy as flaming Larry! I don't know how yer can be so relaxed, yer mustn't have a single nerve in yer body!'

'Ellen, will yer just calm down! What good does it do to be dashing around like a headless chicken, when everything is going according to plan? Take my word for it, me darlin', and be cool, calm and collected. Much better than having a heart attack.'

Ellen sighed and walked into his arms, where she always felt safe. 'We can't all have nerves of steel, love. I know I give meself more trouble by fussing, but Phoebe is the first of my children to marry, and I want everything to be perfect for her, and for you as well. You took my children on, and yer've been a fantastic father to them. They all idolize yer, and like me, they want yer to be proud of them today. It's Phoebe's greatest wish, that when yer walk her down the aisle, yer'll be a proud man.'

'Oh, I'll be that, me darlin', yer can rest assured. There's not a prouder man in Liverpool than meself. And that's how I've felt since the day yer said yer'd be my wife.' Corker held her at arm's length and gazed into her eyes. 'Now go and make yerself pretty for yer daughter's wedding. Time is passing quickly, and before yer know it, the car will be here to take Gordon and Peter to the church.'

Ellen ran the back of a hand across her eyes and managed a trembling smile. Oh, how she loved this gentle giant. Someone up there was looking after her on the day he sent Corker into her life.

Upstairs, Lily had put the finishing touches to Phoebe's headdress, which was like a silver crown holding the veil in place. When Phoebe arrived at the church the veil would be brought down to cover her face. 'Yer look lovely, Phoebe,' Lily told her. 'Absolutely perfect.'

Dorothy was near to tears as she gazed at the sister who had always tried to protect her and the two boys from the kicks and blows aimed at them by their drunken father. Filled with emotion, she wanted to hug her sister, but was afraid of crushing her dress. 'Yer look beautiful, Phoebe, like a fairy princess. I can't find the right words, sis, but Paul is going to love yer even more when he sees yer. And he'll know how lucky he is.'

Phoebe smiled. 'I'm the lucky one, Dorothy. It's not every girl who gets the man of her dreams.'

'Seeing as he's my brother,' Lily said, 'I agree he's really a handsome hunk. Witty with it as well.'

'I don't know about me looking good, you two look terrific. I wonder how the others are getting on?'

'They'll be looking just as lovely as me and Dorothy,' Lily said, laughing. 'Yer dad was certainly good at organizing. The flowers arrived on time and were given out to the two houses, our posies are in the kitchen ready to pick up, and red carnation buttonholes are also in the kitchen for the guests, complete with pins. Uncle Corker left nothing to chance.' She patted Phoebe's hand. 'Don't look so terrified, Phoebe, for I can tell yer from experience that this will be the happiest day of your life. And when yer get to the church, make sure there's a smile on that pretty face.'

'Hadn't we better go next door?' Dorothy asked. 'We don't want Paul to see us, and the car will be coming for him soon.'

'Ye're going out the back way, aren't yer?' Phoebe asked. 'Me mam said no one would see yer if yer went down the yard and into Mrs B.'s. I don't want the neighbours to see yer until ye're getting in the cars.'

'No one will see us, don't worry. Auntie Molly

has left her entry door unlocked. So if you don't mind being up here on yer own, me and Dorothy will leave yer in peace.' Lily followed Dorothy to the bedroom door. 'Don't touch yer veil, Phoebe, I'll see to it at the church. And good luck.'

Dorothy turned to smile at her sister. 'Yeah, our kid, good luck. I'd kiss yer but we'd both end up with lipstick on our cheeks. So I'll throw yer one, like we used to do when we were kids.'

Phoebe raised a hand and pretended to catch the kiss. 'Got it, our Dorothy, and I'll hold it until I get to the church.'

Two doors away, Paul McDonough was pacing up and down, his eyes fixed on the floor, his face rigid with nerves. And while they looked on, unable to get any response to their questions, Nellie and George were finding it hard to believe that their fun-loving, easy-going son had been reduced to a bag of nerves on his wedding day.

'If yer don't sit down, lad, ye're going to wear the lino out,' Nellie told him, 'and I can't afford to replace it.' When there was no reply, she decided to try a shock treatment. 'It's getting near time for the car to call for you and Steve, but I don't think ye're in a fit state to get married, so I'll cancel everything before it's too late.' She winked at her husband, then said, 'George, will you run up and tell Steve not to come down, and we'll explain later why there's been a delay. While you do that, I'll call and tell Phoebe and Corker. It'll be a terrible shock for the poor girl, but better to be told now than be left standing on her own at the altar.'

Phoebe's name had the desired effect, and Paul stopped in his tracks. 'What are yer doing, Mam? Don't yer go upsetting Phoebe. I'll be all right, just give me time.' He pulled out a chair and sat down. 'I got meself all worked up with nerves, and me mind went completely blank.'

'I'll make yer a cup of tea, lad, and that might calm yer down. But yer'll have to drink it quick, because Steve will be here any minute.'

As Nellie bustled out to the kitchen, George told his son, 'Ye're not the only one ever to have had wedding nerves, lad. I was the same meself the day I married yer mam. Running around like a madman I was. Me ma, God bless her, threw a cup of cold water over me face, and that soon brought me round.'

Paul's senses were coming to life, and he managed a grin when he told his father, 'Don't tell me mam that, Dad. I don't fancy having water poured on me new suit, or on me shirt and tie.'

There was a rap on the window, and George hastened to open the door to his eldest son. 'Ye're just in time, lad, 'cos five minutes ago yer mam was going to call the wedding off. Yer brother wasn't able to talk, he was like a man possessed.'

The two brothers hugged each other, then Steve said, 'I went through the same thing.' He was an inch or two smaller than Paul, but just as handsome, with dimples appearing when he smiled. 'The night before I got married I had a nightmare and woke up in a cold sweat. I dreamt I was sitting on the front pew in the church, and Jill never turned up.'

Nellie heard that as she carried a cup of tea

from the kitchen. 'Don't be putting ideas into his head, son, 'cos he was like a bear with a sore head when he came down for his breakfast, and he went from that to being deaf and dumb.' She handed the cup to Paul. 'Drink that before the car arrives, while I get Steve's buttonhole.'

Steve happened to be looking in the direction of the window, and he saw the car go past, then heard it braking to a stop. He put the stem of the carnation through his buttonhole as he walked to open the door, while calling over his shoulder, 'Time to go now, Paul, whether yer feel up to it or not. We can't keep the car waiting. It's got to drop us off, then come back to pick up some of the guests!'

It wasn't often Nellie showed her emotion, but she couldn't hold the tears back when she hugged her youngest son. The last of her children to get married. 'Don't cry, Mam,' Paul said, a shaky smile on his face. 'Yer'll ruin me new suit.'

Then Nellie and George were waving their two sons off, while a few nosy neighbours looked on. A little later on, all the neighbours would be out, and on their way to the church. A wedding in the street brought some excitement into their lives. The Bennetts and McDonoughs always put a good show on, and that was expected. But today was a Corkhill wedding, and no one would miss it, for the big man, Sinbad to the youngsters, was very popular, and very much respected.

Corker and Phoebe were alone in the house. Ellen had gone in one of the cars with Molly and Nellie, after a very tearful goodbye to her daughter and husband. The bridesmaids were on their way to the church, and in ten minutes the wedding car was due to arrive.

'Do I look all right, Dad?' Phoebe's lips were trembling as she looked up into her father's face. 'Will I come up to Paul's expectations?'

Corker, the gentle giant, was so proud he thought his heart would burst. 'Sweetheart, you look very beautiful, like a fairy princess. Paul will be so proud of you, he'll think he's the luckiest man in Liverpool. And I think I have the most beautiful daughter any man could ask for. I'm so proud of you, sweetheart.'

'Me mam looked lovely, didn't she? Her dress and hat really suited her. She should get dressed up more often.'

'If your mam wore a sack, she'd still be beautiful to me,' Corker said. 'I consider meself a very lucky man indeed. Lovely wife and lovely children, what more can a man ask for?' Then he stroked his beard as his loud guffaw filled the room. 'And what about the two best mates, Molly and Nellie? Didn't they both look splendid? Their hats will be the talk of the neighbourhood. And did yer see the way Nellie bowed her head and waved a hand to the neighbours before getting into the car? The only difference between Nellie and the Queen was the curtsy. The Queen would have been treated to bent knees, while Nellie and Molly were treated to shouts of admiration from friends.'

'Dad, the car's here.' Phoebe began to panic. She knew all the people in the street would be out, except those who had gone to the church, and her tummy felt as though it was full of butterflies. 'Do I look all right?'

'No, yer don't look all right, sweetheart, yer look beautiful.' Corker opened the front door and held out a hand to help Phoebe down the steps. And then the women who had waited for this moment shouted out words of praise and good wishes. 'Yer look a treat, queen,' one woman shouted. From another, 'I love yer dress, it's beautiful.' Corker was helping his daughter into the car when he noticed Victoria and Mary Watson standing on the step opposite. He asked Phoebe if she would step out again, just for a few seconds, so Victoria could see her in all her glory. And the onlookers applauded this, for Victoria was respected by one and all. The warmth and friendliness relaxed Phoebe, and she blew a kiss to the old lady before being helped into the car by her very proud father.

The bridesmaids were ready for the bride when she arrived. They were running a little late, and Father Kelly had been out once to see what the hold-up was. So after congratulating Phoebe on looking so lovely, Lily and the other girls quickly took their places behind her and Corker. Lily was paired with Dorothy, Jill with Doreen, then Rosie with Ruthie. And how lovely they all looked in their deep red dresses, with their posies of white daisies. The friends and neighbours who had been waiting in the church grounds shouted encouragement and praise, and were rewarded with a shy smile from Phoebe and a wave from Corker. Then, after Lily had adjusted Phoebe's veil, and made sure the folds in her beautiful dress were hanging right, she handed the bride to be a large posy of deep red carnations. The colour contrast was perfect.

An assistant of Father Kelly came to see if they were ready, and at a sign from him the organ began to play. 'Slowly now,' Lily whispered, 'keep in step.'

Corker squeezed his daughter's hand as he led her into the aisle, and told her, 'This is the proudest moment of my life, sweetheart.'

In the front right pew, Steve stood beside his brother, who was more than a little nervous. 'She looks beautiful, Paul, you're a lucky man. Turn round.'

Paul licked his lips, then turned. And he gasped when he saw the vision walking slowly towards him. He made to run towards her, but Steve was quick to pull him back. 'Wait until she's on a level with us, then you step out and I'll follow. And keep calm, wait until Uncle Corker hands her over to yer. And before yer ask, yes, I have got the rings.'

There were murmurs from the people in the church, which had filled up as those who had been outside had made their way to the pews. The sight of Phoebe, looking so beautiful, and her handsome, towering father, was not something they saw very often. In the pews on the other side of the aisle stood family and friends. Nellie, looking a million dollars, stood at the end of the pew, with George next to her, both looking as proud as Punch. Also in the same pew were Molly and Jack, smiling at their lovely daughters and daughter-in-law. Molly, wearing her new outfit, looked very elegant, and was given the thumbs up by Ruthie.

Gordon and Peter were in the pew behind, with Bella, and looked very smart in their new suits, with their red buttonholes. The seating had been arranged to suit everyone. Tommy, Archie and Phil were behind the McDonoughs, while Bridie and Bob stood behind their daughter and Jack. The rest of the congregation, enough to fill almost every seat, were friends and neighbours.

Everything moved like clockwork. Corker handed his daughter over to Paul, then stepped back to take a seat beside his tearful wife. Ellen gripped his arm. 'She looks beautiful, and so happy.'

Phoebe was happy, and it showed in her eyes and smile. And Paul thought his heart would burst. Somewhere in the back of his mind he remembered her saying she would knock him for six. Well, she'd done more than that, for he'd never known such love and happiness. And when they were facing the priest, holding hands, Paul wanted to share his emotion. 'Isn't she beautiful, Father?' he asked. The priest was taken aback, for no one had ever brought that into the marriage ceremony before. But he couldn't ignore the question completely, so he smiled and nodded before continuing the ceremony of joining two people in holy matrimony.

Corker had booked a professional photographer, and after the ceremony and the signing of the marriage documents, the newly-weds walked arm in arm down the aisle, followed by their bridesmaids. From every pew they passed there were voices congratulating them, and saying it was a wonderful wedding and how they made a perfect couple.

After that it was really hectic. The photographer was ready with his camera on a tripod. First the camera clicked the bride on her own, then with Paul. Then they were asked to stand by a tree, posing this way and that. After that it was with the bridesmaids, the parents, the Corkhill family, the McDonoughs and the Bennetts. Corker was snap happy, he wanted everything on film to remember the day by. And price was no object.

The photographer was closing his tripod, after having taken more photographs than at any other wedding, when Corker approached him. 'Before you pack up, could you just take two more photographs, please? You will be adequately paid for the extras, and your time. You won't need the stand, and I'll keep my eye on it so it comes to no harm.'

'I thought I had caught everyone on the photographs. Who have I missed out?'

'Oh, yer've done a wonderful job, been very patient,' Corker told him, 'but I would like two special photographs. One is of the two ladies standing over there with the fancy hats on, and the other is of the elderly couple with them.'

And so it was that Nellie and Molly were photographed in their finery, with Nellie striking a pose she thought would do her hat justice. Then they gave way to Bridie and Bob, who were overcome to be having their first ever proper photo taken. And it was a toss up who was the proudest, Nellie, or Molly's parents.

Covered in confetti, and looking radiant, Phoebe and Paul returned to the wedding car for the journey to Hanley's reception rooms, where they would stand to welcome their guests. The bridesmaids would follow them in two cars.

When the car moved forward, Phoebe and her new husband looked through the back window and waved to the large crowd of well-wishers who were still shouting words of congratulations. And to the onlookers' delight, making it a perfect ending for them, Paul and Phoebe shared a kiss.

Settling back against the leather seat, and holding Phoebe's hand, Paul asked, 'Well, how does it feel to be Mrs McDonough?'

'Wonderful, wonderful, wonderful! I didn't think there was so much happiness in the world. I feel so happy, and lucky, I could cry.'

'Don't you dare go all soppy on me, Phoebe McDonough, and definitely no tears. I don't want to kiss someone with tears running down her face, or the driver will think I'm kissing yer against yer will. So pucker those delicious lips, and keep them puckered until we get to the reception rooms. In between kisses I'll tell yer how beautiful you are, and how much I love yer.'

The reception room was full, and noisy with many different conversations going on at the same time. Paul and Phoebe were standing in the centre, arms round each other's waists, and talking to Corker and Ellen about how well everything had gone, and thanking them for giving them a wedding they would remember all their lives. 'The Hanleys have come up trumps again.' Corker said. 'The wedding cake is a work of art, and the tables are set with food fit for a royal wedding. They've thought of everything, with wedding napkins, sparkling glasses by each plate, and enough food to sink a ship. I'll nip down after we've eaten, and invite them up this evening after the shop closes. They'll enjoy joining the party.'

'I think it's time to sit down for the meal,' Ellen said, 'because if everyone feels like me, they'll be starving. The bride and groom in the centre by the wedding cake, and there's cards at every setting with the guests' names on. So you and Paul take yer seats, sweetheart, and yer dad and Paul's dad will see everyone to their seats.'

The bridesmaids found themselves on the top table, three either side, with spaces left for Nellie and George to sit next to the groom, and Corker and Ellen next to Phoebe. On one of the side tables sat Molly and Jack with Bridie and Bob. The other side table seated Steve, the best man who would be making a speech, with Archie and Phil. And on the far table were the youngsters, Gordon, Peter, and Bella, who was chatting away, feeling very grown-up and important. Peter was as chatty, but Gordon had eyes only for Ruthie, and he couldn't wait for the meal to be over so he could sit near her.

Glasses were filled, and Steve stood to say the few words he'd rehearsed, before toasting the newly-weds. 'My young brother, he of the dancing feet, has finally realized there is life outside a dance hall. I never thought it would happen, but then I was reckoning without the beautiful

Phoebe. And I think everyone here will agree that Phoebe does look very beautiful today in her wedding gown. We must also give praise to the six bridesmaids, who also look beautiful...'

'Hang on, hang on!' Nellie jumped up so quickly she sent her chair flying backwards, and her hat fell forward to cover her eyes. 'You just hang on there, lad, and give someone else the chance to get a word in.'

She looked so comical, pointing a finger in the direction she thought Steve was standing, and her face visible only from the nose down, that like everyone else in the room Steve couldn't keep the laughter back, and he was chuckling when he asked, 'Who is that woman under the hat? I seem to recognize the voice, it sounds familiar, but I'm blowed if I can put a name to it.' His dimples deep, he winked broadly 'However, would the person sitting next to her kindly explain that I am the best man, trying to make a speech and invite everyone to raise their glasses. But I can hardly do that with a hat interrupting me!'

There were roars of laughter when Nellie pushed the hat back, only for it to fall forward again when she began to speak. 'Listen to me, lad. Hi ham the mother of the groom, hand hi ham hentitled to speak up.' Nellie was sure her posh way of talking went with her hat. 'So just pipe down, hifyer don't mind.'

Steve looked at the piece of paper in his hand, on which he'd written his best man's speech. And to roars of laughter, he screwed it up and threw it over his shoulder. 'Mam, I'm not only best man, but I'm yer son as well!'

'I know that, soft lad, and if it wasn't for me, you wouldn't even be here.'

Corker's guffaw was so loud it could be heard in the shop down below. 'George, ye're not going to let that go unchallenged, are yer? Remind yer dear wife that if it wasn't for you, there wouldn't have been a wedding, and none of us would be here.'

Nellie pushed her hat back and with a determined look on her face she anchored it down with a chubby hand. 'Jimmy Corkhill, big and all as yer are, I'll not let yer talk about my feller like that.' She looked down at George. 'Are yer just going to sit there like a bleeding stuffed dummy and let him make fun of yer? If you won't thump him one, then hold me while I stand on a chair and I'll thump him.'

George eyed his wife and quietly asked, 'Why would yer want to thump Corker when he's right in what he said? I am in a way responsible for this wedding.'

This was too much for Nellie to take in, so she went back to Steve, and was about to say something when he beat her to it. 'Mam, if yer hadn't jumped in with both feet, ready for a fight, then I could have finished me best man's speech, in which I was going to say that, as usual, Mrs Nellie McDonough and her mate, Mrs Molly Bennett, stole some of the limelight as they always do, by looking elegant in their stylish hats and dresses.'

Nellie's mouth puckered. 'Ay, did yer hear that, Molly? Doesn't our Steve make a good best man? Got a way with words, he has. That's 'cos he

538

takes after me.'

George pulled on her arm. 'Will yer sit down, Nellie, so we can all eat our meal in peace.' With her bosom firm after praise, Nellie did as she was told, and no one was more surprised than George.

The tables had been cleared and the chairs pushed back to make room for dancing. And Paul gave his new wife a kiss before telling her, 'I want a word with yer dad, pet. I won't be long.'

Phoebe, surrounded by her bridesmaids and family friends, followed Paul with her eyes. She was so happy she wanted to cry, for her dream had come true. She was now Mrs McDonough. Paul came back and put his arm round her, just as Corker was announcing, 'I'm going to ask the bride and groom to take to the floor for the first dance. Then the party can begin.'

The gramophone picked up speed, and Paul led his wife into the middle of the floor. The record he'd bought specially for the occasion brought a smile to Phoebe's face, and to her surprise and joy Paul began to sing, 'You Stole My Heart Away'. He held her tight, and gazing into each other's eyes they forgot everyone but themselves and their love for each other. And there wasn't a dry eye in the room. Even Corker, all six foot five of him, was moved to shed a few tears of happiness.

It was eight o'clock when Paul whispered in Phoebe's ear, 'Why don't you go and get changed, pet? Yer don't want to get stains on yer wedding dress. I'll come with yer, and yer can hang yer dress in the wardrobe where it's safe, and change into yer going away outfit.'

Corker was standing near, and he said, 'That's a good idea, sweetheart. Yer don't want to ruin yer dress.'

'Yes, I think I will. Paul bought me a new dress and coat, I'll change into them. He calls it my going away outfit, except we aren't going away.'

'Give yer dad a kiss, sweetheart, before yer go.' Corker said, holding out his arms. 'Yer look beautiful, and I've been so proud of yer today. And Paul. Yer've got a good one there, I'll never have to worry about yer.' He beckoned Ellen over. 'Phoebe's going to change her dress, in case yer wonder where she is. Paul's going with her, so she'll be all right. Give yer daughter a kiss.'

An hour passed, and Ellen said, 'They're a long time, love, they should be back by now.'

'Ellen, sweetheart, they've just got married, they're probably kissing and cuddling. Have a heart, be happy for them.'

Half an hour later, Corker waited for a record to finish, then called for some hush. 'I've got something to tell yer, then yer can go back to enjoying yerselves. I've been asked by the bride-groom to pass on a message. Him and Phoebe won't be coming back to the party and he's told me to tell yer he doesn't want yer to think they were mean for not telling yer this themselves. Even Phoebe didn't have any idea, when she went home to change, that she wouldn't be back. Paul had a surprise for her. He'd booked a room in the Adelphi hotel for tonight as a wedding present for her.'

There was silence for just a few seconds, then there came laughter, clapping of hands and cheers. Then Nellie pulled Molly into the middle of the floor for an Irish jig. Molly made sure she was decent by not lifting her skirt as high as her mate, but the little woman went from a jig to a reel, singing at the top of her voice that her son's spending the night in the poshest hotel in Liverpool meant the McDonoughs were going up in the world. And to the delight of those clapping to her dancing, she also showed that even going up in the world wasn't going to stop her wearing fleecy-lined bloomers.

The publishers hope that this book has given you enjoyable reading. Large Print Books are especially designed to be as easy to see and hold as possible. If you wish a complete list of our books please ask at your local library or write directly to:

Magna Large Print Books
Magna House, Long Preston,
Skipton, North Yorkshire.
BD23 4ND

This Large Print Book for the partially sighted, who cannot read normal print, is published under the auspices of

THE ULVERSCROFT FOUNDATION

THE ULVERSCROFT FOUNDATION

... we hope that you have enjoyed this Large Print Book. Please think for a moment about those people who have worse eyesight problems than you ... and are unable to even read or enjoy Large Print, without great difficulty.

You can help them by sending a donation, large or small to:

**The Ulverscroft Foundation,
1, The Green, Bradgate Road,
Anstey, Leicestershire, LE7 7FU,
England.**
or request a copy of our brochure for more details.

The Foundation will use all your help to assist those people who are handicapped by various sight problems and need special attention.

Thank you very much for your help.